Potion Pope & Perfidy

Cover Elements & Credits:

'Vellum' background: RGB Stock, Grunge Parchment: http://www.rgbstock.com/bigphoto/mh1AXVI/Grunge+Parchment

Medieval Manuscript Page: Leaf no. 4 from Otto Ege's Fifty Original Leaves from Medieval Manuscripts, owned by Denison University, Granville, Ohio. Used by permission

Fragment from *Conseil Tenu par les Rats* by Gaston Dore, public domain via Wikipedia Commons

THE BOOK: POTION POPE & PERFIDY

R. EOGHAN HAGGERTY

Bill,

MANY THANKS for YOUR SUPPORT & FRIENDSHIP - HOPE YOU ENJOY READING THIS AS MUCH AS I ENJOYED WRITING IT,

For my wife Bridget.

She will never admit it but she is a better writer than I am.

Of course, this will make her mad.

Acknowledgments

First and foremost my wife Bridget who worked harder than I did on this book. Even more than all the editing and advice was her persistent nagging. Without that I would have ground to a stop.

Then to my sister Renee, whose intense reading and editing helped me to avoid embarrassment. Also my brother-in-law Dennis (the bulldozer). He applied more intense scrutiny than I did and pushed and pushed to bring it to readers everywhere.

Of course, my daughter Cathy, whose continuous stream of ideas made me think more and her extreme faith that I wrote a wonderful book (I'm not as sure as she is).

Also, son Scott Haggerty for cover art direction. If you like the cover it's because of his efforts.

And, not to overlook him, my son Benjamin, who volunteered to be marketing and PR; you will be the best judge of his efforts.

I must thank all the others who read and commented on my first draft. You know who you are and your feedback made the book all the better.

Finally, and significantly, my boundless thanks to the magnificent Barbara W. Tuchman whose book 'A Distant Mirror' provided enormous and critical information on the 14th Century including the plague or as they would have termed it 'The Pestilence'.

Disclaimer

I can't say 'all the characters in this book are fictional'. Some are obviously historic characters (Clement VI, Guy de Chauliac). Some are based on friends of mine. I hope I complimented them. The rest are made up.

Prologue

On the day of Kronos during Anthesterion in the year 737 BC, the healer - Asklepios of Thessaly - was struck by a bolt of lightning. The scorched spot then became sacred ground. The villagers, on being told, gathered and marveled that such a man had offended the gods; they buried him where he lay. From that day onwards, no person would be permitted to tread on the ground the gods had touched so terribly.

At the burial, Asklepios' son Podaleirios, standing near, noticed the beeswax tablet his father carried always to a bedside or injured man - it had melted. *What had thus been lost?* he wondered. He, with his brothers, would now care for their mother, Epione, and their sisters. This would not be difficult. After the cleansing period of forty days, grief would be the only burden the family would have to bear. Asklepios had taught his sons well; they all had learned the skills of healing. The knowledge of healing was not lost nor distorted by memory but recorded on scrolls - all the knowledge. No wound or illness was observed and treated that was not meticulously recorded; first on wax tablets and then on papyrus scrolls at the end of the day. The number of scrolls had grown to fill rooms. Podaleirios' brother Machaon's time was often devoted to sifting, cataloging and consolidating the entries to reduce the space required.

Thus, the family of Asklepios, called to the art of healing, began the task of centuries. Ever changing, ever growing, the family library was in constant use. As the physician descendents journeyed wherever suffering called for their help, a more transportable reference was required. A distillation of knowledge was transcribed. The essential signs of disease; the essential ointments and potions; the essential regimens to good health and the essential blank pages were all included.

Knowledge was gathered by each of the traveling sons. At the end of each Olympiad, the collected notes were brought together. The precepts in the reference book were each scrutinized in the light of new evidence. The entries were debated. Some were confirmed; some were refined; some were rejected. Once agreed upon, the changes were encapsulated in a renewed reference, only to be carried once again to the far lands in another cycle.

By the year 535 BC, the descendent families of Asklepios were forced to hide or disguise their secrets, their reference books and even their ancestry. The name of Asklepios had so filled the people's desire for solace, he had become a myth and a god. Temples were built to Asklepios. The legend of his skill had grown so large, it was said he had learned his secrets from a god. It was said that before he died, Asklepios had raised a man from the dead. This, of course, was unseemly arrogance in a mortal and, for that, he was struck by lightning. So his death was explained.

Faced with mindless worship, the sons of Asklepios would have been unable to work had patients known of their lineage. This worship of their ancestor had so distorted the truth, the progress of the arts of healing were being slowed. In some regions, all research and pursuit of knowledge had been stopped by superstitious worship. The family of Asklepios, during their gatherings, discussed and presented numerous solutions to the difficulty. Some method had to be devised to turn the minds of men to logic and reason. Knowing the simple minds of men, they agreed that argument against the belief in Asklepios, the god, was too arduous, if not futile. A plan was formed and the steps begun. Many years passed before the populace began to discuss and consider two philosophies of healing, with opposing views. One belief clung to the temples of Asklepios; the other proclaimed an end to superstition and, instead, advocated the need for knowledge, skill and medicines.

The worshippers, clinging to the old ways, would bring offerings and perhaps the suffering relative, to the nearest temple of Asklepios. With their gifts and prayers, they would hope for the great god of healing to restore health. It may be the god would perform the service. If not, the worshippers could only believe they had offended or been unworthy. Whether the unworthy was among those entreating or perhaps the patient himself could not be known. To those who believed, all was satisfactorily explained.

The science of learning argued against all of this. Gods or no gods, they proposed that learning and its proper application was more effective. The study of anatomy was conducted extensively; taking advantage of the zoos for comparative animal studies and Egyptian burial craft for human anatomy. Diseases were observed and the early symptoms noted and recorded. Treatments and medicines were tried and the effects carefully recorded and exchanged among physicians. A new occupation was recognized - alchemist. It may be the prescription would perform the service. If not, the philosophers could only believe the information was faulty or incomplete. Whether the flaw was in the diagnosis or the treatment could not be known. To those who believed in science, all was satisfactorily explained.

Although the public did not know that the new science of healing, which discarded Asklepios as a god, was founded and promoted by the very descendants of Asklepios, the science was successful. Ignorance and superstition faded in the strong light of education. The secret reference book of the family Asklepios remained unknown to all but a few.

—####—

In the year 297 BC, a commission was proclaimed by the Athenian exile Demetrius of Phaleron under his patron, Ptolemy I (Soter) - the creation of a great library. The goal charged was to amass all the knowledge of the world in one city, Alexandria.

To begin the task, all the scrolls available were gathered and copied and scholars were invited to attend. The avidity of the successors of Ptolemy Sotar grew. By the reign of Ptolemy III a letter was carried to all the sovereigns of the world to lend their works. When they agreed, the books were copied and the copies were returned, while the originals were kept. Ships docking under Pharos lighthouse in Alexandria were searched for books. If any were found, they, too, were copied and the originals retained. As the fame of the great library spread throughout the world more scholars and writers took up residence. There, the studies of astronomy, geometry, mathematics, medicine and the writings of religion, epics and poetry, would be acquired or created for over six centuries.

In the year 47 BC the first of several fires devastated the library. The Romans attacked Alexandria. When the ships in the harbor were set ablaze, the fire spread to the library.

Earthquakes, other fires and other wars would damage the library, in whole or part, at intervals over the subsequent centuries. Each time, those dedicated to the growth of learning would patiently rebuild and attempt to replace the volumes lost. But, in the end, the pinnacle of the preservation of knowledge would cease to exist.

And what became of the medical reference book of the family Asklepios?

Chapter 1: The library sale

What was that? Seamus woke with a start. It was dark. The street was wet and black. Flashes came from an alley across the square. He reached out his left arm to push Lena behind him and his right hand went under his jacket. He fired back at the attackers in the alley. They stopped and he heard the sound of running steps. He turned, Lena was lying on the hard cement pavement; she was bleeding.

"Lena? Lena!"

A crash from outside cleared his head; there was a thunderstorm in progress. *Oh Lord,* he thought, *this is no way to wake up.* He slid off the side of the bed and looked at his feet. The pain was there, lurking in his mind. *Would every loud noise bring back that terrible night?* Lifting his head he stretched his back and forced the thoughts away. *I must keep myself focused,* he thought. *Well, perhaps distracted is a better word.* He put on his shoes and stumbled downstairs.

“Maeve?”

“Yes?”

“Is there any coffee left?”

“There is, but it’s cold. I turned off the pot about an hour ago.”

“I’ll microwave a cup. Aren’t you afraid of the storm hurting your computer?”

“No Seamus.” She appeared in the doorway. “I’ve told you, I have a UPS.”

Seamus shook his head, “Oh right. I don’t trust any of that. I’ve seen lightning melt metal before.”

He went into the kitchen, poured a cup of coffee and put it in the microwave. After he stared at the panel for a few seconds, Maeve put her arm past his shoulder and pushed the buttons.

He looked sheepish. “Microwaves and copying machines, I’ll never understand them.”

"Or women either, I know. I wonder at the company you put me in."

"You're not a woman, Maeve; you're my sister."

A flash of lightning and the crash of the thunder came simultaneously from just outside the kitchen wall. Seamus flinched away from the sound. Maeve watched as he sat down and hunched over the table, waiting for his coffee and unconsciously rounding his shoulders.

"Are you back there again, Seamus?"

He looked up at her, his face pale.

"Yes, I am. A sudden noise does that. I haven't been able to shed it. Every time there's a bang, I'm back on the street in Dublin and I can see the gun flashes from the alley across from the hotel."

"She's gone, Seamus. She's been gone three years now."

"I know, I know, it's the weather Maeve."

"It's not the weather, Seamus. Not after three years. You were always sensitive to everything around you. That's part of what helped make you a good detective. Now, you're afraid of your own shadow."

Maeve knew what had happened, roughly. Seamus wouldn't or couldn't talk about it, so the details she never found out. Three years ago, Seamus and his wife Lena were in Dublin, walking back to their hotel from a restaurant when they were attacked. Lena was killed; shot dead.

Seamus couldn't get over the loss. He was unable to come back to life, any life.

Maeve was filling up with exasperation. Seamus sat quietly, as always. He thought over what she said. *Am I afraid of my own shadow? A sudden noise makes me jump certainly, but what it does is remind me of the attack. That memory is full of fear, even now. Strange to think of, I had such confidence. If anyone had asked I would have told them no one could attack me without my knowing it in advance. I was wrong. That arrogance had cost me my confidence and my Lena, the love of my life. The Greeks knew*

Hubris is always followed by Nemesis. Do I wish I was that way again? No, I do not; what cost might I pay again?

Another crash of thunder made Seamus flinch. Maeve watched. She had been prepared for Seamus before he arrived but she found all her preparations weren't up to the task. He wasn't getting better and she was frustrated that all her plans and efforts had not seemed to make any difference. *He was…what did they call it? - Clinically depressed. He must be aware of that.* She looked at her brother.

Coldly yet softly Maeve spoke the thoughts she'd been hiding every day of every week.

"Seamus having you about is worse than a wake. There are no guests or drink but I have the corpse all the same. You stumble from bed to table to bed once more and your face makes us all want to fall on a knife. I take a call and you have my heart so crushed the callers all ask me what the trouble is. I expected the time to pass and your grief to pass with it - it hasn't. You won't let it. When I talked you over here to stay with us, the reason was clear to everyone.

It was to put you in a place with other human beings around you. To give you someone to see, to chat with; even to have a joke with. The time is long enough for grief. You're supposed to be alive, Seamus. So get on with your life."

She gritted her teeth. How could she break his infernal depression? The shroud he'd wrapped about himself all those years ago?

She had a thought. *Force him to face the world, kick him out - that's worth trying.* She stooped over to look into his face as she said, "I'm done feeling sorry for you. It does no good. Go out. You won't go freely so I'll push. You are not welcome here today." Maeve stood up. "I can't take you today - go out. Go out and spend the day. Catch a bus and walk the city. I don't mind where you go, so long as you're out. I won't let you back until the end of the day."

Seamus didn't want to go out. He wanted to sit and read or watch the TV. He wanted to snack and drink coffee and take a nap after lunch - as always. He tried another wheeze.

"Should I let you have more for my keep? You know I'm not employed but I'm well fixed. There'll be no hardship."

Maeve exploded.

"Not employed?! Seamus you haven't accepted work in three years - three years!"

She stopped herself, breathing hard. She had stopped herself from telling Seamus he was damn well rich. She realized that would bring him back to the memory of the attack again; he'd think of the large insurance settlement. The old sympathy started to creep into her heart and she shook her head. She couldn't allow the pity she once couldn't help. Seamus sulked over his coffee. *So, my peace is broken.* He knew Maeve was right. *I am depressed. I've been depressed for years. I know it. How could I not know? It didn't matter. Oh yes, some practical thought of it creeps in from time to time, but it's a thought, not a feeling. There was no need to interest myself in anything. I've plenty of funds. My day is spent eating and sitting and sleeping.*

Maeve turned and walked away.

He sighed and straightened up, looking out the window over the sink. *Damn, today's dark and cold. I hoped it might be sunny here but then I wouldn't want to go out no matter how pleasant the weather.* Then he blinked and stretched his neck. *Not freely,* Maeve had said. He stood up and looked at himself. *I'm already well enough dressed. I'll need my jacket, my cap, and my wallet. If I take a bus, I can ride comfortably for hours without being disturbed. That's the thing to do.*

Maeve heard the door as Seamus left. She smiled grimly to herself. *This should have been done sooner. He cannot hide from the world today.*

—####—

Seamus sat on the bus, taking it all in. The bus was much the same as home. Noisy, not very comfortable, with an odor unique to buses. *What combination could produce such a peculiar smell?* He thought. *The ride was interesting though. Perhaps Maeve had touched the spot this time.* As he watched the city pass the windows he found himself wondering. Wondering what some buildings were. Wondering about the lives of the people who lived there or worked there. He startled himself when he thought of the police.

There were so many and they all seemed to have a car. He watched one walking - *to his car* - he supposed with a smile. The policeman was covered with a great assembly of equipment. The gun, the badge and the stick he expected but the collection of electronics looked to be more than was needed.

The trip was short of what Seamus wanted. Just before it ended the bus passed a large square in the center of the city. There was some sort of book fair in progress. The traffic was as bad as Dublin and the bus made less speed than a brisk walk. Just after passing the square, the bus pulled off the street into an outdoor terminal and stopped. It was everybody off. He waited until all the other passengers had left before he stood. *Now what?*

He stopped at the front of the bus and looked at the driver, a ruddy-faced genial looking man.

"When does the bus return to College Hill?"

The driver looked up at him. "It won't be for a while yet, but there's plenty of other buses on this run. You pick them up at Sixth Street. Here, all the times are in there." He handed Seamus a timetable.

He smiled at the driver, "Thank you," he said and got off.

He looked around as he walked away from the bus. There wasn't much to attract his interest. *The book fair! That would take some time. I can browse the mounds of books for hours.* He turned toward the square and quickened his step.

Three hours later the books started to lose their allure. At first, he was enjoying them all; after a while there seemed to be too many textbooks and gothic romances. He had slowly perused the books on table after table. He hadn't purchased even one book. His self-consciousness was coming back. After the attack all those years ago, his senses had become hyper-sensitive. He had always been almost too aware of his surroundings, and the people in them. It was a good habit in his job. Now, he had fear and self-consciousness added on top. He walked away; out from under the tents and sat on a cement bench.

For a while he watched the people passing by. Then he realized he was trying to take too much in; he couldn't absorb or sort it all out. Too many people, too much open space, too much movement and sound for him to feel he was in control. He realized he needed a quiet spot and something to do. This was torture. It had passed lunch but he knew taking the bus back now would be too soon. He decided to find a book to read. He didn't care what book. He only intended to have somewhere to put his eyes and avoid his instinctive habit of tracking everything. As he rose he noticed a sign across the street from the square 'Fifth Street Market Bar and Grill' *Ah, a place to sit out of the weather; now for a book.*

—####—

The wind on the square was stronger, encouraged by the frame of tall buildings. The green copper fountain contributed a fine spray of water to the drizzle. On a pleasant day, the fountain would have its own entourage of people sitting on the edge reading or staring or trying to decide whether to look at another attraction. Today, the fountain was alone.

The rest of the square was filled with large canopies. The nylon tops puffed and sank like cheeks blowing balloons. The canopies' bright colors in the grey weather seemed almost sarcastic.

"We're late." Steve's nervousness had made him whiney.

Jimmy lengthened his stride and threw his answer with a twist of his head.

"Oh shut up, it's only a few minutes."

It was cold, windy and drizzly. The people on the street hurried to find cover. Their heads bobbed as they tried to look down and had to keep lifting their eyes to avoid collisions. No one looked up. The streets were covered with cars, buses and delivery vans. They were motionless most of the time.

Jimmy stopped at the corner. A businessman in an expensive suit, with his insignificant collar turned up, ran across the square and pushed between them with his shoulder. Steve twisted to let him by and tapped Jimmy on the arm. "The sale started hours ago."

Jimmy growled.

"We were supposed to be here at three o'clock; not when the damn thing started."

"Well, there musta been a reason to be here at exactly three o'clock."

Jock usually ignored Steve but his nerves were tight as well. He stepped back and pointed his finger at Steve.

"Steve, one more word out of you and I'll break your nose."

Jimmy took Jock's shoulder gently and turned him around.

"Easy Jock, we're probably being watched."

Jock took it all in and looked around. He hadn't thought of anyone watching him. He tilted his head and whispered to Jimmy, "Who by?"

Jimmy counted on his fingers, "Well, there's the FBI, DEA, NSA - probably the old man himself."

Jimmy's casual list made the idea more unnerving.

They threaded their way between the slow moving cars across the street. As they reached the sidewalk Steve looked back at the street.

"Hey, they could grab us for jaywalking."

Jock leaned into Steve's face. "Don't be thick. They're after the money."

Jimmy looked around the square. "Shut up guys, they could have electronic ears.

Steve didn't have a collar; he held the jacket tight at the neck. Jock's tweed was being blown away from his waist. He pulled it down and buttoned it; then he pulled his cap down by the brim to keep the wind from finding a hold.

Slowly, they walked up the West side of the square; earnestly making an effort to appear disinterested. Jimmy put his hands in his jacket pockets. When the other two noticed, they did the same.

There were four canopies. Each canopy housed eight tables, two lines of four each. The library 'friends' had said 'rain or shine'; the drizzle turned to rain. As they reached the first tent,

Jimmy stopped, looked down at the first table and picked up a book.

Steve adjusted his shoulders and shifted from foot to foot like a child who had to go pee. Scanning the rest of the square he whispered into Jimmy's ear.

"Jimmy, what are you doing?"

Jimmy's exasperation was clear to anyone but Steve.

"Don't be dumb Steve, we're supposed to be here to buy a book, remember?"

"Yeah, but it's three tables up."

"Steve, someday you'll turn that gas chamber into a brain. Just shut up and look at some books, like you're interested."

Jock had already followed Jimmy's example and was standing at the next table, leafing through a book.

Steve looked around. It wasn't crowded; a few people were scattered at various tables.

Steve walked to the next table and looked down at the books.

"Hey guys, here's the history of Mad Magazine."

Jock grinned at Jimmy, "Trust it, that's the first thing the stupid besom sees."

Jimmy walked away without answering. He passed behind Steve and continued up two more tables.

He looked back to Jock, "Here Jock, take a look at this."

Jock came up behind Jimmy and looked over his shoulder. Stepping around, he pressed close to the table looking at the books and then up at the saleslady volunteer standing behind the table.

"Hello," she said.

Jock frowned. "Uh, hello."

"Can I help you find something?"

"Ah'm just spending some time."

"Well, you never know. We have some nice books and they're very cheap. Some are only 50 cents. If you wait 'til

Friday, you can buy a bag of books for ten dollars. But by then, the good ones are all gone."

Jimmy leaned over to Jock's ear and whispered, "Say it again."

Jock said, "Noo, ah'm just spending some time."

"All right, but there are plenty of other books. If you're going to be out in this awful weather, at least look at some of the other tables."

Jimmy pulled Jock away by the arm and whispered in his ear, "Something's not right here."

—####—

"What a singular book. It didn't look like a library book. It didn't look like any book I've ever seen. No, it reminds me of something, but what?" Seamus Cash was in the bar across from the square. He was turning the book over in his hand. The bartender stood in front of him.

"What?"

Seamus looked up. "A thousand pardons, I was speaking to myself."

The bartender nodded. "Uh huh, we have some Irish stouts on tap." The bartender had picked up Seamus' accent.

Seamus made a face. "God help me. I can't stomach the stuff. My father forced me to swallow that tar when I was ill. Don't you have a nice light American something? A local beer perhaps."

"OK, how about a light lager, it's as close to water as I have."

Seamus smiled. "That sounds just the thing."

The bartender left and Seamus put the book on the bar and looked around. The bar was empty. He craned his neck and looked out the window. In spite of the rain and the traffic, he could see people on the square. The book sale was doing more business. Good thing, thought Seamus, otherwise they would be in here trying to get warm. He didn't want people around. *What does this book remind me of?* He shook his head and turned back to the bar.

The almost transparent beer had appeared in front of him. He looked at it suspiciously. *Looks okay,* he thought, and took a hesitant sip. *Ah, there was almost no taste. That was what I wanted.*

He picked up the book again. It was heavy. The paper was very thick. The cover was made of something soft and fuzzy. He stroked the cover with the palm of his hand; it felt like petting a cat. He opened it and looked for a library card or envelope - there wasn't any. *The back then... no, none there either. What kind of library book has no sign of being a library book?*

Seamus peered at the first page of text. It wasn't easy to read. He picked up the book and his beer and walked over to a table.

"You leaving?" The bartender was at the far end of the bar.

Seamus turned his head. "No, I'll have another; very nice." The bartender rolled his eyes.

"OK, comin' up."

Seamus stood and squinted at the book under the table light. *No wonder it's so difficult to read,* he thought, it's not English. *Hang on a bit, it's not printed. Sainted Mary it looks like it's written by hand!* He sipped his beer and turned the pages slowly, trying to make sense of the writing. Finally, he straightened up. His hypersensitivity had picked up something wrong. He felt his stomach tighten. Once again, as so many times in the last years, he wished he had his pistol. He had put it away soon after Lena was killed; realizing he was in no fit state to carry a gun. That was a good decision, since Maeve wouldn't let him in the house with one. Seamus' risk analysis had been so heightened it was almost instantaneous. It was simple, the bartender was watching him. *Nothing else of interest,* he thought. He felt his stomach relax as he turned around. He noticed the clock. "Is that the correct time?"

The bartender leaned over and looked up at the clock. "Yup, you in a hurry?"

Seamus walked back to his bar stool. As he sat down he said, "No, no, I just don't want to miss my bus."

"When's it leave?"

Seamus raised a finger as he downed the last of his beer and put his empty glass along with the book on the bar. Pulling a wrinkled timetable out of his jacket pocket, he looked at the confusing numbers.

The bartender used a hose to squirt beer into a glass and walked over to where Seamus' bag lay on the bar. He put down the beer.

The bartender held out his hand.

"Here let me look, I take the bus a lot."

Seamus handed the timetable to him.

As the bartender looked at the cover, he asked, "Where're you going?"

"College Hill."

The bartender held up the timetable and pointed at the cover. It had 'College Hill' printed in large block letters. He smiled as he said, "Live there?"

Seamus face was warm. He blinked and blurted, "No, I'm on holiday; staying with my sister."

The bartender was looking down at the timetable. He mumbled, "That so." Then looked up.

"So, what stop?"

"Llanfair."

He scanned the table with his finger and then stopped.

"OK, got it, there's one in half an hour and another half an hour later. The bus leaves from Sixth and Vine; that's just across on the North side of Fountain Square." He pointed toward the wall across from the bar.

Seamus looked at the bartender closely for the first time.

"You take the bus a lot? I thought every American drove a car."

The bartender grinned, "I will when I can afford it. I'm going to medical school."

Why do all Americans have perfect teeth? Seamus thought.

He took the timetable as the bartender handed it back to him.

"Thank you, best of luck in your studies."

The bartender nodded and walked back to the other end of the bar.

Seamus went back to the book.

It was beautifully written. At first glance, it looked printed; it was that precise. Very small and squarish letters. *This isn't The Book of Kells but someone had the touch,* he thought.

He turned the pages quickly. There didn't seem to be any illuminated letters but there were illustrations. Some were diagrams and some were rather simple drawings that looked like internal organs. After the first few pages the text was Greek. *Hmm, maybe this was in the bartender's line of work; his future line anyway.* He flipped back to the beginning; that part was certainly Latin.

He tried to read some of the Latin. It took a while before he could get used to the handwritten script. Some of the words he knew; unfortunately, most of them he didn't. It didn't seem very religious, no 'sanctum's or 'te Deum's' anywhere.

When he was an altar boy, back in the days of the Latin mass, he was often called out of school to serve a funeral. He wasn't that expert, he was that fast. The priest liked that.

The bartender came back over to the register. Seamus lifted his glass.

"I'll have another; I'm not driving."

The bartender turned and nodded.

"OK. Good deals on books today?" he asked.

"I should say so. But I had no idea there was a sale."

"Oh, so why were you there?"

"My sister gave me the boot for cluttering up the house."

"Ah." He looked away as another customer came in; then walked down to the other end of the bar.

When Seamus saw the customer he hunched over the book. It felt comforting to have something to focus on.

So, not a library book. Of course it didn't really have to be. The Friends of the Public Library had individual donations mixed in. *Likely someone had donated this book. That didn't seem right. Whatever it was, it deserved better than to be sold at a public book sale.*

He watched the bartender as he served the other customer. *I certainly hope I don't get appendicitis while I'm here,* he thought. *I'd likely have a surgeon who just graduated from bartending school.* Carefully turning the pages, he tried to fathom what it was about.

Okay then, the first part, about a dozen pages, was in Latin. The rest, and the greater portion, was in Greek - with drawings. The writing was small and precise. The hand that wrote it was almost certainly from another age. So what other age? I thought only clerks counting money or medieval monks wrote like this. It could as well be by some monk, but there was nothing very religious looking about those drawings.

He was so caught up in the book; he didn't notice the bartender come back.

"Sorry, I forgot about you; still want another one?"

Seamus flinched and looked up at the clock. It was the middle of the afternoon. The bus ride would take an hour. Add the few minutes walk and it would be after five O'clock. Surely, Maeve would let him in by then.

"No thank you, I'd best be getting to that bus."

"Where're you from? I mean in Ireland."

Seamus stopped half off the barstool. He felt the fear coming but then saw the bartender's expression. *Nothing sinister in that face.* He relaxed.

"Kenmare in county Cork, d'you know it?"

"Yes, I do, my mother's Irish. It's down in the South somewhere, right?"

"That's right, south west, less rain, warmer. It's becoming a little dear though."

"Dear?"

"Expensive."

"Oh, so you're doing all right."

Seamus heart kicked; he felt sick at the thought of being so well off.

"So far."

He busied himself putting the book back in the bag and putting on his cap. The bartender watched Seamus walk out of the bar. As he walked up the stairs, out of sight, the bartender shook his head. *Funny duck,* he thought. *Guess it's just an Irish thing.*

—####—

Jock looked at Jimmy. "Are we sure it was the fourth table?"

"Dead sure."

They were standing out away from the tent in the drizzle. Steve leaned in between them. He whispered,

"Do we have the right tent?"

They both looked at Steve. Jimmy sighed and said, "Absolutely, the West side."

Jimmy went back to the lady at the table.

"Have you been standing here all day?"

"Oh, God bless you, no. I'd be frozen to death by now. We opened early this morning you know."

Jock and Steve slowly walked up behind Jimmy. As they approached, Jock stopped and held Steve back. Jimmy glanced at them and then had a thought. Turning back to the saleslady he asked, "How long have you been here? That wind is fierce."

"I started just a few minutes ago. Gladys had to catch her bus."

Jimmy smiled weakly and nodded then turned away. Two steps took him face to face with Jock and Steve. Jimmy looked nauseous.

"Goddammit. It's the wrong lady."

Jock was confused.

"Could it be here and she just doesn't know?"

"You idiot, we don't know either."

"What?"

"We don't know what we're looking for; think about it for chrissake."

"Oh shite, I ken what you mean."

Jimmy started to walk away, then he stopped.

"Listen, we have to look as normal as we can. Start at the front end, where we came in. Look at every book. If anything looks funny, come get me. I'll start at the far end and work back towards you." He turned and walked up the line of tables.

"What are we looking for?"

Jimmy snapped, "Steve, just keep Jock company OK?"

An hour later the drizzle turned into a hard rain. The books were being blown open and the library volunteers were trying to weight them down and pull the tables back further under the tents to keep them dry. Jock quit foraging through the books and found Jimmy.

"Jimmy, I think they're gonna close up shop."

"You're probably right and we'll never get through them all anyway. Help Steve look over that table. I'll take the one where Gladys was."

"OK, damn I'm freezing."

—####—

Seamus waited for the traffic then slowly walked across to the square. He was the only person walking; everyone else was running to get under cover. The few that stayed were huddled close together under the tents.

He slowed to let a group of people rush across in front of him, then continued past the tents and up a flight of steps.

On the other side was a tunnel lined with shops. Seamus didn't mind rain but it was more comfortable in the tunnel. As he emerged from the tunnel, there was a bus pulling up. A half a dozen passengers were lined up for it. Seamus leaned around to the front of the bus to see where it was going.

"College Hill 17" was on the front of the bus. He joined the queue just as the last of the line started up. He climbed up the steps of the bus and dropped his coins in the odd little gumball machine next to the driver. Knowing he was on his way back to the house helped. He didn't seem to mind the people so much.

"Why don't you take the money?" Seamus asked the driver.

"We're not allowed. I guess some drivers kept it."

Seamus winced.

"Could you tell me when we get to Llanfair?"

"I take care of my riders; I announce every stop. Just don't go to sleep."

Seamus nodded and walked down the aisle. The bus was crowded. He stopped about six seats down on the left. A very large woman was sitting in the window seat. The seat next to her was covered with packages. Seamus cleared his throat. She looked up and blurted, "Sorry." Then she gathered it all up like a bundle of laundry and held it on her lap. Seamus sat down.

She saw the library bag. "Oh, you've been to the library sale. Where's your coat, hon?"

"I have my jacket."

"That can't be warm enough."

"'Tis though, feel it." She felt the lapel.

"It *is* heavy, what is it?"

"It's a wool tweed."

"And the hat?"

"Yes, that too."

"Really, where ya from?"

"Ireland."

"So this is Irish tweed?"

"Yes, from Donegal." She looked at his head. "and the cap too," Said Seamus.

"But what about the rain?"

"The rain runs off like water on the back of a goose."

"That so?"

She lost interest or something outside caught her eye; she turned and looked out the window.

Seamus looked out the window, past her. He couldn't see very much; she blocked most of the view and the window was badly steamed up. *I couldn't live here,* he thought. *Too many fat people; too many cars; too much noise. Even a small city is a worse version of Dublin.*

The usual self-consciousness crept back in and he felt he was being watched. Then he remembered the book. He opened the bag and looked at it without taking it out. *Now that I look at it, it's even an odd size; and shape. It wouldn't stand on its end without help; too soft.* He felt himself start to sweat - *calm yourself Seamus.*

He rolled up the top of the bag and looked out the window. The bus was already out of the city and passing through some residential area. He hadn't even noticed.

Seamus looked at the houses, all different. Some looked to be from Bavaria, some looked like they should have been in Italy.

His stomach growled and he realized he was hungry. *No wonder,* he thought, *I haven't had anything all day. I wonder what Maeve is planning for dinner. Maybe P.J. will be home and barbecue. I'd rather that. Maeve would serve up gray vegetables by the basket, just like Mam. Its not so much the taste he didn't like; more the consistency.*

Again, the bus ride kept him interested. The rain must have discouraged most people. The bus stopped only a few times. Of course, the stops Seamus saw may have been for some other bus route. Seamus didn't know how it worked.

"Llanfair." The bus driver turned and looked at Seamus.

Seamus put up his hand, "Many thanks."

He stood up, swaying with the bus.

"Nice meeting you." He said to the large woman. She looked at him strangely.

"Take care, hon."

Take care of what? Thought Seamus.

The bus stopped. He looked around. Now, which way? As he walked down the steps and onto the sidewalk, the doors closed and the bus started to move. Seamus hurried out of the way. Almighty, if I'd had an overcoat, I'd be dragged to the next stop.

As he turned and looked across the street, he saw the delicatessen. *Ah, past that, second street on the left. I'm all right.*

As he crossed the street it was dark, drizzly, windy and, he guessed, about 45 degrees. He forced himself to walk slowly. He couldn't deny the day had been rather pleasant. *Maeve shouldn't know though. She'd throw him out every day if she thought it would cheer him up.* He made a conscious effort to look blank as he approached the house.

—####—

Again, Jimmy walked up to the sales lady at the fourth table.

"Uh, hello. Did Gladys mention any special book to you when you took over?"

"No, she was in a hurry though. She lives in Kentucky somewhere and she was afraid she'd miss her bus."

"That's too bad. I was looking for something special and she said she'd help me."

"Oh, do you want to talk to her?"

"That'd be great. Is she around?"

"No, I told you, she had to catch her bus."

"Do you have her phone number?"

"No dear. She's a volunteer, just like me. I saw her here last year but I don't really know her. Besides, she's probably not even home yet; the bus is pretty slow. Somebody told me she has a brother who works for the library; but he's not here. He's important you know. She's probably in the phone book."

Jimmy took a chance.

"Can you spell her last name?"

The lady laughed.

"I'll try. It is an odd one. "X-a-n-t-h-o-u-p-o-u-l-a-s, I think. Her husband's Greek you know. She helps at the Panegyri festival at their church as well."

Jimmy wrote down the spelling.

"Thanks very much." He was excited. *There's no way a name like that can be hard to find,* he thought.

Jock and Steve came up behind him. Jimmy turned.

"OK, guys let's get inside."

Steve shivered, "Jeez, about time. I'm an ice cube. Let's get a beer."

Jock raised his eyebrows. "You're an ice cube and you want a beer? Steve, you're sick."

This time, in spite of the rain, they walked to the crosswalk and waited for the light. The mood was somber.

The light changed. Jimmy slapped Steve on the arm. "C'mon."

They went into the lobby of the hotel and started down the stairs. A small neon sign read Fifth Street Market.

"Odd name for a pub." said Jock.

Jimmy smiled.

"It's a bar Jock; not the same thing at all."

The bar was almost full. All those at the book sale had come in out of the rain.

They found a table in the far corner. Steve took off his jacket and held it up.

"My jacket's soaked."

Jock nodded his head. He didn't think much of Steve but he liked him well enough.

A tiny waitress appeared from somewhere.

"Whadda you guys want?" She wasn't chewing gum, but it was the only thing missing.

Steve said, "Gimme a Bud."

"Draft or can?"

"Oo, draft."

Jock made a face. "What other beers do you have?"

"Hudy, Bud, Bud Light, Miller, Christian Moerlein and Guinness on tap. Lotsa other beers in bottles."

"I'll have a double Glenlivet."

"Thata beer?"

"No luv, it's a Scotch whisky."

"Oh yeah, OK. Ice?"

"No."

Jimmy looked at the other two. In Jimmy's mind, what someone ordered was a sign of intelligence. Feeling superior he lowered his voice.

"I'll have an Irish coffee."

She scribbled on her pad.

"Coming up."

She walked away.

Jimmy turned back to the table.

—####—

Seamus walked up onto the porch, opened the screen door and knocked on the front door. Any screen door seemed strange to him.

They must have large numbers of insects, although I haven't seen any. Still, I'm told this is unusually cold for June. I suppose the summer will change everything for the worse.

Maeve opened the door. "Seamus, you do not have to knock. You took me away from the supper."

Seamus looked at the floor. He expected the door to be locked but he didn't want to say so. That would hurt his pride; what little he had left. Still, he thought he should say something.

He blurted, "Would you like a beer?"

Maeve had already turned and was walking away; the words went to her back. She threw her answer over her shoulder.

"No, I do not, but help yourself, you know where to find them and mind your shoes."

Seamus looked at his feet and took his shoes off. His socks were wet. He took off his cap and jacket and hung them by the door. Still carrying the bag, he went down to the cellar to the old refrigerator and took out a can. Coming back, he saw some boxes full of old magazines and brochures on the floor next to the stairs.

A picture from memory blinked into his mind. He was looking at another old cardboard box. The box was damaged from age and water and some small rodent had chewed on it. The flaps were open and it was full of plastic bags. Each bag contained greeting cards, bits of newspapers, brochures and leaflets from holiday resorts. It was Lena's collection - one of Lena's many collections. His eyes misted and he felt a lump in his stomach. Then he realized he was carrying his book in its bag.

He shook the memory away and looked up at the basement door. Pushing the door open with the bag he went to the lounge and fell onto the sofa.

He felt better. Coming back feels good and I can't come back without going out, can I? He took out the book and looked at it. *And here is my trophy,* he thought, *to prove I did the deed.* Somehow the book's comfort grew over time. He felt calm and pleasant. It was his and it was peculiar. He could explore it for a long while without exhausting its novelty. The small thought of learning about the book made him compare it to a jigsaw puzzle. *It may not accomplish anything but it consumes hours of attention. The motion of working on a puzzle pushes all other issues aside. The progress on the puzzle, visible to anyone, gives the illusion of productivity - of accomplishment. Well then, I may as well get started.* He turned his head to the kitchen doorway.

"Maeve, did you tell me you had a friend at the library?"

Her voice came from the kitchen, "I can't hear you."

He got up and walked to the kitchen, holding the book. Maeve was stirring something.

"Didn't you tell me you had a friend at the library?" he asked.

Maeve looked at him. *This was a very different Seamus.* She would expect he would sit without moving until he was called to supper. *Well enough, but will this last?* She came back to the question with a frown.

"No, but P.J. knows a few people there."

"Where is P.J.?"

"He'll be late home. That's why I'm doing the supper.

Seamus sighed, *so no barbecue. Now it'll be the gray vegetables and maybe a bit of meat. There's always bread and butter. Well, something like bread in precise sizes and shapes and butter substitute of yellow grease.* He walked back to the lounge.

Holding the book on his lap, Seamus turned on the television. He watched the local news, then the national news then he tried to watch 'Wheel of Fortune'. *How can anyone sit through this?* He thought. *But I have been, day after day.* It came to him slowly. It had never registered before. He watched but he didn't noticed what he watched.

Just as he turned off the television the front door opened - it was P.J.

"Hullo Seamus, how are you feeling today?"

"Maeve threw me out of the house. I went down to the square."

P.J. froze, taking in the surprise. Then he recovered when he thought his surprise might be obvious.

"Well it was a good day for it; the library started their sale today."

"I came back with a book."

Another surprise.

"You did? What possessed you to do that?"

Seamus didn't want to explain. *The idea that a grown man needed something to focus on; the idea that it would provide comfort.*

"Well, it was rather pressed upon me. It is a singular book. Come and have a look."

P.J.'s head swam; *what happened today? This isn't the man I left this morning.* He needed to collect himself.

With a flurried look he said, "Hang on, let me get a beer. Do you want another?"

"Thank you, yes"

P.J. went around to the cellar door blinking and trying to fathom Seamus. *One day?* He thought, *One day out made this much difference? Seamus was almost normal. Well not quite but the evening before he had all the animation of a shop dummy.* He came back and handed Seamus a can. He was composed now. He would play this through and see if it was true; if it lasted.

"So, show me this book."

Seamus lifted the book from his lap and handed it to P.J.

P.J.'s eyebrows went up. "Huh, this is an odd looking thing to find at a public book sale."

He opened it slowly, as if it would tear if he wasn't careful.

"Well, it's sturdy enough. I can see why you were interested. There can't be many copies of this around. What a strange type it has. What the - Seamus this is handwritten."

Seamus admired the book in P.J.'s hand. He smiled to himself as he thought, *I can't even read it so it should take some time to finish.* He was proud; in the way parents are proud of their children.

He saw P.J. staring at him. *Hm, I may have paused too long.*

He looked away from P.J.'s face and said, "Yes, I noticed that. Do you read Latin or Greek?"

"Excuse me? Oh I see, sure enough, it's in Latin."

"The first bit is Latin; the rest is Greek. I can't read the Greek at all and not much of the Latin, it's been a while since I was an altar boy."

P.J. squinted. "You know, Conor goes to Saint X High School. They're Jesuits. If you want to know what this Latin is about, we could take it over to Father Schmidt. He teaches Latin."

"Schmidt? Is he German?"

P.J. laughed. "Not all priests are Irish you know. But I understand his mother was from Galway. Cincinnati is like that. There's no end to the couples where one is German and one is Irish. They say it's the perfect match. The most intelligent and the best looking."

Maeve leaned into the room. "Ah, and which one is which?" she said. "Come on you two, supper's ready."

"Oh, I almost forgot; I brought something for the table." P.J. walked to the front door and picked up a paper bag. "It's Italian bread. You'll like this, Seamus. I stopped by the bakery on the way home."

Seamus brightened. *Any other bread would be an improvement. Something for supper besides the vegetables,* he thought.

As they walked into the dining room, P.J. handed the bread to Maeve and then laid the book on the sideboard and pointed to it as he sat down.

"Seamus, what did you pay for this?"

"Two dollars."

"What? That seems like a mistake."

Seamus looked over at the book. P.J.'s comment had triggered a nasty thought.

That may be the least of it.

—####—

Jimmy leaned over the table and frowned at the others.

"OK, we're screwed and we've got to figure out what happened."

Jock waved his hand dismissively as he looked at the waitress and said,

"C'mon, the old lady took the book home."

Jimmy grimaced as he said, "Maybe. I suppose she waited as long as she could and had to leave. The problem now is to find her and find out what happened."

The possibility of a real loss finally caught Jock's attention.

"Yeah, and we're being watched. How do we do this without looking funny?"

Jimmy had already thought it over. He lowered his voice and his head.

"Well, first we don't all go in a bunch, we might scare her."

Jock nodded, "So, who goes, where is she and what do the rest of us do?"

"Look Jock, you have to go. You were the one she was expecting, remember?"

"Ah right."

Jimmy went on, "I've got her name. She lives in Kentucky and she took a bus, so it must be fairly close."

Jock pushed his chair back, "Let's finish our drinks and go."

Jimmy held up his hand.

"Jock, that doesn't make sense. She may not even be there yet. She took the bus remember? We don't know if she's got a two hundred and fifty pound line backer for a husband. We don't want our shadows to wonder what we're up to and we'd be walking in on dinner. That's not when you make a social call unless you're invited. Even the Feds would be able to tell we weren't asked over for barbecue. Tomorrow will have to do."

Steve was watching them as if he was at a tennis match. He was feeling left out and he was part of the team - wasn't he?

"Uh...guys. Do we think the old man screwed us?"

Jimmy looked at Steve in amazement.

"That's a good question, coming from you."

Steve ignored the jab. He was used to it and he knew Jimmy was smart; he watched as Jimmy thought. Then Jimmy shook his head.

"Anything is possible. But I don't think so. Let's hope not. We don't even know who the hell he is."

Jock frowned. "Then d'ya think he'll be in a lather about this?"

Jimmy grinned.

"Jock, he doesn't get down this low. If he found out at all, he'd have a good laugh and forget it. He's got his. It's our problem."

Then Jimmy's face went white. "Oh Christ, $250,000 and we don't know where the fuck it is."

Jock took a nervous sip of his scotch.

"Jimmy, that's the first time I ever heard you say 'fuck'."

Steve was worried about Jimmy. He got scared if Jimmy lost his cool.

"Come on Jimmy. It'll be OK. We'll go to the old bag's house tomorrow and get the book."

Jimmy slowly looked from one to the other. His face was set hard.

"You just don't get it, do you? She may not have the book."

"Huh?" "What?"

"Look you two. Can't you see? She may have screwed everything up. She may have given the book to the - wrong - guy."

—####—

After supper they sat in the lounge. Seamus sipped his coffee. He had been living with his sister for a little more than three weeks and this was the first time he had tasted the coffee.

"P.J. What kind of coffee is this?" he said, lifting his cup.

"Colombian, but it's nothing special. We buy it at the local market."

"Well, thank you for that. You couldn't know P.J. but I despise tea. I feel like I was close to drowned in it by my relatives."

Maeve was off to one side of Seamus. She watched, incredulous. Seamus was talking. The unfocused grunts and disinterested silence had vanished.

P.J. laughed. "This is America, Seamus, you'll find hot tea is more a social statement or an affectation over here. Coffee is the national addiction."

Maeve looked at her husband. "P.J. has a talent for sweeping statements."

"And so he should." Said Seamus. "The details would stupefy us all."

Suddenly, Seamus' forehead glistened. He looked around with a frown and blurted, "Where's my book?"

P.J. noticed the look on Seamus' face.

"It's still in the dining room, on the sideboard."

Seamus set his coffee down and rushed into the dining room. As he returned, he was calm. He sat down slowly and placed the book carefully on the settee beside him.

P.J. and Maeve exchanged glances and Maeve looked at the book.

P.J. said, "So, how did you find this book of yours?"

Seamus groaned. "It was odd really. I didn't find it at all. I was idly looking at the tables and the crowds of people. I stopped in front of one table, looking the other way and the lady said. 'Lovely afternoon.' Well, I felt a little foolish and nodded. We had a chat and suddenly she pulled this book from somewhere and said, 'This is the book you're looking for.' I thought I'd made it quite clear I wasn't looking for any book. I was just passing the time. I think I said that to her but she wouldn't take a 'no'. She insisted I take the book - only two dollars. Well, it seemed a small price to be allowed to get away gracefully, so I accepted it." Seamus thought over what he had just said. *That sounded plausible, didn't it? It was almost the truth. It was the truth. It simply left out his desperation and the fact that any book would have done just as well.*

P.J. sensed something was missing but he wasn't going to dig.

"Interesting, Seamus. Most of the people that manage these tables are volunteers you know. They're doing the right thing, but they're not pushy about it."

"Well, she was your exception. She didn't look the type. More like someone's mam offering you another biscuit."

"What did she look like?"

Seamus looked into the middle distance as he remembered.

"She was a little heavy, square face, very pleasant. She was wearing a rather comical rain hat with a wide brim and a purple raincoat. The front was open and her dress was a jumble of flowers. You've seen them, not in any botanical book - just noisy colors in a heap - like the aftermath of a garden show back by the rubbish."

P.J. chuckled at the description.

"Curiouser and curiouser."

Seamus smiled, and looked over P.J.'s head.

"Now that I cast my mind back, I didn't see this one while we were talking. I can't fathom where she picked it up."

"She was a witch and conjured it up to bother you." said Maeve.

Seamus looked at her thoughtfully, "You know, I think she had it in her hand the whole time."

P.J. sipped his coffee. "Damned heavy book - you sure?"

"Yeesss... I am. The more I think on it the more puzzling it is."

Maeve frowned. "What's the book about Seamus?"

Seamus and P.J. looked at each other.

Seamus replied, "I don't know."

"Oh come now, you looked at it."

"Yes, I did. So did P.J. the trouble is, it's in Latin and Greek."

"Latin?"

"And Greek."

Maeve thought and then shook her head.

"Well, anyway, the Latin's easy. We'll take it over to Father Schmidt."

P.J. stood up. "I thought of that Maeve. Do we have his phone number?"

"Oh, yes. It's in Conor's school papers somewhere."

Seamus had a thought.

"Maeve, I have an old friend in San Francisco. He has a degree in ancient languages. Do you have a fax?"

"Sure, in my office."

"Could you fax him the first page tomorrow. I know he can read it."

Maeve's face was blank. *A friend in San Francisco? This was the first she'd known about that. - Good news, indeed. Not the friend. Seamus knew people all over the world. The goodness was Seamus thinking of anyone at all.* She couldn't have guessed the reason.

The thought of going out to see a priest made Seamus uncomfortable. But the use of a fax held no exposure at all.

P.J. walked toward the kitchen. "That's a good thing, Seamus. I don't know how easy it may be to get any time from Father Schmidt. But I'll call him tomorrow anyway. Maybe you'll have the luck of the Irish."

"Which is no luck at all," chuckled Seamus, wryly,

Jimmy reached in his pocket and pulled out a scrap of paper. He handed it to Steve. "Here's her last name. We know her first name is Gladys. Go look her up in the phone book and write the address on the back." Steve took the paper and went over to the pay phone on the wall. Jimmy looked over Jock's head at Steve. "Steve" he raised his voice over the din in the bar, "Remember she's in Kentucky."

Steve looked back and waved. He was engrossed in the phone book.

"Jesus, he makes it look like a project. It starts with X right?"

Jimmy grinned. "Yeah, I know. But he's as strong as an ox and so loyal I'd trust him with my life. I have trusted him with my life."

They both sat in silence for a while, looking at the people in the bar. Jock was obviously thinking hard. Finally he caught Jimmy's eye.

"Jimmy, what makes you so sure Gladys gave the book to the wrong person?"

"Jock, I'm not sure but it's a possibility - a very nasty possibility. We have to consider everything. Look, we're running out of cash. We have every damn government law enforcement agency you can think of watching us through lenses. We - sort of - have two hundred and fifty thousand dollars. We have to think here.

"Why can't we go back to the old man?"

"He did what we needed. He found a way for us to get our money without anyone pinning anything on us. Now he's done. Why should he do anything more for us? We screwed up; we were late. Oh sure, it was only 10 or 15 minutes, but if we'd been there when we were supposed to, we'd have the book in our hands right now."

Jock made a face, "How can you be sure? Suppose the Gladys lady figured out how much it was worth and kept it?"

"OK it's possible. I doubt it. The old man is good because he thinks of everything. The chance is too long to even consider."

"So what's left?"

"Well, she could have waited and she had to leave, so she took the book home. That's the most likely. Yeah, she could have given it to the wrong person, but think of the odds. He had to have a Scots accent. He had to be wearing a tweed jacket and cap. That's all possible, way out there, but possible. Assuming that happened, what about the script? It's a billion to one for chrissake."

Jock shrugged, "So, tomorrow Steve and I go get the book from Gladys. That it?"

"I said just you."

"C'mon Jimmy, I don't drive. Steve can stay in the car. OK?"

Jimmy sighed. He didn't like being caught in stupid mistakes.

"Yeah yeah, OK."

Steve came back to the table.

"Shit, your handwriting is hard to read."

Jimmy looked exasperated.

"Uh huh, did you find her or not?"

"I got her, she's in Covington on Greenup. Must be one of those old brick row houses."

"Good. We can be pretty sure she doesn't work because of all her volunteer stuff. You shouldn't go too early. Maybe about 11 in the morning. That'll keep you from being trapped too long if she wants to talk a lot.

Steve, you're driving Jock over, you must stay in the car. I don't want her frightened. Jock you should be as smooth as you can. If she wants to have coffee, have coffee. I don't just want the book; I want to know what happened. It's just possible the Feds had some hand in this. No, no, she wouldn't know anything about it but she might tell us enough to figure out the game. If there is a game."

The waitress came back. "You guys want another?"

Jimmy scanned the glasses and looked up, "Sure, same again."

She went away. The bar was starting to empty. The office workers were starting to dribble out.

Jimmy continued.

"We can't do anymore tonight. Let's get something to eat. They serve food here. See if you can catch the waitress, Jock."

"Goad, ah could eat a scabby horse."

"Jock, when you get a couple of drinks in you, you're hard to understand."

Jock caught the waitress' eye and she came over. Jimmy asked for menus.

It was dark when they left the bar. Jimmy stopped in the lobby and turned to Jock. "OK, Steve knows where he's going. He'll take you over tomorrow. Remember, if she's got the book, great. Get it from her and call me right away."

"And if she doesn't?"

"If she doesn't, we need to know everything she can tell us. Don't push her; just keep her talking. I've seen you do that before. Just remember everything she says. I've got some things to do tomorrow. We'll meet up at the Ohio River Overlook and figure out what's next."

"When?"

Jimmy shrugged, "I'll call you when I'm in the clear. You two just be ready to show up."

Chapter 2: Three Rewards

The library was enormous. The twenty foot ceiling was crosshatched with ornate oak moldings; in the spaces between the moldings, the panels were surfaced with an ornamental plaster pattern. The walls were composed of bookcases from the floor to a cove molding at the ceiling line. The walls of books were only broken by twelve foot windows. The window's heavy damask draperies were closed; no light entered.

One half of the room contained eight oak library tables each with their own reading lights. The tables were carefully spaced to allow a clear path. Each of four of the tables had four upholstered wing chairs and antique tobacco stands.

The remaining half of the room was arrayed with a series of large chairs in pairs. Each chair had an eight foot floor lamp and a side table.

The floor was carpeted wall to wall and, additionally, three enormous oriental carpets were evenly spaced on top.

The room had only one occupant. In one corner sat a tall, thin, very old man. The light from his ten-bulb floor lamp, shining on the polished wood and the glass from the bookcase doors, illuminated the room - dimly.

A large book open on his lap; the old man held a brandy snifter to the light and gazed at it critically.

It was a good brandy, he thought, *not a great brandy. It had been a good week,* he thought. *Actually, it had been a great week. After all these years a ghost had been exorcised. Exorcised? Oh yes, it had been a dangerous, tricky, irritating ghost. For over sixty years the ghost had clouded any success or any comfort in my family life. Now the ghost was gone. Had all the good works and all the hard work finally been blessed? No likely not. The gods have a nasty sense of Humor. Still, it was truly serendipitous. Jimmy had never been likable, let alone worthwhile. All he ever did was indulge his appetites. His father had been the same way. Nature triumphed over nurture that time.*

Well, perhaps the nurture was responsible too. Either way it was a lost cause.

It was peculiar, he abhorred any action with only one intent, this was three marvelous outcomes with one stroke, presented on a platter. *I increased my wealth. I jabbed a worthless parasite and of course, the ghost was gone. Jimmy would never know who was behind it. That made it all the more savory.*

One of the two massive oak doors opened. There was no sound. A man in his sixties came into the room. He was in formal dress. "Your dinner will be ready in half an hour, sir."

"Thank you Robert. Where did this come from?" He raised his brandy snifter.

"I'm sorry sir, that was the best I could find. I thought better of touching your private reserves."

"You did right, Robert. It's actually quite good enough and there's no special occasion."

Robert bowed slightly, turned and left the room.

But it was a special occasion. Not that anyone would know. I'll have to concoct some specious excuse to open a Napoleon, he thought and smiled.

Good grief, sixty years, sixty five years really. I wonder what the reward is up to by now? Must be millions of dollars. Well, that certainly doesn't matter anymore.

This makes some space in my private library. Not much, perhaps, but I'll be able to open the library and show it off now. That was a pleasure to look forward to. Perhaps I'll invite some friends over for an evening of history and fine wines.

He reached over to set down his glass on the table and winced. *Damn, not until this back of mine stops hurting.*

Chapter 3: The Classicist

Seamus was up at six. He'd stayed in bed as long as he could, wide awake. It had been a fitful night. He knew he had become obsessive about the book. He'd read where that often happened when a person was recovering from a trauma. Still, he was equally aware that the book was a true puzzle - two puzzles. The contents were a fascinating mystery. But another puzzle, more to his taste, was how it came to be at a public sale. The way he acquired the book did not register as odd at the time. He was too nervous and distracted to notice. Now, in retrospect, it seemed very peculiar indeed. If he was to be paranoid, here was a fine place to start. But, wrestle it through as he might, he failed to see any lurking danger. *Well enough, but I sense a chance of danger all the same.* He decided the answer would emerge and he may as soon do whatever else he could. Time to learn about the book itself. *'Sufficient unto tomorrow is the evil thereof'*, he thought as he climbed out of bed and noticed that the book was resting on his bedside table. Seeing it there was comforting. A sense of the significance of the comfort whispered through his mind and then was gone. He shook his head and started to dress.

Even this early, P.J. had already left for work. There was some special meeting that morning and P.J. wanted to prepare for it.

Maeve was in the kitchen making coffee. She turned on the coffee maker just as Seamus appeared in the doorway. Maeve looked, he thought, rather surly, and walked by.

Maeve was still on her guard. It was only the day after Seamus' outing. Prepared for the Seamus she dreaded - his lifeless gloom and continual downcast face - she was tense. All her senses held in reserve.

Seamus watched her go.

"Isn't it a grand day to be Oirish," he said to her back and walked into the kitchen to look out the window. It was raining again," - or a duck," he mumbled. He watched the coffee dribbling into the pot. *A watched coffee pot never fills,* he thought. He put down the cup he was carrying and turned to the doorway. "Maeve, can I fax the first page of the book to my friend?"

Maeve's voice came from upstairs. "Wait 'til I come down. I'll have to do it for you."

He went to the stairs and met Maeve coming down.

"Sorry I left it in my room."

"Well, bring it to my office. I'll do it first and then I'll be able to get some work done."

She poured herself some coffee and went into her office. Seamus fetched the book. "Just fax the first page Maeve," handing it to her.

"What's the fax number?"

"Sorry, here." He handed her a pocket day timer; it was open in the middle. "It's Tony Willet. All his numbers are there."

Maeve took the day timer. "You know, I'll have to scan this. I'm not about to cut it from the book and I can't get this book into my fax." Seamus looked more horrified than merely worried.

"Don't get in a twist, Seamus. It's not a problem. Go get yourself some coffee."

As he made his coffee, he could hear Maeve's scanner Humming.

"Here, Seamus what do you want to say on the cover page?"

Seamus went back to the office and leaned over her shoulder.

"Just say, 'I've a puzzle you should enjoy. Look at this and tell me what, in the name of all the saints, this damn thing is on about. Luv, Seamus'. Will he know where I am?"

"He will. All the numbers are on the cover page."

"God bless you, Maeve." She handed Seamus the book.

"It's all right."

She was relieved and didn't want it to show. This was the Seamus, if not of old then, at least, of the previous night. *I can stand this Seamus around; the other is intolerable.*

"Did P.J. call the Jesuit?"

"Lord no Seamus, he had hardly the time to dress. That's for me to do, as usual."

"Well, don't bother yourself, Maeve. Let's see what my friend has to say."

Seamus went to the kitchen to top-up his cup and sat down with the book. He started turning the pages very carefully from the back – one by one. He stopped.

He raised his voice. "You know Maeve, this has pictures in it."

"Oh, of what?"

"I've no idea. They look rather disgusting to me."

"Ah, you've an ancient book of pornography have you?"

"Not that kind of disgusting. It looks to be some creature's entrails - ugh."

"Right Seamus, leave me alone will you? I'm behind in my work."

Seamus sighed, put the book down and saw the daily paper. *Oh, why not,* he thought.

Seamus read the paper. It wasn't much of a paper. There were a few articles on events in American politics and a few on business. If you looked hard enough there were one or two on international disasters. These tended to be extremely short. The rest of the paper seemed to be devoted to adverts, games, astonishingly trivial items happening in Cincinnati and gardening help - more or less in that order. After forcing himself to look at everything in the paper, he felt obliged to make another pot of coffee. It was apparent he'd had the lion's share.

With a queasy stomach, after all the coffee, he put his head into Maeve's office.

"I'm going for a little air Maeve."

Maeve froze, staring at her computer. *Saints bless us all!* She thought. *Could this be? The saints could skip the rest of us and bless this troublesome book. For all its distraction, it looks to be worth the cost and more.* She took a deep breath and, as casually as she could, she said, "Fine, fine. Just remember, you don't have to knock to come in. I don't want to be disturbed."

"To be sure, Maeve."

He looked out the window over the front porch. The rain had stopped.

He put on his cap and went out the door. The screen door slammed behind him.

He walked down the steps and stopped on the sidewalk. *Hm, which way to go?* Turning right led to the main avenue and it was busy and there would be people. People who would trigger his tracking habit and tire him out. He turned left. For the first time in almost three years, Seamus wanted to think.

So where am I? I'm fascinated by this book. Well, why not? It's certainly a mystery and the world knows I always loved a mystery. I should be just as glad. A mystery found me my sweet Lena. Mysteries filled my coin box and gave us both a good life. Then he felt the grief clutch his stomach. He staggered. Seeing the stump of an old tree next to the walk, he sat down hard. *Yes, he thought, a mystery took her from me.*

His forehead was beaded with sweat and his legs were weak. Perhaps he wasn't ready yet to walk out on his own. *God help me,* he thought, *this is only my second day out and I can't manage to care for myself. Maeve was right; I have to get on with my life.* He lifted his head and focused on a squirrel tightrope-walking the telephone wire. He felt his strength returning and he took a deep breath and considered the book again.

So what was behind this? Was this the work of Saint Raymond Nonnatus, the patron saint of innocent people? Or was this the work of Saint Dymphna perhaps? The patron saint of the insane. It may be I am being guided to help some, as yet unknown, person. Or, as seemed more likely, I'm being given the help I need so much myself.

Not ready to admit the depression that could lead to insanity. He thought he'd settle on Raymond. *So, who was innocent? Myself, surely, and the - not so little - old lady at the book sale. There's bound to be someone; there always is. Of course, this assumes there are opposing forces; the guilty or, at least, the not so innocent. But guilty of what?*

Mayhaps it's time to go back to Dymphna, idiot. There needn't be either; rather a simple, if extremely peculiar, mistake or a straightforward case of bad judgement.

A mistake if someone let a very valuable book slip away accidentally. 'Yes dear, the whole lot of books on the table are for the library sale.'

Bad judgement if someone had no knowledge of its value in the first place. 'Ah, it can't be worth much, it's too old. Give it to the library.'

He stopped. Thinking was more difficult than he remembered. He looked around. *It's beautiful here,* he thought. *All the giant old trees.* Though he was only a few blocks away, he felt he was too far from the house. *I'd better go back.*

He stood up; it started to drizzle again.

He started to think again. *No matter what the reason behind this, I should at least find out the book's value. If it's a truly rare find, it belongs in a museum. If it's just valuable, I can put it up for auction and the proceeds will help Conor get an education. At the least, I'd be helping Maeve for all she's done, putting up with me in my foul humors. If it's worth a pittance, I'll keep it. It'll be good for a bit of conversation over a drink with a friend.*

But then - his steps slowed, *if there's something evil about it?* He shrugged mentally - *one hurdle at a time.* He smiled to himself. *I know Father Schmidt can help. Let's hope he doesn't need his vestments and oils.*

After his lunch and usual nap. Seamus spent the rest of the day looking at the book. *What could explain it all?* he thought. The rest of Tuesday was uneventful. That was all right; he had much to look forward to. Something to look forward to. What a marvelous and long missed feeling.

The supper and small talk took the day to an end and Seamus went to bed early.

—####—

The next morning Seamus had coffee and went straight out for a walk. *This is becoming a habit,* he thought. *It's rather nice and I should make it a regular part of every day.*

Thinking all the while, he didn't notice when he was back at the house. As he went through the front door he heard Maeve call out.

"That you Seamus? You have an answer to your fax. He sounds excited. You may have tripped over something large with this book."

Seamus hurried to the office.

"Where is it?" He looked around.

"Wait up, Seamus. Here on my screen. Let me put it up for you."

She pushed a few buttons and rolled her chair back so Seamus could get a closer look.

"Sweetheart, where have you been?" He read. He looked at Maeve. She had one eyebrow up.

Seamus smiled, his eyes twinkling, "He says that to all the girls."

"Are you one of the girls?"

"Maeve, I still have all my bits and pieces and I know what they're for."

"Ah yes, but do you know *who* they're for? That's my question."

"Now, Maeve." Seamus went back to the message.

What have you found out there? This is fascinating!

You're going to need a priest. For the book, not for you - you sinner.

But don't get an old one - he'll try to steal your book!

The best would be a young enthusiastic Jesuit. A history buff, if possible.

This looks to be between the 12th and the 15th century. Have the paper checked; I'll bet it's parchment - not paper.

But here's the delicious part. This monk was disobeying his superiors!!

He says so right at the beginning! I won't be able to sleep until I see more.

I can't tell you what it's about though; you didn't send me enough. That's the whole point you see.

What I have is one page of the monk's explanation of what he's doing; NOT what he was supposed to do.

Send me some more soon but I'll be out of town for almost a week. So I won't be able to help until I'm back. That would be the 12th OK?

Luv Ya

Tony

Maeve watched Seamus as he read the reply. He was more as she remembered him than he had been in years. The sense of humor, the quick retort and the wit was Seamus with his edge back. *God Bless this book*, she thought again.

Seamus stood up and looked at Maeve.

"Well well well, as Mam would say, 'here's a fine kettle of fish.'"

"Do you want to fax Tony some more pages?"

"Thank you Maeve; I don't think so. Tony has said he won't be there 'til next week. Tell me more about Father Schmidt."

"You've struck the luck this time Seamus. He's about thirty five. Very energetic and brilliant; he reads, writes and speaks Latin. But the part that should make you wonder is that his hobby - if that's the way to put it - is medieval history."

"Bless me and all my parts."

Maeve smiled at her brother.

"Just so, now run along. I'm still behind here."

"Um, it's time for - what is it called here? - lunch."

"Maeve looked at the clock and sighed. "So it is, where did the morning go?"

After lunch, Seamus went up to his room to take a nap. He had started napping three years ago. He had considered staying up but he was tired. Maeve never napped. She went straight back to her office. Seamus could hear her pounding away on the keyboard as he dozed off.

He woke with a vague sense of uneasiness. Turning his head he noticed his book. The usual warm comfort of the book dispelled his disquiet and he sat up. *Time to get on with it again*, he thought. He dressed, grabbed the book and headed down stairs to the kitchen. Again, the coffee was cold. He poured a cup and put it into the microwave. Standing, waiting for his coffee to heat up he looked at the book's cover. *It's magnificent*, he thought. *It must be leather, almost like suede, very thick and sturdy but flexible. If this is really as old as Tony believes, it must have been well cared for all these years.* The microwave bell rang and Seamus took out his coffee. He walked out to the front porch. There were two folding lawn chairs leaning against the side of the house. He unfolded one and sat down to watch the rain and think some more.

So, the book was medieval. Wait a moment, that can't be right. It was bound. They didn't bind books back then; did they? I'm finally up against something with no knowledge to draw upon. Where do I find the answers? How about a printer? He should know. Well, he would if he knew the history of printing. Seamus suppressed a grin. *That doesn't sound like any printer I ever met.*

Hmph, I need a historian. Of what? My luck says I'll have no trouble locating dozens who can explain what American Indians camped under Maeve's house and not one who knows anything about medieval scribes. The library - of course. Aagh, poking about in the library trying to understand their catalog system. I'd fall asleep at the table and they'd lock me in.

I have to get Maeve involved. She's an obsessive. If she get's her teeth into it, she'll find anything that's there.

The wind had died and the rain was coming straight down. Seamus stood up and walked over to the edge of the porch. *How do I get Maeve really interested?* Seamus sighed out loud; *the only hope is the book itself. She is religious, that could be the attraction.*

A car came up the street with its lights on and turned into the driveway. It was P.J. He drove slowly by the porch and back to the garage behind the house. Seamus could hear P.J. closing the garage doors; so he walked over to that end of the porch and looked around the house.

P.J. ran, crouched over, up the driveway in the rain and jumped up onto the porch. "Hullo, Seamus. Nice weather. You must be feeling right at home."

"Not so much; at home it only rains this hard in a gale."

"If you'll set me up a chair, I'll get us both a beer."

"Done."

P.J. went into the house and left the door open. Seamus set up another chair next to his and sat down. After a few minutes, P.J. came back with four beers and handed two to Seamus. Seamus smiled and nodded. He knew P.J. could be a help. More to the truth he realized he had never talked with P.J. before. *How odd*, he was just now realizing how taciturn he had been since he arrived. P.J. was pleasant enough. Thinking back over the previous weeks, Seamus decided he rather liked P.J. but the depression stopped any conversation. *My grief bottled me up and put in the cork. It was well past time to break this wall and find out more about the man my sister married. But what to say? Anything, you idiot, say anything.*

"How was your meeting?" Seamus blurted.

P.J. paused, looking at Seamus with an expression of what? Pride? Sympathy? Then he turned his head to the rainstorm and shrugged.

"Nothing worth talking about. We're planning on a special day next month. I was hoping we could get some authors in for a book signing. You'll like this, we're going to focus on Irish authors."

"Oh? Why would you want to do that? There can't be many left."

"They're not all dead Seamus. There are some excellent Irish writers very much alive."

"I suppose. I know I'm getting stiffness of the brain. It's age you know; but I stopped after I read Ulysses."

"You read Ulysses?"

"Oh yes, it was required reading."

P.J. frowned, "I couldn't get into it at all. I gave up after a few pages. What did you think?"

"I have no idea. I still don't know what the fuss is all about."

"That's a dangerous thing for an Irishman to say."

"I don't tell the world. In the right, uh, wrong situation, I nod and smile a lot."

"You can be quite likeable Seamus."

"And you also, P.J."

" So, any news about the book?"

"Ulysses?"

"No, the one you got at the sale."

"Yes, actually. I got a reply from my friend in San Francisco. He says it's medieval and handwritten by a monk or some such."

"Good Lord, Seamus it must be worth a lot of money."

"How much?"

"Hell, I don't know. I'd have to know more and then get it appraised. It would be the sort of item that would be auctioned. I would expect museums would bid on it. And private collectors too, but they'd be people with a lot of money to invest."

"So the first thing to do would be to find out more about it."

"Uh huh."

"I wish I'd had you call Father Schmidt today."

"I did."

"You did?"

"Yes, Maeve had already talked to him. Must have been about two o'clock. You've been set up with him for this Friday at nine in the morning. Hope that's all right."

Seamus felt surprisingly calm. He waited for the usual fear of going out, meeting strange people, even mild apprehension at having to dress up and look presentable. *Nothing. Peculiar.*

He heard himself say, "I'm delighted. Friday was the soonest he could see me?"

P.J. hid his feelings. *This was not the man who moved in a few days ago. I suppose I'm finally seeing the brother Maeve described with so much admiration. Well enough.*

"You don't know how fortunate you are. He's very busy. From what he told me, he was so excited he shifted quite a bit of real work out of the way. He can't wait to see you but he couldn't clear his desk until then."

"So."

Seamus and P.J. both finished their first beers at the same time. Seamus held up his empty can and looked at P.J. quizzically. P.J. squeezed the middle of the can put it on the porch and stood on it to flatten it out.

Seamus followed his example and they both sat down and opened their second beers at the same time.

"Listen, Seamus. I've got a friend who has one of the last of the Graphics Boutiques - I'll translate that. He does miscellaneous artwork for companies, advertising agencies mostly. The thing is he's an expert on typefaces; loves type in general; designs his own type and knows the history of type. It's more a hobby than an occupation. He would love to see your book and he may be able to tell you something about it. Would you like to meet him?"

Seamus sighed inwardly, *in for a shilling in for a pound,* he thought.

"Nothing could please me more. Hold on, that's a very large exaggeration but you take my meaning."

They both sat in silence for a while, sipping their beers and watching the rain.

Either old Saint Raymond or Saint Dymphna are behind this, thought Seamus. *I would have been bumbling about for a few days, on my own. I wish I knew which saint it was though; it certainly would color my thinking. Still, no complaints. This 'type' person may read much that's invisible to me and it fills the gap between here and Friday.*

He turned to P.J. "P.J. does your type friend know Latin?"

"I doubt it. Does it matter that much?"

"I don't know, maybe it would help."

"You've got Father Schmidt for that. Sam will just tell you lots of interesting stuff about this lettering the monk was writing. He can tell you, more or less, when it was written. Other than that, I don't really know."

"It sounds worth the trip." and it did. Seamus was becoming interested in almost anything about the book. The idea of learning what handwritten typefaces were all about in the middle ages was out of the way knowledge. Seamus loved 'out of the way' knowledge.

The screen door opened, it was Maeve. "Supper's in the offing you two. Do you want me to do it?"

"P.J. looked stricken. He put his hand over his heart.

"Maeve, I'll grill. I promised I would." Maeve was relieved and it showed. She enjoyed any meal she didn't have to cook.

"Well, get on with it then. It's late."

"C'mon Seamus give me a hand."

They got up and went into the house walking through the hall into the kitchen and out the sliding glass doors onto the back deck. P.J. opened the top of the grill and Seamus picked up a bag of charcoal. P.J. waved him back. "No, I don't need that anymore; I have a new gas grill."

Fascinated, Seamus watched. It looked no more difficult than cooking in a kitchen. It was obvious Seamus 'help' was just a way of saying 'keep company'.

P.J. grilled split chicken breasts and potatoes wrapped in aluminum foil. Maeve made a salad. Unusually, Seamus' nephew Conor was home for supper.

"Uncle Seamus?"

"Yes, Conor."

"Father Schmidt told me he's going to meet you Friday."

"That's correct."

"What about?"

"The book I brought back from the library sale last Monday."

"Oh." Conor looked relieved. Maeve noticed.

"Don't worry Conor, it's nothing to do with you."

"It may not be much to do with me either," said Seamus.

P.J. laughed. After supper, Conor went up to his room to play computer games. The adults gathered in the lounge with their coffee.

"This is a fine example of the fruits of civilization," Seamus muttered sipping his coffee. After some confusing chat about local matters, P.J. turned to Maeve.

"Would you be able to take Seamus over to Gilbert Avenue tomorrow morning?"

Maeve looked at Seamus. "I have a lot on my list at present. What time?"

"Nine o'clock."

"It's after the morning rush; that's a blessing. Where am I going?"

"Over to Sam's to show him the book."

Maeve brightened. She liked Sam and she had always been fascinated by his art. As a copywriter, she was interested in language and typefaces. Sam was expert in both.

"May I sit in?"

Seamus was surprised - and pleased.

"Certainly, I'd rather you did."

The talk turned to other topics; Conor's schoolwork, family history, and the differences between Ireland and the States. Everyone called it a day and went to bed early, big day tomorrow.

Chapter 4: The Volunteer

The next day was cold and raining, as usual. Greenup Street was one way headed north to the Ohio River. Steve had come over the big bridge and was going east on Fifth Street in Covington. It was about eleven in the morning. "Are we too late Jock?"

"I doon think it matters that much, Steve. I just hope she's home."

Steve turned right at a street he guessed to be one short and went south a few blocks, then a left and watched for the signs. "There it is."

He turned left again and slowed down. "Her place should be on the left. Hope I can find a spot close."

"No, you don't. You want to be a bit out of sight."

"Oh, yeah, right. I think that's her about three up. I'll take this slot here."

Steve pulled up past an empty spot and backed in. He handed the scrap of paper with her name and address to Jock. "Here, good luck pronouncing the name."

Jock grinned, "I'll just call her Gladys."

Jock got out, looked at the paper and walked up the sidewalk looking for house numbers. Steve was right; it was the third one up. It was a tall, narrow brick house. It looked like it was attached on both sides, but, when you were in front you could see a narrow space between houses. Jock opened the wrought iron gate, stepped through and carefully closed it behind him. *I should be well mannered,* he thought. He walked up the brick path and took the three steps in three steps. "And I shouldn't be in a hurry," he muttered under his breath. It was a wooden porch with four ornate wood pillars. The front door was magnificent; a pattern of three-dimensional panels in old oak and with an oval of beautiful cut glass. Not leaded glass; each piece was framed in oak molding. He knocked using a brass lion's head knocker.

A voice came from somewhere inside toward the back of the house. "Coming, just a minute."

Jock looked around and back down the street. There wasn't a soul in sight. There wasn't even a car, well, not in motion anyway. About a dozen cars were parked and empty; except for Steve about a half a block back.

"Can I help you?" The voice came from the other side of the door.

"I hope so, I missed you at the book sale yesterday."

"The book sale?"

"Aye, the bit about the special book."

The door opened without a sound, it startled Jock. Jock took off his cap and Gladys' eyes followed the cap. A look like recognition lit up her face. She was smiling almost to a grin.

"Oh my. How did I do?" Jock held his smile and thought, *Wha the bloody hell did she mean by that?*

"Oh yah did fane, fane, uh fine. Ahd like to talk about it a little. Can you spare the time?"

"Oh, of course, c'mon in. She opened the door wider, turned and walked down the hall into the house. She continued talking. "I don't have much to do you know. My husband's retired and he's off fishing with some friends."

Jock followed her in, stopped and gently closed the door. Then he walked in the direction of her voice. She had disappeared into the back. *Her husband's fishing? I guess they're supposed to be easier to catch in cold and rain.*

The hallway ended in the kitchen. As Jock caught up with Gladys, she was clearing the paper and some breakfast dishes from the table.

Jock stopped in the doorway. "Well, we were just wonderin if you'd mind telling us exactly what happened."

"What happened? Goodness you have it all on film. Why don't you just watch it?" Jock got a chill. Ah Gaod, was Jimmy right? Had they been set up? He thought as quickly as he could.

"Ah well, it's not like a video tape. It's gone off to be processed."

"Oh, I didn't think of that. Of course, what would you like to know?"

"Ah nothing special. Wha not just tell it to me the way you remember it."

"All right, would you like some tea?"

"That'd be very nice, thank you luv." *Oops, I hope that wasn't too friendly,* he thought.

She didn't notice and started to put water in the kettle.

"Well, let's see. First I was worried about the time. When your director's man came to me, I forgot about having to be home by four. It was all so exciting you see."

Jock smiled, *was this the way the old man did it or were the Feds in the middle?*

Gladys continued, "Well, I was worried at first. But then your man was there. I could see the enormous camera on his shoulder. I felt better then because I knew I could go tell him I had to leave if it didn't go right the first time."

Jock looked interested. *Hmm, I noticed a couple of cameramen. I just thought they were the local news,* he thought.

"Anyway they said it would only take five minutes. So I knew I'd be all right." She put two cups on the table and went to get tea bags in one of the cabinets.

Jock was starting to see that this was not going the way Jimmy hoped.

Gladys had stopped talking, so Jock prompted, "So everything started on time?"

"Oh yes, he came up to my table right on the dot. He was very good; not like an actor at all. He had a wonderful accent, not like yours but very nice." She put the tea bags in the cups and went to the stove to get the kettle.

"He was wearing the jacket and cap. I'd say it was exactly like yours but his was brown not gray. I said my line 'lovely afternoon'. I'll confess I felt pretty silly saying that. Do you people think it's all right considering the weather?" She poured the water into the cups. "Do you take lemon or milk? How about sugar?"

Jock, was staring out the window over the sink. "Sorry?"

"Sugar? Milk?"

"Oh, just sugar, thank you." She pushed the sugar bowl over in front of him and went to the refrigerator and got out the milk.

"Well, anyway, he said his lines, you know, the 'I'm just passing the time'. I didn't expect to actually have a conversation you know. Did that come out all right?"

"It was good." Jock was starting to sweat. *Easy, keep calm,* he thought.

"And then I gave him the book." Not soon enough for me, I can tell you. That was the heaviest book I ever lifted. Well, except for a big dictionary. But you don't actually carry those do you?"

Jock was furiously trying to think of a way to get a description from her. Then he had it.

"How was his makeup?"

"Oh my, it must've been good, I didn't even see any makeup. Unless, were those his real eyes? They were awfully bright blue. I thought they might have been contacts."

"I don't really know, I don't know him personally. So which way did he walk when he left you?"

"Just like he was supposed to; over toward the Westin Hotel. I didn't pay that much attention, I'm afraid. I did look over at the cameraman and he gave me a smile.

"And then you left?"

"Well, I didn't just run away. I thought it was all right but I felt I'd better check. So I went over to the cameraman and told him I had to leave. He looked at me funny but he said OK."

"I see." Jock drank his tea. He didn't sip it he drank it.

"Well, Gladys... may I call you Gladys?"

"Oh yes, of course."

"You've been a dear. I'm glad I didn't bother you. That's all I need now I have to go. Can I call again, if I've forgotten anything? Directors can often be very demanding."

“Certainly, this is the most exciting thing. When will the movie be released?”

“Ah ahm sorry, I don’t really know. They don’t tell me such.” Jock stood up and turned to the hallway. Gladys walked behind him to the door. Jock opened the door. “Beautiful door Gladys.”

“Yes isn’t it, Perry did all the restoration himself. He’s very proud of it.”

“Ah ken that. Goodbye.” Jock walked down the porch steps while Gladys stood in the doorway. He looked back when he reached the gate and waved and smiled. She waved and went back into the house. Jock watched to be sure she wasn’t looking out the door and then realized she wouldn’t be able to see through all that cut glass. He went through the gate, closed it behind him and walked as slowly as he could back to the car. He wanted to run but he realized he might be watched.

Gaod what a mess, he thought, *Jimmy’s not going to like this at all.*

Chapter 5: Paleography

The next morning Seamus was awake at seven. These mornings were very different. For three years or so he had slept until nine or even later. As he dressed, he realized a new and yet much older feeling. The start of a new day with something of interest in the offing. A familiar feeling not there for a long time, *like catching the smell of a freshly turned field or a bog,* he thought with smile.

He was excited, today, someone with special knowledge would tell him more about his book.

Conor got off to school and P.J. was already gone.

It was warmer and there didn't seem to be much chance of rain. So Seamus wore his jacket, but decided to leave his cap at home.

When they left, Maeve told Seamus to wait on the porch while she got out her car. She didn't drive much and the car sat in the garage most of the time. She backed out until she cleared the edge of the porch and opened her window.

"All right, in you get."

Seamus walked around to the far side and got in. It felt strange to be sitting on the right. He kept looking for a wheel and pedals.

Maeve backed out and into the street to go left - away from the avenue.

"Don't we go to the avenue to go anywhere?"

"No, it's too busy and there are too many traffic lights."

She went to the end of the street and then turned right and drove up to a 'T' junction. Seamus looked at all the large houses and even larger trees. It was a beautiful area.

"Some of these trees must be a hundred years old Maeve."

"Oh yes, this is an old part of the town."

Maeve turned to the right, went only a hundred yards, turned left and drove down a long and winding hill. There were no houses, just dense woods.

Seamus was surprised. "Are we still in the city?"

Maeve laughed. "Oh yes. It took me a little time to get used to it. I imagine the hills are responsible. They break everything up and it's more difficult to build on a hillside. The hills never seemed to stop them in the past though."

"It's certainly very pleasant."

"It is."

At the bottom of the hill, they drove past some small houses and stopped at a light. When it changed Maeve turned onto a busy street and then turned again. To Seamus' amazement, they were on a motorway ramp.

After five or ten minutes, Maeve took an off ramp and stopped at a light. Looking to the left, she turned right before the light changed.

"It's a good thing I don't drive here Maeve. I would have killed myself or someone else by now."

Maeve nodded and turned into a parking area behind some buildings.

"Here we are, Seamus."

"That was short."

"Nothing here seems to be more than fifteen minutes from anywhere else, Seamus."

They walked across the macadam to some steps and Maeve started up. Seamus followed along looking around. *Another old area,* he thought. The buildings had been set on the remains of foundations much older. The original foundations were just walls of stones with sand between.

They reached the top of the steps and walked across a wooden deck to the rear entrance. Maeve just walked in, stopped and looked around. "Anybody to home?"

A pudgy young man came around the end of the far wall.

"Hullo, Maeve. You here to see Uncle Sam?"

"Yes, John."

"You can go on up. He's up there mumbling about something he doesn't like."

They walked across and down a hallway to what was the front of the building. There was a reception desk, padded chairs, plants and a very pretty girl reading the paper.

"Good morning Theresa. Not much to do today?"

"Hi, Maeve. There never is; I don't know why Sam insists on my sitting here. He's expecting you. Whaddya got? He's all excited."

"It's not what I have, it's my brother Seamus here. Seamus meet Theresa." Seamus bowed and took Theresa's hand. "A pleasure."

"Nice to meetcha Seamus."

"See you later Theresa," Maeve said, starting toward the stairs. Seamus hurried after her. At the foot of the steps, he looked up. The stairs were very steep and went up three floors with a small landing at each level.

"You'd better not have any extra pounds on you if you're to work here."

Maeve looked down at him. "I suppose you'd be free of any extras soon enough."

After a long climb they came to a single room at the very top. There was no door. There was a very thick plush carpet and a lot of furniture arranged in a lounge setting. In the far corner was a sandy haired man at a desk. He stood up.

"Maeve, it's been a while."

"Too long Sam. This is my brother, Seamus. He said it would be fine if I joined you."

"Hi, Seamus. I've been really looking forward to this. Show me this book. Oh sorry, sit down, make yourselves comfortable."

There were two very large upholstered chairs next to the desk. Seamus pulled the book out of its plastic bag, handed it to Sam and sat down. Maeve sat and leaned over to rest her elbows on the edge of the desk.

Sam took the book with reverence, laid it on the desk and reached over to a double elbowed combination lamp and magnifying glass. He pulled it over to a position just above the book, looked through it to get the focus and slowly opened the book. Seamus looked over at Maeve, but she was watching Sam closely.

"Oh my God," Sam breathed softly. "It's Textus Precissus."

"What is that?" Seamus said.

"Wait a minute would you?" Sam opened a lower drawer in his desk, reached in and pulled out a pair of white gloves. As he started to pull them on he looked around the magnifying glass.

"Seamus, this is probably fourteenth century - 1300's. It may even be older than that but not much, maybe a century. This was before printing had been invented. In those days, a script was called - well it's still called - a 'hand'. This particular hand is known as Textus Precissus. It's very simple compared to what happened next; when the Renaissance got going."

Seamus' brow furrowed, "Um, what does that tell us?"

"Well, this particular hand was used by the scribes to save space. By this time all of Europe was overwhelmed with the need for scribes. Not just to copy old manuscripts but for day-to-day business.

Anyway, as the clamoring for more books increased, the scribes had to find ways to squash more words on a page. That's where Textus came from."

"I noticed it was very small."

"It isn't just that it's small. They changed the hand. They condensed the letters into this. He pointed at the open book. The dark angular sigils increased the number of words in a line. Then they reduced the length of the ascenders and descenders to get more lines on a page. To squeeze in even more, they improved and extended the idea of ligatures."

"Ligatures?"

"Uh huh, a ligature is two letters stuck together. You've seen it and didn't notice; like 'fl' for example. Our eyes don't bobble at certain letter combinations. By putting them together they eliminated any space between. That space added up."

"Why was it called 'Textus'? Doesn't that just mean text?"

Sam chuckled. "You'd think so. Text, texture, it all comes from the same root. All these hands from that period were known as Textus, because they looked like fabric on the page. By the time of the Renaissance, scribes considered this old-fashioned and called any of these hands Gothic - we still call them Gothic."

"So this is one of many Textuses...uh Texti?"

"Yeah, this was probably done in England."

"England?"

"Or somewhere in the British Isles. Might have more of a chance to be from your homeland, Seamus. The Irish monks were in a pocket. They didn't have to look over their shoulders all the time."

"How's that?"

Sam leaned back in his chair. "Imagine what it was like back then. The mainland of Europe was continually at war. England and France were in the hundred year's war but it didn't get to England; most of the murder was in France. Ireland was well away from it all. That meant the Irish were left alone.

This particular hand was called Textus Precissus. There was a Textus Quadratus at the same time.

Now I don't want to mislead you. The Brits did seem to prefer Precissus, but they were both common all over north and central Europe."

"What about Italy?"

"Umm, the southern countries - Italy, Spain - the Mediterranean, preferred a rounder look. They used a form of Textus known as round Gothic, or Rotunda.

"Why did you say this might be earlier than the fourteenth century?"

"It's not a bastard."

"Say that again."

Sam's eyes twinkled. "It's not a moral slur, Seamus. The hands of the fourteenth century evolved from the Textus' into something called Semi-cursive or Bastard hands. In this case, bastard just means 'descended from' or 'child of'. This one could be in the 1200's or it may be the scribe was just off in the boondocks and wasn't up to date. That's part of why I thought it may be from Ireland." Sam grinned. "That, and the fact that you're Irish."

Maeve looked at Seamus. "You see Seamus, you've started distorting the facts already." Seamus smiled.

"How do you know all this Sam?"

"Seamus, I love this stuff. Do you know how hard it is to get to see something like this? He waved at the book. I'd have to go to a museum or the rare books room at the library. Here you go and put it on my desk."

"So the Public Library has books like this?"

"Not many, they have more fragments and not many of those; they're pages from dismembered volumes. Of course, most of those are religious. You know, hymnals and such. I just wish I read Latin."

"You don't?"

"No, unfortunately I don't. I'll have to learn it one of these days. Oh, I can stumble through some of it; but really I'm more interested in the beautiful art these scribes produced."

"You keep saying scribes; weren't they all monks?"

"In the early middle ages, yes they were but, after a time, education became an increasingly important issue. So, 'seats of learning' - universities - were established that were more and more secular. They needed books and documents and monasteries just didn't have enough monks to provide them. Of course, a new occupation was born - scribe. By the way, even in the earlier part of the middle ages, not all monks were scribes. A lot of monks never copied a book."

Seamus nodded, "Like Cadfael, of course. He just fiddled with plants and solved mysteries - like me."

"You're a detective?"

"As much as I don't feel so today - yes I am."

Maeve looked at Seamus.

"Much as I dislike giving the compliment, he's very good at it too. Of course, the relatives don't approve."

Seamus nodded to his left, at Maeve.

"Even Jesus could never impress the people in his own town."

Sam smiled, "What else can I tell you?"

"What kind of paper is this?" Seamus pointed at the book.

"It's not."

"Not?"

"It's parchment, not paper; in this case it's actually vellum, made from the skin of a cow. Sheep were the usual suppliers and that skin was called parchment."

Maeve looked a trifle sick.

"I never thought of what parchment was made from. It's so much more pleasant to just say parchment."

Seamus wrinkled his nose.

"The sheepskin, of course. So that's why the pages feel so thick."

"Yup."

"Then what about the cover?"

"It's leather too. That wasn't common, but it was done often enough. Usually, they would make the cover from wooden boards. That's why they're called boards."

"It's bound; I thought all these medieval manuscripts were just rolled up."

Sam laughed. "That's the movies. Bookbinding goes back a lot farther than this. They were doing Egyptian Coptic binding in the ninth century. You know, it sounds like you're after as much information as you can get. I'm not used to that. Most people listen to me politely, and then after a few minutes, they doze off."

"You're quite right, Sam. I want to know everything. This is truly fascinating."

"All right, let's look a little deeper."

Sam moved his magnifying glass back into place and started to look hard at the first page. After a long pause, he turned the page, then another and another and another. He stopped and turned a page back. Frowned and went forward again a couple of pages.

"This is interesting, Seamus. Your monk's style is the same for the first few leaves and then it changes. Sam looked over the magnifying glass at Seamus. This is just a guess, but I'd say it's more than the content change. Of course he then moves from Latin to Greek but it goes beyond that. As if he started in one mood and then his disposition changed. Of course, it may have been a different monk. It's still recognizably Precissus."

"Hold on Sam, a different monk?"

"Oh sure, this copying business took a long time. One monk might start it and then get sick, go blind or even die. Another monk would be drafted to finish the job. I don't think that's the case here though. The style is much too similar. He may have been tired or weak when he wrote part one and then had a good rest before going on. What the? I just thought of something." Sam closed the book and looked carefully at the cover. Then he turned the book over and looked at the back.

"Huh, that's a question answered. I just realized this didn't have any clasps. It did though, at one time. The amazing thing is how tight and clean the leaves are. When did you get a hold of this?"

"Last Monday."

"Where have you kept it?"

Seamus looked puzzled. "At Maeve's."

"No, I mean what did you keep it in?"

"It's been in that plastic bag most of the time." Seamus pointed.

"You should know you've been very lucky."

"Why is that?"

"Well, this parchment, sorry, vellum is very fine quality; it was scraped on both sides. That means, to me, that this is cowhide. They only scraped cowhide on both sides. Regardless of which it is, if it's exposed to the humidity or even just left alone without any compression, the leaves might cockle and warp."

Maeve's eyebrows went up. "Cockle?"

Sam smiled. "Yeah, I don't think I can explain without using that particular word. You see, left alone without something to keep the cover closed, the leaves are trying to return to their original shape. Sorry to bring this up again, but it *is* animal skin. The fact that it doesn't have boards in the cover makes the problem even more serious." He looked at the book. "I can't prove it, but I'll bet my type collection to a dollar that this book was in a museum or a private preservation vault before you got it."

Seamus eyes stared into space. *So,* he thought. *If that's true, it was no mistake or error in judgement. If it was so carefully preserved, the owner knew damn well what he had. Then why would he give it to a library sale? Maybe he didn't, maybe it was stolen and the thieves were smart enough to get it out of their hands. They certainly couldn't sell it, could they?*

"Seamus? Seamus?" It was Maeve.

"Oh sorry. Have there been any significant robberies lately?"

Sam looked interested. Maeve looked like Seamus had gone mad.

"Did you see any in the paper? You read it. Are you off again?"

"Now Maeve, it is an explanation."

"I see where you're going Seamus. You may be right. This is no ordinary book," said Sam.

Seamus glanced at Maeve then back to Sam. "There you see? Wait a bit Sam; how valuable can it be? I noticed there aren't any illuminations."

"Hell, Seamus, I don't really know. As far as I'm concerned, it's priceless. It's a good question; illuminations do contribute to the value, if only because we admire them so much. Usually though, illuminations would be done to contribute to the greater glory of God. They'll be in religious works, not so often in secular works. I'd say this is either secular or worse."

"Worse?"

"Oh yeah, they may have thought this...um... *diminished* the glory of God."

"Then why would they copy it?"

"The leaders of the Catholic Church in those days tended to be those with money and power. They were perfectly willing, even eager, to preserve knowledge that was useful. But remember, their power came from keeping everyone else busy reading their breviaries. They didn't want the faithful anything more than faithful, if you catch my drift."

"I do indeed, I drifted there myself."

Maeve looked at Sam. "Sam!" she said accusingly.

"Sorry Maeve, it is true. The middle ages weren't referred to as dark without reason. The mass of people, no pun intended, were simple peasants. They were ignorant and superstitious. Only a very small handful were what we would call educated. The Church was - still is - an institution for the preservation of many things; knowledge was one of the good things - power was the natural tendency. Anyway, I didn't intend to bring up a discussion of organized religion. The important point is that this would likely have been preserved; whether it was considered sacrilegious or not. But it must have been considered *useful*."

Seamus frowned. "Sam, didn't these scribes come from the peasant population in the first place?"

Sam looked over at him. "In some cases, yes."

"Well then, wouldn't they be kept in the, um, dark even after they were monks?"

"They would. There were even cases when a scribe was copying manuscripts written in a language he didn't understand. By this time he didn't have to; he simply needed to be a good copyist. By the fourteenth century, the demand for books was way beyond the supply of scribes; so it was a good idea anyway. You see in the early years of the monasteries, they didn't even separate the words. The scribe actually had to read the text out loud in order to know what he was copying. He had to know the language. The scriptoriums were full of monks all murmuring to themselves. By this time, the words were separated and silent reading became the norm."

"So this is not a religious book."

"I didn't say that. It could be it was religious and was copied in a rush. I don't have a hard and fast reason; I just don't think it was."

Seamus thought, then looked at Sam.

"Suppose this was in that category of dangerous; sacrilegious or not. What would the high eminences do to have it copied? Would they do it themselves?"

"Maybe, if they were scribes. I would think most of them were not or considered copying beneath more important matters, like planning the next war." Sam leaned back and stared at the ceiling.

"Just thinking out loud. I would imagine they would find an obscure monastery, away from the threat of attack. Then they would see to it that the head Abbot was a man of unquestioned loyalty, perhaps someone with political ambition. They would charge him with the task, not to do himself you understand, but to give to one of his scribes. Who would he pick? I don't know. Somebody as loyal as himself? - probably not. Another monk with the same aspirations might be considered a threat. Someone particularly pious? Again, depending on what this is, he wouldn't want to risk damaging that piety; it would be like lighting a fuse. The best would be someone who didn't speak Greek. No problem there; the scribe wouldn't know what he was looking at."

Seamus smiled at Sam. "If you ever want to change careers, Sam; come and see me. You'd make a good detective."

Sam laughed. "I'll admit, it sounds like fun. But I think I have enough puzzles to solve as it is."

Maeve jumped up. "God bless us all! I forgot! I have to be back to give Conor his swimming pass."

Sam looked at his watch. "You're right, I even lost track of lunch." He stood up. "Seamus this has been a wonderful morning. You and your book have been the most fun and the most interesting fun, I've had all year."

"Thank you Sam. May I call on you again?"

"Anytime at all, you don't even have to call first. I'm here everyday; usually weekends too."

They shook hands. Sam gave Maeve a hug. They all walked over to the top of the stairs.

Sam looked at Seamus. "How long are you over here?"

"Another two or three weeks. I don't remember what I'm allowed before your government throws me out."

Sam smiled. "OK if I think of anything else, I'll call you at Maeve and P.J.'s."

"That would be fine; thank you Sam."

Maeve and Seamus started down the stairs.

Maeve was leading the way. At the first landing she stopped and turned to Seamus. She looked worried.

"Seamus, if this book is so valuable, why was it at the book sale?" She turned back and continued walking down.

"I've thought about that; I think it was a mistake."

"Oh, please. No one could have been that ignorant."

No, no one could be that ignorant, Seamus thought. *No one who had their hands on this book, anyway.* Maeve had started, well - restarted, a train of thought. *Or maybe it's just a tram.* Seamus smiled to himself.

Sam had not only convinced Seamus to throw out his 'mistake or error in judgement' theories; he'd opened another path that Seamus had been avoiding. *If this had been stolen, why wouldn't the news be in the newspaper? There were new explanations that occurred to Seamus. It may have belonged to a private collector who didn't know it was gone. Or a private collector who didn't want anyone to know he ever had it in the first place. Of course it may not have been stolen; if so why was it there?*

They were on the motorway now. Maeve looked over at Seamus.

"You're very quiet."

"I'm thinking."

"Well, I hope so. I shudder at the alternatives that come to mind."

"Maeve? Is this a very wealthy town?"

"Oh yes."

"Was it always wealthy?"

"Of course not. When it was a muddy bank on the river, I suspect it wasn't."

"You know what I mean."

"Sorry, I didn't know you were serious. Yes, since before the American Civil War. Charles Dickens came here at some point."

"So there are, and have been for some time, very wealthy men in this city?"

"Absolutely! You wouldn't know for example that during the depression, not one bank failed here." Seamus looked at her. "Lord, this would be the place to put away my savings."

"Don't be so cynical. It's quite true, if you were very conservative. They're no longer the entrepreneurial types."

"All right, I'll come right out with it. I should infer, from what you've just said, that there are men here that could be the private owners of books like this?"

Maeve was starting into the driveway. She stopped the car and looked at Seamus. "Oh yes, quite a few. Though not so many as there were, perhaps." She shook her head and drove to the edge of the porch. "Out you hop, I don't want you in my way at the garage."

Seamus got out and walked around behind the car and onto the porch. He stood looking out across the road with his hands in his pockets. *Suppose someone didn't want anyone to know it was stolen; why would that be? Because they had it illegally themselves is all I can think of. Or perhaps?* He frowned. *Perhaps he arranged all of this on purpose? That's nonsense; he couldn't know me at all. Let alone that Maeve would tell me to push off and send me straight to the book. The thought hit him and he slapped his head. You idiot, it wasn't meant for me at all. It was meant for someone else!*

Maeve walked around from the drive and up to the porch. She tried the door, it was locked. "Oh that's a relief; Conor's not been here yet."

"How do you know?"

"Don't be simple Seamus, he has a key and he never locks the door."

"Oh."

"Are you all right, Seamus?"

"Fine Maeve, I'm fine." He walked to her side, leaned past her and pushed the door open for her. They both walked into the house. This time Seamus remembered to hold the screen door so it wouldn't bang. It was warm. He took off his jacket and hung it up.

"Too early for a beer?"

"I should think not."

"And you?"

"No thank you, I'll wait a bit. Don't feel you need the reason, Seamus. You are on holiday."

So I am, he thought. *And never mind that, I do have a reason.* He was sure he was right. The book had been intended for someone else. Everything odd became understandable with that premise. The lady at the book sale was holding the book because she was expecting someone. She was insistent, because she was following a preset arrangement. *She must have been muddled at me. I shouldn't have been a perfect match. She handled it all well. I wonder if she was an actress? No, surely not. She didn't have the look about her. What look? That's the entire reason a good actress is good; they are what a 'normal' person is within the role. Never mind, it had to be the truth that she was part of a plan. A plan to put the book into the hands of someone without anyone else's knowledge.* Seamus had gone down to the refrigerator in the cellar and come back up the stairs with two beers. He stopped. *Well, this is not the answer, he thought. This is an answer but not the answer. All this has done is lead me to the next conundrum.* He opened the door and went to the lounge. *Do I watch television? No, I have to think this out.* He sat down and looked over at the hall table where the book lay in its plastic bag.

Back we go, he thought.

A strange, carefully contrived plan is laid to put this book in someone's hands. Why?

It was stolen. That seems the most likely. This was being 'fenced'. Lord no, if the owner was legitimate he'd cry murder at the top of his lungs. Unless he didn't realize it was gone.

Let's go back again. Why? Tax evasion? That didn't seem right. There are better, and easier, ways to avoid taxes.

Leave all of that. Who is the receiver of this book? Is he legitimately buying it and doesn't want anyone to know? A private collector selling to another private collector? Nonsense, they could do that in perfect secrecy - over a brandy. A pox on this book; I know there's an answer here somewhere.

All right, once more. It's stolen to begin with. Wait a bit, it's stolen sure enough but stolen many many years ago. How's that? I like that, let's go on. By this time Seamus was on his feet and pacing back and forth in front of the sofa. He wasn't aware he'd stood up.

Now, whoever had it; he's trying to get rid of it. He doesn't want anyone to know he ever had it at the start. I think I've got it; 'by George, I think he's got it'. Great film, that.

Hold up, why isn't the seller sitting with his buyer and a brandy?

Seamus sat down. *This theory is flawed; that's why.*

He looked up and Maeve was standing in the doorway with her arms folded.

"Are you finished then?" she said.

Seamus, a little sheepishly, said, "How long have you been standing there?"

"A good while. Your tramping got to my nerves."

She walked into the room and her tone was curious. "I don't want you to get all wrapped in anything risky again."

Seamus groaned, "I know and I appreciate your concern."

"No no, against my better judgment, I have to admit I've become interested myself."

"So?"

"Yes. It's the book. It is a curious thing. It seems to me that the more we know about this book, the better able you will be to uncover any lurking danger. And if that's true, then learning as much as possible will help to avoid that danger. What do you think?"

Seamus kept his face blank. "You're completely correct Maeve."

"All right then, I'll help you. With reservations of course; if I see any sign I don't like - you with a gun for instance - I'll drop it straight away and have you deported."

"Of course, thank you Maeve." She turned and walked back into her office.

The phone rang. Seamus could hear Maeve pick it up in her office. "McCarthy. Yes? Hello Sam. Oh I don't think so. Wait, let me put him on. Seamus? It's for you; it's Sam."

Seamus stood up and walked over to Maeve's office. She was standing in the middle of the room with the cordless phone in her hand. She walked over and handed it to him. "Go on. He wants to know if he can see you and the book tomorrow."

"Sam?"

"Hi, any chance of you coming over here tomorrow with the book? I've had some other thoughts and I'd like to look at it again."

"Sam I'd like to but I'm seeing a priest tomorrow morning and I don't know how long it will go."

"Hmm, well how about next Monday? I'm out on my boat with some friends over the weekend."

"Hold on Sam." He held the phone away from his ear and turned to Maeve. "Maeve could you take me back over to Sam's on Monday?"

"Yes, of course." Seamus put the phone back to his ear. "That's all right with Maeve and she's the boss."

"Great Seamus, I'll see you Monday morning. Anytime after eight in the morning and I'll have coffee. Hell, I'll even buy lunch." Seamus laughed. "You are enthused. See you then."

"See you Seamus, have a good weekend." He hung up and Seamus handed the phone back to Maeve.

"Well, I wonder what he's thought up. He seems to be quite taken with it all."

"I expected that, he loves old books and you've shown him one of the oldest of them all."

"So I have. I wonder what Father Schmidt will think."

"He'll love it too Seamus. As long as you have that book you will make many friends."

—####—

Seamus was sitting on the porch when P.J. pulled in to the driveway. Seamus went in and down to the cellar while P.J. put the car away.

When P.J. walked around to the front porch, Seamus handed him two beers.

"Ah Seamus, you have the customs down now." He sat down on the lawn chair.

"So, anything interesting to report?"

"I like your friend Sam."

"Yes, he's a great guy. What did he think of the book?"

"Quite fascinated."

"I expected that. Was he helpful?"

"Indeed he was. I learned very much. I'm to have an appointment to see him again Monday."

"Really? He *was* fascinated. He's a busy man you know. It's not easy to get any of his time.

So tell me all about it." Seamus told P.J. as much as he could remember. Maeve came out on the porch in the middle of the talk and then retreated into the house. She came out again and listened until Seamus had finished; then she interrupted.

"All right, that's about it. It's supper." She went back in and P.J. and Seamus followed.

Conor had come home earlier and was at the table. This was two days in a row and very different; he usually fetched his own snacks and went to his room or a friends' house.

"So Conor, to what do I owe the pleasure." Seamus said.

"Huh?" said Conor with a mouthful.

P.J. looked at his son. "Conor, your Uncle Seamus is right. You're never here for supper; this is two nights in a row."

Conor looked uncomfortable and blurted, "Oh, I was thinking you might talk about seeing Father Schmidt tomorrow."

"To show him the book."

"Is that all?"

"Oh Conor, I expect that's enough." Maeve grinned at her son.

Conor was relieved, "He's a good coach," he mumbled.

"Do you like him?"

"Yeah, he's more - uh - regular than the other teachers. Sometimes I think he gets in trouble."

Seamus looked at Conor.

"Why Conor?"

"Well, he gets excited and, I dunno, he just doesn't act like the other priests."

"I think we'll get along," said Seamus to Maeve. Maeve looked at Conor. "Made to order." She said sarcastically.

After supper, Conor went up to his room. Seamus, Maeve and P.J. sat in the lounge with their coffee and talked. P.J. got up and looked at the other two. That's all the coffee I dare have, how about you? Anyone want a refill?"

Maeve looked into her cup. "I'd better not P.J. Early morning tomorrow. I don't want anything between me and my sleep."

Seamus stood up. "I'll have another P.J. I want to do some more thinking. Here Maeve give me your cup and I'll put it in the kitchen." P.J. and Seamus walked into the kitchen.

"So Seamus, you haven't figured it all out yet?"

"No not even most of it. I still can't fathom why it was at the sale to begin with."

"You've given up on the theory it was a mistake."

"Completely - Sam gave that the coup de gras when he told me it had been carefully preserved up to now."

"Stolen?"

"I don't think so, I can't make it fit unless it was taken a long time ago.

Although it's just possible." Seamus was pouring his coffee. He looked at the wall.

"Look P.J. if the book had been stolen and the owner knew it was gone, he'd raise a fuss. There's been no sign of that. But then, if he didn't know it was gone, he'd either be a very busy man or he didn't look at it very often. Or..." Seamus paused and looked around at P.J. "Suppose he was very wealthy and had an extensive collection of such things. Is it possible this wouldn't be missed?"

P.J. frowned, "Hm, It's possible. Anything's possible. Doesn't seem very likely."

They walked back into the lounge. Maeve looked up at them. "I overheard that. Seamus, the only way to know, is to find out just how special this book actually is. After all, this shadowy owner, you're speaking about, might have dozens of them."

Seamus sighed, "Ah Maeve, you're right of course. God give me patience. Father Schmidt will help tomorrow."

They chatted a while longer and then went to bed.

Chapter 6: The Latin Teacher

The next morning everyone was up early and all in the kitchen together. Maeve had an Irish breakfast on the table - eggs, rashers of bacon, some fried tomato. She looked at Conor. "You're a lucky lad this time. You can ride in with us." "Conor looked up at his mother. "Do I have to?"

"You'd rather not?"

"Well, it's just that the guys will all be on the bus and I won't know what's going on."

"Oh." Maeve looked at Seamus. "All right then go on and take your bus. I certainly don't mind. Seamus?" Seamus had a mouthful. He looked at Conor and then Maeve and finished chewing. "Fine fine, Uncle Seamus never wants to be in the way."

Conor got up and ran for the door. Maeve looked at Seamus. "We don't have to leave for a bit. I'll have time to clear up." She started clearing the table.

Seamus went to the front hall and looked at the thermometer on the porch. It was seventy degrees Fahrenheit. *Uh oh, I can leave the cap behind,* he thought. *I suppose I'll be all right in my jacket. I'll stay in the house this afternoon, in the air conditioning.*

Maeve walked by to get the car out. "It's going to be a warm day."

"I noticed that."

Seamus followed her out onto the porch and waited. She walked down the driveway to the garage.

Seamus stared at an enormous Plane tree on the other side of the road. *Good heavens,* he thought. *Dear old Ireland could use more trees like that. They're trying at least. Many trees have been planted in recent years.* Seamus sighed, *They take so long to grow.*

Maeve backed up beside the porch and rolled down her window. "In you get." Seamus walked around and got into the car. "Shouldn't I lock the door?"

"It'll be all right, we won't be away long." She backed the car out into the road and drove toward the Avenue. "Why aren't we avoiding all the traffic you talked about?"

"Can't do that this time. The school is on the other side."

It was a short drive. They were only on the Avenue for two blocks before Maeve turned right onto a residential side road. She drove all the way to the end and turned left. "This avoids all the school traffic, buses mostly. They stop to let the children on and you have to wait each time. It's maddeningly slow." Seamus nodded as he thought, *everything was so crowded in together. The center of the village was everywhere. You never left it.*

They were driving along another residential section and ahead on the left he could see the school. It was enormous. The car park was larger than a football pitch and there were at least a dozen school buses there. Some of them had streams of students getting off. Most were empty.

Maeve drove around the parked buses to a visitors parking area and found a spot.

They got out and Maeve locked the car. "I don't leave it open here. Some of the kids might be tempted." Seamus nodded and walked around to her side. "Lead on MacBeth."

"That's 'lay on MacDuff' and don't tempt me."

She walked toward the largest building. Seamus followed and noticed when they got closer they were not separate buildings at all; just one large one with multiple wings. They went through a large entrance with glass doors and down a hallway. There was an office on the left and Maeve went in. "Good morning. We're here to see Father Schmidt." An older lady behind a counter looked up. She looked exhausted already and it wasn't yet nine o'clock.

"Do you have an appointment?"

"Yes we do."

"Name?" Maeve turned and looked at Seamus.

"Well, it would be either McCarthy or Cash."

The lady picked up a phone and punched three numbers. "Father Schmidt? Someone to see you. That's right. I'll send them right over." She hung up and looked up at Maeve.

"Do you know where to go?"

"Oh yes."

"Then would you sign this sheet." It wasn't a question. Maeve signed where the lady pointed. Seamus watched with interest.

After they left the office and were walking down the corridor Seamus leaned over to Maeve's ear.

"You'd think we were seeing an inmate in a prison," he whispered.

Maeve grinned.

"Yes, I know. After all the strange doings in schools over here, they're frightened half to death."

The hallway was empty. All the classes were in session. They came to a door with glass in the top and painted on the glass was the title 'Language Department'. Maeve opened the door and went in; Seamus right behind her. There was a young girl at a desk just inside the door. Maeve went up to her.

"Good morning, we're here to see Father Schmidt."

"Oh yes, he's expecting you. Just go down that hall and it's the third door on the left." She pointed to her left and back. They both looked at the hall and Maeve said thank you.

"You know Seamus, it's much worse in many other schools. They would have put you through a metal detector and your bag." She pointed at the book. They stopped in front of the third door and Maeve knocked on the glass. A voice from inside said, "Come in." Maeve opened the door and just inside she stopped.

"Hello Father. What are you doing?"

Seamus looked over her shoulder. Father Schmidt was young; about thirty five, Seamus guessed. He was standing on a chair and peering out a narrow window set high in the wall. The window was so narrow he had his head turned on its side.

"Hello Maeve. I can't remember whether I locked my car." He turned around and got down off the chair.

"You must be Seamus, very happy to meet you." He put out his hand. Seamus shook hands and lifted up the plastic bag.

"Here it is." he said.

Father Schmidt's eyes lit up. "Oh my. Let's take a look. Sit down; sit down." he waved at two chairs in front of the desk.

Maeve and Seamus sat down and Father Schmidt sat down behind the desk and took out the book. He started to pull the book out quickly and then saw what he had and stopped. "God bless us," he said and very slowly put the book on the desk. He handed the plastic bag back to Seamus and carefully opened the cover. He frowned. He was muttering to himself. "Thirteenth century? No, fourteenth century? Strange, it looks like a little of both. A Textus hand and vellum."

He looked up at Seamus. "This is priceless."

Seamus smiled. "It's a singular book. I expected you to like it."

"Like it? It's wonderful!"

He turned over the flyleaf and looked at the first page. Then he turned over the next page and the next; just as Sam had done. He was completely absorbed. Seamus leaned over the desk. "Father?"

Father Schmidt looked up. "Yes?"

"Can you tell me what it's about?"

"Oh, hang on let me read a bit more." He turned back to the first page and started to read. He was reading aloud but so softly, Seamus couldn't make anything out. Worse, he wasn't saying the translated words but the Latin. Seamus thought it sounded exactly like his memory of the priest saying Mass in his youth. Seamus looked at Maeve and Maeve looked back. She raised her eyebrows. Seamus looked back at Father Schmidt. He was still reading but now he was starting to frown. He turned the page and continued to read. The frown was beginning to change to more of an expression of surprise. He turned his head to the next page. Father Schmidt had an expression of sadness; his eyes were wet.

Seamus was watching the Jesuit's face intently. "Father?" Father Schmidt turned the page. "Father?" He looked up at Seamus and then looked at Maeve.

Maeve leaned forward. "Are you all right Father?"

Seamus frowned. "You look ready to cry."

Father Schmidt looked at Seamus and said.

"You're wrong you know. It's not a singular book; there are three of them."

"Pardon? There are three of them?"

Father Schmidt smiled, peering up over his reading glasses. "Well, actually four, if you count the original; but they're different. Apparently only two have this fascinating Latin preface. The preface was written by the monk after doing the copying. It's not part of the original codex. I'm sorry, when my mind went back to this man. Back to where he was and when he was. It… it's rather moving. My heart just went out to him; I'm all right."

Seamus looked at Maeve, "I had a friend tell me the monk was disobeying his superiors. Is that in there?"

Oh yes, right on the first page. He was pretty upset about it; concerned for his immortal soul, of course."

"Well what does he say?"

Father Schmidt leaned back in his chair. "Well first this was written during, what has been called, the Babylonian Captivity. The Pope - six in a row really - was in Avignon. The Pope of this book's time was Clement VI; the monk mentions him by name. This particular transcription was a special request from the Papacy. He was only told to produce one copy. The funny thing is, he was expressly told to only produce one copy and to keep it quiet. I don't know why; the monk doesn't say.

Anyway, the monk disobeyed, a very serious thing to do. He duplicated the original twice more. So, the original, the copy requested and then two more adds up to four.

Seamus and Maeve were staring. The priest looked from one to the other and then laughed softly. "You should see your faces. I wouldn't attach any earth shattering meaning to this. In those days any commoner's whole life revolved around the Church; let alone a monk in Ireland."

Seamus' jaw dropped. "Well I'll be...Sam was right. He's Irish then?"

"Oh yes, his name's Colum. A pretty shrewd man for his day and more independent than you'd expect. He didn't just run-off a couple of copies for himself. Although he doesn't explain his reasons, he must have had a very strong motive for this. A medieval monk was more disciplined than a marine. They just didn't *do* this kind of thing. I can't really fathom what prompted him to do it. To my eyes he seems very upset by what he has done but it is difficult to attach the appropriate intensity to his words. In those days blessings and prayers saturated everyday life. Some one saying 'may God protect and keep you safe' was the equivalent of modern America's 'have a nice day'."

Seamus leaned back.

"Oh, so maybe a religious mystery or revelation?"

"No, nothing like that. Your nose went where I was going; that was the first thought I had. But I think we're both wrong. He refers to himself as a "weak vessel" and "poor clay." Then he says he is truly contrite for his failings. There may be more meaning here than I can glean; his Latin's pretty rough. It's also more like a vernacular the way he uses it."

"What about the original?"

Father Schmidt looked down at the book; then gently leafed through some of the following pages.

"I'm afraid, although I do read Greek, this is too difficult for me; but it looks like a medical text. Did you notice the drawings?"

"I did indeed; they struck me as rather revolting"

The priest laughed. "I'll agree with that. So much so, I'm convinced they're anatomy diagrams. It would figure they'd be Greek. The medieval Church prohibited autopsies. That didn't stop everybody though; a few still did autopsies for their own medical research. You should ignore that; if a medieval surgeon, well more likely a physician, did an autopsy, he wouldn't write his notes in Greek. They'd almost certainly be in Latin."

Seamus dropped his head. Then smiled and looked up at the priest from the corners of his eyes. "So, what do you think became of this...uh felonious monk?"

Father Schmidt grinned. "I could learn to like you Seamus. Even if Maeve does think you're a heathen."

"Just cynical, Father. What do you think became of him. Was he...um defrocked?"

"Oh no. I doubt anything happened; beyond a long contemplative life, like most monks. I don't think anyone ever found out what he did. He was very careful. He describes his intentions in his preface."

"He does?"

"Uh huh, he was giving one copy to the scriptorium. That was usual, it was common practice that any codices copied would be copied twice and the second copy kept in the monastery. Of course, this was being forbidden in the case of your book. I wonder that he had this preface in the scriptorium copy; he could have easily been discovered and given a penance, or worse."

Father Schmidt looked down at the book and turned back a few pages. "Ah, here it is."

He scanned the page, muttering to himself.

"Here we go, the last copy he would keep to himself. Carefully concealing it in his cell. That may have been rather difficult. They were not supposed to own books themselves you know or anything else, for that matter. They were supposed to go to the library in the scriptorium. Oh Lord save me; look at the time. I have to prepare for a class. I'm really sorry Seamus. This has been wonderful. Please let me know whatever else you find out."

Everybody stood up. Father Schmidt put out his hand. "A real pleasure Seamus; perhaps we can get together again and talk about the flaws of religion."

Seamus shook his hand. "I'd like that Father; but it's never religion - just people - as usual."

Maeve rolled her eyes. "Come along Seamus, before *I* end up doing a penance."

As Maeve and Seamus walked to the car, Maeve stopped and turned to Seamus. "Well, some leprechaun has stopped making shoes and arranged for your entertainment - what now?"

Seamus walked on a few steps and then turned. "I don't know Maeve. I suppose I'll have to sleep on it; ask me again after my afternoon nap. I'm on holiday."

Maeve hurried up to where Seamus was standing by the car. "You're not going to let this rest. This is what you love, a real mystery to winkle out of the shell."

Maeve unlocked Seamus' door, opened it and touched the unlock button. Then she walked around to the driver's side. They both got in and turned to each other. "No Maeve, I can't leave it. But it isn't spoiling in the bag. I have time and I need to think."

She started the car. "So; and I suppose you'll not tell me until the thought is birthday wrapped."

Seamus chuckled. "If I thought it would inflate your curiosity the more, I may be tempted. But no Maeve, don't suppose you'll be kept in the dark; I'll be talking all about it to you. More than you'd like before it's through."

Maeve smiled. "I believe you're right. I'm to be hoisted by my own petard."

They sat in silence until Maeve was just pulling into the driveway.

Maeve stopped the car. "Out you get; but keep thinking. I want something tangible before P.J. arrives."

Seamus got out, and then leaned in the open car door. "You'll not get a cogent thought until after I've had some food and a lie down." He closed the door and walked around and onto the porch.

A cogent thought; now there's a good goal. Can I sort out this tangle and make a straight line to follow? Of course I can as soon as I find one end.

Maeve walked around the corner of the house. "What are you smirking about?"

"Just musing on my inadequacies."

"Come in then. I'll make us both some lunch."

Maeve made sandwiches and some salad. It was quite good. Seamus went up to have his siesta and Maeve went to her office with some tea and a handful of papers.

Two hours later, Seamus walked into Maeve's office. "Is there any coffee left from the morning?" Maeve looked around. "I don't think so Seamus; you'll have to make fresh."

"Grumble; will you have some if I do?"

"Uh, yes, I think I will."

Seamus went to the kitchen and started the coffee. He sat down in a kitchen chair and looked out the window. The sun was bright; so bright it hurt his eyes. He got up and closed the curtains. *Everything seems to be up and about except me. I'll have my 'cogent thought' after some coffee - perhaps.*

Maeve voice came from her office. "Seamus? Have you decided what to do next?" She was keying some work into the computer; he could hear typing behind her voice. *Ugh, it may be I'll need a change of air before my foggy brain clears. Tony! Why not pay him a visit. It had been some years and San Francisco is supposed to be a very pleasant town.*

"I'm still thinking Maeve. Sorry. It's a sin to tell a lie; I haven't started yet. Let me have my coffee."

Maeve appeared in the kitchen doorway. "I'll have coffee too; is it ready yet?" Seamus looked over at the pot. "Not quite."

Maeve sat down. "I've had a few thoughts of my own. You may be guided enough doing nothing."

"How's that?"

"You have Sam to visit on Monday. He said he had something to talk about. And then there's your friend in

California. What was his name? You sent him the fax - Tony?"

"Yes, I could send him some more of the book next week."

"No no, take him the book and let him see it."

Seamus was startled; he'd just had the same thought not two minutes before.

"Umm, I suppose I could. How would you manage without me around to counsel you?"

"Very funny Seamus. Shift your chair a little and see it from there. You'll not be going back home with this enigma haunting you. Your time here cannot be indefinite. The American authorities will come after you. And anymore of that and I'll say "That's him sitting there; the illegal alien himself." If you're a good man, I'll let you hide in the garage."

Seamus leaned on his hand. "Suppose you pour the coffee and I'll be more of a match for your keen mind."

Maeve turned around and took down two mugs from the upper kitchen cabinet. She squeezed some honey into Seamus' cup and poured the coffee. "I'm happy to know your friend's a pouf. Then he can be sure you don't do yourself an injury."

"Your sisterly concern is very touching Maeve."

"Mam swore me to look after you; her saintliness has saved you from my justifiable wrath."

"Just so."

Maeve put the coffee down in front of Seamus. "And so?"

"I'll think on it Maeve. It is a good approach. Tony would be assuaged by a visit. He might be in a snit if I go home without seeing him. More to the point, he reads Greek and he'll spend the time to uncover whatever the book's about." Seamus took a sip and looked up at the ceiling. "I know I could find a reader of Greek down the road, but he wouldn't be a friend. I want to be there during the unveiling and get excited without being self-conscious."

Maeve looked over her cup at Seamus. "I'd rather like to see that. Your self-consciousness makes you quite likeable. More like a younger brother than my older brother."

"Ah, then I dare not show myself. You must always have me to look up to Maeve."

"Some paragon you are; you don't even go to church."

"I'm never out of church Maeve."

"Um, pass that. I am pleased with you Seamus. You've done very well. How are you doing?"

Seamus knew she meant Lena. He felt the old familiar knot in his stomach. He took a deep breath and thought of the book; the knot unraveled. He looked up at Maeve. "I still miss her Maeve; I always will."

Maeve looked into her cup and softly said, "She's still with you Seamus; she always will be."

"I know Maeve, but there's too much room in the bed all the same."

Maeve swung a playful slap at Seamus and missed as Seamus leaned back and said,

"You'll spill my coffee."

"So are you going to see Tony then?"

"Hmmm, yes I think it would be the thing to do."

"For the book?"

"And for the sake of my friendship. He's not someone I want to neglect."

"If you're concerned for my well-being in your absence, would you mind if I joined in?"

"Come along as well?"

"And why shouldn't I?"

"No reason. I'm certain Tony would enjoy having you there. He fancies himself something of a cook and a decorator."

Maeve smiled. "They always do."

Seamus laughed. "I suppose so. What about P.J. and Conor? I would think they might enjoy having their mam to themselves. I've been here for quite some time now."

Maeve frowned. "Yes that's true. Perhaps it would be as well for you to have some time on your own besides. When do you want to leave?"

"I have another talk with Sam on Monday; Tuesday is soon enough."

"I'll book the ticket. When do you want to return?"

"Whatever is a week after. Now, as to time of day, please yourself, I'll need a lift to and from the airport and I don't mean to inconvenience."

"That's fine. I can find the odd hour without interrupting my work. I'll be sure not to have you going or coming in the early hours or when we should be eating."

She topped up her cup and went into the office.

A minute later Maeve slowly walked back in the kitchen.

"Ah Seamus, I must confess, I wish I was joining you."

"It's probably just as well, Maeve. I need to be a little more on my own. I need to be back to work."

"I know what's best for you; haven't I been saying so. You can go to the devil; I want to know more about your accursed book."

Seamus chuckled. "A good thing I'll be saving it from your prying fingers."

"You need to leave all the numbers to get to you."

"Surely. You'll have his home and office and you already have his fax."

"Some portion of all that will serve well enough. Do you want him to know you're coming?

Seamus looked at her. "I knew I'd forgotten something - yes I do."

"You'd best call as soon as. Some friend you are; you'll be expecting him to meet you at the airport. You should say your prayers he's in his rooms or your arrival won't be noticed."

"Oh no, Maeve. He's not in his rooms. Remember? He said in his fax, he wouldn't be home until the 12th."

Maeve thought a second.

"That's Monday, Seamus. You'll have to call after you see Sam. Just don't forget."

She looked at Seamus. He wasn't listening he was lost in thought.

"Seamus? Where are you?"

He blinked and smiled sheepishly.

"Sorry, Maeve, I was just trying to imagine what it must have been like. You know, in the fourteenth century. Not how they lived as much as what they thought. Nobody lived very long then. What did they want? What did they look forward to?"

"Well, Seamus they were very devout and not just the monks; I know that much. You could learn something from that."

Seamus shook his head.

"Yes Maeve, I know. I don't think it will bother me, though"

Chapter 7: Papal palace

Avignon, 1342

Pierre Roger could not believe his good fortune. Of course, it had cost a fortune but it would be repaid tenfold. He felt benign, he felt beneficent, he felt hungry. As he walked through the consistory, the morning light glowed on the walls. The butler's pantry was at the far end. Perhaps there would be some scraps from the morning meal. If not, he could simply continue to the kitchen tower. The palace was adequate but to his mind, incomplete. The chapel, as an example, was worthy of a small noble family perhaps certainly not up to the needs of Christ's Vicar on earth. He would see to all that. A feeling of satisfaction slowly cleared the pangs of hunger. Pierre, now Pope Clement VI, felt himself a master workman, with the great task of building before him. His genius, with the help of God, would provide comfort for himself and every Pastor Aeternus who would follow him.

Great sacks of coins, mostly pennies, lay in heaps of various sizes almost covering the consistory floor. His Holiness had to walk a crooked path around them in order to reach the far doorway.

These should be moved at once, he thought.

They would make the faithful even more receptive to the strident cry of simony. He sighed, *what would they have him do? The Church needed funds to provide for itself; to then provide for the people. The salvation of the Immortal soul was surely of more value than the wealth of the Church.* He frowned. *The nobility have become proud; so proud they would attack the Pope. They did attack a Pope. We must have the funds to defend ourselves and demonstrate superiority to those who would try to hold themselves above the Church. What next? Above God?*

Two priests, a page and two nobles hurried past him; dodging and stepping over the sacks. One of the priests looked at the Pope quizzically.

Clement VI stared ahead in unruffled dignity. *I should not wander around the palace alone,* he thought.

It was suddenly more than he could bear. The continuous cacophony of Curia, nobles and dozens of simpler souls were assaulting him always. Each with their own scheme for themselves; all draping their requests in the cloth of holiness. Daily, he was presented with propositions of income or tactical advantage in exchange for benefices. Some few may even be worthy of the appointment. At this remove he could not tell.

No one enjoyed the comforts that came with wealth and power more than he. But there were few in these days that cared a sou for the common man. *Of course, it wasn't easy to find a love for these villeins. With their lice-ridden hair and smoking feet, a priest's gorge would rise while administering the last rites. Assuming the priest was from a noble family of course; a peasant priest would not notice. They seemed to be unaware of their own filth, ignorance or even their own misery.* Clement sighed. *Ah, indeed, they are not like us.*

As Clement reached the butler's pantry he realized he needed to piss and the latrine tower was just beyond the kitchen tower, immediately in front of him. A too long walk back to his chambers made him decide to continue to the latrine. After he finished, he put his head to the opening in the wall. The air was foul. Not as foul as most other castles. The palace in Avignon was fortunate; there was an underground stream that flushed away the bottom of the latrine but still foul enough. As he breathed in the clean air he saw a team of horses down on the river embankment. It was pulling slowly into view a large barque du Rhône. *Likely one of a string of barques laden with goods for the city.*

They are so slow, he thought, *the furnishings I require will arrive at different rates as they proceed down river from Lyons or up river from Arles. I must choose carefully. Those up river being preferred that they may be sooner provided. Ah, but what of the quality?*

—####—

Fouinon – The Cutpurse

Fouinon stood on the deck of the barge watching as the embankment at Avignon drew closer and scanned the porters gathering to unload. They jostled and elbowed each other to be first. Crowds of other people moved along the bank behind the porters. He watched from the corners of his eyes as he kept his attention on the task of sharpening his dagger with a small whetstone. He had to sharpen his blade often; a cutpurse could not afford to have a dull knife at the critical moment. *Avignon's reputation appears to be sound.* He thought. *The pilgrims and those in orders are there, as I expected. But more impressive to the mind are the wealthy merchants and tradesmen. I should do well here. If not, the fault will be my own.* As he watched he mused on the clothes they wore. *The style in these days is not to my advantage. All wear such bright colors and bold patterns. Even some priests are arrayed in garish style. He looked at his own quiet dress. I stand out in my dull grays and browns; I look like one of the porters. I must think on this and determine what would make me difficult to see in the crowds of the market. Perhaps a bold black and white pattern of squares and red hose would be most commonly worn. Still, my dress may make me out to be a poor porter. That would be some advantage.* He felt his own purse. As he already knew, it was not full. He would have enough coins to eat and have drink at a tavern. After that, he would have to replenish his wealth from some unfortunate he marked. The effort would be to choose the best tavern for the custom that frequented it. *They must needs be well enough to provide a good catch but not of noble estate. The nobles would entail too much risk.* Fouinon wanted a living but did not wish to risk the loss of a hand or arm - or his life. He stood up and stretched. *Well, some repast, a glass of something warming and then to work. I cannot afford to shirk.* He smiled to himself as he walked off the barque down to the embankment.

—####—

A River Warehouse on the Embankment

Gervais and Alard groaned and woke on their sleeping mats. Gervais sat up and shook his head then leaned over to his friend and shook him by the shoulder.

"Wake up you river scum we have another day of misery to work off our excesses."

Alard rolled over and swatted at a fly near his head.

"Enough, I have an anvil in my head and the devil pounds it."

Gervais turned and put his arms around his knees. "No doubt and that serving wench would serve you the same, had she the chance."

"She wanted me Gervais, I could smell her passion rising when she filled my cup."

"Pah!, she had much the same smell for all and that stench was not her passion, fool. She needed a dousing in the river, as do you."

"Mayhaps, I had nothing of the days wages left to me by then."

"And you rise on another without the means to start the day."

They stood up, already dressed, and kicked their bed mats up against the storage crates. Jervais felt his purse, then turned his head to Alard. "Move soon enough and I still have enough for a hot cup to start our day. There should be work enough portering a barque or two this morning."

Alard hurried to keep up. "And you, my good friend, shall be repaid in heaven for your generosity."

"I shall be repaid by yourself; why should heaven pay your debt? Come quickly, a line of barques may now be tying to the bank and others will have the work...and the reward."

—####—

A Market Street Shop, Avignon

Fabrice shouted down into the shop. "Edwige, more heat to the pot. Lift those slab feet and fetch water. Open the shutters and unbolt the door. The custom awaits. My neighbor will have my profits, all the blame to you."

Edwige scurried to the fire and added some wood. As she turned, she looked down, pulled up her gown and beat out a small flame. Rushing to unbolt the door, she put her burned hand in her mouth. As she struggled to pry up the latch bolt, Fabrice came up behind and pushed her aside. He lifted the iron latch and shoved a bucket in her stomach. "Fetch the water." he glared at her. She grasped the thick rope handle in both hands and hurried toward the back.

Fabrice opened the door and stepped into the street. He began to take off the shutters and stack them against the wall of the shop.

"Fabrice." It was his wife's voice, from inside the shop. "Fabrice, we are near the end of our silk. The remainder is within the stores on the river's landing. What would you do?"

Fabrice carried the shutters into the shop. "God stop your tongue, Ghislaine; I shall send Edwige. She is beneath the attention of even the rats."

Ghislaine made a face. "Edwige, ha! The day arrives when Edwige and the stores will depart together."

Fabrice looked at her and thought a moment. Then he said slowly, "Mayhaps, I think not. She has neither the wit nor the strength for it." He waved a hand dismissively. "Talk has no purpose here. I will pull the devil's tail before I descend into that river air. Do you say you prefer yourself there?"

Ghislaine's eyes opened wide. "No! Edwige may be sent; she has so before."

"Done, layout the goods Ghislaine, the day wears on."

Fabrice turned his head to a noise from the back of the shop. Edwige stumbled into the shop from the back by the stairs. She was carrying the water bucket in front of her with both hands. The water was sloshing and spilling. Fabrice walked over and took the bucket. He pulled back his hand, as if to slap her, then lowered it. "You filled the bucket to overflow. The saints weep at you Edwige." He pulled a key from his belt and handed it to her. "Go to the stores and fetch two bolts of silk. Be sure to return directly. I shall stop your food a day if you do not."

Edwige nodded, wiped her hands on her tunic and took the key carefully. As she turned, Fabrice shouted. "Foolish wench, hide the key in your sleeve." She hesitated and put her hands in her opposite sleeve as she left.

Edwige walked out the back door into the alley; through the alley she watched her feet - and the rats. Some, sitting on the refuse piles, stared at her and continued to chew contentedly. Others ran ahead and dodged quickly to avoid her. When she reached the street, she paused and then turned toward the river. The noises of the street faded behind her as she walked. Finally, it was quiet. A cartwheel scraped off to her right, perhaps one street away. She heard some men talking. The shops and houses were all shuttered and locked. In the silence, she could hear the sound of the rats in the alleys as they scuffled and ran. Occasionally, there was a rustle or thump as they knocked over part of the trash. She unconsciously found herself carefully walking in the very center of the narrow street. The mist on the river was rising and thinning. She stopped to watch a barque and a small ferry move across the water; they were hard to see - dark shapes.

Then she remembered Fabrice's threat and hurried to the storehouse. At the large iron gate, she bent over and peered at the lock. She backed up a step and carefully inserted the foot-long key. Fabrice had spoken of a trap for lock pickers. A sharp blade would slice off their fingers. That was the reason for the long key. She wondered if it was true or a rumor started by Fabrice to discourage the attempt. She turned the key and heard the scrape and click; it was difficult to turn. Suddenly the latch cleared and the iron gate sprang in a few inches. She turned the key back and pulled it out. As she pushed the gate enough to pass through, it creaked and she looked about nervously. She put her hand on her dagger hilt for reassurance. Inside the storehouse yard, she turned, put the key in from the other side, pushed the gate closed and, holding it with her foot, locked it. A rat ran passed at her feet, she flinched and, as she watched, one of the storehouse cats raced after the rat.

The two animals turned at the far wall and the rat escaped between the bars of the iron fence. Then she noticed, against the far wall, the decomposing remains of a cat and a few rats. She shuddered, crossed herself, and ran to the storehouse.

—####—

The young monk sat at the high copying desk in the scriptorium. A large gray cat sat on the floor beneath him. He read out loud from a single page of parchment.

"I and Pangur Ban, my cat,
'Tis a like task we are at;
Hunting mice is his delight,
Hunting words I sit all night.

Better far than praise of men
'Tis to sit with book and pen;
Pangur bears me no ill will;
He, too, plies his simple skill.

'Tis a merry thing to see
At our task how glad are we,
When at home we sit and find
Entertainment to our mind.

Oftentimes a mouse will stray
Into the hero Pangur's way;
Oftentimes my keen thought set
Takes a meaning in its net.

'Gainst the wall he sets his eye
Full and fierce and sharp and sly;
'Gainst the wall of knowledge I
All my little wisdom try.

When a mouse darts from its den.
O how glad is Pangur then!

O what gladness do I prove
When I solve the doubts I love!

So in peace our tasks we ply,
Pangur Ban, my cat and I;
In our arts we find our bliss,
I have mine, and he has his.

Practice every day has made
Pangur perfect in his trade ;
I get wisdom day and night,
Turning Darkness into light."

Colum looked down at his cat.

"Do you hear that Fergus? We are all alike under God, even in the olden times. Did you know, as wise as you are, that this was written over 400 years ago in a far away monastery? Penned by a good Irishman of course."

The cat stared at Colum, then stood and rubbed his head against Colum's leg. Turning away, Fergus looked toward the door of the scriptorium. Outside in the hallway they could both hear the noises of the morning. The scriptorium was empty. The senior antiquarii scribes and the junior librarii scribes were seldom occupied as they had been in years past. The new diocesan cathedral schools and the professional scribes had taken over much of the copying. The precentor still found reasons to apply the talents of the monastery's scriptorium, but they were few and seldom sponsored. Colum didn't mind. He was young. His talents for copying were admired but it was the times that had given him the chance. In years long ago, his talents would have been ignored since he was so young. Instead of his morning recital for Fergus, and himself of course, he would have been put to work stirring the vats or scraping the hides. He did that now but the time spent was small enough. The need for parchment and ink had been reduced to a fraction of what it had been in his father's time. He was content. He had a book to do. One of the chieftains on the mainland had requested a breviary for his daughter. Colum smiled. It was a favor, he knew. The chieftain was a friend of his father. The chieftain also knew that the precentor would give the task to Colum. It was good to have such friends. Of course, the precentor might have given it to Bron. Colum would have shared his friend's joy at that. Bron was still an oblate however, and even in these times, an oblate would not have such an honor. Colum looked at the cat. He was in a corner under one of the writing tables; he'd found something. *I hope it's his breakfast,* thought Colum.

The scriptorium was as it had been for centuries. Perhaps a little dustier. The writing tables were all on one side and the library was above. The library was full of codices. In centuries past there had been many bare shelves. *That was reason enough to be here,* thought Colum, as he looked up at the shelves consumed with beautiful books.

He had been asked to read a few weeks ago. The codex had been copied and illuminated over two centuries ago. It was so beautiful he had been dazzled. The Abbot had coughed twice before Colum realized he wasn't reading. He was relieved when he noticed the Abbot and precentor hiding their smiles. He knew it was a part of every brother's duties to read. He was actually required to read at least one book each year. When he had first arrived he was afraid he would not be allowed to read at all. At least not until he had proven himself worthy to the Abbot. It may have taken years. It had taken years to finally read to his brothers. Praise be to God, he was commanded to read to himself and for himself and for the glory of God from the very first.

The daily work was tiring but the Divine Office provided rest and peace enough. As he looked around the quiet, empty scriptorium, he was filled with joy. His life was given to God, yes, as it should be. Yet his life was also as he had dreamed it might be. The blessing of the Lord had been on him.

Colum turned to a loud bang on the door of the scriptorium.

"Colum, the currach is here. Your strong back is needed."

Colum heard the precentor's sandaled feet walk down the stone-floored cloister in the direction of the large gate. Colum grinned then straightened his face. *The knock had been very loud,* he thought, as he walked to the door. *The precentor must have used his baton cantoral.* Colum smiled again. *God smiles when we smile as long as it is in His praise.* Colum opened the door then held it as Fergus ran out after him into the cloister.

"Fergus, you are needed in the storehouse. We both have our duties to our brothers."

As if the cat understood, he ran ahead to an archway and out into the sunlight. Colum watched Fergus stop to sharpen his claws on the giant yew tree in the center of the courtyard; then he walked along the same path and turned toward the high steps that led down to the sea.

As he walked, he glanced over at the wooden parchment vat. Thinking that the hides may be ready, he changed direction and went to look. The hides had only been soaking for four days but the weather had been warm. Colum looked in, and picking up the tongs, lifted a hide out of the lime solution.

Not quite, he thought. *Perhaps by tomorrow he could begin to wash and mount each hide on a stretching frame.* He released the hides, pushed them deep into the liquid with the tongs and, hanging up the tongs, walked back over to the steps. The steps had always filled him with awe. Centuries ago they had been carved into the solid rock. The Brothers of those days chipped painfully day after day and threw the pieces down the mountainside into the water. Colum had wondered if they had started from the top or the bottom. The bottom, he supposed. That would provide a better place to stand. He started down. In his first days as an oblate, he had been afraid of the steps. When he first arrived he had managed to climb them - slowly. Looking up as he climbed, he could feel he was ascending to God. He could touch the steps he would tread next. Descending was beyond him. He had asked Brother Malachi if any had ever fallen. The antiquarii had looked away.

A year later, Colum had a day of weakness. He felt he would never be worthy and wished to leave. Brother Malachi suggested Colum go down to the water and contemplate. Some time later, Malachi sat beside him and asked him for his thoughts. They both looked across the water for a time. Finally, Colum turned to Brother Malachi, there was a smile on the older Brother's large face. "Why are you smiling Brother?" asked Colum. "See where you are Colum." Colum looked up at the three hundred feet of stone steps. He suddenly realized he had walked down without being aware of his fear. Goose bumps on his arms, he looked at Malachi with astonishment.

"What does it mean?"

"It means God is always guiding us; more so, when we are least aware of His hand. His hand was on your shoulder Colum."

Colum had stayed.

It was good that he had; and it was sad also. He came to his vocation late. As a young boy he had seen the beautiful books and marveled at the time and skill it took to create them. He had hoped always, that God would guide him to become a scribe. He had prayed to his namesake Saint Columcille to intercede. His prayers were answered. God had agreed, but God wanted Colum to do more than just copy the books. He wanted Colum to serve his brothers and all God's creatures.

As the simple son of a farmer, Colum was unaware that the monastery had few books to copy in these later years. The need for ever larger numbers of books had created a profession of scribes. These scribes were educated laymen surrounding the seats of learning - the cathedral schools.

Colum would become a scribe quickly. True, he was still a librarius but he was very young, even for a junior scribe. The reason slowly became clear; the books were few and those that were created here were smaller and plainer, without the great illuminations.

Rubricators, miniators and illuminators found more time for their devotions because their skills were needed less and less for the books. Correctors were still required of course. Colum smiled to himself. *Thanks be to God for the correctors.* Colum's grasp of Latin was still less than he wanted it to be. The correctors had raised their eyes to heaven before Colum's work. Their patience and quiet explanations reassured Colum. He learned. Now they smiled when they began their task.

Colum reached the last of the stone steps. He walked across to the currach. Some of the other brothers and many oblates were emptying the boat. He stooped picking up a large sack of oak galls, placed it on his shoulder and stood up.

"That's the last you'll be seeing before next harvest season Brother."

Colum turned. It was one of the boatsmen who spoke.

"Thank you, Finian. These will be all that are needed. God's blessings on you and your family."

The boatsman blessed himself.

"Thank you, Brother Colum."

Colum turned to the steps and began the climb up, with the sack on his shoulder.

The boatsmen never climbed the steps. Colum had thought it was because of the walk down. He later found that the Abbot discouraged them. Brother Malachi had explained.

"The Abbot believes we should take the danger and the struggle for the glory of God. Many of these boatsmen have given of their time and the fruit of their fields for our sake and God. They have done enough to bring these gifts here. Their families await; we should do the rest."

Colum had nodded. Life was hard enough for these good men.

Colum climbed. Even for one as young and strong as Colum it was arduous, but his heart was light. These oak galls would help to make the ink needed for his book. He would have to start soon to have the ink he needed to finish; and then? God would tell him. He knew, in his heart, he should not be selfish, but he could not evade the hope that he would be given another book.

Chapter 8: Ohio River Overlook

"Well? You've been looking for him all week. What have you got for me?"

"Aw Jimmy gave us a break. We don't know who the guy is; we don't know what he looks like. It's impossible!"

"Jock?"

Jock shrugged. "Steve's right. We dinna know where to start," he said.

Jimmy was mad. He knew it would be tough but he expected them to think of something. Obviously they didn't think at all. He pointed at Jock and looked at Steve.

"What a load of crap. You've spent the whole week going to bars. If the asshole walked in and announced himself, you'd both be too blind to notice. Besides what made you think he'd go to bars as often as you do?"

Jock looked back with an accusing face. "Why can't you ask the old man?"

"I'm thinking about that. I have to figure out how to contact him again. We don't know how often he checks the drop box."

Jock felt vindicated. He held out his hand. "He's the only one in this town with a network large enough to track somebody."

Jimmy's anger had passed; he was thinking it over with a frown. "I know, I know. Let's go over it again. The guy was dressed like Jock; but brown tweeds instead of grey."

Jock thought back. "Tha's right, and he had an accent; Gladys said she liked his accent."

"But it wasn't like yours."

"Noo, so he was speaking English with... with what? An English accent?"

"There are a dozen English accents."

"More than that Jimmy."

"But what would Gladys like? Not southwest, she'd say he sounded like a pirate."

Jock laughed. "Ar, from Penzance."

"Probably not Eastender or Welsh; red brick maybe?"

"That would sound very pretty to Gladys."

"Yes it would; and I doubt he would speak fraffly."

Steve grinned. "Fraffly?"

"Yeah Steve, like the queen; you know 'sew fraffly gled t'see yew'."

"Oh, weird."

"So, we're looking for a well educated bloke?"

"I think so Jock. But it doesn't help much."

"Then what's the point of this analytical crap?"

"Hey, it will help us if we just run into him in a bar. But the real reason is so we can tell the old man what to look for. That would help a lot."

"Ah yes t'would."

"You two go get us something to eat. I've got to figure out what to say to the old man."

Steve was walking in circles - he looked up at Jimmy, baffled. "Shit, just tell him we didn't get the book."

"It's not that simple Steve. Why should he give a damn? It's our problem. No, I've got to make it look like a threat to him. Otherwise he just won't answer."

"Tell him you'll blow the whistle on him."

"About the robbery?"

"Yeah, the job your old man did for him way back."

"He's too smart for that Steve. First, who's going to believe me? Against him? Forget it. Besides he knows I need him more than he does me and I won't kill the goose."

"Goose?"

"Yeah, the golden goose. You know the goose that lays the golden eggs."

"Uh yeah OK."

Steve looked puzzled. Jock turned away and waved to Steve. ""C'mon Steve you and me will get the food while the mad scientist writes his letter. We'll be back in half an hour." Then to Jimmy. "Ay, what do you want?"

Jimmy looked over the wall at the river down below and waved his hand behind him. "I don't care as long as it's not haggis."

Jock smirked and got into the car. They backed out and drove around the horseshoe road out of the park.

Jimmy watched them leave, shook his head and thought.

What do I say to the old man? I don't have much to threaten him with. Lying about anything isn't the problem; it's making it believable. I don't even know who he is - dammit.

Wait a minute; could I figure it out? I know he's old. My dad did that sweet sweet job for him back in, what did he say, 1926? The old man was a young man then. Well, no older than his early thirties. Jesus! He has to be, what, 90 years old? Yeah it's possible; you see these 100 year old farts on the Today Show all the time.

OK, how many stinking rich people are there in Cincinnati that are 90 years old?

Jimmy had been sitting on the back of a bench with his feet on the seat. He got down, walked to the wall and sat sideways looking down at the river.

This could work if I can figure it out.

If I know who he his, I don't have to come up with some fairy story threat. I can just tell him I'll blow his head off if he doesn't help. That'd do it.

Unless he's so fucking old he doesn't give a shit anymore.

Ah, one thing at a time.

OK where do I start? Chamber of Commerce! There we go.

Crap that sounds like a lot of farting around for a long shot. Wait a minute! Who do I know? Who's the fattest customer I've got? Uh or whose the fattest father of any customer I've got?

Preferably someone whose up there a little. In his fifties anyway.

Into what? Real Estate? That's a good choice; the old man probably owns a bunch of buildings by now. That's what they say: 'property is the best investment'.

Jimmy started to walk down the side of the wall toward the bridge onto Victory Parkway, wrestling with the top three best choices to talk to. He got to the end and turned around to walk back. Jock and Steve pulled in from the other side of the park with the food.

Jock was gathering the bags of food. "Where is he?"

"I don't... there he is! He's over by the bridge.

Jimmy!" Jock held up the bag.

Jimmy walked across the grass and then stopped and waved them over.

"C'mon over here we'll sit at one of these tables."

Steve and Jock jogged over and sat down.

"So, have you puzzled out the letter to the old man?"

"No, I'm not going to."

Steve looked up. "Why not?"

"We..." he looked back and forth at each of them, "are going to figure out who he is." He smiled.

Jock was about to take the first bite of his burger and stopped. "How the shite are we to do that?"

"Who do we deal to that come from big money?"

"Steve had a mouthful. "Thersh lots of 'em."

"Exactly."

Jock looked into space. "Ah see it now; one of them has to know our old man. Even if he doesn't know it."

Steve looked at Jock. "The old man?"

"Yah, you eejit; the old man's one of the richest in town. Any other rich ones will know about him, even if they don't have him over for tea. Got it?"

"Yeah I see what you mean. So we need to ask the rich boys that want us around a lot."

Jimmy tapped Steve on the arm. "Damned good Steve. That's exactly it. These pathetic souls need us to deal to them. They'll tell us whatever they know. It doesn't sound like secret shit to them; why shouldn't they?"

Jock was chewing and wiping his hands with a napkin.

"Yah know Jimmy if it wasn't for the glop they lather these with, yah wouldn't be able to tell 'em apart. What animal is this do yuh think?"

Jimmy laughed. "Kangaroo for all I know. Listen Jock you and Steve have some setups to do and we need to find out what we can as soon as possible. Re-book the fat kids to the top."

"Ah'd do that anyway."

"No, I mean all the way to the top; stall the appointments and stop the 'on call' stuff."

"Aye, alright. What am I asking them?"

"Easy. Who's the richest bastard in town, who's 90 years old or more and has been rich all his life. Say that anyway you like and it'll work."

"I'll wager t'will. How many can there be for Gawdssake?"

"You may be surprised. I'm thinking there'll be as many as half a dozen. They've got money you know; they stay alive longer."

Jock smiled. "I always thought they died of heart attacks in their forties."

"Yeah, well some of them do I guess. But we know the old man's alive and still kicking...hard."

Steve looked eager.

"But not for long huh?"

"Hey, I don't want to kill him. I want him to work for us. He can find our book if anyone can."

"You'll have to say hello to him Jimmy. He won't do shit unless you tell him you'll kill him."

"Yeah, I know. We can always do some other damage to show him we're dead serious

Steve said quietly, "I've still got my assault rifle Jimmy."

"I don't ever want you to use it Steve. But if we must we must. Don't forget guys, we're still being watched and assault rifles are very very noisy."

Jock and Steve frowned. "Do'ye ken they've listened in to our talking?"

"No, I've been careful. We're under trees with a wind. It chops up the reception. They still have to have 'line of sight' to get a clean signal. Besides, they have other bad guys to catch you know; we're not the only ones. Just never forget it; the one time we get sloppy? - that'll be the time they have four agents on us at once."

Steve was excited, he liked action and guns.

"So Jimmy; we get the bastard marked, crack his head and get our book; then what?"

"Then the book goes to Marcus in New York for auction. The old man said something more than two hundred and fifty thousand. I think it'll fetch more. Museums will bid big bucks for this."

Steve was relieved and felt a little smug.

"Whew, a clean bag of cash and a profit for our trouble; that's something to dream about."

"Look forward to Steve; not dream about. Don't forget though, Marcus takes 25%. If it goes for two hundred and fifty thou, we get about $187,500."

"Steve beamed, "I can live with that."

"Ay, such a shame, only a hundred and eighty seven thousand dollars. I'll have to cancel the paper; watching me pennies y'know."

"You're weird jock."

They finished the lunch and threw the wrappers in a trashcan.

"Steve you drive Jock and get on this right now. It'll take a few days. These kids will need to get what we want from their parents probably. That means we won't get our answers until they see us again for the next fix."

"Yeah, OK c'mon Jock."

Jimmy yelled at their backs. "I've got to take care of suppliers. We'll meet right here same time next week."

Jock turned, and walked backwards. "I'll buy lunch again."

Chapter 9: The Margin Notes

Maeve was driving down the hill on the way to Sam's. Seamus was lost in thought. By the time they pulled onto the expressway, he shook his head.

"Maeve, this book is nagging me. I have the feeling - not that I can explain it - there's more to this book than just being old and valuable."

"Well, the monk disobeyed his superiors. Is that the bothersome part?"

"No, but you're close. It's why did he disobey them. The good father touched the spot. These men were more disciplined than the marines. This mutinous behavior didn't happen without very good cause."

"Surely, but our monk may have religious fervor that overcame his judgment."

"I don't think it's religious."

"The book or the monk?"

"The book of course; the monk would be religious, I should think."

They pulled into Sam's parking lot. When they got out of the car, a voice called from above their heads. "I saw you pull in. I was by my window, getting coffee." It was Sam standing on the deck behind the building.

Seamus looked up. "Sam, how was your weekend?"

"We had a great time. I got the boat out; first time this year."

They climbed the stairs up to the back deck. At the top, Seamus shook hands with Sam.

"When you go out in your boat; where do you go?"

"Just up and down the river. It's the idea that counts."

Seamus chuckled.

"I suppose so and it seems much more tranquil. Not to mention safe."

They followed Sam through the back door and around to the inside stairs up to Sam's office.

"God save us, these steps again."

Sam turned back to Seamus. "Sorry about that. It is good for you Seamus. I don't feel the need for jogging, that's for sure."

"I should say not; I never feel the need myself."

They walked into the large room on the top floor and Sam went to a coffee maker by the window.

"I still haven't had my quota. Do you two want some coffee?"

"Yes thanks, Sam. My wits could use a waking up."

Sam poured the coffee and they sat down around Sam's desk.

"So, I heard about the priest. What did he tell you?"

"You were very accurate Sam. He concurs the book was done in the 14th century."

"Ah, I was sure it was."

"You found more than that Sam. The priest says the Latin preface was a sort of apologia. He wasn't supposed to be doing that copy."

Sam leaned forward. "That would explain the subtle difference in the hand."

"I suppose so."

"Do you have it here?"

"Oh yes, I wouldn't dare leave it."

Seamus took the book out of a plastic bag. There were two pieces of plywood on either side with large rubber bands sandwiching the book.

" Seamus, you listen well."

"Ah yes, after you talked about cockling and warping I thought I'd better take more care. P.J. put this little rig together for me."

"This'll do fine. After all these years the pages aren't likely to move; but it's still a good idea. The cover will be well protected and the pages will stay tight. Sometime, the sooner the better, this should be stored in a cool, dry place. The humidity in a Cincinnati summer could do damage."

Sam took the rubber bands off, reached in his lower desk drawer and put on the white gloves.

"Where can I get some of those gloves, Sam? Are they really necessary? The whole world has been fingering the poor thing."

"They're just cheap cotton gloves Seamus. You should carry a pair with you when some one looks at this. The oil in your hands could hurt the pages."

"Maeve?"

"We'll get a pair on the way back."

Sam opened the book.

"It's absolutely magnificent."

He was turning the pages very slowly.

"Did you find out where the monk was?"

"Yes, Father Schmidt said he was Irish."

Sam looked up with a grin. "Am I good or what."

Maeve laughed. "You're good Sam."

"So, Sam. Why did you want to see it?"

"Well, I'll confess. I did just want another look but I had a few thoughts after you left and I needed to check my memory."

"And?"

First, it's almost certainly not a religious work. You've looked at the Greek part no doubt. It's a pretty safe bet it's a medical text."

"T'would seem so."

"So, if this monk did the book 'on his own', he must have done the binding and illustrations also."

"Ah, I see what you're thinking. He couldn't let anyone else see it to do the work."

"Exactly. Let's assume that he did the whole job and look for clues that we're right. The first point that hit me after you left was the lack of boards."

"Boards?"

"Yes, all these books had the problem you're solving with the plywood. They usually had actual wooden boards for the cover. Sometimes they were ornamented. You know, carved and painted prettily. They usually even covered the wood with leather. Either way, they all had boards to keep the pages flat. They even had a metal clasp to hold the boards together. This, otherwise beautiful, book doesn't have any of that."

Seamus looked into space.

"So. He must not have had either the materials or the talent to make these boards?"

"That's the way I see it, but to give him the credit he deserves, if he bound this himself - and he almost must have - he did a remarkable job. I don't know much about binding, but it would seem to me more difficult to bind a softcover book than hard."

Seamus looked at Maeve, then back to Sam.

"Should I try to find a bookbinding expert?"

"If you like, but I wouldn't bother; seems like a lot of trouble."

"Umm maybe so. What else Sam?"

"The ink and the vellum."

"What can you tell of that?"

"Well, I can see quite a bit actually. For example, these pages were very nicely prepared. The pouncing was finely done and took some time."

Maeve laughed.

"Pouncing? The skin still has that much life in it, eh Sam"

Sam smiled. "I know, I know. Strange words; I don't know where they come from. No, pouncing is the preparation of the vellum so it would be a good writing surface. We're so used to paper, we don't think about this problem. Imagine trying to write on an unprepared animal skin. Even a well stretched and scraped animal skin."

Seamus leaned over. "So, what is pouncing?"

"Well the skin was usually wet again; after it had been soaked and scraped the first time - remember? Then it was rubbed with pumice to smooth it even more. Hold on."

Sam pulled his elbowed magnifying light over to the book and bent over it. He turned a few pages and then gently rubbed one of them in the bottom corner.

He looked up over the light. "In this case, the vellum was then rubbed with chalk."

Seamus sipped his coffee and then smiled.

"So they wrote on chalk instead of with it."

Sam moved the light out of the way. "Yup, think about it. It made the surface even smoother and whitened it as well - couldn't be better. I love this stuff but I have to admit - it doesn't prove much."

"You mean our Irish monk could just as easily have gotten this from central supply."

"I think it's possible - sort of. It was very unusual for a monk to do multiple skilled tasks, but they did do different tasks. He may have made all of this himself; just for the books he copied. Then again, he may have had some - not so talented - monks in training doing all the vellum and ink work for him. They broke the copy work down; I know that. There were rubricators, illuminators, miniators and even correctors."

"Wait up Sam, what did all these specialists do?"

"OK a rubricator was a monk who did bits of the manuscript in red. He'd do chapter headings, section headings sometimes even underlining of words - all in red. That's why the title 'rubricator'; it comes from the word 'red'. He also would likely use a special archaic text - to make it stand out."

"The miniator did little teeny pictures?"

Sam laughed.

"No, miniator comes from 'minium'; which was orangey-red. So, the miniator did work in an orange-red also, but his stuff tended to be imbedded. The rubricator was the headings and titles man. Illuminator is obvious; that's the really ornate first letters and any other pictures. The corrector was the proof reader."

"Maeve stood up.

"Can I have some more coffee Sam?"

"Sure, I could use some more myself."

They all walked over to the coffee and Maeve picked up the pot.

Seamus put his cup on the table and turned to Sam.

"Does this mean anything to us Sam? This book doesn't have any work for all these monks."

"You're right. There isn't any fanciness to it. Maybe there was in the original and our boy left it out; or maybe there wasn't and that made it all easier for him. It is a Greek medical text, as far as we can tell."

Seamus looked over his cup at Sam.

"True, the Greeks didn't fiddle around with fancy lettering - pagans that they were."

They walked over to the desk.

"You know Seamus I'm being somewhat contradictory."

"How's that again?"

"Well, by the 14th century, most books had dropped the illuminations and the hard wood covers anyway."

"They had?"

"Uh huh. But now we know he was a monk - thanks to Father Schmidt. We know he was in Ireland, again thanks to the good Father. So when I said it was dated to the fourteenth century, I was right. I shouldn't be even looking for illuminations or rubrics, let alone boards."

"So, why are you?"

"Because he was an Irish monk. I've already said he was in a pocket - away from what was supposed to be civilized Europe. So, I'm trying to find signs of the old ways. I guess I'm assuming he would still be following centuries of method and procedure. Of course, he is using a hand - call it a typeface - that was in use later in the game. At least well after the 11th century. I don't want to send you down a blind alley."

"Don't mind that. I'll soak up all the knowledge you can give Sam. What about the ink? What can you tell of that?"

"Sam pulled back his light and bent over.

"About the only thing I can tell is that it's good ink."

"Bad ink would, what? be faded or clot, or something?"

"No, this ink was good because it didn't do any damage to the vellum. After all these years bad ink would have eaten the pages."

"It was acid?"

"Oh yes or alkaline. They used something called Iron-Gall ink. It was made from oak galls. The lumps the tree grows over damage - from insects, I guess. These galls were crushed, fermented, whatever and then mixed with other stuff, gum arabic and ferrous sulphate - if I remember right. The point is, if the mixture was off, it would be acidic or alkaline and that would eat the vellum. If it was mixed correctly, it'd last a very long time without doing damage. Thing is, they didn't know whether it was right or not. A lot of wonderful books were eaten away over the years. Oh, I almost forgot."

Sam leaned over the magnifying light and turned pages until he was almost halfway through the book. Maeve and Seamus watched and after a while started to look around.

"Ah ha, I thought I remembered this right. Someone made notes in the margins - in Latin no less."

Seamus' head snapped back to Sam.

"Sorry?"

"Someone made notes in the middle of the Greek text - in Latin. I think your Irish monk actually copied them in as close as he could. He probably wouldn't know what else to do. It's a little different hand and I'm sure it wasn't the monk himself. These look to have been done on the original codex."

"Hmm, how can you tell it wasn't done after the monk produced his copy?"

"Because I can spot the handwriting of the monk in these notes, even though he was copying someone else's. I've become something of a handwriting expert along the way. I couldn't help it."

"The plot thickens or quickens."

"It's a good plot. Somebody was seriously chewing through this book, before our monk got the job. Trouble is, we don't know when. The notes could have been done anytime; scattered over a few hundred years."

Maeve looked at Seamus.

"Will you be going back to Father Schmidt?"

"No, Maeve. Since I'll be seeing Tony in a day or so, I'll have him tell me about it."

Sam looked puzzled, "Tony?"

"An old friend Sam. He's a natural linguist with a degree from Harvard in ancient languages."

"Whoa, he can read the whole thing."

"He certainly can, of course that's not enough."

"It's not?"

"No, he needs - and I need - to know what it all means."

Sam laughed.

"That sounds more like a job for your priest than your friend. You should get them together."

"Well said, I wish I could. It's not likely though. They're two thousand miles apart."

"Where's Tony then?"

"He's in San Francisco, well, Berkeley actually. He has an apartment not far from UCal."

"What does he do? Teach there?"

"No, oddly enough he's a computer scientist. He'd say he was a programmer but he's more than that."

"Hmph, I wonder why he didn't use his language knowledge."

"I don't think he wanted to be an academic. Of course, the idea of a language school was probably appalling to him. Helping Americans to learn enough French to wander about Provence - ugh."

Sam chuckled.

"I can see that. But computers? That seems like an odd choice."

"Well, it's not really. Most of his work revolves around language; even if it's a computer programming language. At one time MIT allowed Fortran to be applied as language credit for their bachelor's degree. I don't know if they still do."

"Huh, who'd have thought."

Seamus smiled.

"The problem is that Tony is really brilliant. He was interested in Far Eastern Religion at one point, so he taught himself Tibetan in six months. He wanted to read the Tibetan documents in the original language you see."

"Good God!"

"Indeed, there was even a story that during some software project, there was a delay of some sort. Tony turned bored during the delay and started to translate IBM's most technical manual, the 'Principles of Operation' into Latin."

Sam's face had a look of disbelief. He shook his head. "So you're off to San Francisco; sounds like a pleasant trip."

"I'm looking forward to it. So's Maeve; she'll have a few days days without her brother underfoot."

Sam stood up.

"Well, I promised I'd buy lunch. Let's go down to the kitchen and see what it is.

Maeve glanced over at Seamus.

"Sam has a caterer bring in lunch for everybody on Mondays and Fridays."

"Oh I see."

Lunch was long. They talked about Ireland and its history and the book. It was after two when they left to drive back. Maeve was on the expressway again before she spoke.

“I may actually miss you Seamus, now that you’ve returned to the brother I remember.”

Seamus chuckled to himself and looked at Maeve. “Yes, I know I’ve been a trial. I hope to never be so again. Still, you don’t know what may happen; think of the book.”

Maeve grinned. “I would wish I could take credit; obviously the book was divine intervention."

Seamus thought, *yes, and just when it was needed most. I wonder if I will ever know who to thank. Saint Dymphna, likely.*

When they got back to the house Maeve tapped Seamus on the arm.

"Don't forget, you're to phone Tony."

Maeve went into the office and returned with the phone. While Seamus went down to the basement for a beer. Maeve met him coming up the stairs. “Here, get on with it,” she said, handing him the phone.

Seamus pushed the buttons and gave Maeve a sheepish look. It only rang once.

“Willet.”

“Tony, thank the lord above you’re there.”

“Seamus?”

“And who else would call you the day before to say he’ll be standing in your parlor the next day.”

“Hey that’s wonderful. You’re flying in tomorrow?”

“Just so.”

“You’re a lucky old sod; I have the day off. Give us your flight information and I’ll be at the gate with my teeth glinting in the sun.”

“As only they could Tony. Hold up, I’ve Maeve here with all the numbers.”

Seamus handed the phone to Maeve.

"Hullo Tony. We meet - well as close as can - at last."

"Maeve, I've heard so much about you."

"From Seamus? You're a liar Tony. He wouldn't remember my name long enough."

Tony laughed. "Well, I actually have Maeve. I won't say everything but then I can't remember it all."

"Here you are; do you have a pen?"

"Shoot."

"Shoot?"

"Go ahead Maeve."

Seamus went for a pee. As he came back into the office, Maeve turned.

"Tony, here he is back to you."

She handed Seamus the phone.

"So are you angry with me?"

"I should be. No gay man would be so inconsiderate you know."

"Ah well, I am contrite. You have my permission to subject me to your cooking and thus take your revenge."

"Oo you can be nasty. I will do that and may God have mercy on your stomach. Now, I have to run out to the market and buy the instruments of torture. I'll see you tomorrow."

"'Til then."

Seamus handed the phone back to Maeve. She pushed the disconnect button and set it down on the file cabinet.

"Does he mince?"

Seamus choked laughing.

"Tony? Nothing could be more unlike. He's well over six feet; I'd guess about six foot six. He must weigh over seventeen stone and he's built like a weight lifter. The last I saw him, he had a black moustache and you'd run for your life if he came at you out of a fog."

"Good heavens above and he's gay?"

"Oh yes. They come in all shapes and sizes you know; just like the rest of us. Tony, however, is a bit out of the ordinary. He's been in some trouble more than once. He's so brilliant he's bored easily you see; so he found his entertainment starting fights in the pubs at three in the morning. I think he outgrew it. A wonderful person to know. The sort that keeps your interest up."

"I should say so. Not someone to follow about but fright does keep one focused."

"No no Maeve, he's really a gentle soul and as good a friend you'll be hard put to find. I may as well start packing."

Seamus opened his second beer and went up to his room. Maeve went back in her office.

Oh Seamus, she thought, *Nothing else could have done so well as this book. Now with luck and God's help you'll be off on a quest. Lena's death and all that pain can be dulled long enough to fade. Dare I wish for you to meet someone? No, not yet. Another woman now would be too filled with faults. Not that Lena didn't have her own; but poor dear Seamus came to love them so, they weren't faults at all.*

Chapter 10: Hibernia, 1347

"Michaeleen og! you look well enough. How is your father?"

"Thank you Brother Colum. He's been off the work. He's tired I suppose is all."

"He's in his bed?"

"Still. He's been weak since the day of Saint Becan."

"Ah, blessings on him and his; that is too long a time. You're managing?"

"I am."

"You're a good son Michaeleen; I will remember you and your family - not forgetting himself - in my prayers. What have you brought us?"

"A good set of hides Colum. These will fill many a book and you asked for a stone to sharpen the lunellarium."

Colum chuckled.

"I thank you and Brother Bron thanks you more. He has many days of scraping ahead and he was weary at prime devotions."

Michaeleen grinned.

"Then he'll be wearier still Brother Colum; I brought the copperas for your ink."

Colum's eyes widened.

"Bless you! I will mix the ink myself. Brother Bron's occupations are enough for him. You should know; this was sorely needed.

"I don't understand."

"The ink must be prepared in careful portions, Michaeleen; else it becomes too strong and the pages are consumed."

Michaeleen looked back at Colum with his mouth open.

"Brother Colum, that must be more pain than you - of all - could stand."

"Ah I know it, but I can never see it. The corruption takes many years; more than God will grant me I'm sure."

"The corruption taking so long a time, how can you know this?"

"I have seen its infernal work in other good works; works done by antiquarii hundreds of years ago."

"Ah, then why do you concern yourself?"

"Michaeleen! We strive to provide for those that follow us and the glory of God; not for our own times or our own pride."

"Brother Colum, I am sorry."

Colum put his hand on the young boy's shoulder and smiled. "Don't enlarge the thought; you are still young and a good heart is what God wants most."

Michaeleen went back to the currach and lifted a small linen bag. He walked back to Colum.

"Mam sent this, Brother Colum. She told me it might help your studies."

Colum looked inside. He looked up at Michaeleen.

"And so it shall. Take home my special blessings for your mother."

Michaeleen blessed himself.

"What is it, Colum?"

Colum noticed the missing appellation and ignored it.

"It's a dictionary; a very special dictionary. This provides the definitions for Greek words in Latin."

"Do you know Greek?"

"Not as well as I wish, but I improve. The library contains but a few Greek volumes; this will help."

"I must leave Brother; the markets will be open now and I have some fine fish to sell."

"A long day for you."

"Yes, the market to sell, then the market still to buy and finally home. I hope these hides I brought will suffice for your work."

"Sadly, they will more than suffice. We have few books to copy now. The travel discourages so many. Even the mendicants may easily find scribes closer, so they go to them. Unless some such singles us out, we may have these gifts from you next year; as blank pages in the scriptorium."

"God may yet change this Colum; Bron should be prepared."

Colum chuckled. "I know and so should the hides. Go with God Michaeleen og."

The boy returned to his boat and loosed the lines to leave. Colum loaded the hides on his shoulder and started the long climb up the stone steps.

—####—

A Street in Avignon, 1347

A juggler tossed around some bones at the entrance to an inn.

A group of passers-by stopped and crowded around the door. Fouinon looked over his shoulder and slowly backed to the side by the door. A fat swarthy-faced fat man pushed him aside; almost knocking him down, saying, "Make way you wart." Fouinon slowly withdrew his dagger and slid behind and beside the fat man. In a blink, he cut the cord of the fat man's purse and dropped the purse into a bag under his surcoat. The bag was of the same material as his tunic. He carefully replaced his dagger. The fat man looked down and, seeing Fouinon, elbowed him again; pushing him back against the inn wall. Fouinon bowed submissively and slid sideways along the wall until he was clear of the crowd. As he turned to walk away, he thought, *Once more I provide a boon. Reducing that toad's bulk will be a blessing to him.* He smiled to himself.

Gervais nudged Alard, "Do your eyes capture that?" He nodded toward Fouinon's back. Alard smiled and dropped his mouth to Gervais' ear. "Would that I had the skill. A more profitable living and the effort is small." Gervais grinned, "you speak the truth but the risk is too large for my stomach. One mistake and you might lose an arm or even your head." Alard grimaced and rubbed his neck. "Now you make me dwell on evils as would not chance avoid. I would, had I the skill, retire with a fortune before such could end the sport." Gervais chuckled and slapped Alard's shoulder with the back of his hand. "Had you the skill? The world will end before I see that miracle. You are safe in God's mercy, Alard. Your lack of talent protects you."

—####—

A Market Street Shop, Avignon, 1347

Fabrice turned from the door of the shop and shouted toward the back. "Edwige! The horses of those nobles just here have fouled the street before us. Fetch the shovel and a basket and clean it off. Don't neglect to wash the spot." He frowned and raised his voice. "Make haste Edwige; the custom will turn away from such a blockage to my door."

As Edwige emerged from the gloom at the back of the shop and passed Fabrice with the shovel in hand, Fabrice pushed her from behind. "Show some speed you wretch," he said, then, "Pah, your odor is bad enough; the horse dung will be unnoticed." Holding his nose, he walked back to the base of the staircase and shouted up the stairs. "Ghislaine, do you still intend to count receipts? This should be done before we crowd with buyers."

Edwige shoveled the horse manure into the basket and lifted it to her shoulder to carry to the rear of the shop. A cart passing slipped from a stone and slid into a pool of horse piss, splashing Edwige. She flinched, then ignored it and carried the basket away.

Fabrice opened the door to the shop and shouted at Edwige. "More haste, you lump, when you finish fetch a bale of cloth from the warehouse. The warehouse key hangs by the alley door."

—####—

The Papal Palace, Avignon

His Holiness Pope Clement VI sat at his desk sipping a particularly uninspiring Medoc. He made a face.

God help those who have to say a Mass with this sour wine, he thought We may have been fooled here. Bordeaux? I wonder at that, sigh, is any soul to be trusted in these times? He rang a small bell.

The Grand Butler entered the room.

"Your Holiness." He bowed.

"Marceau, what must I endure next?"

"Your Holiness, both your architect and your physician wait to attend you."

"De Louvres first, Marceau. What does De Chauliac want with me; does he tell?"

"No, your Holiness. He seems excited and in some urgency."

De Chauliac paced in the corridor outside the papal apartments, thinking furiously. *How do I approach my request? This Pope is not so pious as most. Although the threat is not to the souls of the faithful he still must see his charge to care for his flock. He is wealthy and sensual and pursues luxury to satisfy his wants. Perhaps his learning is the key. He has a fondness for knowledge no doubt to enhance his own self. Could I appeal to his interest in ancient medicine?*

Clement paused and thought, *I have no pain, what urgency does de Chauliac consider.* He looked at the tabletop without seeing it. Then, to Marceau, "Well, let him wait a moment; it will be good for his own liver. Even physicians need to moderate their habits, eh? He likely seeks a dispensation for some tart anyway." Clement VI looked at a tapestry and muttered to himself, "Hmm no, not de Chauliac; he is too consumed with his craft. Well, he can still hold for a few moments."

The Grand Butler bowed and turned to the door.

Clement leaned back; he was tired. Looking at the paintings on his walls, his thoughts tried to sort the issues by importance.

God grant me the strength to continue. The Romans and that gadfly Petrarch wish me to return to Rome; that decayed and squalid wreck of a city. True it was once worthy but now? He shook his head. *Do they not see, I have no time. Germany will be in civil war without my efforts. The Jubilee is not just three years hence. The palace is almost complete and must be furnished.*

"Your Holiness, Monsieur Jean de Louvres."

"Jean, what have you for me?"

Your Holiness, I but ask if you may find the occasion to view the work almost at an end."

"With pleasure. Will the morrow morning be too late?"

"No, indeed."

"Then you may prepare yourself at the Peyrolerie Gate as soon as Prime devotions are completed."

"I shall stand aside to the door of the Great Audience Hall your Holiness."

"De Louvres bowed and turned - the Grand Butler looked at Clement."

"Yes, Marceau. Against my feelings, I shall see the physician."

The butler left and then returned; holding the door, he announced the physician.

"Monsieur Guy de Chauliac."

The physician walked into the room and up to the desk.

"Your Holiness."

The physician dropped to one knee.

Clement lost sight of him below the desk.

"Yes yes - stand up! - what is it Guy?"

"Your Holiness, I have received disquieting news."

Clement was admiring a newly acquired painting on the wall; he turned to look at de Chauliac.

"How disquieting? Can it compare to imminent war? I have consequences in my day that affect the souls of thousands of the faithful, physician."

"I beg your indulgence Holiness. A great pestilence has been told to me. It has been reported that it arose in Cathay. I have now recently been informed it is in Tartary, Egypt and Persia. Whole regions are laid waste; fields of corpses - man and beast - rot untended."

"Where did you hear of this?"

"Stewards, bringing furnishings for the completion of your apartments, reported to me. Genoese traders from the east describe the scene with horror, Holiness."

"What is this to me? I recognize your passion for medicine but the pestilence is there, not here. They are heathens and worse, Guy. God may well have intended they should be so afflicted."

"As you say Holiness, but I fret that the skies may intend this. Are we not also subject to the influence of God's heavenly bodies? I am concerned for your safety and would beg your permission to pursue preparations. If we are spared, by God's good grace, the learning would not be wasted."

"Are you suggesting you leave? You may not leave Guy."

"No your Holiness. I wish to gather my knowledge."

"You have complete freedom of my Bibliotheca Secreta; what more do you wish?"

"Your Holiness, I fear that I myself could bring the corruption to the volumes. May I have leave to copy the work most useful to me? I may then take a copy and thus preserve the purity of the original."

Clement looked over the physician's head. *How trivial,* he thought, *and yet it has merit.*

"So then, how do you propose this be done? Do you have the copyists?"

"No, your Holiness."

"How many volumes will there be?"

"I cannot say Holiness. With your countenance, I can select those of most value by the Feast of Corpus Christi."

"You may not exceed two volumes. My copyists are currently engaged in an important effort for my nephew."

"Thank you your Holiness. That which I require most is but one codex."

"That is well, physician. These copyists take time." Clement stood up and walked over to a window. *This requires more thought. What if the physician is right to be alarmed. Could the pestilence come to Avignon?*

Could this be God's blessing? Could this remove any of the enemies around me? A grim smile passed over his face. Without removing myself, of course. He turned back to the physician.

"Make more haste, physician. If the protections you seek are in these ancient texts, we must have them before we are in need."

"But the copyists your Holiness; where are they to be found?"

"Hm, yes, physician. What is more, they must be trustworthy. Questions will be asked. Some ambitious scribes may see this as more opportunity than threat."

"Holiness?"

Clement was thinking. *Opportunity, hmm. If this was known to the physician, others already are aware. A clever man may see this as a chance to further himself while others are engaged. Fear is a terrible weapon. If the invisible death of a pestilence waits outside the door, why fear death from a knight's sword? Why not consume all you can before being rushed to eternity?*

This will take much thought to arrange the players to the advantage of the Church - and myself.

Speed is the ingredient to make this sauce...and secrecy.

The physician may find a potion to effect a cure in this ancient knowledge - or not. The chance is long but too significant to neglect. More importantly, should the answer be found it must needs be in the hands of the Church.

It would be unfortunate if some greedy noble held the physick - for ransom! He turned and looked hard at the physician.

"Physician, say nothing of this to anyone. Should you be asked of this audience, tell that you begged a dispensation for a kinsman. Your presence in the library is common enough and will not be remarked. But press your search; we may be forced to send the codex some distance to ensure its safety. You may take your leave."

de Chauliac bowed and murmured, "Holiness."

The physician kissed Clement's ring and backed out to the doorway; the Grand Butler held the door.

"Leave us Marceau; I must stir this new ingredient into my plans."

Clement walked to a couch and stretched out on it. *Copyists, God save me from them. They take too long. The time could destroy the most perfect stratagem. And that time must be reckoned from when they start! Hm, How to place the work on the desks rapidly. They cannot be in Avignon. No secret could be preserved here. The journey over land is perilous.*

The freebooter knights rob whatever comes to them on the road. They would not care for ancient texts, but they would slay the travelers and burn the baggage, which was of no use to them. And even if they arrived safely at Sens, Fecamp or as far as Arras, what then?

These knights with no battles to fight, would not scruple to attack and loot the town - including the abbey.

Wait! The English! No no, were Edward to hear of this, he would sequester all and play it as a card against France. Worse, I would be forced to treat with him against my own.

Hmmm, that risk aside, there...is...something...here.

Clement sat up.

Of course! Hibernia! They stand in isolation. The war does not pay in that gloomy isle, he smiled, and to sweeten the choice, they might babble to the multitude with little effect.

Their words would fall silent in some morass or clatter on their rocks.

The monastery I would select - where would that be?

And to travel there? Ah that is simple enough - a merchant vessel - Spanish. One to stop in Avignon to trade and then depart for the west coast of Hibernia - they're fond of Spanish wines. Small wonder, what pleasures can they have besides?

Clement stood up and walked to the bell on his desk. *There, I've settled with that; a more pleasurable task remains - the banquet this evening.*

He rang the bell.

The Grand Butler walked noiselessly into the room and bowed. "Your Holiness?"

"Send for the kitchen steward and my secretary."

"At once your Holiness."

Clement walked back over to his couch and sat down heavily with a sigh. *God grant they received the capons and veal,* he thought, *the rest is assured. Two, deeply stirring, beauties tonight; all must be perfect to charm them. True, their wealth is in their bodies.* He smiled. *Both bodies, the one which is so wondrous to the view and the other, of no less value - their bodies politic. Four prizes to win, I will assess my fortunes by Matins.*

The door opened and the kitchen steward stepped just inside the apartment.

"The capons and veal are here your Holiness; all is being prepared for the banquet as I speak."

"Excellent, that is why I called for you. I expect your best tonight. I assume you will serve the fine white butter sauce you prepare so well." "Yes, your Holiness, such was my intention."

"I approve, you may go."

As the steward turned to leave, he held the door for the secretary. The secretary walked in to the room and bowed. "Your Holiness."

"Ah Jean, I need a notation for two days before the Feast of Corpus Christi."

The secretary pulled a book from under his arm and opened it. Turning the pages he walked over to the desk and laid the book on the desktop. He reached for the writing quill. "A task your Holiness?"

"An appointment, Jean, for the physician de Chauliac. Have I the interval of a long psalm between vespers and compline that day?"

"Yes, Holiness."

"Then record this as soon after vespers as may be. I may lose sleep but not to the conversing with my physician."

The secretary was writing and finished. He sprinkled some ground cuttlebone on the page, shook the book and poured the cuttlebone back into its container.

"It is done your Holiness; shall I inform the physician?"

"Yes, Jean. You may tell him I expect to hear of his progress."

"Your Holiness."

The secretary bowed, turned and left.

Chapter 11: San Francisco

Seamus woke with a start and looked out the window. The plane was landing, the bump and screech of the tires had awakened him. *Aagh, I did it again! When will I stop doing that?* he thought. *Every time I get on a plane I fall asleep. The answer is never, you old man. You're not thirty anymore. Ah such a shame, I had so wanted to see San Francisco from the air. Nevermind, I'll see it when I leave, um...maybe.*

As they arrived at the terminal, dozens of people stood up and started rummaging in the overhead compartments. Finding what they carried on; they stood in the aisles holding their bags. *Amazing,* he thought as he watched, *and so predictable. They do it on every flight and it does no good. They must have the airplane version of what? - cabin fever? They don't help, they don't get off any sooner and it must be uncomfortable to stand there for who knows how long. Watch for it, yes, now they're resting their bags on the backs of the seats. In the way of other passengers and completely oblivious to the irritation they cause. Sigh.*

'O wad some Power the giftie gie us

To see oursels as ithers see us' - indeed.

Seamus settled back in his seat and looked out the window, as he always did. Only after most of the passengers had hurried off would he get his bag and stroll down the aisle.

As he came out of the tunnel into the crowded terminal he saw a large sign being held up; 'Leprechaun Limo Service', it read. He grinned and walked toward it. Tony's face appeared from one side. He looked Seamus over. *Hmmm, poor Seamus looks old and tired,* he thought. *But then it has been a long time and after losing Lena he probably didn't sleep or take care of himself, never mind, I have to be cheerful and distracting now.* He shook it off and smiled at Seamus.

"You're too large; only leprechauns will fit in my apartment."

Seamus grinned. Tony dropped the sign down in one hand and grabbed Seamus around the neck with the other arm. "God it's good to see you, give us a kiss."

"Over my dead body."

"Aw, Seamus, this is San Francisco. It happens all the time."

"Not to me, it doesn't. When did you grow that beard? It would take the skin off a crocodile."

"Hmm, that may be what happened to my last lover. Is that the only luggage you have?"

"That's all."

"You're a light traveller; it looks heavy though."

"It is but it's one of those with the wheels."

"Then let's be off." They started to walk slowly out of the concourse. Tony waved his hands and talked as much to himself as to Seamus. "It's beautiful weather today; that's actually unusual for San Francisco, it should be all over fog. I've planned a slow and pleasant tour before we tax our memories."

Seamus smiled and strolled slowly along enjoying the sights and Tony's company.

"I'd like that and I'd rather not tax anything until tomorrow."

Tony looked down at Seamus. *Damn,* he thought. *I forgot this problem. I hope he's not too upset.*

"Sorry, Seamus I have to go to work in the morning."

"Um, well, I'll have to worry out what to do in your absence."

"You're welcome to my liquor cabinet, my music and my library. I'll be back, ready to think intensely, by the time you rise from your usual siesta - how's that?"

"Well enough, Tony. I'll be well rested and ready to wear you to a nub."

"I'd be cute as a nub."

They drove into the city and parked the car; Tony had already planned to spend the afternoon on foot and cable car. After a tour of the city, Seamus finally begged to stop and take a break. Tony found a coffee shop with outdoor tables and they sat and talked about old times. Tony thought, *What do I say about Lena? Do I bring her up at all? Yes, I better; it will clear the air.*

"So, how are you doing?"

Seamus knew what he meant and brushed it off.

"I'm fine Tony."

"How's Maeve doing with you doing fine?"

"Ah she's careful but I know she wants me to get by it all and click me heels in the air."

Tony chuckled. "She's a woman Seamus and she wants you to have a mate. They're fond of saying they don't need men, but they know men need women. Do you still think of Lena all the time?"

Seamus looked wistfully out the window, "Not all the time, but often enough."

Tony watched his friend, "There are 'triggers' you know. Perhaps if you tried to avoid them."

Seamus looked at his coffee and shook his head, "No Tony, I miss her every time I get into an empty bed. She used to warm her cold feet on the back of my legs."

Tony saw Seamus' eyes misting up. "I'm sorry, Seamus, let's talk about something else. Someday you'll find someone else."

Seamus looked out the window again and smiled.

"Yes, yes but I'm not ready to look for one now. It will be a while yet. Of course, if a young beauty found me that might make me pause."

"You're right, it'll be a while yet."

"Ah, you're no fun."

"I'd be more fun if you were gay."

"Sorry."

"You should be; that young beauty would show up by tomorrow."

"Uh huh, I'm sure - a real beauty."

Tony grinned and stood up. "Shall we? We can beat the traffic across the bay bridge. I have plans to show you Muir woods, Golden Gate Park and Chinatown but that's all for other days. How much time are you going to give me?"

"Lots, Tony. I told Maeve to give me a week. Don't forget though, I want your brilliance shining on this book I've found."

"Oh yes. I haven't forgotten. I'm looking forward to this. It's smack in the middle of both of my passions."

"Meaning language and religion?"

"Yup."

"I counted on that."

They got the car and left the city; driving across the Bay Bridge to Tony's apartment in Berkley.

"Tony, why are you still in an apartment? You should be living on the fat of the land with your salary."

Tony laughed.

"There's not enough housing fat in this land, Seamus. To get what I might want - urban guerilla that I am - I'd have to fork out over a million bucks."

"Ouch! sorry I brought it up."

"It's all right, I have a very nice place; wait'll you see it. Besides, I don't have to repair broken pipes and such - or even pay to have them repaired. I'd rather have the time and the lack of worry than the pride of ownership."

"Surely, if I had thought a few seconds longer, I'd never have asked. The idea of you pushing a lawn mower is truly incongruous."

There was a silence, broken only by the drumbeats of the expansion joints in the bridge surface. Seamus admired the view across the water. In the distance the mist obscured the north shore of the bay. Not surprisingly, considering it was quite a few miles distant. Finally, Tony broke the silence in a serious tone, "Seamus, do you still avoid church?"

"Yes I do, but I don't feel I'm ever out of church. What prompted that question?"

"Oh, curiosity. I've been musing on it myself lately. I haven't decided whether to follow your example or avoid it. But I do need to know what that example may be."

"Avoid it. I'm no example at all."

Tony was turning into his driveway. He glanced over at Seamus.

"Oh yes you are, live with it. This book will be interesting you know."

"Oh I know."

"No, I mean from the religious perspective."

"Say again?"

"You're - well we - are about to peer into the mind of a man whose whole life was driven by religion. In a time where all of society was driven by religion. That culture compared to today is even more different than New York compared to Benares."

"It was Christian wasn't it?"

"Not as we know it Seamus. They had no clocks to speak of; you know how they measured time? By the time of their prayers - about a dozen a day. Do you know how they said 'I'll see you in two weeks'? They'd say I'll see you by the feast day of such-and-such a saint. Everything they did, even saw, was distorted by the Catholic Church and the latest bull from the Pope."

"Right, the latest bull indeed."

"Now, now - tolerance Seamus, tolerance."

Tony had driven down to a garage and used a remote to open the garage door. While they were talking, he pulled in and they got out of the car. The garage was very large. It was obviously made for two cars with ample additional space for a workbench and storage for garden implements along the back wall.

Seamus pointed at the empty space in the garage.

"So, only one other tenant?"

"Oh that's mine too, but I only have one car."

"The entire garage is for your use?"

"Yup, I told you it was a nice apartment."

They walked through a side door in the garage and along a flagstone path towards a very large house.

"Ah, I see now, you rent the entire house."

"No, you're close though; I rent the bottom two floors. The top floor and the basement are used for storage. Honestly, I'm not sure who actually owns the place. I think it belongs to the University. I send my payments to a real estate outfit."

Seamus was looking up at the house.

"A very nice apartment indeed."

Tony walked up some stone steps and unlocked the back door. He held the screen door open with his foot for Seamus. They walked into a large kitchen all in white and butcher block. Tony walked through to the front room facing the street and pointed at a huge overstuffed chair.

"Try that but watch out, it'll put you to sleep if you're not careful."

Seamus sat 'into' the chair - you couldn't sit 'on' it.

Tony walked over to a liquor cabinet on the far wall. Opening the drop down door on the cabinet he rummaged around and then turned, lighting up a cigarette.

"So, a drop of the Irish?"

"You've the blood of a prince Tony."

"I know that; I think I'll have a little myself."

He turned back to get the drinks.

"Still smoking, I see."

"Now and again. I don't smoke at work and I smoke a lot when I'm in a gathering of other smokers. I like the idea of thumbing my nose at the American baby-boomer hysterics."

"You don't think they have a point?"

"Oh these things aren't good for you, perhaps. But with the massive pollution in this country, how can they tell? You know Seamus, in Ireland they've almost all smoked since Sir Walter brought it back from the Indians. According to what I've read, they've only recently seen the rates of heart disease and cancer rising. Now why would that be? I'll tell you. Because they've only recently started to create pollution of their own."

"Hmm, you may have something there. But there's always the expense."

Tony winced. "I won't argue with that."

Seamus looked closely at Tony and a puzzled expression formed on his face.

"What is that a miniature cigar?"

Tony took the cigarette out of his mouth, looked at it and smiled.

"No, it's a Sobranie."

"A what?"

"A Sobranie, Black Russian. They're pure Turkish tobacco and extremely good. Trouble is, they're almost impossible to find. They don't import them into the States or even Western Europe."

Seamus raised his eyebrows and shook his head.

"Of course, you would find an obscurity. So, where did you get them?"

I ordered them through the Internet. I thought I was dealing with a company in Gibraltar, but they turned out to be in Baku." He tossed the black and gold box to Seamus. It had a large white box on the lower half, with lettering in cyrillic text.

"Where?"

"Baku, Azerbaijan. On the west coast of the Caspian Sea. In the end, they were shipped to me by an agent in the Ukraine. Wonderful isn't it?"

Seamus stared with a comic open mouth. Looking at the box.

"It's amazing, what does that Russian text say?

"I have no idea; I don't speak Russian or Ukrainian or whatever it is, but I'm going to learn."

Seamus snorted.

"So, you're going to learn Russian just to read the writing on your cigarettes?"

Tony looked offended.

"Of course! This is the sort of thing that makes life fun. I imagine it just says 'smoking is bad for your health'; even the Russians have climbed on that bandwagon."

Seamus grinned back at Tony and then a thought struck his face.

"Ah! Tony, I just remembered. I left my case in the car."

"So, we did. I'll go; you stay; even if your clock's ahead of mine."

Tony went out the doorway carrying his drink. Seamus smiled. *What a great lad he is. A shame he's all these miles away.* He sipped his drink and looked out the window. The back door slammed and he heard Tony taking his case up the back stairs.

"Tony!"

"Yes, what?" Tony's distant voice came from the other side of the kitchen.

"Hold up, let me get the book out."

"Come on back here and follow me. Then you'll know where you're staying."

"Right, on my way."

Seamus went to the back and looked up the stairs. Tony was stopped halfway. He waved Seamus' case to indicate up the steps.

"Follow along."

They went up to the first room on the left and Tony left Seamus to unpack his bag.

When Seamus came down with the book, Tony was at the liquor cabinet

He pointed at Seamus' drink.

"Shall I freshen that up a little?"

Seamus lifted it up to Tony.

"Thank you, a fine thought."

Tony handed Seamus his drink and sat down.

"So, is that it?" He pointed at the book in Seamus' hand.

"It is. This strange rigging..."

"Is to keep the parchment from warping. I know."

Seamus stared at Tony.

"How do you know all this?"

"Come Seamus, you know I'm a religious student. Where is all the chewy stuff to be found? In old manuscripts of course."

"Of course; have a look." He handed it to Tony.

Tony took the book; removed the large rubber bands and gently lifted off the plywood sheets.

"Oh Lord!" His face became suddenly very solemn. He set the book on the arm of his chair and went over to a chest of drawers. He opened a drawer and took out some gloves. He went back to the chair putting on the gloves.

"I have to get some gloves."

"You damn well better. This is a priceless relic Seamus. If you damage it, I'll be after you with a torch and a pitchfork."

Seamus sat back in his chair and sipped his drink; looking sheepish.

Tony had begun to read the first few pages. He was amazingly fast; as if he were reading a magazine.

"Tell me what you read Tony."

"I'm reading the words of a man telling me to go back to church."

"That's a bit dramatic."

"It's true for me though. This monk was one of the few of his time."

"The few of what?"

"A religious man who was truly religious. He reads like he was in spiritual pain Seamus."

"Whatever for?"

"Do you remember I told you he was disobeying his Abbot? It's much worse than that - he was disobeying the Pope."

"The Pope! - good heavens."

"Exactly, heaven is the key. Poor man thought his soul was in real trouble."

"I thought he was an obscure Irish monk."

"He was, from what I can tell; way off in the middle of nowhere."

"Then how could he disobey the Pope? Something he did to violate more bull?"

Tony laughed. "No, nothing so remote. He was given instructions explicitly from the Pope and he disobeyed."

"Why would the Pope be instructing some simple Irish monk in anything?"

"Good question. I haven't figured that out yet. It seems to revolve around this book. I'll keep going here." Tony read another page.

"Hmm Seamus? I think I've got it."

"Go on."

"This monk was given the task of copying this book."

"Right."

"He was also specifically told to only make one copy."

"That's what the priest in Cincinnati said, very Odd."

"Yes it is, what's even odder is the monk apparently made three."

"Yes I know. The priest mentioned that also."

"That's a lot of work. The question is - what possessed him to do it? Particularly in direct disobedience of his orders."

"He doesn't say?"

"Not clearly; or maybe I haven't gotten there yet. He talks about his failings and his arrogance. He was wrong to forget the humility that all men must remember; particularly himself, in holy orders." Tony continued to read.

"Seamus, it's this book. Not the stuff I've been reading; it's what comes after. It must be the Greek part. The monk is saying this book can prevent some suffering. That's why he made additional copies. Well, that and his inadequate talent and inadequate effort."

"So, then what is this Greek book saying?"

"Let me take a quick peek. The beauty of Greek is that it hasn't changed much."

"Oh come now."

"Really Seamus, Greek hasn't changed substantially in all these past two or three thousand years."

"Tony, are you trying to convince me that they would understand us? What with airplanes and instant coffee, I find that hard to credit."

"Oh they would have the devil of a time with modern vocabulary of course. That's not the issue. We're trying to read them - remember. Their vocabulary isn't that arcane. I can read it easily. The modern Greek can read the inscriptions on temples chiseled back before the days of Alexander the Great."

Tony pulled over a handful of pages; starting at about the middle of the book.

"Well I stand - er sit, corrected."

Seamus laughed. "Ah ha, so what's the difficulty?"

"The Greek's all right. I can't fathom what this one is trying to tell me. It's ingredients and procedures for...um. Here we are. It's a treatment or maybe - and, a prescription for some ailment. That doesn't help Seamus. I'd say we're going to need a doctor."

"You do look a little green around the gills."

"Very funny. I mean it looks like this is all medical stuff. Actually, it's worse than that."

"Why?"

"We're going to need a doctor who's familiar with medical history I think."

"Maeve was right, the plot sickens."

"Ouch. That was uncalled for Seamus."

"So, who do you know? I don't know a soul here."

"Hm. I suppose I can ferret out someone. The best would be a teacher I guess."

"Only if he teaches ancient Greek medicine."

"Not too many of those around. Don't snort though; they do exist. Medical history is fascinating to many people."

"Are we stumped?"

"Lord no! I have some friends over at UCSF and there's Berkeley, just up the street. If they don't fill the bill, they'll find someone who does."

"UCSF?"

"University of California at San Francisco."

"Ah."

"Tony, I had a couple of wonderful talks with a man in Cincinnati. He was a type expert but his passion is old text - like this."

"Uh huh."

"He went into great detail about the 'hand' and the paper."

"Vellum."

"Right you are. I'm ignorant of the history of books. I thought the old manuscripts were all on scrolls."

"Well, that's the history of bindery."

"All right, what about the animal skins? I thought they had papyrus."

"Oh , I see where you're confused. Yes, they did have papyrus; great stuff. It would outlast anything we use today, I suspect."

"So why did they go to skins? It must be much more work to produce."

Tony laughed. "You can bet on that. What happened was a long, long time ago. There's a myth and the facts."

"Give me both."

"OK. The myth is that back during the Ptolemys - that's the line of pharaohs that started after Alexander conquered Egypt - they cut off the supply of papyrus."

"Who did?"

"The Egyptians."

"Cut it off from who?"

"OK, let's back up. There was in ancient days a magnificent library at Alexandria."

"I've heard of that."

"Right, well, after a while, a second library started up in Pergamum and the Egyptians got jealous. Pergamum was growing so fast, it was starting to rival Alexandria you see."

"So they cut off the papyrus?"

"Yup, they wouldn't allow it to be exported. They had the market cornered - right? All the papyrus came from Egypt."

"So, that's the myth? It sounds plausible to me."

"I guess that's why it lasted so long."

"So, what is the fact?"

"The fact is that Epiphanes invaded Egypt in about the second century B.C. and that disrupted the supply of papyrus. Parchment was the alternative, there were always plenty of sheep around. Anyway, it was adopted all over the ancient world; not just at Pergamum."

"Enough! My tiny brain is reaching the point of overload."

"You're tired. Let's have a brilliant supper, worthy of the finest restaurant, and collapse. I have a nasty conundrum to unravel tomorrow and I need my beauty sleep."

"Sounds right, Tony, but I don't think you'll ever get enough beauty sleep."

"Aagh, follow me to the kitchen. After that remark, I feel encouraged to poison you; so you should be there to watch."

Chapter 12: The Collector

The phone lay on the floor next to the couch. When it rang, Jimmy pinched the end of the roach and reached down without looking. He slid up against the armrest as he picked it up and pushed the talk button.

"Yeah?"

"Jimmy?"

"Yeah."

"It's Jock, I think we've got him."

"The old man?"

"Yah."

"That was too quick; are you sure?"

"It was easy. There are only three and two are out of town."

"Ah Jock, he doesn't have to be in town. He could have done it all from anywhere."

"I didn't think of that."

"Well, hang on, I'll get a pen."

Jimmy could hear Jock shouting away from the phone. "Steve, watch the car - he's going for a pen."

"OK I'm back, give me all three."

Jimmy listened and wrote on a yellow pad.

"Good enough, where'd you get the addresses?"

"Little Willie."

"Yeah, I thought he was a good bet."

"Better'n that, Johnson and the playmate gave me the same names."

"That's enough, I think we're good to go."

"Do we still meet Saturday?"

"I'll think on it. No, skip that, yes; we'll meet as planned. If anything changes, I'll call."

"Right."

The phone went to a dial tone. Jimmy looked at the receiver and then hung up.

You'd think these guys would learn a little etiquette, he thought. *Shit, they could at least say goodbye instead of leaving somebody hanging.* He walked over to a chair and looked at the pad.

OK now, which one are you? I think I've got you, old man, and where you live.

We'll have to scout the houses out. I'll bet they have big expensive security. He may even have armed guards with all his bucks.

Damn it, I'm getting way ahead of myself. I don't know which of these old farts is you!

I don't feel like bashing down the doors of two other guys trying to figure it out. The cops would be looking for a new burglary ring.

How do I figure this out?

What do I know about you? My old man told me he did that job for you back in the twenties. You were a fat cat then. Old money in Cincinnati didn't get hurt much by the depression. Besides, you answered the drop box, didn't you? So, I know you're alive and I know you're old and I know you've still got the bucks. I guess you'd have a great big old mansion, but that doesn't help. You had one then but it may or may not be the same one. Besides, you probably have more than one.

So what did my old man say? You had him pull a major burglary. Shit, I guess. If my old man had kept some of it, I'd be a rich man now; instead of screwing around with dope to make a living. Jesus, my old man said he'd cleared almost half a million. 'Course he could have been lying; he did that well.

Come on Jimmy, focus.

The client - that's you, you old fox - wore a tux. He had a moustache. He belonged to the Cincinnati Country Club. He loved old stuff, books, art, sculpture, architecture. Wait a minute! He...loved...old...stuff. So you probably still do - right? Of course, where else would you get the book. Obviously, you have a lot of very valuable old stuff.

So, I'm looking for a collector. Sure, all three of you are probably collectors and I could be screwed. All old guys, with big money are collectors but you - you should be a standout. Jimmy smiled.

I wonder if you'd bite at some really hot sounding merchandise? Why not, your scruples are low.

Hmm, were low. You could have got religion by now.

But if you're going straight, why answer the box?

Hey, I could paralyze my head this way. Two Hundred And Fifty thousand bucks is two hundred and fifty thousand bucks. Still...

This book is worth as much or more. More - hmm, now that I think about it, why did you bother? Why not ignore me and just keep this book? You're the nut about really valuable old stuff and you've got plenty of money - so why?

Because you thought a lot of my dad - sure, when pigs fly.

Because you wanted the money - just auction the book.

Because you thought I'd give you a hard way to go. Well, I might try but you know I don't know who you are.

How did I get here?

Shit, why did I take so long to get here?

It doesn't make any sense. If I was the old man, I just would have ignored me.

The phone rang. Jimmy walked across the room and picked it up. "Yeah?"

"Jimmy it's Jock."

"Yeah?"

"You'll never believe it; one of our old guys is in the paper."

"Huh, what's the deal?"

"Cincinnati collector donates ten million dollar art collection to the art museum."

"Oh yeah? What's it say about him?"

"It says he's one of the most respected art collectors in Cincinnati. It says, he's been known for his generous donations for years. Ummm... fifty years! Sheesh! It says he's a renowned expert on art and antiquities."

"Go on."

"Jimmy, It says he doesn't get out and travel around buying, anymore. He's, uh, infirm."

"I'll bet. We'll be infirm ourselves if we get to his age. Jock, get anything you can on the other two."

"The other two? Why?"

"Because I want to find out, you dummy."

"Ah, more work for me."

"Look, I think this one in the paper has got to be him. I've been thinking about what my dad told me and the old man loved and collected stuff; but I want to be sure. I don't want to get on the radar of our friendly neighborhood police - got it?"

"All right, all right. I'll check the library."

"That should do it, these guys go back and they're public figures."

The phone clicked and the dial tone came on.

Goddammit! Why does he do that?

Jimmy hung up the phone.

Crap I'm tired. Jimmy stretched out on the couch and fell asleep.

Jimmy woke, startled and reached for the phone.

"Yeah?"

"It's Jock. You sound awful."

"I just woke up. Thinking is hard work Jock, try it sometime."

Jock chuckled.

"Noo thank you. Ah just want to have a comfy place in the Bahamas."

"Yeah yeah, what've you got?"

"The other two don't have much to do with art or any old stuff."

"What do they have to do with?"

"One of them's a big developer. Spends all his time down in Florida, swimming. He's a physical fitness man."

"At ninety?"

"Guess so, he's been a sports kinda guy all his life."

"OK, what about the other one?"

"He's a traveller; that's why he wasn't in town - he's never in town."

"Christ when do these guys start acting their age?"

"This one has a crowd of people taking care of him. There's a bit in an old newspaper that says he wants to see all the great wonders of the world before he dies."

"That's good enough for me Jock. You were right the first time. The one at home is the only one left."

"Yah. When do we go get him?"

"Take it easy. First of all I'm the only one who's going to see him."

"Ah, Jimmy."

"Listen, I want him to find the guy who's got the book, remember? I don't want to blow that chance by blowing a hole in the old man."

"OK, but what if he won't go along."

"Oh I think he will."

"How can you be sure of that?"

"I've been thinking and I've got some questions for the old man about the book."

"Questions? What about?"

"Not sure yet, Jock. Just wait and it'll be all clear. Anyway, give the address to Steve. We're going over to see the old man tomorrow."

"Tomorrow?! Soon enough."

"Yeah, no point in wasting time. That book could be on its way to New York by now."

"Dammit Jimmy, don't talk like that."

"It's OK Jock. It may be even better if it is."

"What? Are you out of your mind?"

"No Jock. I told you I'd been thinking. I think the book is stolen."

"Yah damn right and it's ours."

"No Jock, s-t-o-l-e-n...stolen."

"Uh, I don't ken."

"By my old man."

Jock was silent.

"Jock, it could be we were set up. Come over and pick me up at ten tomorrow morning. Now say goodbye."

"Ah...right... goodbye."

"Goodbye Jock."

Jimmy smiled, hung up the phone and lay back down on the couch.

Sleeping must have done it. I didn't put it together until Jock was on the phone.

That's the reason the old man would do what he did. That book was hot and the old man wanted to get rid of it. 'Course it didn't have to be stolen by my dad; could've been anybody. But I'll bet the old man would like the turn of that. Give some hot stuff to the son of the guy who stole it.

Do I care? I don't think I do really. After all, dad's been dead for over twenty years. I'd think the statute of limitations would keep me out of receiving stolen goods.

What about the book. If someone tried to sell it, and they found out it was stolen; would they have to give it back to the rightful owner? Maybe I should call lawyer Chris and find out. Even so, odds are good nobody would know.

If they ever did catch on, I'd be on a very private beach. If they found me, I could be indignant and if enough time went by, I'd pay it back out of my investments; while stalling as long as possible of course. Anyway, it'd be in the hands of a museum or a megabuck collector by then and they wouldn't want to give it back. Hell, they'd fight and stall more'n I would.

Nice try, old man, I still think I'm all right - when I get the book.

And if you don't get the book - clever Jimmy?

That's straight, I get my money back, or another valuable something from the old man's collection, or... or I blow his brains out and take whatever looks good?

Nah, I could get nailed for that. I'm just not the violent type; I'm a businessman.

Steve could do it though; I could make that clear to the old man. Or... I could threaten to blow the whistle on him?

Maybe. If he's got all this respect, a scandal would hurt his family.

Ah shit, I'm back to where I was last week - who'd believe me?

Chapter 13: San Francisco day two

Tony was up at six and made a pot of coffee. He wrote Seamus a note and then left. Seamus woke up at 6:30. The house was very quiet. He knew Tony was an early riser; well, had been an early riser. He got dressed and went down stairs. The coffee pot was full and the note was next to a clean mug.

Seamus,

I'm gone - to solve my problem. If I'm lucky, getting in this early will get me back sooner.

Have coffee, think about your problem. If you run out of ideas or amusement, I'll be calling about ten - answer the phone.

Tony

Seamus smiled.

Ah Tony you are a sweet man. You'd have made someone a wonderful wife. Seamus chuckled out loud.

He's got the right thought there. I need to gather my wits and all this new information and make a manageable outline of it. So, there's the thought; where's some paper?

He walked out to and through the front room to Tony's office. Sure enough on top of the desk was a blank yellow pad. Bringing it back to the front room he sat at the table in the front window, sipped his coffee and looked at the pad.

So, it's a book.

It's from the 14th century.

Copied from an original that was sent from the Pope - himself?

Ah, question number one. Couldn't this have been just as well sent by the Pope's librarian?

Seamus wrote that down.

Now. The book was copied by an Irish monk who was expressly told to only make one copy.

Hm, question number two. Why only one copy?

Seamus started to write, then stopped. *Hold up, the real question is: can I find out why? That seems a bit unlikely.*

Well, we'll write it down anyway.

He scratched out the second line and wrote beneath it.

I know the monk disobeyed; and worried himself about it.

I know mountains of fascinating details about 14th century books and how they're made and what they're made of.

Hmph, doesn't tell me a damn thing.

He looked out the window. A bird was perched in a tree a dozen feet away; the bird was staring through the window at Seamus.

What does that bird think he's looking at? I may not be pretty, but he's seen the likes of me before, surely.

The bird cocked his head to one side.

What is this bird on about?

Seamus turned his head back into the room.

For the love of Mary! I'm waay off the path.

He turned back to the bird; it was gone.

So, do I have you to blame, uh... thank... you peculiar bird?

The puzzle isn't why did the monk do this particular book; the puzzle is how, and why, did Seamus Cash become the proud owner?

Weelll...the puzzle of the monk is still there, of course. Ah hell, let's work on one puzzle at a time. Why did I get the gift - or curse - of this book? Have I learned anything that can help with that?

No!

I know a great deal about how the book was made.

Does any of that help?

Not that I can see.

Sigh, back to Saint Dymphna no doubt.

All right, I have to think I was right in believing it was intended for someone else.

So. It's horribly valuable. He'll be wanting it back.

Back...um, I'd best be watching mine then. If there's anyone after this book, he's after me.

He'll be sure he's the rightful recipient - not me.

Umm, wait a bit; I see a mistake. I've not thought of the whole thing; there must be two ends.

One end is the one that could well be after me. The other end is the one that sent it there.

He chuckled.

There must have been a real Donnybrook when one end didn't get what the other end sent.

I wonder if it was large enough to show in the newspaper?

Ah! Maeve, I forgot to call her.

He walked back into Tony's office and picked up the phone. Then he noticed the time.

What time is it in Cincinnati? About noon, um no, eleven o'clock? I shouldn't call her now, she's just coming up to her lunch. I'll call a little later.

He walked back into the front room and sat down.

Where did I leave off? Oh yes - two ends.

I doubt I can ferret out the lad who was to receive the book.

Can I find the one who sent it? Perhaps.

I have more to work on; I have the book itself.

Hmmm, this might be possible. After all, the owner of a book such as this must be a little out of the ordinary.

Who are the likely candidates: a very well off private collector?; a very skillful thief?; someone associated with a museum?

I must balance probabilities here. The most likely versus the...uh less likely. Clearly, I would expect a theft of this magnitude to appear in the papers. The lack of noise would point to a private collector. Then again, suppose I was on the right thought back in Cincinnati.

The theft may have occurred a long time ago. It would make the papers in a very noisy way; then it would become old news.

Hmmm, I'm in the wrong place once again. If I were still back in Cincinnati, I could go to the newspaper archives and forage.

Seamus made some more notes on his yellow pad. Then set the pad on the arm of the chair and went back to the office. The clock read 9:45 and he sat down in Tony's office chair and picked up the phone.

I suppose Maeve will be through lunch by now. I should remember to pay Tony for the call.

He dialed and the phone rang twice, then, "Hello, McCarthy"

"Maeve?"

"Seamus, you were to call me when you arrived."

"I know, I do apologize. Tony put me through his first day of tourism after I got in."

"I thought as much."

"You're not angry then?"

"I was completely prepared to be, but I did think something would get in the way."

"Good, all's well. The entire time was quiet and painless."

"So, what have you discovered?"

"Not so very much. Tony is trying to find a medical historian to help us with the book."

"Hmm, that's a fine thought."

"Yes, it's seems right as far as it goes."

"That's not far enough for you?"

"I've been thinking Maeve."

"Of course you have."

"Yes yes, I know. Here's what I didn't think of. Where did the book come from? I mean to say, who did it come from. At the sale."

"Oh, I see. We're back in the present day."

Seamus grinned. "Right, back to the boring modern times."

"Well, and what did you miraculously discover?"

"Nothing. I do have a theory though."

"And that is?"

"That if it was from a theft, it would be a very unusual theft. The poor benighted victim would not be poor. The victim may even have been a museum. So, even if it was a long time ago, it would surely be in the newspapers."

"As you put it, I cannot but agree."

"Could anyone go to the local newspaper archives and look for it?"

"I've never looked into it. I believe so."

"Would you mind?"

"I'll be happy to learn how it's all done. I won't say I'll do it Seamus."

"Thank you, I don't need you to spend all that time Maeve. I can look into it when I return. I have to go now. Tony left me a note to say he'd be calling about now."

"Right, call me again at the weekend."

"I promise Maeve."

"Uh huh and so you did before you left."

"Maeve."

He heard her chuckle.

"It's all right Seamus, enjoy yourself, goodbye."

"Bye Maeve."

As he hung up the phone, it rang. He looked at the clock. It was exactly ten.

"Willet residence."

"Oh very nice Seamus. I think you should stay and answer my phone for a year or two. My friends would be so impressed."

"Hello Tony."

"What have you been doing?"

"Thinking and making notes. I did call Maeve. I've just rung off as you called."

"Oh right, we forgot to call last night. Well? Come up with anything?"

"Not much, but I do think I should be trying to uncover who this book belonged to."

"Can't help you there, but I think we're on our way with the book itself."

"So?"

"I talked to a friend over at UCSF. He told me there's a national organization for just this kind of thing."

"Marvelous!"

"Isn't it? It's the AAMH - the American Association of Medical History. One of the websites - I browsed the net for it - says to pronounce it with a Boston accent - Awmuh. Good eh?"

"Yes, so when do we go see them?"

"Well, we don't. It looks as if the best approach is to find out what member, with the stuff we want, is here in town."

"Oh? how do we do that?"

"Well, I have a list of members here in the Bay area. I'll ask them. They should be able to point us to someone in the AAMH who's into ancient Greek medicine."

"Hmm, sounds right. So when will you be back?"

"I solved my problem, so as soon as I make these calls, I'll be on my way. Say, an hour at worst. That means you must wait for me before you have lunch."

"I see, this is part two of your revenge."

"You got it, see you then. Bye."

"Goodbye Tony."

Wait for Tony; only fair of course. I'll be hungry by then' I'm hungry already. My clock says I'm an hour past dinner. Lord, going back to Cincinnati will be painful. Then there's the trip home but that won't be quite so bad; by then I'll be off a good eight hours. Why couldn't Maeve live just past the date line? Then my clock wouldn't change; just the day of the week. I lose track of the days of the week often enough as it is.

Seamus walked back through the front room to the kitchen and poured himself more coffee.

I suppose the owner of this book can wait until I return to Maeve's. The book puzzle is much more interesting anyway.

He went back to the front room and sat down, sipping his coffee.

In spite of the coffee, Seamus dozed off. He woke to the sound of the rear entrance door opening.

His pad had fallen on the floor. As he reached down for it, Tony walked into the front room.

"Ah ha, caught you."

Seamus looked up.

"At what?"

"Taking exercise. I knew you had been lying to me all these years."

"Caught indeed, now that arm is done for the rest of this month."

"C'mon, I'll get us some lunch."

Seamus stood up and they walked into the kitchen.

"So, did you find us the expert?"

"Yes I did, how about that?"

"I am impressed. Who and where is he?"

"Close, no cigar. *She* is just down the street - almost. The best part is she's a fanatic about ancient Greek medicine. You know, Hippocrates and all those guys."

"Hippocrates is the only one I know of."

"Only one I know of too but there would have to be a couple of others - I hope. Otherwise this will be even more boring than I feared."

"Tony! I wouldn't have thought this would be boring; particularly for you."

"It's all relative Seamus. I'm just afraid this'll be so full of clinical terms for boils and constipation, I'll be forced to doze off - bad manners that."

"Oh now, surely we can guide her in her explanations."

"Let's hope. Anyway, we're seeing her at eight this evening."

"This evening!"

"I thought you were eager."

"Oh I am. No, I mean, that's all right. I'll have had my nap and I should be in fine fettle."

"Whatever a fettle is."

"I don't know either. What's her name?"

"Doctor Margaret Farrell."

"That's good, she's Irish."

Aagh Seamus, why does everyone have to be Irish."

"Starts the conversation off well."

"What if she's gay?"

"Will I know?"

Tony closed one eye and looked at Seamus.

"No, you won't."

"Is that a rebuke?"

"No, just a defect. For all your great detection skills, there are a few spots where your antennae are too short."

"Ah, You'll not mind if I make no attempt to improve that."

"Suit yourself."

Tony made sandwiches and they sat at the kitchen island eating and talking.

"Well Seamus, you'll be off to your nap I suppose."

"If you don't mind."

"Not at all; mind if I look over the book while you're snoozing?"

"I wish you would. You could well find something of use. I certainly can't read it."

"Yeah, but I'm going to look hard specifically for those 'guides' you mentioned."

"Say again."

"To point Doctor Farrell."

"Oh I see, yes. If we don't have a specific place for her to start, we'll spend oceans of time."

"Unnecessary, wasted time. I'm going for the sections that have margin notes. It looks to me like they were of most interest to someone centuries ago."

"Which may be the part that Colum the monk thought was so important."

"Exactly, look, if your book and handwriting expert was right, then someone else wrote those notes. If he knew enough to write the notes, he may have been a medical man himself. Anyway, somebody - according to your friend - other than the monk, Colum - wrote those notes; that seems like a good place to start."

"I'm convinced - and sleepy."

Seamus went up to his room for his nap and Tony went to the office taking the book with him.

An hour later Tony heard Seamus coming down stairs.

"Seamus? That you?"

"No, it's a very groggy house breaker."

"Right. Come in here; I have something interesting."

"Let me fetch some coffee."

"Sure, anything to wake you up. I need you alert enough to digest this."

Tony could hear Seamus pouring the coffee and shuffling toward the front room.

"There you are, sit down and tell me what this means. This Greek is Doric."

"Doric, as in columns?"

"Yes, as in columns. Also as in a dialect of Greek."

"What's unusual about that?"

"Well, most works were written in Ionic. It's like the medieval writers using Latin instead of French or English."

"So this was written by the uneducated or the country peasant."

Tony laughed.

"It's not that bad. The idea of it written in the Doric does seem significant though."

"How so?"

"My guess is it was intended to be used personally or by an insider group. Not for publication, if you like."

"Oh, I see. Whoever did this was writing a working manual or something."

"Exactly, sort of 'just us pro practitioners' would have this."

"That is interesting."

Chapter 14: Feast of Corpus Christi 1347

The Grand Butler entered the room.

"Your Holiness."

"Marceau, has de Chauliac arrived?"

"Yes, your Holiness he paces in the corridor."

"Send him to me."

"At once, your Holiness."

The butler left and returned.

"The physician, Monsieur Guy de Chauliac."

The physician walked into the room and bowed.

"Your Holiness."

"Guy, what have you discovered?"

"I have one codex of importance, your Holiness."

"Describe it to me."

"It is a treatise on medicine from Greece, your Holiness."

"Guy, describe it to me."

"My apologies, Holiness. The volume is large, with many leaves. It is in Greek and there are simple drawings of anatomy interspersed."

"How many pages do you imagine?"

"I would surmise a figure somewhat less than three hundred, Holiness."

Clement made a thoughtful face. "Hmm, not insignificant. This will challenge the time.

Physician, we have all in readiness. You will turn over the volume to the grand constable."

"So soon? But your Holiness, I have numerous notations in this work. I cannot trust to my memory."

"You must, physician; if, as you have suggested, this pestilence emerges, we cannot permit the original to leave the palace. So have you said yourself. The time cannot be trusted. The copyists must needs begin."

"Is there no recourse, Holiness?"

"There is but one, physician. No copy is commissioned. The exemplar remains here in the palace. If a pestilence strikes Avignon, you now vow to your Pope and your God, you will not leave these grounds."

"I cannot, your Holiness, what of those who may suffer. I cannot deny them my help."

"As I thought physician, but what of your Pope? You may well doom the souls of all, in exchange for those few. A bargain that wagers the salvation of countless souls against the chance to prolong some few miserable and brutal lives."

"Your Holiness, I beg your forgiveness. I must still remain true to my purpose. I know not any other way to serve God."

Clement's face softened.

"I see. Your heart is a physician also. As you will, physician. But then the matter still stands; the book must leave at once. If it is not returned before next Eastertide, we may both despair at its absence."

"Why would the time be so long, Holiness?"

"This codex is not a simple trade contract. A copyist, scribe or monk, may skillfully manage three or four pages a day, physician. Such a time must be increased more to allow for ruling the pages. After the writings are complete, the quires must be arranged and cut. Then the leaves must be bound. All this is enough without the time to transport the exemplar and its return."

"The time in travel is so great, Holiness?"

"You could not know Physician; I have arranged for the work to be given to a monastery in Hibernia."

"Hibernia? So far from us?"

"Yes and from prying eyes and eager ears, physician. The journey sounds longer than it should be. One of my couriers will carry it to Bordeaux; that will be swift - perhaps six days. A barque will receive our package there and carry it up the coast, perhaps another eight days, to Brittany. I have been assured the crossing to Hibernia will be short from Brittany. A Spanish navigator is to accompany my courier. We pray the entire interval will be less than a month."

"Once there, the Abbot can assign the task. If the copyist is skilled, it could be returned before the beginning of Lent, Holiness."

"I dare not make my plans on that, physician. It is simple, without a need for rubricators or Illuminators. That much I know. You have said it has images, however; the copyist must go more slowly and carefully."

"Holiness, what of my notes?"

"Do not concern yourself. The instructions to the copyist will state clearly to make the copy in statu quo."

"Is there time to have more than one copy, Holiness?"

"No. More so, since I will not allow it. It is not in your mind to see such things, physician. This may be a very dangerous volume. Your need allows one copy to be produced - no more."

"Dangerous, Holiness?"

"Indeed, I cannot tell and nor can you. We have yet to discover the volume's worth. Just consider, if this contains the alchemy to stay this pestilence, what power it may provide to the unscrupulous. Now carry the volume to the Grand Butler and ensure it is well protected for the journey; oilskins will be necessary."

de Chauliac bowed. "Your Holiness."

Hibernia

"Brother Colum!" The Abbot was walking across the courtyard from the chapel.

Colum was helping Bron remove the hides and mount them on the stretching frames. He looked up and handed the wooden tongs to Bron.

"Yes, Father Abbot."

"Colum, strange and wondrous news has been told to me by Fisherman Fahy."

The Abbot took Colum by the arm and turned pulling Colum along.

"You must leave Bron to this work and turn your attentions to the scriptorium."

"What is this news Father Abbot?"

"A Papal courier is, at this moment, on his way to us with a commission. Think Colum, a commission from his Holiness Clement VI himself. I know no more than this; but you will be immersed in your heart's work for many a month."

Colum brightened.

"From his Holiness the Pope?"

"Yes Colum." The Abbot smiled. "What is more significant yet; the volume is arriving in the hands of a Papal courier. As you should know that is rare and indicates a very important codex."

"I am to perform the task Father Abbot?"

"Indeed Colum. You are the best choice. You are young, skilled, diligent and, above all, happiest when you are writing. All here have been consulted, I should tell you; and all here have suggested you."

Colum smiled to himself. *He knew the antiquarii had so hurt their eyes, the Abbot would not allow them to work in the scriptorium for fear they would become blind. The other librarii, although younger and strong of sight, thought of the task as a penance. Only Bron loved the books and he was still inexperienced.*

With all these thoughts, he held his silence and only said, "Thank you Father Abbot, I will do all I can."

"I know you will Colum. Now you must prepare the scriptorium, your materials and yourself."

"Yes Father Abbot, when do we expect the courier to arrive?"

The Abbot released Colum's arm and turned to Colum.

"We shall be pressed Colum. The courier may stand on our steps as early as the Feast of Saint Peter and Paul."

They walked across the courtyard and paused at the great yew.

"How do we hear of this?"

"Fahy heard from a merchant. He had landed from Bordeaux that same day. The merchant talked with a navigator responsible for the courier - 'a latere', Colum. This Spanish navigator wished to sail directly, but the courier was afraid. They were to proceed up the coast to Brittanny before crossing."

Colum pictured the voyage in his mind.

"I see Father Abbot, then they could be delayed the days spanning three Sabbaths."

"Yes, Colum. A blessing for us. With gratitude to the Lord, we may still not have enough time to prepare."

"I will begin at once Father Abbot."

The Abbot stopped and Colum walked on; through the arches of the cloister. As his sandals slapped against the stones, he heard Fergus cry and looked out into the courtyard. The cat was running toward him. Colum continued, and ahead, through an opening, the cat walked onto the stones and sat; waiting for Colum to reach him.

"So Fergus, you have heard the news."

The cat got up and fell into step with Colum.

"You are timely, Fergus. I will need you to discover and discourage any rats or mice that may have set up their homes in the scriptorium."

As Colum reached the scriptorium and opened the door, Fergus ran into the central chamber and began to stalk around the skirting boards.

Colum watched for a moment.

"No mercy, Fergus. They must not escape us. No doubt they will only move their belongings to the storage rooms; that being preferred by them. The Abbot will object of course, but not until after the Pope's courier has gone."

The cat stopped and looked up at Colum.

"Well go on, go on. When our distinguished guest has left you may then go to the storage rooms and be welcomed all the more."

The cat resumed his search.

"Now, Fergus, I must reckon my materials. Parchment will be too coarse for a Papal commission. I must have vellum. Thanks be to God, and Michaeleen og, we have some fine pages. The oak galls and the copperas were also from young Michael. I pray himself is no longer ill and may receive my thanks and prayers. The cleaning will occupy my labors for some time; pray God I am ready before the courier arrives."

A mouse scurried across the floor with Fergus in pursuit.

"Praise the Lord Fergus. You will improve your chances."

Colum's friend, the Oblate Bron walked into the scriptorium. Colum smiled.

"Bron!"

"Brother Colum, I heard of the book. You are blessed and so will be the owner of your labors."

"Thank you Bron. The owner is his Holiness the Pope. I must believe he has blessings enough without my contribution."

Bron smiled. "I had more than hopes for this, Colum. I knew in my heart God would not allow your skills to wither from lack of use."

"His name be praised Bron. How could you be so strong in that faith? God may as easily have wished me to harvest weed from the sea."

"Ah but this year Palm Sunday falls on the Feast of the Annunciation, Colum. That is always a sign that events of great moment are impending. What better proof than this commission?"

"Mmm, you should not allow these old omens to color your thoughts Bron. They may not be as God wills. More than that, I recall that old omen may portend ill as soon as well, thus we say ominous."

"Yes Brother Colum. Yet, the book is a truth, if the old tale is not."

Colum smiled. "Enough of that, my thanks for your gladness at my new task and we must prepare. Come and show me the stores of vellum, ink and quills. I shall also need a good corrector knife Bron. My faith does not go so far as to believe I will make no errors. Titivillus, being a demon, does not rest."

"Titivillus?"

"Yes, Bron, the demon with the sack. He encourages mortal scribes to err in their work by diverting their attention. He captures the errors in his bag and ensures they are presented on the day of reckoning. I struggle to add to my prayers and good works to help balance my account; already heavy with mistakes."

Bron frowned and thought, then his face cleared. "Brother Colum, your dedication to God and the preservation of his works is well known. I expect the weight of Titivillus' bag will be as a pebble to a millstone."

—####—

A River Street near the Docks, Avignon, 1347

Fouinon leaned against the wall at the end of the street, sharpening his dagger. From a distance down the street coming up from the docks he heard a thump and a squeek followed by the sound of something sliding and the clacking of wooden shoes. He looked in the direction of the noise but could see nothing and resumed his sharpening. Another thump and the scrape of something sliding made him look up and, as he watched, a large bale emerged from behind the corner. The bale moved a foot and stopped then another foot and stopped; then a girl's head emerged bent over as she pushed the bale. She was small, ragged and dirty. He assumed she was a domestic servant. He pushed away from the wall and walked slowly over to the bale; just as she pushed the bale into his legs. She grunted and then looked up. When she saw Fouinon she stood up quickly and curtseyed.

"Oh, I beg your forgiveness, good sir."

Fouinon grinned. "And I beg yours m'lady, where do you travel with your burden and how may you manage such a large bale."

Edwige blinked and smiled quickly. "I am charged to deliver this to my master's shop six streets up this hill." She pointed.

Fouinon looked her over. *If she was washed well and dressed otherwise, she would be pleasant enough.* He thought. He stooped down and lifted the bale to his shoulder. As he turned he waved his hand to Edwige. "Come and lead the way, I will take you to the door. God may credit my account for this small favor."

Edwige beamed and ran past Fouinon, turning to him she bowed a little and blinked again.

"Oh, good sir, you have spared me a beating; it is this way."

She walked in front as Fouinon followed. As she walked she turned her head and smiled at Fouinon.

She is no beauty, he thought, *but she attracts me. Perhaps, after some wine, I could enjoy her company.* He looked at Edwige's matted and tangled hair and the smudged dirt on her face. *Um, after she was bathed.* Fouinon staggered up the street behind Edwige, his head tilted by the bale of cloth. Edwige ran a few steps in front, stopped, turned and smiled, then ran a few steps more. Thus they progressed up the hill. Fouinon watched her, smiling to himself and wondering. Finally, he said, "Your master must credit your strength to send you on such an errand. What are you called?" Edwige answered over her shoulder, "I am Edwige. My master is my Uncle who took me into his care after my parents died." *Oh ho,* thought Foinon, *A chance that God gave for labor at a low price.* "Does your Uncle treat you well, then?" Edwige paused, then replied, "Well enough. I have no skill or worth and I am fed and have a mat on which to sleep away from the rats." Fouinon frowned. *Enough to use this slip of a girl for hard labor. As so many merchants have always done before him. Still, the family should have some leave. Ah, none of my concern.* He shouted up to Edwige. "What of your parents then; did they not leave you something?" Edwige snorted and kept walking ahead. "All my parents had belonged to the Bishop; themselves in the bargain. A band of knights with no colors took it all." Fouinon nodded, "They shall suffer under God," he said. Edwige stopped and turned to him. "While we suffer now? I wonder that God cares a sous." She started walking again. Fouinon mused on the thought. *I believe in God's care. How else could I be so helped? I break the commandments always and yet I am fed and clothed and sheltered. Only God could arrange such a long chance.* He smiled to himself. *Of course, I may do some good in God's plan. Relieving gluttony of its excess and showing the way toward a blessed life. He trudged on after Edwige, thinking her more attractive as he walked.*

—####—

A River Inn, Avignon, 1347

Gervais looked over his cup and muttered from the side of his mouth. "Alard, the old Jew has done well at the expense of the faithful." Alard followed Gervais eyes to the old man at the table across the Inn against the back wall. An old man laughed as two serving wenches refilled his cup and his plate. They hoped for his generosity; he enjoyed the attention. Alard's face held an expression of disgust. He turned to his friend. "They all fill their pockets with the fruit of usury. The Church permits only the Jews to lend money."

"As you say, and is this as it should be? That those who murdered the Savior should grow fat while the faithful who obey the Church are in want?"

"Of course, you refer to ourselves with only the means for four cups on a dark, chill night."

Gervais looked at Alard with a crooked smile. "I feel the need, nay, duty, to redress the balance. What say you?"

Alard watched the old man putting his hand up the gown of one of the wenches and stroke her leg. "You have touched the spot, Gervais. We would be doing God's will."

As the old man made ready to leave, Gervais and Alard stood up and hurriedly left the Inn. Outside the night was dark with only the sliver of a moon providing light past the windows of the Inn. A mound of bales blocked the roadway to the side of the door. Gervais motioned and they walked around the bales and crouched, watching the door. The old man staggered out, leaned for a moment against the wall and then started around the bales.

Alard stood up quickly and pinned the old man's arms as Gervais found his purse under the tunic and cut the cord. The dagger was dull and Gervais cursed as he sawed at the thongs holding it. As the old man struggled he started to shout, "help, mercy, blackguards." Alard stooped and picked up a stone fragment from the gutter. He struck the old man on the side of the head and he went limp. As the old man slumped, Gervais' dagger finally severed the cord and Gervais waved the purse in front of Alard's face. "Come," he whispered, "We have it." Alard dropped the old man to the ground and they turned and ran.

They reached the warehouse where they slept and stumbled up to the door in the dark.

The door to the warehouse creaked open as Gervais pushed hard with his shoulder. Alard put his hand on Gervais arm. "Hold a moment, there is no light inside, let us see what we gained."

Gervais stopped and turning to the dim moonlight, opened the old man's purse and put in his hand. As he pulled out the coins he gasped. "Alard, the old man was a great success indeed." Alard stared at the gold in Gervais hand. "We have blessed ourselves this night. There is enough to care for our wants for a span of three, perhaps four, Sabbaths." Gervais grinned. "We shall do our reckoning on the morrow. If God smiles, we may trade our mats in this rat filled warehouse for a soft bed of rushes in a good Inn." Alard returned the grin,"Ah, with a comely wench to add the warmth. First, Gervais, you should have a new dagger with a cutting edge."

"Or, you, Alard, can remove the next prize." Alard pushed past Gervais and through the door into the warehouse. As he passed Gervais he said, "My dagger is no better than your own." Gervais followed, "Is the Jew alive?" he said into the dark. Alard's voice came back in a hollow echo. "I cannot say nor do I interest myself."

—####—

A Market Street Shop, Avignon, 1347

Edwige staggered into the back of the shop from the rear alleyway carrying the large bale of cloth. Fabrice and Ghislaine were leaning over a table under the stairs to the second floor. On the table between them was a large open strongbox. Fabrice turned to watch Edwige.

"Edwige, open the bale and sort the bolts by color." Edwige dropped the bale and walked over to Fabrice. "Master may I have the use of an edged knife for the bale." As she spoke she saw the open strongbox; it was full to the brim with gold. Fabrice followed her eye. "What say you to that, eh?" He waved at the box.

Edwige's eyes were wide. "God has blessed you indeed, master."

"God, Pah! My wit and my labors are what are rewarded here. Soon I shall sell this filthy shop and buy a fine country house a goodly distance from this foul-smelling place. On that day you shall have to find another master to take you in, if you can." He laughed as he handed her his knife.

Chapter 15: The Doctor

"So Tony, what poison awaits me for supper?"

"I intend to toy with you for awhile, Seamus. We're going out to a restaurant on the way to the doctor."

"This would mean I'm safe for another day."

"You were in danger sooner but you refuse to eat breakfast."

"You could flavor my coffee."

"You're too observant. To deceive you I'd have to do the whole pot and I like my morning coffee too much for that. Besides, that's Starbucks and I won't waste it to watch you make a face."

"Well, I suppose I should clean up a bit."

Tony looked at Seamus' wrinkled jeans and shirt. "Yes you should, otherwise I'll have to leave a larger tip."

They left the house and went to a small family restaurant that specialized in Italian food.

"Seamus, I hope you don't mind Italian."

"Mind, I should say not; I do believe it's my first choice."

"Oh good, I feel the same way myself."

It was a quiet supper. Neither spoke often; they were too busy eating and enjoying the food. It wasn't until they were sipping the after dinner coffee that Seamus leaned back.

"So, how far are we from the good doctor?"

Tony looked out the window at the traffic. "At this time of night on a weekday? About five minutes."

"Did you decide where she should start?"

"Yup, first page that has notes in the margins. It's odd really; the notes are all in a few consecutive pages; not scattered around as I expected."

"Sounds like someone found a specific reference."

"That's all I can think of. He was looking up something and then read and commented on what he found."

"Can you tell what it is?"

"Uh huh, it's a disease."

"Right, wouldn't any of it be a disease?"

"Oh no. There are general diets, exercise recommendations, wound healing - different kinds of wounds - and even specific conditions."

"Such as?"

"Cataracts, acne or at least something about bad skin, dentistry and the delightful bowel movement issues."

"I see what you mean. Well, what about this disease?"

"It's a description of a historic breakout of the disease. How bad it was and how it was treated. Then, what was wrong with that treatment. Of course, the correct treatment follows that - a potion of some sort."

"Does it actually tell you what the potion was?"

"Yes, two of them. One was to be taken if the disease was contracted and then one was taken to prepare for the disease; I guess, if you heard it was coming. Fascinating really. It's very detailed and involves doing things during certain days of certain Gods."

"I would think the good doctor will be interested."

"If she's not, we've got the wrong doctor and we can go shopping for another opinion. Shall we?"

Tony stood up and left the tip. They went out to the car.

"Listen, Seamus. I don't expect you to sit like a dummy while the doctor and I debate the Greek you know."

"Oh have no fear of that. I'm not the quiet type." *But I used to be*, he thought.

They drove for about six or seven minutes and Tony was on a quiet residential street lined with old and fairly large houses.

"I didn't know we were going to her home."

"Didn't I tell you? It seemed the best to her; she didn't want to be in her clinic."

"It would be incongruous?"

Tony chuckled. "I would say so. She's apparently quite the history nut. It figures she'd focus on medical history."

Tony spotted the house number and pulled into the driveway. As they got out of the car, the front door opened and a woman stepped out and watched them while she held the screen door.

"Tony?"

"Yes, Mam it is I."

Seamus looked at Tony.

"It is me, Tony."

"No it isn't you, it's me."

"Aagh, I concede."

"This is the owner of the book?"

"Yes, Doctor Farrell; my name is Seamus Cash."

"Call me Margaret, Seamus."

"May I call you Meg?"

Margaret Farrell laughed.

"Yes you can. That's what my father used to call me."

"Whew, that's lucky."

They walked up the path to the door as they were talking. Margaret held the door for Tony and Seamus took it from her as they walked into the house.

"Seamus, how on earth did you get hold of an ancient Greek medical book?"

"That's a story of its own, Meg."

She walked away from them into a sitting room and then through that to a study on the far end. Seamus turned to Tony and whispered. "I like her already."

"So do I Seamus. It's always nice to meet a doctor who is real people."

"Real people?"

"Umm, down to earth, you know, no pretensions."

"All the better when they have a right to pretensions, yes?"

They walked into the study and Meg was standing at a liquor cabinet on the left hand wall.

"Drink?"

"Ah Meg, and you a doctor."

"Don't be silly, good for your heart."

"If Seamus is going to be good; I'm certainly not. I'd love a scotch and water."

"Seamus?"

"Well then, I'll have the same. It would be impolite to say no and I'd miss it anyway."

"Would you rather have Irish?"

"Thank you, no. I like the scotch."

"Coming up. Sit down and be comfortable."

She made the drinks, went around to her desk and, opening a drawer, she pulled out a pair of white cotton gloves. Then came over to the two chairs where Seamus and Tony were sitting.

"Here you are; I had the scotch myself. I really like scotch and don't make the choice often enough. Now, let me see the book before I explode."

She sat in a third chair in the group and pulled on the gloves. Her desk was behind her.

"Don't you want to sit at your desk?"

"Oh no, the light's good here and we're going to talk a lot I suspect."

Seamus pulled the book from under his arm.

"The rubber band contraption..."

"Is to keep the pages from warping, I know."

Seamus turned to Tony.

"That's what Tony said; everyone knows all about this except me."

Meg laughed. "Don't feel bad Seamus. I've spent a lot of time in old libraries and museums looking at books like this. After all this time, this probably isn't necessary anymore."

She took off the rubber bands and plywood and set them on the floor. Then she opened the book.

"I thought you said it was in Greek?"

Tony leaned forward.

"Keep going, Meg."

She turned page after page, slowly.

"God, it is beautiful; even without the illuminations. The painstaking work they did. I'm always amazed by it. Ah, here's the Greek part."

"Meg, I had a long look through it this afternoon. We'd really like you to start at a very specific spot."

"I'd be happy to, but you have to let me look through the preface."

"Preface?"

"Oh yes, it should have some explanation of what the book is."

"Nope. I thought that was odd myself."

She was frowning.

"I'll be... you're right. This isn't what I expected at all."

Seamus frowned.

"What were you expecting Meg?"

She looked up at Seamus.

"Well, I rather thought it would be another Hippocratic Corpus; or some portion of it. The medieval books from the Greek usually were - or Galen maybe."

"And this isn't?"

"No no, not even close. I'm having a little trouble with the Greek though and I've seen 'Hippocrates' a few times before. Tony?"

"It's Doric, Meg."

"Doric?"

"Uh huh. Not the usual dialect for a publication - that was usually Ionic."

"Your knowledge of ancient languages may save me here. Why would it be in Doric?"

Seamus looked at Tony.

"We wondered that too. The best explanation we can think of is that it wasn't intended for publication really. But many things were written in Doric. It tells us it's from classical times and Doric speaking Greece. I'm going more from the rather casual style. I need you to tell me what you get from the content."

"I see. Then this could have been a physician's notebook."

"That's what we thought."

"Oh my, oh my. This could be almost unique. How in the name of heaven did it get copied all the way to this and not show up before?"

Tony chuckled.

"Now there you have us. We don't know enough about Greek medical history to know it didn't show up. Are you sure?"

"Ah no, I'm not sure. If you can help me with some of this language though; we might be able to tell if it's scarce."

Tony had a thought, "Meg, where was Hippocrates from?"

Meg was engrossed in the book and answered without looking up, "Hippocrates was from Cos."

Tony's eyes widened, "They spoke Doric on Cos."

He looked at Seamus. "it's time for you to say the plot thickens, Seamus."

"Pass."

Meg laughed and went back to the book.

"Well, where are the parts you wanted me to look at?"

"I put a piece of paper in to mark it. It must have slipped down."

Meg started fanning through the pages with her thumb.

"Here it is. Let me see. Hmm, it's about some disease; marked by dark skin lesions."

She turned the book over to show Tony and pointed at a spot.

"What's this Tony?"

"Let me see, Meg."

Tony took the book and read, then turned back a page and read forward.

"That's Thucydides, Meg; the writer is referring to the history of an epidemic in Athens. It doesn't actually give a date, but I put it - from the references - at about fifth to sixth centuries B.C."

"That's approximately the period we associate with Hippocrates."

"So far, so good. Here." He gave the book back to Meg.

Seamus watched and then looked back and forth between Tony and Meg.

"Here, wait a bit, are we in the part that has the notes?"

"Yes, right at the beginning."

"So, this is the history of the disease you mentioned to me before; is that right Tony?"

"Yes, he's talking about some disease that caused a lot of deaths and wasn't treated properly."

Meg had been reading and stopped to look up at Seamus.

"No wonder it wasn't treated properly. I doubt they had a clue on this one."

Tony stared at Meg.

"Why?"

"It looks like plague to me."

"Plague?"

"Uh huh, Black Death, Great Pestilence. It was around a long time before Monty Python did The Holy Grail."

Tony made a face.

"Very funny, Meg. I realize it was around centuries ago. I didn't realize it struck ancient Greece."

Meg stared up into space for a moment. Then she looked down at both of them.

"This was recorded. I thought this particular epidemic was put down as typhus by archeologists, but I know exactly what he's describing. A couple of years ago the city of Athens was building a subway. During the excavation they hit some ancient ruins; know what they were?"

They both shook their heads. Meg smiled.

"A graveyard with mass graves. They dated the find to about 400 to 500 B.C. The worst of it was the loss to the archaeologists. They scrambled as fast as they could and then the government stamped in and destroyed the whole site."

"What happened; I mean what did they discover?"

"I don't remember any details about artifacts. I just remember being really angry. After all that, the government decided not to build that part of the subway after all. The last I heard there was a big empty hole and they were going to put up a parking garage on the spot."

Seamus shook his head and looked at Meg with a sad face.

"I suppose the Greek man in the street is so used to those ancient ruins, they don't hold any wonder anymore."

Tony nodded.

"I can believe that. It's like us living next door to Muir woods. The last time I went to gaze at those astonishing trees was when a friend stayed with me two years ago."

Seamus laughed.

"And the next time will be to show them to me."

"Right."

Meg grinned.

"OK…ok, it is true, but this is still a terrible mistake. The archaeologists had pretty well decided it was evidence of the epidemic described by Greek historians."

She thought a minute. "Annnd... you know, I think they even mentioned Thucydides accounts of it."

Seamus waved his hand at the book in Meg's hands.

"Does our doctor say he was there? If he was, he was awfully lucky."

"Meg looked at the book, then at Tony.

"Did you get that? I don't see anything that makes me believe the writer was present."

"No, I don't think he was. It's written as an account. Very detailed though; as if he got the story from another physician who actually was there - or knew someone who was."

"Did you read the whole thing Tony?"

"Lord no, I enjoy reading Greek manuscripts as a rule. I break that rule when I see stuff like this. The treatment of bodily problems is not interesting to me."

Meg smiled. "I suppose I understand that. Well, let me read through some more."

Meg read in silence for quite a while. Tony and Seamus sipped their drinks and watched her face. They had finished their drinks and were starting to fidget when Meg looked up and sat back. She noticed their empty glasses and expectant faces and grinned.

"Well let's top up the glasses first. This is wonderful. I thank God I was the one you two stumbled on."

She got up and collected the glasses. Seamus stood up.

"I'll carry hod, you'll have trouble carrying three back to us."

"Carry hod? I've never heard that one before." They walked over to the liquor cabinet. Tony reached in his pocket.

"Meg can I have a smoke?"

"There's an ashtray next to you."

"I noticed, that's why I asked."

"You may, I have one or two a week myself. But your limit's two. This study has bad ventilation."

"Thanks."

Meg looked at Seamus as they walked to the cabinet bar. "Hod?"

"Oh yes, it's a term used in bricklaying. The hod is the triangular wood thing on top of a pole. That's what they carry the bricks in."

"How strange. I've seen it in pictures; up on their shoulder, holding onto the pole to balance it. I didn't realize it was called a 'hod'."

"Peculiar name, I admit. I don't know the etymology."

She made the drinks and they walked back. Seamus handed Tony his drink and turned to Meg as he sat down.

"You're being coy, Meg. Too quiet. Come now, what have you discovered."

Meg smiled and Tony looked at her over his glass.

"OK, I want to check some of this with Tony. But, for a start, I'm trying to digest what he's saying. He thinks he has some empiric evidence for a cure. That's what I read. I have trouble with that idea."

"Why?"

"Good Lord Seamus, this was somewhere around 400 B.C. Can you imagine what I must think about a Greek doctor who found a cure for plague? Why wasn't this referred to somewhere else? Anywhere else."

Tony leaned forward, putting out his cigarette.

"I sympathize Meg, but isn't it possible at least?"

"Oh, it's very remotely possible, I suppose. But veerry remotely. The plague is still with us you know. It can be cured by serious antibiotics."

Seamus frowned and looked up at the ceiling.

"Meg, are you implying that this Greek would have to have antibiotics?"

"Yes I am. Not just any old antibiotics but streptomycin, chloramphenicol, and tetracycline.

The best is streptomycin, but it can be toxic if used for too long. You have to prescribe tetracycline with it to allow the dose the necessary extension of days. About five to ten days does the trick."

Tony and Seamus looked at each other. Then Tony looked back at Meg.

"So how could he have found those?"

Meg laughed. "Raw luck and a very odd mixture of ingredients worthy of a witch doctor. It does sound a little like that to read. The only things missing are toads' feet and eye of newt."

"Right, hung in a corpse's shroud by the light of a gibbous moon."

"It's not that bad; but it's pretty far-fetched."

Seamus held up a finger.

"So, one, he thinks he's found the cure. What about two? Did he say he actually used it?"

"Oh yes he does. He says he cured whole families."

"Whoa, Seamus this book was stolen from the AMA and they're trying to kill whoever has it."

Seamus looked at Tony.

"Bite your tongue; even in jest that is soft ground. Maeve would have me deported to die in me own homeland." He turned back to Meg.

"I thought the plague killed people overnight?"

"It can be that fast but only if the patient is susceptible - weak or very old or very young, and, even then, it would almost have to be the pneumonic form."

"There are different kinds?"

"Two kinds: bubonic and pneumonic. Bubonic is contracted by infection of the blood - something like a fleabite. You have a little bit longer to go before it gets you. Pneumonic is contracted by inhalation; it hits the lungs - hard and fast. Anyone with that would be lucky to make three days."

Tony shivered.

"Ugh, creepy stuff."

Seamus looked fascinated.

"Meg, wouldn't our Greek have to treat these people right away?"

"Oh yes, indeed he would. That's another serious problem. Even today, people die because it's not diagnosed quickly enough."

"Then he would almost have to know it was coming?"

Meg thought a moment.

"It would help. Then he could have just treated anything that moved - in case. The thing that just occurs to me now is the preparation time. It's not a mixture he can whip up overnight. He has to have a couple of weeks at least. Then there's the physician himself; how did he do this without dying himself?"

"Leave the dying part for the moment. Couldn't he just have a stockpile of the potion; tucked away in his shop?"

"No he couldn't - it doesn't last. The concoction would lose its potency over time. That's true of any antibiotic. Who knows what the shelf life of this is." She pointed at the book.

Tony had been listening. Finally he waved his hand between them.

"OK hold it for a minute. I can certainly see this Greek may have been mistaken. Even if he did see his cure work, who knows what actually cured them. What I've been wondering for a while now is how did this show up in a 14th century monk's cell to be copied. That's a long way to travel, let alone a very long time after. Yes, I know they often brought back ancient Greek texts to Italian City States. I know they would be coveted by the wealthy Doges. It's incidental that it could end up in the Vatican's secret library. How did it get from Cos - we guess - in the fifth century B.C. to a form like this?"

Meg looked quizzical.

"I must admit I didn't register that this was 14th century. I'm not used to that. You have a point though. This would have been on papyrus to begin with; then it would have been transcribed over to the parchment."

"Vellum actually. I told Seamus the story of how parchment and vellum came to be; so I guess that's where we start."

Seamus looked confused.

"Wait a minute. Why is this strange? You explained the library at Alexandria and the competition from the library in Pergamum later on. Wouldn't that cover it?"

Tony sighed, "Not to my satisfaction. Volumes going into either one of those libraries would have been in pristine condition or immediately copied to be sure they were. Most of the books that were in Alexandria were destroyed by fire. I don't remember what happened to Pergamum. Either way it's not a - for publication - book - remember? This was some guy's notebook. What convoluted path did this take to get here?"

Seamus watched Meg's face as he answered Tony. "Tony, you're in my department now. We'll never know; so there's no reason to dwell on it. I imagine more than half of the puzzles I ever solved are incomplete. I just have to be resigned to not knowing."

"That would drive me crazy."

"Make a vow, now, not to do my work for a living. I will be very lucky if I discover how the blessed thing got into my hands in Cincinnati - of all places."

Meg was looking at the open book on her lap.

"You know Tony, this had to come from someone's private library. Maybe even a family heirloom."

"You mean for Seamus to get it?"

"Uh that too; but I meant to end up in medieval Europe."

"Oh I see what you're getting at. Some Genoese trader or sailor bought it from some Greek who'd had it in the family for a few hundred years."

"What other explanation is likely? Even at that, the family would have had to copy it sometime; from papyrus to parchment - if nothing else."

"Why would they do that?"

"It's not that strange. They could have been a family of physicians. That happened a lot in those days. This was a serious working tool. They would hand it down from one generation to the next."

"Hmmm, and maybe add to it as they went."

"Sure, that would be perfectly reasonable. Finally, somewhere along the line, the last doctor died, or the last generation decided not to be a physician."

"OK, I give up. Seamus is right, we'll never know anyway."

Meg looked at Seamus.

"Seamus, you have something here that is priceless."

"How well I know. I'm told so by everyone I meet."

Meg laughed.

"I suppose so, but my reason is probably different."

"In what way?"

"I think this may be truly uncharted knowledge of Greek medicine. It isn't just the book I consider valuable, the contents may well be priceless."

"OK Tony, here you are. The plot thickens."

"Groan, it had to happen."

Chapter 16: Buyer Meet Seller

The door to the library opened silently. The butler walked into the room and coughed.

The old man looked up from his book and turned his head.

"Yes, Robert?"

"Sir, my apologies for disturbing you. There's a rather uh... oddly dressed young man here to see you."

"Did he say what his business was?"

"No sir, he is wearing the coverall uniform of a repair man but he said his name was Jimmy. He may well be *our* Jimmy. Would you like him evicted; or perhaps diverted?"

The old man turned his head back and stared into space. *Well, well, has Jimmy found me? Not so unlikely I suppose. There are fewer and fewer of my age left to find. Do I let him in or throw him out? Let him in I think. This could actually be rather interesting. He may be dangerous but he wouldn't be here to threaten or rob me. He wants something; I'm curious.*

"Sir?"

"Did he arrive at the front entrance?"

"No sir, he rang the bell at the tradesman's door."

"Mmm, that's good. Don't concern yourself Robert. I imagine I'm perfectly safe. Show him in and bring him here to me."

"Yes sir."

Robert left, closing the noiseless door behind him. The old man went back to his book.

A few minutes later the door opened and Robert walked into the room. He spoke to the back of the chair the old man was sitting in.

"Um, Mr. Jimmy, sir."

The old man waved his hand around the side of his chair and pointed at a chair opposite.

"Sit down Jimmy; don't make me get up."

Jimmy's cockiness had worn down; he walked nervously over to the chair and sat facing the old man. His knees were together, both feet flat on the floor.

Robert leaned over to the old man's ear. "Sir?"

"Oh you can go Robert. I'll ring when I need you."

"Yes sir." The butler left closing the door. This time the door clicked.

"Well Jimmy. You must be proud of yourself."

"Yeah, I found you."

"Yes you did. Not so hard really. Excuse my obvious concern in not wishing to be associated with you. How shall I explain your visit to the law officers who may have watched you arrive."

"Don't worry about that. I wasn't tailed."

"And how can you know that?"

"I've been at this for a while. I went to the museum center; went into the men's room and came out in this workman's outfit. I know the guy who's on me. He didn't catch it at all; probably still sitting there wondering how long I can piss."

The old man chuckled. "I appreciate your discretion. Why would you bother to be so careful?"

"I don't want anybody to know about you either. That'd cut your value too much."

"I see. So, what do you want to talk to me about?"

"I um... need your help."

"You do? I thought I'd already taken care of that."

"Well I, uh - we - didn't get it."

"Didn't get...oh. You didn't get the book?"

"No dammit, the old lady gave it to somebody else."

"My my, that's unfortunate. Who did get it?"

"That's why I'm here; shit, we don't know who he was."

"I see. So you want me to find him for you. Is that it?"

"Yeah."

The old man was silent - thinking. *Oh blast. So now we know how nasty the gods can be. It didn't work. Although, Jimmy's loss doesn't really matter - except to Jimmy.*

What does this comic twist have to do with me? I suppose I would be better prepared if I knew who this unknown party was. Of course, if I'm not careful my own research could present questions I don't wish to answer. Why do anything?

"If I don't help you find this other man, what will you do?" he said.

"I'll blow your head off."

"Oh Jimmy, I know you better than that. You haven't the heart for it. Besides, I may consider you defective but I don't believe you're stupid. Adding murder to the list? The three letter law enforcement agencies would certainly add more money to the 'get Jimmy' budget."

"I can get one of my guys to do it."

"Hmm, I still doubt you would. You have an incongruous sense of loyalty - to low-life I know - but you'd feel bad hanging that on one of your friends. Even at that, I'm old, Jimmy; all my days have been surprises for quite some time. No you'll have to come up with something else."

Jimmy was frustrated; he knew it might go like this and he was running out of his advanced planning. Well, last chance.

"I'll tell the authorities about you and my dad."

The old man laughed.

"Jimmy, Jimmy, who on this good green earth would believe you? Your word against mine?"

The old man thought. *Is that true? Of course it is. Still, I wonder if I have any enemies left who would want to chase it. It would be impossible to prove anything but it would put the question in the minds of the great unwashed. They're always ready to believe that people of wealth were crooked; no matter what good they might do.*

"So you won't help me?" Jimmy was starting to look desperate.

"I didn't say that Jimmy. You have to accept that I won't be threatened. Then we can discuss this in more civilized tones."

"Alright, no threats. But something's been bugging me for a few days. Why did you do it in the first place? I didn't expect it; you were a real long shot."

The old man had his head on his hand and was watching Jimmy carefully.

"Go on."

"The only thing I can figure is you wanted to get rid of that book. Was it hot?"

"You're quite the thinker Jimmy; I'm impressed."

"Did that come from the loot my old man got for you?"

"Oh Jimmy, I'm not going to answer that. Besides, why would it matter to you? Your conscience won't be bothered by the knowledge it used to be someone else's property."

"You're right, I don't give a shit. The guy that had it is dead and so's my dad. If the cops ever did pick up on it, I'd be so gone they wouldn't bother to look. So are you going to help?"

"I haven't made up my mind. Here's what you should do. Write down what you know about the afternoon at the library sale. If I decide to look into it, I'll want any scraps of information you have. If I do anything and if I find out anything I'll let you know - how's that?"

Jimmy was thinking. *I think he's going to do it. He won't say that, but he wouldn't bother with this last crap unless he was curious or nervous. Hell, I'll play along. Damn, the problem is time; how long could this take?*

Jimmy looked over the old man's head and said, "That's no good, I'm running out of cash and I've got two guys to feed. How long do I wait?"

"Hmmm, you have a point Jimmy. I don't want you hanging around here for the rest of my life; no matter how short it may be. After you give me the information you have, give me a couple of weeks and I'll give you an answer. Meanwhile, moderate your habits. I know you're still dealing right here under the noses of the Feds. Not smart Jimmy."

Jimmy looked at the carpet. *I guess I can't push this guy anymore. So what, I think he's pushed enough - he'll do it. Funny thing is, I don't know why he'll do it. He's right about one thing though, we've got enough to cover us for a few months. I'd better lay off the transactions for a while.*

"OK, it's not smart; but it's my business. I'll send you the bits we picked up. Now, how do I get outta here?"

The old man pushed a button on the table next to him. The butler entered the room almost immediately.

"Yes sir?"

"Robert, would you show Jimmy the way out?"

"Yes sir."

The old man went back to his book. After he finished the chapter he was reading, he pushed the button on the table.

The butler entered the room.

"Sir?"

"Robert, please come over here and sit down. I know your feet aren't what they used to be."

The butler smiled, walked over to the chair and sat down. There was a questioning look on his face.

"Yes Robert, that was the Jimmy."

"I thought it might be, sir."

"Do you know what he wanted?"

"No sir."

"He didn't get the book we sent. Someone else picked it up by mistake."

Robert's eyes widened.

"Yes, it seems impossible to me also. I instructed him to send me a document outlining what he knows. Of course, he wants us to find the proud owner and recover the book for him."

"Sir?"

"Yes, tell me what you think."

"Why haven't we heard about the book before now?"

"A good question Robert. I can only assume that our Mr. X has no idea of the value and has simply thrown it up on a shelf above his television. Either that or he dimly perceives the value and is exploring the process of turning the book into a new car"

Robert chuckled.

"Shall I contact some of our people in place that day?"

"Yes, you should. Don't give them any knowledge; just ask for a post-mortem."

"Yes sir."

"Robert, if Jimmy decides to tell the story of his father. What reaction would you expect?"

"No reaction sir. I cannot imagine anyone paying any attention to him or his remarks."

"No, I suppose not. It's a shame though. Jimmy's little mind and even smaller knowledge sees me as the Moriarty of the 20th century."

"He has nothing other than his father to direct him, sir."

"Yes, I wonder if I wasn't too generous. The Lord already knows I was too rash."

"You shouldn't criticize yourself sir. The Reginald was a sewer rat."

The old man laughed.

"He was that; world class. Thank you Robert, I think I would like a brandy. I want to muse on this turn of events."

Robert stood up and bowed.

"Yes sir. Perhaps a particularly fine brandy is in order?"

The old man looked up.

"What made you suggest that?"

"I should think you deserve to enjoy some of your earnings before they belong to others, sir."

"Ah, how true, Robert. I accept your suggestion. It is appropriate to putting my mind back to the wheel."

"Yes sir."

The butler turned away as he smiled. His fondness and admiration for the old man would have shown on his face. The old man wouldn't have understood that. Through all the years Robert had been with him, the old man had always been involved in charitable work. His generosity was well known. Yet the old man never considered his efforts significant enough to warrant admiration. Robert shook his head. There are some, perhaps far fewer than in the old days, whose modesty was natural. The old man was one of these.

The Old man looked at his book after Robert left. I'm tired of this one, he thought. I need something more inspiring. He slowly stood up and walked over to a wall of books. He was looking though the volumes when Robert returned.

"Your brandy, sir."

"Thank you Robert, just leave it on the table."

"Yes sir." Robert placed the glass on the table beside the book.

The old man had found a different book and turned around with it in his hand.

As he walked back to the chair he had a wry smile on his face.

"At least I don't need a cane Robert. Too bad really, a good walking stick is a dapper touch to a fine suit of clothes."

Robert smiled. "yes sir." He watched to be sure the old man was seated again before leaving.

The old man sipped his brandy, opened the new book and then looked up, lost in thought.

Sewer rat. Yes, Reggie was all of that.

Reggie Decker! I haven't even thought of you since...when? - when you died I suppose. I still believe you were murdered, you vicious bit of work. There were numerous candidates who would have been proud to do you in. So many, I never could settle on a suspect.

My my, the first time I met you I was actually impressed. Ugh, my feelers were numb that day. You were showing off some new artifacts to us all. What were they? Oh yes, pre-Columbian weapons as I recall. I was fascinated by them. I had collected a few items myself, but yours were museum quality. Odd, I'd never thought of collecting museum quality pieces before that.

When did I have my first inkling of what you were?

Only a few weeks later at the Cincinnati Club on a dreary, rainy night. I'd just purchased my first palimpsest and was eager to discover what was hidden. You, loud and showy as ever, were holding court in a group by the fireplace. I stood behind some other members and listened. You greedy, grasping creature! I can still feel the chill as I heard you describing how you had found out about poor George. You had bought his mortgage from the bank and within a week you foreclosed due to non-payment. All perfectly legal of course. The sale of George's house had paid for the self-same artifacts you had shown me just a few weeks before.

Sigh, that was the end of George. His house was all he had left. With the sale of his house he may have been able to pull himself back up. What did you say, Reggie?

I remember too well. 'Old George never knew what hit him. Since I was a friend he thought I was going to help. You know the bank had threatened him already and George was so relieved when I took over the mortgage. He actually thought I'd give him the time.' Then you laughed and laughed.

The old man shook his head and sipped some more of his brandy.

Chapter 17: Newspaper Archives

Meg finished her drink and looked at her watch.

"Oh no, it's eleven o'clock and I have patients to see tomorrow. I don't want to stop."

Tony grinned and looked at Seamus.

"Don't feel bad, Meg. For Seamus it's two o'clock in the morning. You may consider this part of my revenge, Seamus."

"That's well enough Tony. I deserve worse than this. I hadn't even noticed the lateness of the hour."

Meg was putting the plywood and rubber bands back on the book.

"Well, I feel better about throwing you out. But I meant it you know. I don't want to stop."

Meg stood, handed the book to Seamus and walked over to the cabinet to set down her glass.

"Will you keep in touch with me?"

Tony and Seamus stood up and Tony walked over to Meg, saying,

"Would you like to continue tomorrow? I'm not a bad amateur cook and I really love to do dinner for company."

Meg looked melodramatically shocked and touched her neck with the tips of her fingers. "You mean come over to your place for dinner? Tony, this is so sudden."

Tony laughed and pointed at Seamus.

"I'm not the one to watch. The dangerous male is over there."

Meg smiled.

"Actually, I had rather gathered that."

“Good eye, Meg, Seamus is completely incapable of such perception.”

Meg leaned around Tony and pointed her finger at Seamus.

“Be warned Seamus, never plan on living in San Francisco. You’d be a social pariah within a week.”

Seamus walked over to join them.

“I suppose I would, but that wouldn’t really be so different. I’m not much of a mixer, I’m afraid.”

“Oh Seamus. It sounds as if you could use a mentor.”

“I thought Tony might help. Regretfully, he’s been a disappointment.”

Tony bumped Seamus with his shoulder.

“You can’t be helped with true sophistication Seamus. I despair of you."

He stroked his chin and looked at the ceiling.

"Perhaps an *Irish* fairy.”

“Do you two always carry on like this?”

“Oh Meg, we don’t carry on at all. What can I say; Seamus likes girls.”

“I’m a girl.”

Seamus bowed.

“And a very attractive example, Meg; I do like you.”

Meg leaned her head over.

“Thank you Seamus and I like you as well - very much.”

Meg looked at Tony.

“I like you both of course.”

Then back to Seamus. “But it’s not the same thing.”

Tony looked over at Seamus. “Are you blushing, you old lump of peat?”

Seamus glanced at Tony, then back to Meg.

“Uh well, tomorrow then? I would feel better, Meg. There’d be less chance of Tony poisoning me if you were there.”

Meg laughed.

"That settles it, I'll be there. My job is to save lives. What time?"

"Say seven o'clock? I'll call you with directions tomorrow morning."

"Fine, seven o'clock."

They walked out to the front hall.

Seamus was dozing in the car on the way back.

"Seamus, wake up! We're here."

"I'm all in Tony. I'm going straight up."

"Wise of you; I'm ready myself. Hell, it's almost midnight."

Seamus went up the stairs to his room. Tony stayed downstairs for a few more minutes, locking up, turning off lights and setting up a pot of coffee on the timer.

—####—

The next morning Seamus came down early. Tony had set the coffee to start at six and Seamus moved it back to five to start it perking.

He went into the front room and watched through the window as the paper flew across the front lawn and bounced off the front door.

Hmm, I might as well see if this one is any different, he thought.

After getting the paper and his coffee, he sat at one of the tall chairs at the kitchen island and looked over the front page.

Not that much better. I suppose it's because it's America. The rest of the world is very far away. Not like Ireland where they, at least, involve the European issues.

He was halfway through when he heard Tony stumble coming down the stairs.

"Hold up there; watch your knees."

"Same to you. What got you up so early?"

"You forget; my body thinks it's almost nine o'clock."

"Oh God, that's right. I'll have you at my mercy tonight though; that'll help compensate."

Tony poured himself coffee and walked into the front room. Seamus heard the answering machine squawking in Tony's office. A few minutes later Tony walked back into the kitchen.

"I'm still asleep. Here I walked out to the front door to get the paper and you were right in front of my eyes reading it. Just as well, though. Maeve left you a message last night; sounds interesting."

"What did she say?"

"She said P.J. went to the newspaper archives yesterday afternoon and found some good stuff about a burglary."

"That's nice to hear. Not just the good stuff part; that man has saved me some aggravation and likely embarrassment as well."

"Delighted to hear it. We wouldn't want you be embarrassed. But what's your interest in an old burglary?"

"It's about the book. I could not fathom why such a valuable artifact popped up at a book sale. When I thought about it, it seemed to me it might be stolen."

"I get it. There wasn't anything in the paper."

"Correct, so I wondered if there may have been something in a previous paper I'd missed."

"Wouldn't Maeve or P.J. had said something?"

"I think they would have; if they had read about it."

But they said nothing, so you assumed it wasn't there?"

"P.J. reads the paper thoroughly every day. If such a story had been printed on any day in the last few years, he would have remembered it. He remembers the comics."

Tony chuckled. "A valuable resource."

"Yes, and he had no recollection of anything bearing on something as unusual as this book."

"They don't often list what was taken in the paper, you know."

"Of course not, but this book would be news, surely."

"Hmm, perhaps so. So what do you think he found?"

"I've no idea."

Tony looked at a clock on the wall.

"You can call anytime; she must be up."

"You are more than right, Maeve is up and about by seven; She's been working for hours by now."

Seamus handed Tony the paper.

"Here you are; it's of no use to me. I'll be getting dressed I think."

"Thank you, I just read the horoscope and the comics and do the puzzles."

Seamus came down a half an hour later.

"Tony?"

"I'm in the office."

Seamus walked around to the front room.

"Have you seen me book?"

"I'm looking at it now."

"Are we going touring today?"

"I thought we'd go up to Muir Woods. But better this afternoon, it's damp at the bottom of those trees. We'll wait for it to warm up a bit."

"There goes my kip."

"No no, we can go about three. I want you to see them not hug them. We'll only be there an hour or so."

"What about the time spent traveling?"

"It's not far and most of it is freeway."

"What are you looking at or for?"

"I'm looking at the margin notes. They're very interesting. Whoever this guy is - he's a physician I think."

"Hmmm, what does he think of the Greek?"

"He's as dubious of the Greek as we are of him, from the sound of these notes. He has serious doubts and not a little fear of this potion."

"I wonder about that. What harm can it do?"

"Oh ho, Seamus. That's how Dr. Jekyll got into trouble."

"Um, he has to drink this I suppose?"

"Yup, and it sounds pretty icky, if not nauseating."

"More eyes of newt and so on?"

"No, but you mix these very organic ingredients up and let it go very bad - and smelly. Then you squeeze it to get the good juice out - yuck."

"What's left at the bottom of the kitchen scraps pail?"

"Something like that. I would have to be very scared or dangerously sick before I'd try it."

"But Meg said the Greek was administering this to whole families."

"Yes, Seamus she did and curing them. They must have been more trusting in those days."

Seamus shrugged, "Well, the old witch doctors cured psychosomatically."

"Plague? I don't think so. If you or I came down with the Black Death, I can't believe we'd be OK with just a cheerful attitude."

"You have a point there."

"Anyway, our note maker seems to be serious about his consideration."

"Tony, does he say he's going to try it?"

"He doesn't say that. It's just that he's not looking at this out of idle curiosity. His notes are the notes of a man looking for a solution; and looking hard - almost desperately."

"Hmm, I wonder who he was."

"Dunno, but you'd better call Maeve now; if you wait, she may be having lunch."

Seamus had a sarcastic smile, "Right, she may know."

"You can be truly sarcastic some times Seamus. Here you go; I'll get us both some more coffee."

Tony pushed the phone towards Seamus, stood up and and, taking the cups, walked out to the kitchen. Seamus sat down at the desk and picked up the phone.

"Good morning - McCarthy."

"Good morning Maeve."

"Ah, as soon as there's news of your book you call promptly. I'll have to remember that."

Seamus chuckled. "So why call, if it's not urgent?"

"It is - for you. Grist for your mill you know."

"Tell me all."

"P.J. had a tedious meeting; the whole day for that; or so he said. He decided to walk over and look at the newspaper archives."

"So you said in your message. What did he look for?"

"He searched for any robberies where valuable antiques or art were taken.

He found a few over the years, but, as he put it, they didn't smell right. Then he caught one in his net that seemed perfect. There is a problem with it though."

"What may that be?"

"It was long, long ago - 1926, Seamus."

"Lord, that seems much too far from here."

"So I thought, but P.J. insisted. He says it's perfect. You see the booty included priceless medieval manuscripts."

"Be still my heart. Who was the victim - a museum?"

"No, some, disgustingly wealthy, private collector."

"Huh, did they catch the thief?"

"They did not."

"Uh, did it look that they tried?"

Maeve snickered.

"As far as they ever do. But P.J. found two other stories about it."

"Oh? Police are looking for...to help with enquiries and so forth?"

"No, the first was a description of the brilliance of the work. They seemed quite taken with the skill of the thief. The other was a reward offered."

"Good idea, that. The owner took a good step there."

"A reward is often a help, but it wasn't the owner. It was a friend of his; also disgustingly wealthy of course."

"Of course, how much was offered?"

"Ten thousand dollars."

"Hm, not so very much."

"In 1926? That was a fortune Seamus."

"Uh oh, right, sorry. Bless me, now that I think on it, he must have been a very good friend."

"I should say."

"Good work P.J.! What else does he tell us? I'm more interested in the victim."

"P.J. was as well. The man's name was Reginald Decker. He was a real estate mogul. His was old money; he inherited a mound of dollars from his parents. Apparently he was a collector of any sort of antiquities."

"I should go show him the book."

"That may be difficult. P.J. checked on that, he died in 1965."

"Blast. There's a cold trail."

"Just so."

"Well, I thank you Maeve and P.J. of course. Did he save any of the articles?"

"Surely, he copied them all."

"I shall give them my full attention when I'm there next week."

"Alright, I need to ring off. Don't you dare forget to call me the weekend."

"I vow Maeve."

"Uh huh, goodbye Seamus, have a splendid time and tell me all about it when you call."

"I vow again. Bye Maeve."

Tony had been standing by the desk for a while.

"There's your coffee; anything good?"

Seamus picked up the coffee and looked up at Tony.

"I think so, but I don't know what as yet."

"Oh come on, tell me what she found."

"P.J. went to the newspaper archives." Seamus recounted what Maeve had said. Tony looked at the wall and sipped his coffee.

"Hey, the original poor little rich man is gone. What about the guy who posted the reward?"

"Tony, you're brilliant. He could tell me all about it."

"I don't know about that. Lord Seamus, if he's still with us, he'd be in his nineties. He may not remember what he had for lunch."

Seamus chuckled.

"He may not be able to eat lunch. Still 'n all it's worth looking into."

Chapter 18: The Scriptorium

Hibernia 1347

"Brother Colum." The voice came from the cloister outside the scriptorium. Colum turned as the door opened. The Abbot was excited. "Colum, a Papal courier has arrived on the mainland. Fahy hurried his donation to bring the news."

"What should I do Father?"

"Prepare my son. I must believe he intends to visit our insignificant retreat. Most immediately, he will have some interest in your work. It would be well if he was pleased with your effort."

"I understand Father. I will arrange the scriptorium and myself."

Fergus ran past the Abbot's feet. The Abbot watched as he disappeared behind the tables and said, "I pray the courier appreciates Fergus' importance."

Colum, smiled as he watched the table legs for Fergus' reappearance.

—####—

The courier bowed to the Abbot and looked up nervously at the steps cut into the cliff face.

"Gerard de Pont Saint Esprit my good Abbot; at your service."

The Abbot put his fingers together, bowed in return and followed the courier's eyes up the steps.

"Welcome, I pray you to excuse my ignorance; with what title should I address you?"

The courier smiled. "Gerard, Father, I am a simple man from a small village near to Avignon. The reverence may only be appropriate to the missives I carry."

The Abbot looked up at the cliff then back at Gerard and smiled. "Gerard, I recognize your concern. The path is sound and the footing is wide. You will have no cause to fear once you begin the ascent."

Gerard looked back at the Abbot. "I trust your faith, Father. It is my faith I must pray for."

The Abbot turned and invited Gerard to the steps. Gerard inhaled deeply and began to climb. The Abbot followed behind him. After some minutes Gerard turned to look down at the Abbot, then, turning back quickly, he leaned his hands on the steps in front of him.

"I was prompted to remark on your confidence, Father. I see that was rash; may I rest a moment and regain mine?"

"It would be better to continue, Gerard. There are but a few steps left to take."

Gerard sighed and continued to the top. At the wall, he walked away from the steps and rested his hands on his knees. The Abbot leaned over him.

"Some meat and drink, Gerard and your calm will be encouraged."

Gerard looked up and then past the Abbot at the sea and the shore beyond.

"I may now feel I have earned the right to appreciate this view. My eye is well pleased, good Abbot."

The Abbot followed Gerard's gaze. "Ah, we become accustomed so readily, Gerard. My thanks for bringing God's beauty back to me."

Gerard stood up and the Abbot led him past the yew tree to the guest quarters. As they passed the cloister, Fergus walked in front of them, watching them over his shoulder curiously.

Gerard watched Fergus as he sharpened his claws on the tree.

"You have cats, Father. I have two myself. They are useful, but I am more taken with their grace and beauty. Only God would have created such a creature."

The Abbot looked puzzled. "God created all creatures, Gerard. The companion cat is but one among the many."

Gerard hesitated, then answered. "As you say Father." *So the witchery and the devil seekers had not found their way to this lonely place,* he thought, *I can only pray they never will.*

Gerard was left to rest. The Abbot was pleased with him. *A good and simple man,* he thought, *God shows me, once again, not to anticipate my fears. The man he had feared would be a patrician; laden with his importance and ill humors. Such a man would find fault, no matter. Thanks be to God, Gerard was plain and content to be so. He could be trusted and he would be kind. Brother Colum might well find a kindred soul and a friendly reception for his labors.*

He entered the scriptorium.

"Brother Colum, the courier has arrived. He rests at present. His first thought when he wakes will be of the refectory. God has blessed you, and me also. A fine man with a warm heart or I doubt my sanity."

Colum turned. "All is ready father. Does he speak of his purpose?"

The Abbot laid his hand on Colum's shoulder. "No Brother, do not concern yourself. God wills as He wills."

"Bless your refectory Father, my hunger was great. I have fasted, against my will, from the start of the sea journey."

The Abbot looked at Gerard in surprise. "God bless you, how many days?"

"Four days, father. I had no will to eat. Your refectory bread and cheese cured me."

The Abbot smiled. I shall share your words with Brother Brendan. He prepares our breads. Though I may be thinking it would add to the sin of pride."

Gerard chuckled. "Consider the recognition of God's gift, Father."

"Ah, a fair thought and now, Gerard, what blessing for us - he paused - and mayhaps trial for you, sent you on this journey."

"I know not, good Abbot. I have the answer in my bag; from his Holiness in Avignon. I was instructed to open this in a private place. Only yourself, the scribe, and I, are to be present."

"We anticipated as much. Only the commission from his Holiness would prompt your presence. Our Brother Colum is the scribe in your instructions. It only remains to follow your direction."

"Thank you, I do not wish to return soon. I was made for solid ground. Would the morrow, after Prime devotions suit?"

"Just as you wish. Our simple home is yours. You may wander as you please."

—####—

Gerard looked around the scriptorium. *A placid room; the odor of learning and the fruits of tireless monks over centuries lining the shelves,* he thought. The Abbot introduced, perhaps more pushed, a monk toward him. "Gerard, here is Brother Columcille. He is the scribe referred in your instructions."

Gerard, bowed. "God be with you, Brother."

Colum looked confused and bowed quickly in return. "And also with you...ah"

"Gerard, Brother; I have no noble lineage."

"Gerard."

Gerard walked to a small table under the library shelves and, setting down his leather bag, he reached inside and removed a pouch sealed with hard red wax.

The Abbot and Colum followed him and stood. Gerard sat down and motioned to the others to do the same.

"Perhaps I should bolt the entrance?"

Gerard looked up at the Abbot. "I doubt the necessity, Father." Fergus walked up to the table and sat, twitching his tail. I shall even accept Fergus' presence." Gerard had asked after the cat the previous night and Fergus had taken to him.

The Abbot smiled and sat, motioning to Colum to do the same.

Gerard removed a sheet of parchment from the pouch and then a leather bound book, Setting the book on the table, he read the parchment. As he read he frowned once or twice and then looked up at Colum.

“Brother, all is simple. His Holiness would have you copy this exemplar.” He flicked a finger at the book on the table.

“There are only two stipulations. first, that you make only one copy, his Holiness is quite emphatic on this. And, second that you copy the exemplar in statu quo. You are to take care to copy all and reproduce whatever may fall on the pages. Is this a difficulty for you?”

Colum reached for the book and said, “May I view the exemplar, Gerard?”

“Of course, Brother.”

Colum carefully began to turn the pages, then stopped and looked puzzled.

“Gerard,” he said, “there are illustrations. I am not so gifted that I may trust to copy them perfectly.”

Gerard smiled. “As you can, Brother and have no fear of a lack of perfection. The simulacrum would be supported by the text.”

Colum sighed and replied in a resigned tone. “I will do as well as God permits me, Gerard.”

Gerard stood up and placed his hand on Colum’s shoulder. “As we all must, Brother Colum. Have no fear.”

Colum bowed to Gerard. “God grant safe journey, Gerard.”

Gerard bowed in return. “Thank you Brother. I may travel here again. If God wills; I would be well pleased. The Abbot and Gerard left the scriptorium. Colum turned to his table.

“Fergus?” The cat cried from behind the storage shelves, then walked slowly out to the tables.

“You may thank our Lord that Gerard is fond of cats, Fergus. The Abbot assured me he would have locked you in the peat room.” Fergus sat, then stood up looking at the door. He turned to Colum and cried.

Colum looked at the door and then the cat.

“Yes, Fergus, I must be sure to see Gerard off safely. He is a good man.”

He went out to the cloister, holding the door open for Fergus.

The Abbot and Gerard were standing close to the yew tree. As Colum approached, he heard the Abbot ask. "Are you well enough prepared for our steps?" Gerard smiled. "On my arrival my body was weak from lack of nourishment, Father. My safety is not a concern. Your Brother Brendan's kitchen has strengthened my body and my will."

They turned as Colum approached and Colum spoke to Gerard. "May I accompany you to the currach?"

Gerard chuckled. "You see Father Abbot. God reassures me. Brother Colum may precede me. He looked at Colum, - not too quickly."

The Abbot bowed to Gerard. "God speed."

Colum led Gerard the way to the cliff. As he approached the steps, he turned, "You are welcome to prolong your stay, Gerard. The Abbot is fond of your company, as am I."

"Thank you, Brother but I must make up my time. I would arrive before the pestilence."

"Pestilence?"

"Yes, Brother. You could not have received word in this isolated place. A great pestilence advances toward Avignon. I wish to reach Avignon and take my leave to return to my home."

"Are there no physicians?"

"Ample Brother, and all their knowledge and physicks are to no avail. Or so I have been told."

Colum's thoughts were confused. He turned and started down the steps with Gerard following - cautiously. In his care for Gerard, Colum was silent until they reached the landing. As he turned, Gerard jumped the last few steps to the ground and let out a breath.

"God's mercy, Brother."

Colum smiled, then frowned.

"God's mercy, Gerard. You leave a small danger for a greater one."

Gerard's expression was solemn. "Yes, Brother. I understand. And does He not hold us in His hand through all our days. These are but more days ahead." Gerard bowed and turned to the currach.

Colum burst out, "Will you know if the pestilence has won the race?"

Gerard's expression was sad. "Yes, Brother. The dead will show the way. The boatmen have told me they will have black eggs ringing their necks."

Colum shivered involuntarily. "God protect you, Gerard." He bowed.

Gerard bowed sat down in the currach and then held up his hand as the boatman rowed from shore.

—####—

A River Inn, Avignon, 1347

Gervais looked over his cup at Alard sadly.

"We are at the end of our sustenance Alard."

Alard smirked and drained his cup

"And not solely in the cups. What would you have us do?"

Gervais slumped and twisted in his seat.

"I would wish for another Jew but they are few in these Inns."

Alard nodded and looked at the table.

"As you say, and more in my thoughts. I fear the risk of retribution."

Gervais scratched a tooth and looked disgusted.

"Don't waste your fears on that; the world and God care little for a Jew. We are in no danger. I care not for a punishment. The puzzle is where to find a store of riches for our talents to pluck."

Alard grinned as he whispered, "and unable to fend us off."

Gervais smiled back.

"As you say, I would not want to be harmed for some coins. We must come against a weak or old benefice to help us carry our habits without effort."

They both laughed.

Chapter 19: Medieval Medicine

"Tony! She's here."

Tony's voice came from the kitchen.

"Well, let her in, you dolt. I'm preparing appetizers."

"Yes of course. Right."

"Are you nervous?"

Seamus walked into the kitchen.

"Yes, I am a little. I'm rather taken with her."

"You should be, she's very attractive as women go. Not to mention being articulate, intelligent, with a sense of humor and she's probably a good dancer."

"She does have a good sense of humor."

And that's rare in women; or so I hear. Now, go open the door for pity's sake. She'll be wondering if she's come to the right house."

"Yes yes, I'm going."

Seamus walked through the front room to the door. As he passed the sidelight, he could see Meg coming up the walk. He paused, then opened the door just as she stepped up on the porch.

"Seamus, how are you?"

"I'm well, Meg, good to see you. Come in. Tony's still fussing about in the kitchen."

"Thank you; nice house."

"It is isn't it? Tony rents the lower two floors he tells me."

"There's a third floor?"

"Apparently. It's used for storage."

Seamus walked Meg into the front room and waved his hand at the overly soft chair. Meg sank into the chair."

"Drink?"

“Um yes please, a scotch and water and perhaps a more uncomfortable chair. I feel as if someone is about to put a top on me.”

Seamus laughed as he walked over to the liquor cabinet.

“I recommend the one across from it. We’ll arrange for Tony to be immersed in that one. He turned his head toward the kitchen and raised his voice. “Drink Tony?”

“Good of you to offer. I’ll have some Irish in your honor.”

“Right, should I bring it out to you?”

“No thanks, I’ll be there in a second.”

Seamus poured the drinks and as he walked over to hand Meg her glass, Tony walked in from the kitchen carrying a tray.

“Perfect timing Tony; yours is on the liquor cabinet.”

“I’ll exchange that for the tapas. I hope everyone has a healthy digestion. I’m doing Mexican.”

Meg brightened. “Oo, I love Mexican Tony. What is this?” She pointed at the tray Tony had set down on a stand.

“Jalapenos stuffed with cheese. Common but tasty.”

Seamus looked at the tray.

“I have to admit, I don’t know whether I like Mexican or not. I don’t know if I’ve ever had Mexican food.”

Meg smiled. “You’re in for a treat Seamus. I imagine Tony knows what he’s doing in the kitchen.”

Seamus watched Tony walk out.

“You may have the truth, Meg; if not, we may both have cause for regret. However, I will not shirk; apprehensive though I be.”

He picked up one of the peppers and took a bite.

“Mmm, it’s actually quite good.”

Tony walked back from the kitchen. “I expected a rigorous evaluation, Seamus but the least you could do would be to hide your surprise.”

“Apologies, Tony; involuntary I’m afraid.”

Meg watched Seamus and Tony with her eyes twinkling.

"You are both worth the price of admission."

"That tells me what my wit is worth." Tony sat in the mushy chair.

I see I was maneuvered into this. If I doze off, it will be your responsibility to lever me out. Have either of you brought up the book yet?"

Seamus looked over at Tony with a sad face.

"Blast Tony, and things were going so well."

Meg smiled at Seamus. "Now Seamus, I was invited because I wanted to go into the book some more - remember?"

Seamus bowed to Meg.

"I will be apologizing all night it seems, you're quite right. I'll go fetch it. I must confess, I'm starting to wear a little from this book." He walked across to the study and came back with the book.

"Here we are again. Tony was looking at it this morning."

"Anything in particular, Tony?"

"Yes Meg, the notes in the margins. I think our note writer was a doctor."

"I didn't really look at those carefully last night. What you say makes sense." She opened the book and leafed through to the beginning of the notes.

"Do I have time to read them before dinner?"

"Oh sure; I decided not to get too fancy. We're just having fajitas. All the time is spent putting them together and I let the guests do that."

"Oh good, I was looking forward to this. I'm slow at Latin Tony. Stand by to help."

"With pleasure."

She started to read and Seamus settled into his chair and watched. After a quiet few minutes, Tony got up. "Anybody ready for a refill?"

Without looking up, Meg held up her glass and rattled the ice. Seamus shook his head, yes. Tony got the drinks handed them out, then sat down again. Leaning over to Seamus they started talking in low tones, while Meg read.

After ten or fifteen minutes, she looked up at Tony. "What is this Tony? It seems way out of place."

Tony got up and looked over her shoulder.

"It's a prayer, Meg. entreating God to save us - whoever us may be - from the trials and tribulations that are to come and asking God to help him - that would be our note writer, I guess - overcome his fear and do his duty."

"Oh God, that poor man."

Tony looked fondly at Meg. "You are a certifiable softie, Meg. Your reward is dinner. Come both of you or it will be indigestible and I'll take the blame."

Everyone walked out to the kitchen.

"Here, Seamus, watch what I do and follow along."

"Oh Tony, let me just make his for him."

"If you do that, he'll get used to it and I'll have to wait on him after you've gone."

Seamus waved his hand, "That'll be enough. I don't want anyone fighting over me. I'll watch Meg; then I'll know I'm not misled."

After dinner Tony started a pot of coffee and Seamus and Meg went back to the front room. They both sat down, then Seamus stood up and walked over to look out the window. "If only we knew who he was."

Meg looked at Seamus' back. "I'm afraid I can't help there. My research has always been way back in ancient Greece. Is it so important?"

Tony walked in from the kitchen. "I know Seamus; he wants all the information he can gather."

Seamus turned around. "Of course I do. I would like to know what he was writing about. Why was he reading this ancient text in the first place? Surely medicine had advanced beyond this Greek book."

Meg chuckled. "If only that were true. Sometimes I think we could learn from these ancients today."

"Meg, you must be joking. They had no scientific method."

"Oh yes they did. The Greek philosophers had more rigorous logic than I've seen applied lately. They didn't have our massive political or money interests either."

Tony went back to his chair and sat down.

"Can you give us an example?"

"Umm, yes, I think so. The theory of evolution."

"What?"

"Anaximander and Empedocles both believed that all the animals of the world - including us - evolved. They were quite clear about it and specifically talked about the survival of the fittest. What doesn't work dies out."

Seamus walked back and sat down.

"Well you have me there. We lost that one; didn't we?"

"That wasn't all that was lost. The Greek philosophers and physicians were closely allied. They were sometimes the same people."

Tony turned his head to Seamus with a wry smile as Meg went on...

"The dark ages were well and truly dark. It wasn't just a question of the Church not approving. Medieval Europe was immersed in religious cant. Knowledge was discouraged if it wasn't explicitly related to God and the Church."

Seamus waved his hand at the book. "That explains our note writer. We know he was in the depths of the middle ages."

Tony nodded, "Yes, the Latin points to that. So does his prayer. But this looks to be toward the end of the medieval period; the toes of European thought were over the threshold of the Renaissance. That covers a lot of ground, Seamus. I don't think we'll find out who he was."

Meg looked back and forth between them.

"I do know another doctor who's a medieval specialist; he's in the AAMH too. Want me to call him?"

Seamus and Tony raised their eyebrows as Tony said "Sure; think he's home?"

"We'll find out. Where's the phone?"

Tony got up. "In the office, follow me."

As Meg and Tony walked into the office. Seamus turned toward the kitchen.

"Do you two want coffee? I was going that way myself."

Tony stopped, leaned around the doorjamb and extended his glass to Seamus. "Coffee sounds good. Here you go; drop this in the sink."

"Meg?"

"No thanks Seamus, I'd have trouble sleeping."

George Litchfield

Tony handed Meg the phone. "Who is he?"

She pushed the buttons. "A very nice man - George Litchfield. It's ringing."

"George? It's Meg."

"Yes, it has been a while. Listen, I have something you may find interesting."

Seamus walked into the office while Meg was talking and handed Tony his coffee. "How does it go?"

"We'll know in a minute."

Meg turned to Tony. "He's excited and wants to come over right away; is that all right?"

"You bet. Does he know how to get here?"

"No, here you better give him directions." She handed the phone to Tony

Seamus smiled at Meg. “Did you talk him into it?”

“I’d like to say I did, just for the points, Seamus, but no; he is truly thrilled and can’t wait to see your book.”

“Ah, is he far away?”

“Oh no, if he doesn’t get lost, he should be here in about half an hour.”

Tony was just hanging up the phone. “He’s on his way.”

They all walked back to the front room.

As Meg sat down, she cleared her throat and looked back and forth at them significantly.

"Do you realize how amazingly lucky you are? Right at this moment you need an expert in Medieval medicine and with a quick phone call you have just the man coming over in a matter of minutes. I'm actually amazed myself."

Tony nodded smugly.

"Since you point it out, it is remarkable. Still, I'm right in the middle of many famous universities. UCAL is just up the street, Stanford is just down the peninsula and there are others all over the Bay area. Actually, UCSF is a medical college. This is one of the intellectual capitals of the country.

Meg nodded.

"You know, I think George may teach at UCSF."

Tony shrugged.

"There you go. Location, location, location."

Seamus grinned at the others.

“So, now what do we talk about?”

Tony looked at Meg. “We went to Muir Woods.”

Meg raised her eyebrows. “What did you think Seamus?”

“I was honestly astonished. It was like being transported to the jurassic. All that was needed was Tyrannosaurus Rex.”

They were still talking about Muir woods when Tony rose up in his chair and looked out the window.

“I think that may be your boy George.”

Seamus groaned.

Tony was up and walking toward the door. "You're welcome Seamus. Yes, he's pulling into the driveway."

Tony went out to guide George to the door. A few minutes later they both came in. "George, this unlikely looking character is the worthy Seamus. Of course you know Meg."

They shook hands. "A real pleasure, Seamus; hi Meg; I was facing a dull evening until you called. This may be the high spot in my year."

"I think it may, George. Here sit at the table and I'll get the famous book."

Tony was standing next to George, leaning on the table. "Drink, George?"

"Don't mind if I do. Uh, what do you have?"

"Almost anything you like in mixed drinks and coffee. I don't have any wine or beer."

"Wonderful, I'll have a gin and tonic."

"Coming up."

George sat at the table and Meg, standing on his left, opened the book to the place where the notes began. "It's just the Latin notes we want you to look over, George. They are referring to an ancient Greek medical...umm... workbook is what we think. We want to know if you can identify the man from his notes."

Seamus was standing on George's right and looking over his shoulder. "We know it's 14th century. Wait a minute, we know it's during the tenure of Pope Clement VI."

George looked up at Seamus. "Do we know whose book it is?"

Meg answered. "We don't know who wrote it, if that's what you mean."

Seamus looked at Meg with a wry smile. "But I would assume it belonged to Clement. He was the client who asked for it to be copied."

Tony walked up behind and reached between Seamus and George. "Here's your drink. I would have to believe this was either Clement's personally or it was part of the Papal library; such as it was in those days."

"Thanks Tony. Well then, this was probably from the infamous Bibliotheca Secreta."

"The what?"

"The secret Vatican library. It wasn't much in those days but it had many books that the Popes would not allow anyone to see. Unless they were given special permission of course."

George looked down at the book and started to read. "Hmph, this guy knows his stuff, I'll tell you that."

Meg looked interested. "You think so George? I couldn't tell."

"Oh yeah, for the medical blackout of the middle ages, this one was very bright."

Tony looked at Seamus. "Hey, I guess we got the doctor here."

George chuckled but kept reading. "This is my turf. But don't hold your breath. There were a lot of physicians back then that never did anything but let people die."

"I thought they helped to kill them."

"That was usually a barber surgeon. The physicians traditionally never picked up a knife. Ah... except to bleed the patient I suppose. There were a few physicians that were unusual; they actually tried to learn. Of course, what they learned was over a thousand years old in most cases. Like this one. He's reading ancient Greek medicine. You can bet he thinks he's going to get something good out of it."

Meg smiled at Seamus. "Actually, we think he may well get some good out of it."

George was frowning in concentration. He was reading and turning the pages back and forth to compare and remind himself of earlier passages.

Seamus walked over to his chair. "I shouldn't expect much. Wishful thinking, I suppose."

George was still reading. "You know, I can't prove it but this may well be one of the brightest physicians of the day."

Tony leaned over. "And that would be?"

George looked up and grinned. "The amazingly talented Guy de Chauliac."

Meg looked at George in disbelief. "How can you possibly know that?"

"Oh, Meg, I can't prove it. I don't see his signature anywhere. But here's the thing; de Chauliac was the physician to three Popes. The Popes were all in Avignon. Clement VI was one of those three. This, Seamus tells me, was Clement's book. Who else is going to be looking at old Greek medicine, besides de Chauliac? De Chauliac was not just a physician. He was a shining star of his day. He advanced medicine - that was tough in those times. We know a lot about him actually. He wrote a massive medical text called Chirurgia Magna. This was about as complete a medical text of the period as ever was. The guy - no pun intended - was just plainly and simply outstanding."

Seamus had turned around during this and walked back to the rest.

"So, if these notes were written by de Chauliac, what was he after?"

"Well, I don't read Greek. What are the notes attached to?"

"Let's hold that for a moment. I don't want to lead you. What does de Chauliac have to say?"

"You read them. He appears worried about something imminent and he's looking for treatment or treatments to prepare. He doesn't seem to have any knowledge of any treatment of his own and he thinks this Greek text may - I stress may - be the answer. Without knowing what the Greek is saying; my guess is its plague."

Meg and Tony both burst, "Bingo" at the same time and looked at each other.

George turned around in his chair to look at Seamus.

"Bingo?"

Seamus laughed. "Bingo indeed George. The Greek seems to have a potion for plague. Rather foul to take from Tony's description."

George looked blank, then he looked at the floor and shook his head. "That makes no sense."

"Why George?"

George looked up at everyone. "Because de Chauliac did save the Pope and he claimed to have saved himself after he got plague, but not with any treatment even close to this." He pointed at the book.

Tony frowned and Meg's face went blank. Seamus was the first to speak.

"Wait a minute George, how do you know?"

"Easy, you said this is a potion. That matches the notes. Presumably, you concoct something and drink or eat it. That's not what de Chauliac did for Clement or himself."

"Maybe this wasn't de Chauliac after all," said Tony.

Meg said, "What did de Chauliac do?"

"For the Pope he made him sit in a chair between two huge fireplaces. The fires were kept burning day and night. This was even in the heat of the summer. Of course, the fleas wouldn't get near him, but then he was so isolated it probably didn't matter. Anyway the Pope survived."

"And de Chauliac?"

"He claimed he contracted plague - this was rather late in the game of the Black Death. And he said he cured himself by burning the boils with a hot poker. I just figured he was wrong and he didn't actually get the plague. For a start, he said he was sick for nigh on six weeks. That doesn't sound like plague to me."

Tony shuddered. "A hot poker - Good God! - even the Greek's nauseating elixir would have been better than that."

George grinned up at Tony and pushed his chair back.

"I'm with you. Those were very strange times. They thought nothing of, what we consider horrible, physical pain and self-inflicted damage. Yet they had a wealthy class who indulged themselves in ways we gaze at in disbelief."

Seamus and Tony walked back to their chairs and both turned them to face George. Meg sat down and George turned his chair around. Meg wrinkled her nose.

"I've heard of the flagellants."

Tony got up and went to the drink cabinet. "So've I, they whipped themselves to atone for everybody's sins - right?"

George watched him. "Yes, and they were highly regarded by the common folk. The Church objected after a while because they got too big for their britches. They even took to hearing confessions. The point was that everyone thought the plague was a punishment from God for a wicked society. The Church didn't look very holy in those days and the priests, and even high ranks - Bishops and Cardinals - died just like everyone else."

"How far did the plague reach?"

"Oh hell, all the way to Iceland. The best estimates we have today indicate that over a third of the population of Europe died."

"I thought the fire of London wiped out the plague in England."

"Different plague; well, same disease, different occasion. The Black Death or pestilence is the plague that hit Europe in the 14th century. The Great plague hit in the 17th century. That's the one that was going on when London burned. The fire had little effect though."

"Why not; didn't it burn up all the fleas and so on?"

"Nope, it burned a part of London that was fairly clean and uninfected. The foulest part of London, the part that had the highest death rate, was untouched. Still it did help some; the plague victim counts dropped after the fire. Nowadays we think the rebuilding and overall cleanup made more of a difference."

"So it did help - indirectly."

"Uh yeah, I guess so." George pointed over his shoulder at the book. "Anyway, different outbreak than this one."

He looked at this watch. "Oh lord, my wife is not going to be happy. I'd better go."

Everyone stood up with George. Meg shook his hand. “Nice seeing you again George.”

“Nice to see you too Margaret. I want to be kept involved in this; is that all right?”

“I’ll tell you everything I find out George but the book belongs to Seamus and I think it’s going back to Cincinnati?”

Seamus looked at Meg. “Ah, next Tuesday - unfortunately. I’m having a better time than I expected.”

Tony chuckled. “Well I like that.”

“Sorry Tony, you know what I mean.”

Tony looked at Meg. “Oh I do, I do.”

Meg smiled. “Now Tony; I always thought gay men were more subtle and suave.”

“Not this one. I have a tiresome friend to look after. Any chance of turning over the job will not be overlooked.”

Meg grinned and looked at Seamus. “How do you put up with him?”

“I suppose I’m just used to it.”

George walked to the front door.

“So, you promise to tell Margaret whatever you find out and I’ll get it from her - right?”

Tony stood on his toes to look over Seamus. “Right. More likely from Seamus to me to Meg to you George, but you never know.”

George stopped at the door and shook everyone’s hand as Tony opened and held the door. “Thanks for coming over George; you were very enlightening.”

“My pleasure, by the way I’d love a copy of that book. Is that possible?”

Seamus thought for a second. “I don’t see why not. It will be another puzzle for me. I suppose we can snap pictures; I’d hate to break the binding - would that be all right?”

“Absolutely. No rush, whenever it’s convenient. Good night.”

Everyone walked back to their chairs after George left. Seamus and Tony sat down, Meg stopped and stayed standing. "I'd better be going myself. It's late again; you two are really a bad influence."

Tony and Seamus stood up again. Seamus put out his hand and Meg took his hand. "I've had more fun than I expected."

"Why's that?"

"It's you two of course." She looked at Seamus. Tony noticed she still held Seamus' hand.

"Listen Meg, I'm taking Seamus over to see Chinatown tomorrow. Why don't you join us for dinner there?"

Meg turned to Tony and back to Seamus. "That's sounds like fun. I haven't been to Chinatown in years. Um, I'd love to; what time and where?"

Tony was grinning. "How about seven thirty at the Gold Mountain."

"Where's that one?"

"It's at Broadway and Stockton; don't drive - the lines are long and it is Chinatown."

"Yes indeed, lousy parking. Why go there if it's so much trouble?"

"In two words - Dim Sum. They serve it on carts and they have great pastries. Then there's the sesame seed balls." Tony smacked his lips.

Meg laughed. "All right, it sounds good."

She was still holding Seamus' hand and suddenly realized it. She let go slowly and turned to get her purse.

"I don't know what I'll do for entertainment after you leave Seamus. I haven't been out this much in a long time."

Seamus followed her to the door. "That's a surprise and why is that?"

"I don't really know; I guess I just get lost in my work."

"Tony opened and held the door. "Why don't you walk her to the car, Seamus?"

Meg smiled at Seamus. “No really, I’ll be all right. I’ll see you tomorrow night.” She walked out. After she was gone, Seamus turned to Tony.

“What are you about? The matchmaker was more unobtrusive than that.”

Tony laughed. “C’mon Seamus, you two like each other - a lot - any fool can see that. I’m trying to get you to discard your confounded reserve.”

“I can manage my own courtships, if you don’t mind.”

“But I do mind; you won’t do a thing without prompting and Meg’s too good to lose.”

Seamus looked out the window as Meg left. “Mmm, I cannot but agree Tony; she’s a sweet lady.”

“Well, don’t expect me to apologize. If you two throw any sparks, you may expect me to be suddenly missing.”

“Aagh, I’m going to bed.”

As Seamus was walking up the stairs to his room, he could hear Tony singing softly ‘back in the saddle again’ - he shook his head.

—####—

The Gold Mountain

Tony and Seamus had been at their table for about a half an hour.

“Do you think she’s lost?”

“Don’t be impatient. This is a really awkward part of town. She wouldn’t drive so she’s suffering the vagaries of public transport.”

“Which is not predictable?”

“No, then there’s the walk and trying to find us in here after she actually arrives.”

“Public transport is like Ireland?”

“No, nothing’s like Ireland. The beauty of the Irish transport is the people.”

"There is that; they are agreeable."

"Yes they are but that's not what I meant. They don't seem to care whether the bus is on time or not."

Seamus chuckled. "A much slower life; thank the Lord."

"There she is." Tony stood up and waved. "Over here Meg."

Meg walked up to the table, slid her bag off her shoulder and hooked it over the chair. Seamus had half risen from his seat.

"Don't get up for me. She waved him back down. "Been waiting long?"

"No, just long enough to get a table and some tea. Except Seamus won't drink tea." Tony looked at Seamus' teacup. "Will you."

"This is Chinese tea. I'm not going to sing about it but it's tolerable."

Tony waved at the waiter. "Some more tea?"

Tony turned back to Meg. "Hope that's all right."

"Just what I needed. I've been looking forward to this all day and it's been a hellish long day."

"What do you do Meg?"

"I'm a simple internist. Lots of patients and more trouble with insurance companies than medicine. The AAMH is my passion and my hobby."

Tony was leaning on his hand. He lifted his head. "I guess we came with the right carrot then."

"You certainly did."

Seamus turned to Meg. "Last night you said you didn't go out. Is the work so much of the time?"

"We used to go out a lot."

"We?"

"My husband and I."

"Oh sorry, I didn't mean to touch a sore spot."

"You didn't. He's been gone for over eight years now."

Tony looked puzzled. "Gone?"

"Yes," she sighed, "he was killed in a car accident. It was almost instant; he didn't suffer."

"But you did."

"Oh yes, way back then I was a basket case. That's the way it is. The ones left behind are hurt the most."

Tony looked at Seamus. "The unreasonable and painful truth, Meg."

Meg caught Tony's look. She looked seriously at Seamus. "You too?"

"Yes Meg, me too. My wife died just about three years now."

"Oh, your spot is still tender. I'm sorry. It does get better, you know."

Tony smiled fondly at Seamus. "It should but Seamus has too few chances to forget."

Meg looked puzzled, "What do you mean?"

Tony turned to Seamus, "Seamus? Will you let me?"

Seamus lowered and shook his head in exasperation, "If you like, go ahead Tony."

Tony looked at Meg. "First of all Seamus lives in a small village in Ireland. Everything he sees there reminds him of Lena."

Meg frowned. "I know how that is Seamus. I had the same problem. I solved it by moving down here." She turned to Tony. "Did you know her Tony?"

"Lena? Oh yes; wonderful gal. She was so sweet - and smart - it was one of the few times I thought of going straight."

Seamus chuckled. "Watch it."

Meg looked at Seamus. "You know, I am a doctor; you should be talking about this yourself. It's good for you."

Seamus smiled. "It wasn't just a car accident, Meg; or even a disease. I might have coped with that."

"Will you tell me."

Seamus leaned back. “You know I’m an investigator - a detective.”

“No...I missed that.”

“That’s the noose this all hangs on.”

Tony waved his hand. “Ok, ok, look Meg, Seamus has it in his head that he’s responsible for Lena’s death.”

“Good Lord , what happened?”

“Seamus was on an assignment. Lena was with him. He was gathering information on some very nasty characters. Lena and Seamus were walking back from a restaurant and two of these criminals started shooting at them. When it was over, Lena was fatally wounded and the bad guys were dead.”

Meg looked at Seamus with her mouth open. “You killed them?”

“Oh yes, I killed them. I would have killed them twice if it had mattered.”

“Do you always carry a gun?” Meg looked nervous.

Tony waved his hand. “No no, Seamus never carried a gun; before or since.”

“Why that night?”

“I was warned by a friend at Interpol to be careful. He suggested it.”

“How can you blame yourself?”

“Easily, I should never have let her come with me.”

“How could you know?”

“Well I had some signs and I did know these men would stick at nothing. I tried to keep her at home but she begged and pleaded.”

He paused and shook his head.

“No not really - she just told me she was coming and that was that. She was that kind of woman.”

“Good for her. I’d have done the same thing.”

Seamus smiled at Meg. “I think you would have.”

"Well now that you're over here every corner doesn't bring her memory back. What about going home?"

"I don't know. At least I've had a rest."

Tony grinned. "If you can call this a rest. I'll bet Maeve is just having her rest since you left."

Seamus looked down into his teacup and shook his head.

"Poor Maeve and God bless her. She carried the burden of Seamus."

"Who's Maeve?"

Tony turned to Meg. "Oh sorry, Maeve is Seamus' sister."

"Why has she had to suffer?"

Seamus grimaced, "Remember what Tony said?; that everything was a reminder? It was. I pestered Maeve by phone for almost three years. Then she finally was full up and had me over to visit. That's where I've just come from; she lives in Cincinnati."

"Oh, I see. So you'll be going back there and then home to Ireland."

"That's right."

"I've never been to Ireland; I'd love to see it. My grandparents were from West Cork."

"I'm from West Cork now."

"Now?"

"We moved down there from Galway six or seven years ago. Lena yearned for the warmer and dryer climate."

"Where exactly?"

"Kenmare; a very nice village but it's become over crowded with tourists in summer."

"I don't really know where my grandparents were from; somewhere around Bantry Bay."

Tony waved at the waiter. "Confound it, you can never catch these guys when you want them."

He turned to Meg. “Around Bantry Bay is all pretty; doesn’t matter much where.”

“You’ve been there then.”

He nodded towards Seamus. “That’s where I ran into Seamus.”

Seamus chuckled at Tony, “Almost, but you missed me.” He looked at Meg. “He swerved to avoid a sheep and almost hit me; driving on the wrong side of the road.”

“There wasn’t enough room on that road for two sides.”

Meg laughed and made a cutting motion with her fingers. “Enough, enough. I can’t think when you two get me laughing. How long ago was that?”

Tony looked at Seamus with a frown. “How long ago was that?”

“God help us, it must be all of twenty years.”

“Nearer twenty five now. Doesn’t seem so long.”

Seamus smiled at his friend. “No it does not. Many sheep in that road.”

Tony finally got the attention of the waiter and the talk turned to the food. After dinner and the dessert, Seamus insisted on coffee. Tony held up his hand in a ‘stop’ and looked at Seamus in disbelief.

“Seamus, you are in a Chinese restaurant. They would consider coffee an insult. They might actually bring something they call ‘coffee’ but you would not want to drink it. Let’s check out of here and walk to a cafe nearby. I know a very good one. The Café Trieste, it’s on Vallejo street; it’s a nice walk and there’s little fog coming up. We can pretend we’re in a Charlie Chan movie.”

Sipping her coffee, Meg looked over the cup at Seamus. “Has your...uh, occupation always been dangerous?”

“No it has never been dangerous; just the one time.”

“Is the book part of some investigation?”

“As a curiosity only - so far. I can’t let any oddity go past me without a look.”

"Well, it is an oddity, at least. How did you stumble on it?"

"It found me." Seamus went on to tell her the story of the book sale.

Meg still looked puzzled, "So you don't think there's any lurking danger surrounding this."

"I didn't say that. What I mean to say is I don't know of any. I have to confess, it's too strange to be entirely accidental to my mind. Of course the book is so valuable there may well be some danger."

"Are you worried?"

"No no, I've been at my game for over thirty five years. I never thought of any looming risk and the years have borne that out. I won't dismiss the possibility, but it won't keep me awake at night."

Meg put down her cup and looked thoughtfully at Seamus' shoulder. "It's rather fascinating to me. I have such a dull life."

Seamus nodded and said, "May it never be anything else; ask the waiter about the ancient Chinese curse."

"What is that?"

Tony answered. "May you live in interesting times."

Seamus followed with, "and possibly survive them."

Meg showed her teeth, but it wasn't a smile. "I see the point but I'm not getting any younger. I'd like to have something to remember besides my last patient's aches and pains."

Tony turned his head to Meg. "Good thing you're not getting any younger. You'd be chewing gum, bouncing your head on your shoulders and incapable of completing a sentence without using the word 'like'."

Seamus' eyes sparkled. "I agree with Tony; you're as young as I would ever wish for."

Meg cocked her head. "Be careful for what you wish."

Seamus chuckled. "My ego isn't so large that I'd be worrying about that."

"Oh, you should worry. You're a handsome man. Seamus."

"Did you leave your glasses in your other bag?"

"No, I see well enough to realize you don't know what you look like. That's appealing but it makes you an easy mark."

"Easily flattered I suppose?"

"Of course."

"Then I'll start to worry. Tell me about your mother."

"She's a battle axe but she wouldn't live with us."

"Oops, hold it Meg. Tony said he would vanish if he heard us talking this way."

Meg smiled at Tony. "A very perceptive man is Tony."

Tony grinned. "We always are, at least, that's what I read in the fashion magazines."

Meg turned back to Seamus. "So, this is your last weekend in San Francisco."

"Yes, sad to say; my first and my last."

"You could always come back."

"I'll have to sometime. Tony would be forced to come to Ireland if I didn't."

Meg sipped her coffee and softly said, "I wouldn't mind that."

Tony nodded at Meg. "I know it's a beautiful place. It's just that I have this tendency to doze off."

Seamus said, dryly, "I could always step out and blow the horn in the car every few moments."

"It's not the same; there's no smell of pollution to comfort me."

Meg laughed and waved her hand between them. "OK ok. But Seamus, it might be years."

"Ah...yes...it might well be."

"If this is the last two days, I don't want to sit at home looking over patient charts. Why don't we all go sightseeing?"

"Why not? When?"

"How about tomorrow? I'll drive. I could come over and pick you up in the morning. Say, about ten; and we could go to the vineyards."

"I'd like that."

Tony was watching the two of them talk. "I think it is a wonderful idea. And I think you two should go without me. I can find some trouble of my own and Seamus has kept me from my bad habits all week."

Meg, rather insistently, said, "Oh Tony, I don't want to exclude you."

"You're not. It's not just 'no problem' I'd be happier if you two left me at home. I'll find something to do, don't worry about that."

"Are you sure?"

Seamus patted Meg's arm. "He's more than sure Meg. That's Tony's way of insisting."

Meg looked at Tony knowingly. "Matchmaking Tony?"

"If anything happens you can be sure I'll take all the credit. The truth is, no matching is needed and I don't want to be a human bundling board."

"Tony we can't get up to anything in a vineyard."

"Sure you can; I have."

Seamus looked at the ceiling. "I don't want to hear about it."

"And you won't; it was far too exciting and romantic for your crusty old ears."

Meg grinned at Tony, then turned to Seamus. "Alright, I'll see you at ten tomorrow."

Chapter 20: Post Mortem

"Well Robert? It has been all of four days. What have you discovered?

Robert moved the glass to the table and picked up the tray.

"Well sir, as you know, we received Jimmy's letter and it wasn't of much use."

"Yes I know, I expected that. The question remains: can we verify his assumption that the book was misdirected?"

"We should know presently sir. It turns out that Jeff actually retained the raw footage."

"He did? I thought he used an 'English load'."

"No sir, he was more resourceful than that. He went to the news director and suggested filler on the book sale for the evening news."

"Good for him. So he, as the camera and cutter, could be honestly useful to his station and ourselves."

"Yes sir, he studiously ensured no footage of the book transfer appeared on the news, of course."

"Of course; but how did the source tape survive? My understanding is that they are invariably overwritten."

"Again Jeff thought for us. He discovered the station was short of cameras that afternoon and arranged to borrow one from the AdVid Productions Company. Since they had some older cameras idle he had no trouble."

"What was the importance of that?"

"The older cameras are much larger sir. The model he used was more the size of a film camera, thus being more likely to be acceptable to Gladys."

"Ah, she may have been curious had the camera been a tiny digital unit - I see. But the tape?"

"The tape was a rather large Betacam SP cassette, sir. The station and even the production house had little reason to use the tape. They were both more likely to reuse the new technology cassettes."

"So, where is the, miraculously still intact, tape?"

"On its way to us as we speak sir."

"Excellent, we can see it all happen - as they say - in the comfort of our living room."

"Yes sir but I think I'll bring the cart in here."

The old man grinned up at Robert. "Robert I do approve, but you must allow me to walk around a little more. If I'm any more sedentary, I'll need wheels."

"Yes sir."

Robert turned to leave.

"Robert, I just thought; can we play the Betacam tape?"

"Oh yes sir. We can play any tape, even the old half inch beta format."

"Obviously you've kept up with all of this."

"Yes sir, your antiquities are shown worldwide on tape and film. It was necessary."

"Yes of course, thank you, Robert."

Robert walked out closing the door.

—####—

The old man walked into the study and sat down. As he picked up the book from the morning, Robert opened the door and wheeled a professional multi-media cabinet into the room.

"Sorry to disturb you sir. The tape has arrived and I have prepared everything for you to view it."

"Good Robert, my curiosity gets in the way of my nap - roll tape."

Robert turned on the power and started the tape with a remote. Then he set the remote down on the table and turned to leave.

"Don't leave Robert. I want your comments on this."

"Yes sir."

He stood behind the old man's chair. A few seconds of static and the player adjusted the tracking. As they watched they saw the table at the book sale with Gladys standing behind it. She looked nervous. Seamus walked slowly into the shot from the left. Gladys said something and Seamus stopped. They talked for a few minutes and Gladys pulled her hand from below the table. The book was in her hand and she handed it to Seamus.

"Robert that looks like Jimmy's boy."

"Yes sir, but he's too old."

"You're right. Jimmy told us his assistant - I should say accomplice - was only in his late twenties. This man must be nearer fifty. Why didn't Gladys notice?"

"Well sir, we never mentioned age to her."

"Not at all?"

"No sir, with all the other signals involved, it didn't seem to be an issue."

The old man thought a minute. They watched Seamus pay for the book and Gladys hand him the plastic book bag. Seamus walked out of the shot to the left.

"You're right of course. Even as I watch, it seems beyond belief. This violates all the laws of chance."

"Yes, sir. At least we know what he looks like."

"That's not very helpful Robert. The gods of chance are truly against us. It would be a complete accident to find him. It's not like a missing person you know. We can't put his picture on the evening news with a caption 'have you seen this man?'."

"Yes sir."

They watched as Gladys came around from behind the table and approached the camera. The camera panned over to the fountain and they heard Gladys telling Jeff she had to leave.

"So she wasn't there any more than a few minutes."

"Yes sir, just as Jimmy said."

They watched Jimmy, Steve and Jock hurry into the scene.

"There are the terrible trio now. They're late."

"Yes sir and the book might have well walked past them on their way."

"Jeff is taking a lot of footage."

"He is sir. He told me he wasn't sure how much we wanted. There may be a break coming up. I suppose Jeff would have to change the tape."

"He may have started a scratch from the middle; otherwise he should have more than enough."

"Yes sir."

They continued to watch until Jimmy's gang walked away to the left. Jeff continued to tape them as they crossed the street into the hotel. Then the screen went black.

Robert turned off the monitor, picked up the remote and started the rewind. The old man leaned back and looked up at Robert.

"Well, now we know everything and everything we know is of no use to us."

"No sir. Should we give this to Jimmy and let him search?"

The old man thought, looking up at the artwork on the far wall.

"No Robert, I don't think so. I'd rather Jimmy didn't even know about this tape."

"Sir?"

"There are interesting possibilities that didn't exist before. I must chew on this for a while."

"What should I tell young Jimmy when he calls sir?"

"Hmm...tell him we have no information as yet and that he should be patient."

"Yes sir."

"Robert."

"Sir?"

"How was the transaction with Jimmy managed? More precisely, what were the mechanics?"

“After the message was received from Jimmy, and you gave me your instructions, I composed the details of Jimmy’s part on one sheet of paper.”

“Did you write or type?”

“I typed his directions on flash paper.”

“Flash paper?”

“Yes sir, it burns completely. There are no ashes.”

“Good heavens, that must have startled young Jimmy.”

“I never heard sir.”

“Go on.”

“I arranged for the page to be left in the drop box. In the light of recent events sir, I would like to suggest you change the drop box placement and even the marker.”

“I agree Robert. Although Jimmy is the only surprise that was - or is - possible, I would prefer he no longer be capable of unforeseen requests. Then what followed?”

“The directions were quite simple and Jimmy followed them carefully and correctly sir. He left the cash package the following day.”

“I wondered if he would be prompt.”

“Yes sir. I could only infer that he was prepared.”

“Mmm, he is bright; among all his failings.”

“Yes sir. I carefully arranged for the package to be transferred to the Seventh street vault.”

“It is still there?”

“Yes sir.”

“Untouched?”

“Yes sir.”

“Did you describe Jimmy’s script in the first message or was that part subsequent to receiving the package?”

“Subsequently sir. I thought it would be better.”

“Most certainly Robert. So the actual time, place and script were separate. Was that on flash paper?”

"Yes sir. The instructions specified that Jimmy should copy the document to a separate sheet, due to the fragile nature of the paper."

"Excellent Robert. Then, were the directions found, they would be in his own hand. Do you think Jimmy was burned by this paper?"

"Unlikely sir, the paper burns so quickly there is almost no heat thrown off. It is often used by magicians for the moment they say Abracadabra."

"Or whatever they say nowadays. I see. How did you know to cast Jimmy's cohort for the role?"

"I didn't sir. I requested Jimmy describe the individual who would actually receive your compensation."

"And Jimmy nominated his friend from Scotland."

"Yes sir."

"Mmm, well done Robert; changing the drop box would eliminate the last possible link to us.

"Yes sir. Sir?"

"Yes?"

"I hope this is not impertinent."

"Go ahead Robert."

"I must admit I was surprised that you chose the book. You loved it so much and it must be terribly delicate."

The old man's eyes softened and he looked at a spot on the wall opposite.

"Mmm yes, you're right." He turned and looked up at Robert. "Not impertinent at all Robert; a good question is implied. You are correct, I do love that book. Unfortunately, it must find its way back into the world. As you know, I couldn't emerge with that book in my possession. The problem has been on my mind for some while now. The opportunity presented itself and I took it."

"Sir, can the book survive its own debut?"

“It certainly can Robert. It is peculiarly sturdy. Most of its centuries of life were spent in a hermetically sealed box. After I retrieved it from that troll, I was careful to keep it under very comfortable conditions.”

“If you hadn’t sir, it would probably no longer exist.”

“Robert, that certainly has been the salve for my conscience all these years. But, truthfully, those wonderful old codices are robust. If someone, like Jimmy, were determined to destroy it, he could, of course. You may be surprised when I tell you he would have to work very hard to do so. The book would survive almost anything outside of burning it. The volumes produced after the middle of the nineteenth century would almost dissolve. So you see, my conscience balm is more a contrivance than a fact.”

“Your conscience should not need a balm, sir. Your conscience should be healthier than any other man I know, sir.”

The old man smiled. “Thank you Robert, but we all have our regrets. This is mine; however justified I may believe myself to be.”

“Yes sir.”

“If it is not an inconvenience Robert. I would like to discuss some possibilities arising from the latest events. Could you arrange your schedule to meet with me this evening.”

“Whenever you like sir.”

“Then let’s say eight tonight.”

“Yes sir.”

—####—

“Ah Robert, punctual as ever. Extend my compliments to our new chef. His chateaubriand was excellent. He must be French.”

“No sir, he’s Japanese. He does have a cordon bleu certificate.”

The old man blinked. “The world is much smaller than when I was young, Robert.”

“Yes sir.”

“Sit down Robert. I want to think in your direction.”

“Yes sir.” Robert sat in the wing chair facing the old man.

"Here is my synopsis of the current position. Tell me if I overlook anything."

"Yes sir."

"We have Jimmy's cash. It is intact, just as he wrapped it and safely tucked away."

"Yes sir."

"Jimmy did not receive his compensation; that is - the book."

"So he says sir."

"And so have we verified with Jeff's tape."

"Yes sir, unless Jimmy arranged for this other person."

"Hm, you have a point there Robert. A crafty thing to do; he could then cry foul and demand more. That would be his style and furthermore, it would explain how the clothing and the script so uncannily violated all the laws of probability."

"Yes sir, he was able to instruct this unknown person in the role."

The old man thought, then shook his head.

"No I don't think so. Whatever he knew, Jimmy couldn't know we would have a videotape of the transaction. True, he may have surmised that; but that is a fringe chance. I have commented before that Jimmy is bright. I will now credit him with the thought that we would not be able to verify his claim."

"How does that help us sir?"

"He would not have come to me - that took some courage by the way - with his hat in his hand. He would have arrived with confidence. No, I don't think he knew and I don't think he arranged this. I think he was simply late. It is so simple and so trivial, it fits the personality."

"I see sir."

"So, to continue; Some unknown party is in possession of the book. It is clearly problematic whether we ever find him or the book. What questions does that conjure up in your mind Robert?"

"Do we want to find the book at all, sir?"

“A good start, Robert. We were trying to get the book out of my vaults and back into the world; now it is. So why concern ourselves with - where? What else?”

“How do we appease Jimmy, sir?”

“There are only two courses open that I see. The first is to compensate Jimmy; the second is to threaten him.”

“Threaten him?”

“Yes, simply deposit the cash package back on his doorstep and call the authorities.”

“I see. Then he would be quickly put away.”

“Yes, and by the time he re-emerged, I would not even be alive. Unfortunately, my children would be and they would be pestered, if not in physical danger. I may be overly paternalistic, but I don’t expect they would be able to cope with Jimmy.”

“I agree, sir. They have led placid lives.”

“Exactly as I wished Robert. It would be a shame to ruin that from beyond the grave.”

Robert looked solemnly at the old man. “Then there is one other possibility.”

“And what is that Robert?”

“As you put it, sir. The elimination of Jimmy.”

“That is a hard choice of words Robert, but correct. The more specific issue is how and to what degree.”

“He could be removed, sir. With little or no exposure.”

“Ah Robert. I have very little time left. I’m not a religious man and I’m not cramming for my finals. I’m a humanist and that’s enough. I could not condone it, let alone command it. There must be another way.”

“You leave only one remaining way, sir - compensate him.”

“I know. The logic is inescapable. The riddle is - how?”

“Cash, check or money order, sir?”

The old man laughed. “I don’t expect that is a good approach Robert. The authorities watch our boy Jimmy. They may observe this; they would almost certainly observe something that large.

The conclusion? That I am the largest consumer of drugs in Cincinnati or, worse, that I am one of the kingpin dealers. No, it must appear legitimate. This is not an easy task. Jimmy does not involve himself in much that is legitimate."

"He must win the lottery - so to speak."

"Yes, or some, more controllable, streak of luck."

"The Library sale is over, sir."

"Your irony is well taken Robert. The book was just the right method to solve the problem. I suppose we must concoct something similar."

"You will still have the original cash package from Jimmy."

"Oh Robert, I can't use that. I wanted it retained just in case it had to be returned. Now, I don't want it returned. I'm in the odd position of needing to protect Jimmy from his own crimes. We will hold it until the matter is resolved and then burn it."

"Are you sure, sir?"

"Yes, I'm sure. There is no doubt that some of those bills are marked. I'm conversant enough with modern times to know they are very clever and very subtle in the way they mark money these days."

"Yes sir."

Chapter 21: Pestilence

The physician was excited but held himself in check. As he bowed to the Pope, his face was grim.

"Holiness, the pestilence we feared has shown itself. A trading vessel from the Levant attempted landfall in Genoa. The sailors were dead or dying. They were driven off and continued west along the coast seeking a haven. Many of those nearby have died of the same curse they carried."

"Do you say it progresses?"

"Yes Holiness, it is said those who die may kill others by their very glance."

"West, hm, how near do your rumors say?"

"Frejus, your Holiness. The merchants and sailors are only calling it the Pestilence. I have been told it is also known as black flesh."

"Black? Why is that?"

"It is said that those who contract it are covered shortly with black boils, your Holiness."

"Hm, a bad sign. The populace will surely consider this the work of God."

"They already say it."

"Mmm, consider Guy, this may well reach Avignon before the volume copying is completed."

"Is there any message from the copyist, Holiness?"

Clement VI shook his head. "Physician, apply your thought. Would they dispatch a missive a month's journey to tell their Pope the codex is not complete?"

De Chauliac looked down. "Forgive me Holiness, I am consumed with worry."

"Forgive yourself Guy, we must continue as God shows the way. You read this codex before its departure. Can you recall the instructions?"

"I cannot tell, Holiness - perhaps."

"Then go to your recollections, Guy. Your path is lighted."

"Yes, Holiness."

The physician bowed and kissed Clement's ring. As he turned and left, Clement sighed and walked to his desk.

Clement sat down and thought.

Mayhaps I should forbid trade to Avignon. That would delay, if not prevent, the pestilence from reaching us.

No, it is not possible; the planets move beyond any touch of mine. So, also, would that prevent the necessaries of the Church from reaching Avignon. And what of all the travelers that come seeking benefices and dispensations? What of all the revenues?

Does God send His punishment to the wicked? If so, He will spare His Church.

Clement looked at his fresco art with a wry smile. *He may not spare all within His Church however. How many, even in tonsure, are some way short of Holy. And His vicar on earth? How well have I conducted my affairs?*

With relish and appreciation; not with forbearance or abstinence. God's will be done; I cannot assume my will is able to this task. I must not concern myself. That way removes all that life entails.

—####—

de Chauliac interviews Alcadio

"Monsieur de Chauliac, the navigator is at your door."

"Thank you Simon, show him to me."

The manservant left and returned while the Physician paced nervously beside his desk.

After a few moments, Simon returned with a Spanish sailor. The sailor looked at de Chauliac and bowed.

"Physician you asked for me?"

"Yes, Senor?..."

"Alcadio Monsieur, simply Alcadio."

Something in Alcadio's tone and a tension in his muscles struck De Chauliac. The physician raised his eyebrows. "I pray not to be taken as a threat, Senor."

Alcadio was still on guard. "What would you ask of me Monsieur?"

"To be seated, enjoy the wine of my cellars - a quality not found in the river Inns - and tell me all you can of the Pestilence of Genoa."

The Spaniard let out his breath, smiled and looked about for a chair. He chose a leather-topped bucket to the side of the desk and sat down.

"My explanations are tiresome Monsieur. Let me say there are those who would not scruple to do me an injury."

"I understand." De Chauliac picked up a small bell and rang it. The door opened and the manservant stopped, holding the door.

"Monsieur?"

"Simon, bring us two clarets from the cellar and glasses."

"At once, master." He closed the door.

"I should begin physician, before your claret clouds my thoughts."

De Chauliac smiled and waved his hand at the Spaniard. "As and when you will, Senor."

Alcadio looked confused. "What question do you ask?"

"Too soon to know Senor. Tell me what you have seen and heard. The questions will present themselves."

"To begin then, it is not the Pestilence of Genoa, physician."

"Of whence then?"

"The entire coastline to our south is suffering; almost to Marseilles."

De Chauliac frowned. "So soon?"

"Prepare your shrouds, physician; your physicks cannot avail anyone."

"Describe the condition; have you witnessed this?"

"Yes, God give me comfort, an old friend, recently from Messina."

"What did you see?"

"The first day he had labor in walking. He explained to me that some growth was in his groin. I warned him of the poxy women he bedded and we laughed.

The second day an oarsman said to me my friend was abed and wished to see me. I went.

When I arrived another seaman was with him and terribly frightened."

"What could you see, Alcadio?"

"Nothing at first, my friend was on his back and wrapped in bedclothes."

The Spaniard looked up at De Chauliac with glazed eyes. "Physician - he was on fire, the bedclothes were as plump with water as an anchor sail."

"Were you afraid?"

"I had not the wit to fear. I was overcome with puzzlement and confusion."

"Did he say why he called for you?"

"Yes, he reached out from the folds and paid me a loan I had forgotten from two years before. I took it and I took it ill; the sign of a man who is settling his debts before God."

"And then?"

The Spaniard gave de Chauliac a grim smile. "He asked for the pot. I looked about and found a rusty vessel at the end of the bed and held it up. He twisted to get to the side of the bed and the linen fell from his neck. Then I felt fear. I set the pot on the bed and stepped back beyond his reach."

De Chauliac gave Alcadio a quizzical look.

"His neck and armpits were covered with black growths; like to the size of a good farm egg or even an apple in one or two. His flesh had black splashes but nothing was spilt - the color was in the man."

"His eyes?"

The door opened and the manservant came in with a tray.

"Thank you Simon, pour for us."

After they were holding the glasses, the Spaniard sipped and looked at De Chauliac.

"A fine price for such talk; this would call for more wit and flattery." He raised the glass.

De Chauliac smiled. "I am repaid in my profession Alcadio. Your wit may be saved for the appreciations of the prettiest wench in your next port."

The Spaniard grinned. "Well said."

"Now to your friend, Alcadio; his eyes?"

"His eyes were shining and they wandered as he talked."

"Does nothing other stand large in your memory?"

"Yes and I hope God dims it, physician."

De Chauliac looked at the Spaniard and the Spaniard's eyes were far away. "Yes?"

"The smell, God wash that smell from my nostrils."

De Chauliac's expression was blank. He drank some wine, then twisted in his chair and looked at the Spaniard.

"Was there no blood?"

The Spaniard thought. "Forgive me, yes there was enough and to spare. It seeped from the black bulbs, he coughed it up and I saw blood in the pot after he pissed."

Looking into his glass, the physician thought. *Growths, foul odor, fever and bleeding from inside the body; it almost shows as if from a violent blow - but for the black growths and flesh. Even black flesh has been seen after a fall. Could Alcadio be mistaken?*

"Your friend went to God, Alcadio?"

The Spaniard looked surprised. "Four days, physician, it took but four days."

"Were you there?"

Alcadio shook his head. "No, I could not. I had a trade ship to pilot. I thank God for that. I may as easily have followed my friend soon after."

"Your friend was but one man Alcadio. Why worry God with your fears."

Alcadio's face was solemn as he sighed. "Yes, he was but one man. The one man I was saddened to miss."

He looked at De Chauliac, his lips pressed hard together. "Not the only man, physician, his crew all are gone the same way. As are half the portage workers, clerics, travelers at my Inn, guildsmen, sailors and merchants in Sicily and Genoa." Alcadio paused, then looked up through his eyebrows at de Chauliac as he said quietly.

"This is not bad cheese, physician, this is the breath of God."

The physician looked away sadly and muttered. "More like to the vapors of hell."

—####—

De Chauliac was admitted to the Pope. Walking up to the desk, he bowed.

"You sent for me, Holiness?"

"Yes, Guy. Are you preparing yourself?"

"I am, Holiness, as my time allows."

"You have heard, no doubt, the pestilence ravages Marseilles."

"Yes, Holiness."

"And the Greek apothecary?"

De Chauliac paused, then looked into Clement's eyes. "I am not hopeful, Holiness."

"You have tried it then."

De Chauliac shook his head. "No, Holiness, I have yet to obtain the total of ingredients."

"On what do you base this hopelessness you speak of?"

"I believe my remembrances are accurate, Holiness."

Clement waved his hand. "Then we have nothing to fear."

"Holiness, the Greek demands that certain mixtures be performed on the days of certain of his god's. Were I to follow his strictures to an exaction, they are pagan gods of pagan days. I cannot build on ground as soft as this."

"You are saying these formulae may not stay the pestilence?"

"I believe not, your Holiness."

Clement's face was grim. "Physician, I have scholars steeped in Greek knowledge. We cannot allow this to lie fallow."

"Has the book returned then?"

"No, Guy. I will send a courier soon enough to elude the planets. My instructions will go to the copyist - sealed. You understand?"

"I am...unsure, Holiness."

"My see is under siege, physician. Whether from God or Satan, I know not. I will do all I must to protect the Church. I will instruct the copyist return the copy of all he has -if it includes your annotations - unbound. He may keep the exemplar to complete the volume, until the walls of his monastery crumble. You shall have the Greek's guidance within two months."

"What then, Holiness?"

Clement leaned forward and glared at de Chauliac. "Then...physician, you shall consult my scholars and prepare the physick. I care not for your fears of pagan thought. God shows us the way as He wills. Would you have me believe God hid Himself at the sight of a Greek physician?"

De Chauliac stepped backward, blinked and stammered. "Nuh...no, your Holiness."

Clement turned back to his chair and sat down. Looking up at de Chauliac, he put his fingertips together. "Guy, do not fear. Fear is a useless occupation. Gather your tools and your courage; I will assist as I can - God as He will."

De Chauliac bowed. "Yes, Holiness."

"Now go and engage your talents; as you leave, send Marceau to me. I must prepare the copyists message and assign the courier."

"Yes, Holiness."

“Fergus, this is a strangeness. I have annotations. Where are you?” A squeak came from the library above Colum. He looked up and the cat was staring down at him; its tail switching back and forth.

Colum looked up at Fergus and said, dryly, “So, you peruse the volumes. That is a useful application of your talents.” Colum looked back at the exemplar held open above his writing surface. “I was instructed to perform the copy in Statu quo. I must, perforce, include these remarks. Can you agree?”

The cat had turned back to the shelves. Colum looked up and could only see Fergus’ rump.

“Hm, you are doubtless correct. His Holiness specified the copy be as it is; I shall be true to that stipulation.”

Colum peered carefully at the writing in the margins muttering to himself.

“My duty aside, my interest need not be quelled.”

He read the comments carefully then looked up at the library. Not seeing the cat, he raised his voice, “The personage who penned these notes could only do so with high rank.” He looked back at the exemplar; talking under his breath. “Mmm, I think too quickly, he may have been the once fortunate owner. No matter, his mind was devoted to medicine; that much is clear.”

Fergus came down the staircase to the floor of the scriptorium. Colum looked over at the creak of the steps. “I hesitate to interrupt your labors, Fergus, but the annotations are of great import. They are the work of a physician, I will swear by Saint Cieran.”

Colum’s expression went suddenly somber as he read. “May God bless his tortured soul,” he mumbled to himself. “This man is in fear, Fergus. He seeks God’s help in this very book.” Colum lifted his head, his eyes blank, as he thought.

A commission from his Holiness? Delivered to this unsheltered rock? God’s will is not to be understood, but such a volume as this, with such deep concern. He looked at the other copies on the table against the wall. *Time! His Holiness and this physician are in urgency. I have made a grievous error; one copy, one copy to shorten the time. May God forgive me.*

Fergus rubbed against the leg of the stool. Colum looked down.

"Fergus, we must make a change. I must quicken my writings. My anticipation of the Abbot's joy is not to be rewarded. God has blessed me with understanding; there can be one copy and one copy only to hasten the work. My pride has been shown to me and God has meted out a just penance. There will not be a copy to improve our library."

Fergus blinked, and then scratched his ear.

"Your concern over my exertions is appreciated, Fergus. I promise my utmost efforts in ensuring you do not share in any penance I may suffer."

—####—

Bron caught the rope tossed from the ferryman and tied it to the dock pylon. As the currach neared, the stranger stepped onto the dock and bowed.

"God's blessings good brother."

Bron bowed.

"God's blessings sir and how may I direct you?"

"I am Gerard de Pont Saint Esprit, brother. I have come to visit your Brother Colum"

Bron's eyes widened.

"You are the courier of his Holiness. It is the space between the prayers of the divine office. Brother Colum will be at his task in the scriptorium; I shall take you to him."

Bron turned to the steps and started up.

"Stay brother." said Gerard, "I entreat you to follow behind my steps. I would be more secure with your presence at my back."

Bron smiled, nodded and stepped away from the steps as Gerard began the ascent. Bron followed a few steps behind.

As they reached the top and started across the yard towards the cloister, Fergus ran over to Gerard. Gerard reached down to pet the cat and the cat joined them as they walked.

"Gerard." It was the Abbot.

"Welcome, we had no news of your arrival."

Gerard stopped, waiting for the Abbot to reach him.

"I had no time to send notice good Abbot. I was hurried to the journey. Your welcome reassures me that I was not a disturbance in so peaceful a place."

The Abbot placed his hand on Gerard's shoulder.

"You could not be less than a pleasant surprise, Gerard. But what has brought you to us, so long a journey and so soon. Brother Colum has not yet completed one half of the work."

"Thank you, good Abbot. I understand. It would appear there is some new thought from his Holiness that would not allow delay. I have his wishes in my pouch."

Here Gerard swung his elbow forward to show the pouch carried over his shoulder.

The Abbot's face, at first puzzled, brightened as he turned toward the cloister.

"Then we should go to Brother Colum and all hear of the news together."

They walked to the scriptorium. Colum greeted Gerard warmly.

"Has the pestilence then gone, Gerard?"

Gerard winced.

"No Brother Colum, it has not arrived. I expect that I shall find it waiting on my return."

Colum's face was shocked.

"Then you must remain with us."

Gerard sat down and smiled at Colum's concern.

"Ah, Brother, I cannot. I must continue my work. My hope is to retire on my return; if his Holiness grants my request. Now, to the task at hand."

He lifted the pouch onto the table and, opening it, he pulled out a fold of parchment.

Gerard broke the seal, lifted the fold, removed a single sheet of parchment and began to read.

"His Holiness would entreat all here to secrecy. He does not require that we be so sworn but trusts we are men of God and the church. He asks that I view the commission in progress and judge its worth. He is confident that all will be of quality." Gerard paused and read a few moments more.

Then looked at Colum. "I am to ask the scribe... that is you Brother...have you reached a page in the exemplar containing Latin annotations?"

Colum looked at the Abbot. "I have."

Gerard looked back at the parchment. "Have you then, as the commission specifies, copied these in situ?"

Colum looked at Gerard, nervously. "I have."

"Good Brother, not much more. Have you reached the end of these pages?"

"I have."

"Excellent Brother. His Holiness will be most pleased."

Colum relaxed visibly.

Gerard read on and then laid the parchment, face down, on the table."

"Father, Brother, I am to take your copy back to Avignon. His Holiness so stipulates."

Colum and the Abbot sat startled. Colum again looked at the Abbot. "and the exemplar?"

Gerard smiled. "The exemplar stays with you Brother. His Holiness also requests, with apologies, that you begin again. Thus creating a complete and fully bound codex."

Colum's eyes wandered to the writing table. *God's mercy, I can complete all. The Abbot may have a new codex.* His excitement pushed aside his modesty. "Does his Holiness instruct as to the time allowed?"

Gerard frowned briefly and picked up the parchment. His eyes swept down the page.

He looked up. "Forgive my carelessness Brother. He writes 'as God's time and your duties allow'."

The Abbot thought to what Colum had already grasped. "Brother Colum. you shall need all your ink and vellum."

"Yes, Father."

Gerard looked at both monks and smiled to himself. *Thanks be to God, I have brought a joyful end to my journey. Would that it was always so.*

He stood up. "Brother, you may lead me to your work."

Colum was already walking to his writing table. The Abbot stood and watched as Gerard followed Colum.

Gerard stopped and looked at the pages laid open. *Beautiful,* he thought, *as simple as some may think of this.* He looked at Colum and smiled.

"Quality enough Brother, as His Holiness foretold."

The Abbot spoke over Gerard's shoulder. "Brother Colum's attention to his work is only surpassed by his fondness for the task."

"I am assured the two are seldom apart Father."

"As you say, Gerard."

Colum carefully gathered the vellum leaves together into a section and rolled the entire section into a cylinder. "I have no suitable way to protect the leaves Father."

Gerard looked at the Abbot. "Father, could we wrap the pages in oilskin?"

"Yes, Gerard. I will take this to Brother Brendan. He will ensure they are well sealed." The Abbot took the vellum from Colum.

Chapter 22: Vineyards & Goodbye

Seamus was standing in the front room when he saw Meg's car pull into the driveway. He turned and shouted to Tony in the kitchen.

"Meg's here, Tony. Are you quite certain you won't join us?"

"No thanks, Seamus. I'll be fine. You two go and have a good time.

Tony walked in to the room carrying a cup of coffee. "What's the problem, Seamus; you nervous?"

Seamus turned around. "A little, yes. I haven't done this for some while."

"Done what?"

"Taken a lady out."

"You're not taking a lady out. She's picking you up to show you the sights."

"I should be helping her have a good day."

"Yikes, Seamus; you certainly haven't done this in a while. She's in the driver's seat, in every way - just let her. Besides, you and Meg have no trouble talking; you'll be OK."

"If not, you would be sure to make it all the more difficult."

"Only if I had the chance to show off my wit."

Seamus turned around and saw Meg walking to the front door.

"Right, I'm off."

"See you Seamus; have a good time."

Seamus went out the front door and met Meg. Tony watched as Meg stopped and they both turned around to leave. A few minutes later he saw Meg back out and drive away.

He sipped his coffee and went over to the liquor cabinet to add a little eye opener. The phone rang.

—####—

Tony heard a car pull into the driveway. He picked up the remote and turned the music off. He got up and walked over to the front room window. After a few minutes, Meg and Seamus walked across in front of the window, then stopped - talking. Tony watched, he could hear them talking, but couldn't make out any of the conversation. Finally, Meg took Seamus' hands, leaned forward and kissed him. It wasn't a long kiss; just a 'see you soon' kiss. The sort that couples give each other who have been together for many years. Meg turned around and walked back. Seamus walked over to the front and came in the door.

"Tony?"

"Right here."

"Oh there you are. How was your day?"

"Terrible; the comp center called just as you left. It took me all day to solve the problem."

Seamus' smile faded. "Sorry about that. I suppose you should have joined us."

"Yes, but it was a good thing I was here. Anyway, forget that; what happened?"

"We had a marvelous day. The wine country is beautiful."

"Uh huh, I've been there. You know what I'm interested in hearing about."

"Ah, I suppose I do. She's a remarkable woman."

Tony made face. "So remark a little. This isn't my style but allow me a little vicarious romance."

"A gentleman doesn't tell, Tony. Truth is there's nothing to tell."

"So, I'm expected to believe you two just bumbled about Napa Sonoma babbling about grapes?"

"Blast it, Tony; find me a drink."

"Sure, coming up. Now go on."

"All I can say is we both know our histories, our tastes and our hopes for the future."

Seamus sat down. Tony made drinks, walked over and handed Seamus his glass and sat down.

"OK Seamus, don't blush; I saw the kiss you got. You looked like you were already married."

"Seamus smiled thoughtfully. "It would look like that, yes. But the reason is not what you may think."

"Want to explain that?"

"It is all too obvious, Tony. We both know we could just as easily fall in love. The world is against us. We discussed it. I was surprised. We drifted to the future; all unaware - our future. I cannot say what Meg felt. I only know I found myself wistfully accepting that we would go our different ways."

"Just like that? You both agree to just give up on each other. Where's the tenacity I remember?"

"Tony, Meg has her whole life here in San Francisco. Mine is home in Ireland. I would not live here. She cannot imagine herself there - the end."

"Bah, what life? You know you'll fester there. I know Meg will miss you terribly if you're not here."

Seamus looked at Tony with a sad face.

"I won't move here, Tony; Meg knows that."

"Hmm, so I have to convince Meg that Ireland is the place to be."

Seamus grinned. "Oh, it is, it is." He frowned. "and don't you ever try. I won't chance Meg's well ordered life or her suspicion that I put you up to it."

Tony got up, finished his drink and walked over to the front window. As he walked he mumbled to himself, "I'll chance that." He looked out the window for a few seconds and then turned around.

"So, the good Meg has taken care of the last of my preplanned events. What do you think of just staying home tomorrow. It is Sunday; a day of rest."

"I vote yes, Tony. A day of sitting around is the best for me."

"Done."

—####—

"Good God, Seamus, hasn't your bioclock adjusted yet. Its been almost a week."

"And a good morning to you, as well. It is a quarter after eight."

"Yeah, and it is a Sunday morning. Don't the Irish sleep in?"

"An agricultural country cannot indulge in slug a bed. Unless they're Dubliners, I suppose."

"Your memory goes back too far, Seamus. I have complete confidence that the modern Irish do damn well indulge. Anyway, I intend to."

"Rather early for you to be so adamant."

"It was the smell of the coffee, damn you."

"Mea culpa."

"I see your days as an altar boy haven't been wasted. You know, I'll never be able to hear Latin again without thinking about your accursed book."

"I also."

Tony poured himself coffee and sat across the island. Putting his elbows on the counter, he sipped and looked at Seamus over the cup."

"Do you think we have any way of knowing whether the Greek's potion actually worked?"

Seamus looked at the far wall. "I've thought on that. There are only two ways to know. One, mix it up, take it and then make a concerted effort to catch the plague."

Tony grimaced. "My curiosity just faded."

Seamus smirked and went on. "And, two, find hard evidence in historical records."

"That's more palatable and less likely - no pun intended."

"Is it so unlikely?"

Tony sighed. "Fraid so, this was 1347. They had records but not that would discuss this. Beside the sad fact that most of the records were lost. Hell, after the plague, entire towns vanished."

"Say that again."

"Vanished, disappeared. A small town would be wiped out by the plague. Anybody left alive…left. The growth of nature and the decay of man's buildings left nothing but some vague outlines in the weeds."

"Ugh." Seamus shook off a chill.

"What about the Monk's preface; doesn't that help us?"

"Not that I can see. Oh, we may figure out where his monastery was and then look up anything we can find about it. Assuming we were very lucky, it may even still be around. Active, I mean."

Seamus shook his head. "I doubt it. We think it was on a small rocky island. I don't think any of those are anything but ruins."

"Well, OK, then we find some great records in Ireland that pertain to nothing but the writings and diaries of the monks that were there. We still won't have much chance of finding out about this book."

"Wait a bit, Tony. Can't we assume that the Pope got his original back?"

"Tony straightened up and his face brightened. "Son of a bitch, you're right. The original and one copy should both be in the Vatican Library."

"So, we should at the least be able to find out what became of them."

Tony looked thoughtful. "If we knew how. From what I know, it takes a lot of work to even get into the Vatican Library; let alone find a single book."

Seamus made a face. "It's worse than that. Even if they are both there in all their glory, we don't know what happened in 1347; or any other year. I wonder what happened to the fourth copy?"

"The monk gave it to a relative or a chief or someone, remember?"

"Perhaps, I've been assuming that was the copy I have."

"Hmm, Oh - he kept it."

"Ah yes. That is the only other with the preface."

"Right, and that's all four of them. The original and a copy without the preface went back to the Pope. At least, that's what we have to assume. The other two were kept in Ireland. One the monk had and the other he gave to some layman."

"Which one we think is in our hands."

"Yup. hey, you know something, there is some value to finding out if the Vatican has the other two."

"And that would be?"

"The medieval physician. He would have had it - or access to it - and... you know something; he would likely have mentioned it in his own writings."

"Why would he do that?"

"C Y A, - cover your ass. He would have quoted sources in his own writings to lend credibility and let himself off the hook if it didn't work."

"A very good thought, Tony. How can we find out?"

"George, let's give him a call."

"Call! I promised to call Maeve."

—####—

Seamus walked back from the office to the kitchen. Tony was finishing his lunch. He looked up.

"Well?"

"Maeve was quite pleasant. She tells me the good Father Schmidt called for me with something he thought was exciting."

Tony looked at Seamus with a sarcastic smile. "That's nice. What did George say?"

"Oh, he was out. I left a message."

"Rats, well, you'll be off for your nap. I'm going to run down to the corner store and pickup some smokes."

"What if George calls?"

"I'll only be a few minutes, Seamus. Don't worry."

"Right."

—####—

Seamus walked down the stairs into the kitchen. Tony was sitting at the island doing the crossword.

"Any coffee?"

"Fresh pot; I've got your habits down to an art."

Seamus poured some coffee and sat down.

"Any news?"

Tony looked up from the crossword.

"Yes, there is; George says de Chauliac always gave credit. Apparently he refers to numerous Greek and Arabic surgeons throughout all his writings."

"Excellent! and?"

"George says he's read just about everything De Chauliac ever wrote. Well, at least everything they have today."

Tony paused. "There's no mention of anything even remotely similar to this book."

"Confound it. Then do we assume he never had it or perhaps never saw it?"

"That's what it looks like."

Seamus frowned and sipped his coffee. After a few minutes of silence, he looked up at the ceiling.

"Tony, who did write my book?"

Tony looked blank. "Huh, well we don't know. I don't remember any mention of the author or authors anywhere in it."

"Ah ha! It is just possible that the good doctor didn't refer to it simply because he couldn't credit anyone. How does that sound?"

"Pretty damn reasonable but it doesn't answer our original question."

"Hmm, you're quite right, unfortunately. Still, it remains possible that he did try it."

"Yeah, and we have no clever way to find out. As you so succinctly put it; either we try it or we look for records. If you want to try it; I will run. Actually, I will gallop; with a bottle of carbolic acid under each arm."

Seamus smiled. "I have no more interest in that path than you. What possible source of records might we have missed?"

"Unless you want to go on an archeological dig, the only thing I can think of is the - always readily available - surmise and conjecture. Look Seamus, this isn't like you; you're getting stuck on something you may never know. That's not good; you've said it yourself."

"You have me there, Tony. I don't always follow my own logic; this is just one example."

Tony smiled. "Oh goodie, I've always wanted to catch you at it. Now, forget that; where are we? Isn't it time to review?"

"Hmm, yes it is - past time. To start, we know a lot more than we did about the book's contents."

Tony raised a finger. "And we know, as a result, why this book was likely being copied in the first place."

"I think so, if you're thinking as I am. It was for the good doctor de Chauliac."

Tony nodded. "That's what I think. Our Pope was doing himself and the doctor, a favor."

"We believe he was trying; of course, we don't know if it worked or even if he tried it."

"Seamus, what about the monk?"

Seamus was pacing. He stopped and turned to Tony.

"The monk?"

"Yes, the monk; wouldn't he have as much interest as the doctor?"

Seamus shook his head. “I shouldn’t think so. He may not have even been able to read the Greek he copied. If he did understand Greek, he wasn’t a physician.”

Tony looked out the kitchen window. “Mmm, I see what you mean. Even if he was a Greek linguist and a monastic physician, the plague probably didn’t touch him.”

“Uh, it may have. As unlikely as it sounds, Ireland was hit by the plague just like almost everywhere else. The plague even reached as far as Iceland. Remember he did have to receive some items from England or the continent.”

“OK, let's hope his monastery was in a nice bog or, better yet, on the rock island off the coast we’re guessing at. That would make it pretty far-fetched.”

Seamus chuckled. “Yes, it would be; and a good thing for the monk.”

—####—

One day left - one day. I never thought I would be so sad to leave. Seamus sat at the kitchen table sipping his coffee.

Tony walked in from the living room.

"Well, you have two days left."

Seamus' head jerked up and he turned to Tony.

"Two days? No, no, I only have one day, surely."

Tony had a crooked smile as he said,

"Well, technically, yes but your flight tomorrow doesn't leave until eleven at night. Sooo..."

Seamus turned back to the counter and thought, *So, I won't see San Francisco from the air at all. Hello! I can see Meg tonight - for a bit anyway.*

"Tony, what excuse can we have to see Meg again before I leave.?"

"Why do you need an excuse? And to think you said you could manage your own courtships - there's a laugh. I'll give her a call and ask if she would like to stop over for a farewell lunch. Just sit like the lump you are and I'll get back to you." He walked into his office and Seamus could hear him on the phone and then talking. After a few minutes, Tony came back.

"Well, the news is mixed. First you will be subjected to my cooking again, my last chance to inflict real damage and second, Meg's coming to dinner. I apologize for not being able to arrange a private tete-a-tete for the two of you. It seems she still wants to focus on the book."

Seamus looked out the window of the plane. *What a fascinating place. San Francisco is, certainly pretty from the air - at night.* He smiled remembering Tony giving him a rib-cracking hug at the entrance to security. *Too bad Meg couldn't break free of her clinic; I would have enjoyed seeing her before leaving. Still, all of the trip was a surprise; Meg most of all. Could I live here? No, I know I couldn't. Ah, how strange is life.*

He settled down in his seat and fell asleep.

Chapter 23: Return

Seamus slept very late, skipped lunch and went up for a nap as usual. His clock was still halfway between Cincinnati and the west coast. When he came down P.J. was standing in the hallway.

"P.J.!"

"Hello, Seamus. Good trip?"

"A brilliant trip and all the surprises were pleasant."

Maeve walked past them and went into the kitchen. As she passed she turned her head. "Fetch the usual two beers, you lot, and find a chair. I blathered about Conor all the way home from the airport. We need a complete report."

P.J. disappeared down to the basement. Seamus looked bemused, shook his head and sat down.

Maeve came back from the kitchen with a cup of tea. "Where's P.J.?"

Seamus pointed down just as P.J. came up the stairs.

"Here you are; how's the beer in San Francisco? I hear the steamed beers are great."

"Sorry P.J. I wouldn't know. Tony fed me Scotch and Irish the whole time."

"Oh, shame; well, you know what I mean."

Seamus laughed. "Yes, I do."

Maeve leaned forward. "Well, come on; what did you learn?"

"Ah, it's the book you want to hear about."

"Of course."

They listened, while Seamus recounted everything he had discovered about the book. It was well past supper when Seamus finally stopped.

"So, that's all I have or can remember. Now, you have news for me; right?"

Maeve looked at P.J. “P.J. kept copies of the newspapers for you but you know about that.”

P.J. looked at Maeve. “There’s Father Schmidt.”

Maeve turned to Seamus. “Oh yes, I told you. He called last Friday. He asked for you and when I told him you were out until today, He said he’d call back. He was very excited, I thought, but he didn’t tell me what it was about.”

Seamus looked disappointed, then laughed. “It can keep. I’m nackered; if I heard anymore I wouldn’t be able to keep it in my head.”

—####—

The next morning Seamus came down to the kitchen and Maeve was pouring coffee. “This is for you; I heard you stumbling down the staircase.”

“Bless you Maeve.” He sat down and Maeve handed him the coffee and sat down opposite.

“So, what did you leave out?”

Seamus sipped and looked over the cup. “Patience; but now, what do you mean?”

“You are more chipper than I’ve seen in many a month. What caused that then?”

“I had a good rest and a pleasant time without any thoughts of the past, Maeve. Isn’t that enough?”

“No.”

Seamus chuckled. “That’s all you are going to get, my dear sister. You shouldn’t pry so obviously.”

The phone rang in the office and Maeve got up and went to answer it.

“Seamus, it’s for you; it’s Father Schmidt.”

Seamus looked up as Maeve walked into the kitchen and handed him the phone.

“Here you are; I don’t want any coffee spilt on my computer.”

Seamus took the phone. "Good morning Father, how have you been?"

"Excellent Seamus, I have some interesting news for you."

"Oh, so?"

"I have an old friend from years ago when I was in seminary. He's a Monsignor in the Vatican. He's been working in the library, Seamus."

Seamus' face lit up with interest. "You have all my attention Father."

"Yes, you may guess. I asked him to scour the library for your book. Well, the original of course, not your book. This wasn't easy. All I know and could tell him as a guide wasn't much. I told him it was 14th century; Greek Textus and medical."

"I understand."

"Seamus." There was a pause. "It's not there. At least, not all of it."

"Again?"

"My friend could only find a portion of it. He's pretty sure it's the same content apparently a Greek medical text from that century is rather rare but there's no Latin preface."

"That doesn't surprise me, Father."

"Oh, I know; there shouldn't be a preface. The point is there should be two codices in the library. The original and the copy that was asked for. There is no original; my friend is certain of that. The only thing he could find was a, fairly large but incomplete, portion of, what he believes to be, the copy."

"That is odd."

"I thought so and, even more interesting, it isn't bound and my friend says it never was bound."

"Bless me. How can he tell?"

"Apparently, there are no signs of stitching. I guess there should be little holes in the pages and there aren't."

"Hm, I've heard there are often loose pages. Don't they cut them out?"

"I asked about that; could the holes be cut off. He says no. The pages are not individual, as they would be if they were cut. They are still folio, or bifolium in a stack. The stack is then stitched in a gathering and multiple gatherings make a bound book."

"Of course, the single sheet straddled the bound edge; two pages really."

"Exactly. If it were bound the stitching marks would be obvious."

"So, what else did your friend have to say, Father?"

"Um well, he would like your book for the library, of course. He was quite excited about it."

Seamus smiled. "We shall see, Father. I haven't settled my mind on the rightful owner yet."

"I understand. Well, let me know how it all develops; I'm very curious myself."

"You may rely on me, Father. I promise to keep you well informed."

"Thanks a lot, Seamus. I've got to run; classes to do. Goodbye."

"Goodbye Father."

Seamus held the phone out and looked at it. Then pushed the disconnect button and handed it to Maeve. "The good Father has been investigating on my behalf. He had a friend in Rome look for the original. It is not there; only a portion of the copy."

Maeve stared and then got up to the coffeepot and came back to top up their cups. "How can that be? The copy you have couldn't exist without the original; it must have been lost."

Seamus looked up at her. "Or destroyed."

"Why would it be destroyed?"

"Many reasons are possible. Dangerous knowledge of the human body is one; that may have damaged the faithful trust in God."

"Ah, you would think of that. Let's leave it; what do you intend to do now that you have all this knowledge of the human body."

"Good one, Maeve. I would like to look through the copies P.J. brought back from the newspaper archives."

"I'll fetch them and then you can have your peace. I have work to do."

Maeve brought a stack of paper out to the kitchen and laid them on the table. She left Seamus reading and went into her office.

Three hours later, Seamus heard Maeve turn off her computer.

Seamus raised his voice. "So, is it time for the dinner?"

She came into the kitchen and sat down. "I'll just bring out the leftovers from the deli; P.J. brought them home yesterday. So, what do you make of all this?" She waved her hand at the papers spread all over the table.

"I think it has all the marks of being the wellspring of the solution, Maeve. It explains almost every oddity."

Maeve got up and started bringing out the packages for lunch. "It doesn't explain why you have the book."

"No, well caught. Still, I sense that my book came from this Mr. Decker's collection. I have to work out what happened after the robbery."

"That seems even more troublesome."

"Not to me. This way I have some point of origin and I have some threads to catch hold of."

"What threads?"

"The one that comes to mind is the friend who offered a reward."

"Hmm, I see the value there. If you could find him."

"If he's alive, I'll find him."

—####—

"Sir?"

"Yes, Robert?"

"I have taken a telephone call from a Mr. Cash."

"Yes?"

"I am sorry if I overstepped my bounds."

The old man turned in his chair and looked at Robert. There was something in the butler's voice.

"Robert, are you all right?"

"Yes sir, it's this Mr. Cash, sir. He would like to see you.

Sir...he has the book."

"Good Lord! Are you sure?"

"Yes sir, I am positive. He believes it was part of the articles missing from Mr. Decker's after the robbery."

"Astonishing." The old man paused.

"But then, why does he wish to see me?"

"That is also rather extraordinary, Sir. He is hopeful you will be able to identify the book; since you posted a reward."

"Well well well, he's a veritable ferret, this Mr. Cash."

"I should say so sir. He permitted me to state a day and a time. I arranged for him to visit tomorrow at ten in the morning. I apologize for the presumption; I felt you would want to meet as soon as convenient."

"Your judgment was exactly right, Robert. What decided you to avoid asking him over immediately."

"I assumed you would prefer some interval to collect your thoughts, sir."

"Excellent, Robert; My thoughts must stop whirling before I can collect them."

"Yes sir."

Seamus turned to Maeve as he opened the car door. "Are you sure you won't come along." Maeve was looking up at the mansion through the car windscreen.

"I'm quite sure, Seamus. I'll be comfortable in the car."

"This may take a bit of time, you know."

Maeve looked at Seamus. "Enough of that. I'll be in the way of the conversation and well you know it."

"All right, all right, I'm going." Seamus climbed out the car, closed the door and walked across the cobblestoned drive to the high wide steps. As he walked up the steps to the entrance, the right most door swung open and an older man in a tuxedo stood in the doorway. As Seamus reached him, the man stepped back.

"Welcome sir, I assume you are Mr. Cash?"

"Yes I am. I hope I won't take up much of your time, sir."

The man chuckled. "You won't take any of my time at all. Please follow me; I'll take you to the master."

Seamus followed, feeling chagrined. *Of course you eejit, this is the butler. I never thought of that.*

"Mr. Seamus Cash, sir."

"Thank you, Robert. Please, take a seat Mr. Cash."

"Thank you. You may just call me Seamus, sir."

The old man chuckled. "Then let me reciprocate; you may drop the sir."

Seamus smiled. *What an astonishingly well preserved gentleman,* he thought. *He must be ninety or better and he looks more around his mid-sixties.*

"Sir, I was brought up to address my seniors and betters as 'sir'."

"I can't argue with the senior. I, myself, have difficulty finding a senior these days. As to the better? I stopped considering such things many years ago. And now, apart from enjoying your company, what can I do for you?"

Seamus sat back in his chair, relaxed and thought, *I like this old man. He has a, worn-in-place, charm. There are few men who have his dignity and poise.*

"Well sir, I recently came into possession of a rather strange book. I was hoping you could identify it for me."

"You have it with you?"

"Yes sir." Seamus reached down to his bag on the floor and brought out the book. He handed it over to the old man. As the old man took the book, there was a tenseness in his body. His eyes opened slightly; then he blinked twice and his expression relaxed. Seamus noticed and wondered but kept silent. The old man held the book affectionately and opened it slowly. He turned a few pages; then looked up at Seamus.

"A remarkable book, Seamus. You know how fond I am of antiquities?"

"Yes, sir; I did a touch of research before I came."

The old man nodded.

"Then you can appreciate how valuable this book is and how I admire it."

"Yes sir. Do you recognize it?"

"What? Oh, yes I do. Your surmise is correct; this was one of the pieces in Decker's collection."

Seamus caught a tone in the old man's voice. The way he said 'Decker's collection'. *Hm, I thought I heard a disparaging word. Could the old man still harbor some ancient dislike? No, surely not; why would he post a reward? Still, I read men rather well.*

"Sir?"

"Yes?" The old man was looking through the book; lost in his own thoughts. He stopped and looked at Seamus.

"You posted a reward for the recovery of Mr. Decker's collection. Is that right?"

"Yes I did."

"So did you know the collection well?"

"Quite well."

"And this particular book?"

"Oh yes; I recognize it. I never was allowed to actually look at it. This is my first opportunity."

"Mr. Decker kept it under lock and key?"

"Yes, he displayed it in a bullet proof glass case. The book was open at a central page, on a stand, with a light carefully placed. It was valuable of course, but there was more significance than that."

"Oh?"

"He was proud of the way he acquired it."

"How did he acquire it?"

"He paid an old Irish ostler fifty pounds for it."

"God save us, fifty pounds?"

"Yes, rather sad, really."

"Apart from his display, did he tell you about the book?"

"Not very much. It was clearly a medieval manuscript; a medical treatise of some sort. It follows that it was hand written by a monk. I believe it is fourteenth century. Other than that." The old man shrugged his shoulders.

"Do you read Latin , sir?" The old man was looking at a few pages in the middle of the book.

"Umm? Oh no, and this is Greek to me."

Seamus grinned.

"Indeed, sir; to me also."

Something about the old man's expression prompted Seamus.

"It appears to be badly damaged in places. Do you know where I may have it repaired?"

The old man looked surprised and then relaxed.

"I would start by contacting Hebrew Union College. They have the skilled people or would help you find someone."

"I'll call them. It is a shame; I'm afraid some of the content may be lost."

The old man looked at Seamus thoughtfully.

"The Vatican library might help you there. I imagine at least one of theirs would still be complete."

"Except for the preface."

"Yes, except for the preface." The clock on the library table chimed.

“I’m sorry Seamus. I’m afraid I must hasten our talk to a close. At my age, I am compelled to be overly careful with my health.”

He handed the book back to Seamus.

The door opened and the butler stepped into the room and stood next to the door.

“Seamus looked over at Robert.

“Of course, I understand completely. May I call again?”

“Please do, I always enjoy intelligent company.”

Seamus stood up. “You flatter me, sir.”

The old man looked up from his chair.

“I don’t think so, Seamus. Your modesty is courteous but inaccurate.”

Seamus smiled and, nodding briefly, he extended his hand. The old man reached up, shook his hand and smiled with a twinkle in his eyes.

“Please do visit again, Seamus; I think we have more to discuss.”

“Thank you sir; I agree.” He turned and walked out. Robert followed and closed the door behind him.

Seamus turned to the butler as they walked. “The old gentleman has a keen mind. What is his age?”

“I don’t know exactly, sir. I know he’s well into his nineties.”

They walked in silence to the front hall and the butler opened the massive door. As Seamus walked past the butler through the doorway, the butler smiled.

“The old gentleman has a mind like a cheese wire, sir.”

Seamus looked at him, smiled, nodded and walked down the steps. *That was a message*, he thought, *don’t underestimate this man.* He smiled to himself, *I like the way this plays. Let us keep the ball in spin.*

He opened the car door and dropped onto the seat. “You missed something, Maeve.”

"Did I?"

"Indeed, a very impressive old patrician."

"I should hope. The house looks the part."

Seamus looked out of the window and up at the mansion. *Saints protect us, this looks a match for any crowned head of Europe.*

Maeve drove around the long curve of the driveway and down to the street.

"So?"

"Yes."

Maeve glanced over at Seamus. "It is from the old burglary! Then how and why would all those years pass without a glimpse."

"Ah, that's for me to discover." Seamus felt a warm glow of satisfaction. This was familiar ground and always a pleasant path.

Chapter 24: The Black Death

A barque du Rhone fought its way across the river current, trying to turn to the docks. The docks were almost full. A dozen lay at their moorings while a hundred men and boys hurried to unload their cargo. The walled bank was piled with goods and the mud-splattered storage sheds, wine houses, crumbling inns and sailors wenching houses were almost hidden by the towering crates, barrels, wicker hampers and cloth bales. The stench was overpowering. The wind was from Avignon; there was no outlet for waste. The streets were thick with slime; a muck of human ordure, decaying dead animals and the slop from the kitchens. Rats were everywhere; standing arrogantly on the cargo; racing to fight over scraps or sniffing for food. They ran, then stopped, then ran again. The people walked, ignoring the rats, as the rats dodged human boots.

A scattered few nobles, with cloths held over their noses, waved their arms and hands, giving directions to the porters. Monks, nuns and priests walked in two's and three's. Hurrying to depart the docks and reach their destinations.

The docks were always swarming and drunken men staggered trying to avoid the overseer's eye.

Ferand looked about and counted his porters as they carried their loads past him. *One, two, three, four - God's blood! where was the Sicilian?* He walked to the wall of cargo as Giuseppe shifted a box from his shoulder. "Giuseppe, where is Pietro?"

The Italian turned his head from the box and looked up. "In the Porter's Inn, Ferand, he had a terrible thirst."

"How long ago?"

Giuseppe squinted at the sun. "Two bells, maybe."

Ferand grunted and strode toward the inn, a crooked path of only a few hundred yards, he reached the open door and stepped inside. He stopped to let his eyes adjust to the dark and saw Pietro on a bench against the north wall. He clenched his fists and as he came closer he made his boots stamp loudly on the stones. Pietro did not move.

"Pietro! We have two boats to clear before nightfall. Move yourself! or by all the saints, I shall send you back to your wife's brothers."

Pietro did not move. Ferand grabbed his shoulder and shook. "Are you so drunk this soon?"

Pietro slid from the bench to the floor. He was dead.

Ferand jumped back and crossed himself. He bent over then recoiled. Pietro's smell was even more foul than the Avignon air. The rough spun shirt Pietro wore had fallen open at the neck. Ferand could see the black bulges under his armpits. "Satanas," he cried and ran from the inn. The other sailors and porters had stood up as they watched. They shouted at each other to make way and ran from the inn behind Ferand, knocking against the chairs and benches.

As Ferand came out into the sun, he turned aside and shading his eyes with his hand, he stood still and scanned the throng on the docks. A porter walking to fetch another barrel was twisting as he walked. As though his understrap had loosened. Another porter, shifting cargo from the same barque, was sweating heavily and his eyes wandered. As Ferand looked over the heads in front of him, he noticed the barque in the river, turning to find a berth. Then he thought of his own. Looking hard down the docks, he strained to see his porters. The others, unloading between his eyes and his own berth, allowed only a few seconds view, at intervals. Giuseppe was still unloading steadily. A bull of a man, he worked as if he were an ox under plow. Ferand smiled and stared intently. *Where were the Frenchmen?* For an instant the walkway cleared. One of them was sitting against the bales, while the other two bent over him. He was white with fever. *So soon? Impossible.* A hand touched his arm.

"Ferand, why are you here? Your concern for your cargo cannot be helped at this remove." Ferand turned a frightened face, then let his breath out.

"Alcadio! You are a sight of comfort. Pox the cargo. Walk with me away from this evil inn." Ferand turned and slowly worked his way down towards his barge, staying close to the walls. Alcadio followed, then gripped Ferand's arm and pulled him around. He looked Ferand in the eyes. "A frightened Ferand? What cause could make this wonder?"

Ferand's face hardened. "Pestilence, Alcadio. It is here."

Alcadio froze, then looked around at the crowded docks. His eye saw the two porters Ferand had seen. Stretching his head he stared across the length of the berths. Looking for the signs he remembered so well. Two or three slips north, he saw a group of porters unmoving. A priest and two nuns were looking on. Suddenly, one of the porters ran across the walkway and disappeared between the storehouses. He turned back to Ferand. "What did you see?"

"One of my porters is in that inn, dead."

"Then, quickly man, we must leave the river landing, while we can."

"My cargo - I cannot leave it."

Alcadio held Ferand's arm. "You must or leave your coins to the gravedigger. Remind yourself of Marseille, Ferand."

Ferand looked down and shook his head. "God save me and my crew."

Alcadio pulled Ferand's arm. "They are already dead, Ferand, if God wills. Come, I must give this news to a man I know." Alcadio let go, turned and walked away; Ferand followed, looking behind him as he walked.

—####—

Gerard de Pont Saint Esprit

Gerard de Pont Saint Esprit leaned against the stone of the old Roman wall. He was watching an ostler friend groom a horse. The ostler turned his head as he brushed. "So, Gerard you are finished."

Gerard laughed. "An awkward word, Michel. I intend only to return to my home."

Michel stood up and stretched. "For fear of a pestilence that may never arrive, you abandon a vocation."

"Vocation?"

"How else to call it? You are paid well indeed and in the service of His Holiness; such occupations are not called out to common man."

Gerard looked out at the town thoughtfully. Then smiled at Michel. "Ah Michel. I travel to carry the pouch. My labors are not the exertions of a noble or a learned man." Michel loosened the straps and pulled the brushes from his hands. Setting them down on a water barrel, he turned back to Gerard; rubbing the backs of his hands. "Oh his modesty is much admired," he winked at Gerard, "and misplaced. "He walked up and placed his hand on Gerard's shoulder. "When do you intend to begin your journey? When do we drain a cup together? I would numb the pain of your absence."

Gerard pushed away from the wall with his foot. "To answer that - this very moment, my good friend. I ride before prime devotions on the morrow."

Michel held his hand up and nodded at a stable boy to tend the horse.

They turned and walked through an opening in the old stonework, talking. As they walked beside the wall, a friar ran up from the river. He was headed to a gap in the wall that led to the Benedictine Nunnery. As he approached them from the right, he stumbled and crossed himself as they approached. His shining eyes were flickering, confused and frantic. He paused and then ran again to pass Gerard. Gerard reached out his hand and gripped the friar's arm. "What trouble good friar? May we help?"

The friar stopped and bent over, gasping for breath, holding his knees. He looked up at the two men. "I have come from the river; men are stricken. Three poor souls have gone to God. I need oils and assistance to administer extreme unction." He waved his hand at the church in the shadow of the nunnery.

Gerard and Michel looked at each other. Gerard frowned at the friar. "Of what cause, brother; man or God?"

The friar crossed himself. "Quod avertat Deus! God forbid! These men had skin like unto badly burned black bread." He blessed himself again. "I must go." He gave a short spasmodic bow, turned and ran on towards the church.

Michel touched Gerard's sleeve. "I would choose to drink behind the palace. I know of an inn in the shadow of the Palace of the Commune; toward the Ghetto. I salute your clear eye, my friend. I wonder at any delay."

Gerard was watching the friar disappear on the other side of the wall. He turned his head to Michel as they turned East at the end of the wall and walked briskly past the Templars. "You should depart this place Michel. I will travel to the east and north. The wind also blows north by northeast. I fear, but I trust to God."

Michel shook his head as they strode towards the synagogue. "You and the friar have shaken my bones, Gerard. I shall not be long behind you."

—####—

The River docks, Avignon

The porters recoiled from their friend and slowly stepped back. Their faces were mixtures of horror, surprise and fear. Giuseppe walked past and dropped a bale against the storeroom wall. As he turned he saw the French porters and followed their stares. He froze.

His eyes went to the two confused Frenchmen and realized they had no knowledge. His face hardened and he spread his arms as he herded them back.

"Leave, leave now. Go to your homes, and families, if you have them."

One stood and stared at Giuseppe blankly. "In God's name what do you do?"

"Do not delay nor question my friend. I have the memory you lack. This is the pestilence. You have but one hope and that is to run. Run far and run fast. Do you know of Ferand? Has he been seen since he left to fetch the Sicilian?"

The Frenchman pointed to the hillside. "I saw his back on the embankment some time past."

Giuseppe twisted and looked in the direction the Frenchman indicated. Shading his eyes, he scanned the slope.

Turning back to the porter he waved at him with the back of his hand. "Go, go, go with God - I give you a small hope to live."

The Frenchman stumbled and turned. He glanced back at the body and, terrified, he ran after his friend.

Giuseppe looked at the dead porter against the wall. One hand covering his mouth and nose, he blessed himself, turned and strode quickly away. Perhaps he might find a northbound barque or a cheap horse. As he walked he pulled out his money pouch and felt the coins through the leather. *Not so many.* He took a long breath. *I need to discover Ferand; he will help.* A grim smile slowly formed and his eyes went cold. *If he lives long enough.*

—####—

The House of Guy de Chauliac

Alcadio stretched his stride as he threaded through the filth on the narrow streets. Ferand kept up easily; following closely. He touched Alcadio's shoulder. "Where do you take us?"

Alcadio spoke from the side of his mouth, without breaking the pace. "A physician, Ferand."

Ferand shook his head. "A fool's choice, Alcadio, as you know too well." Alcadio chuckled without humor. "Yes, Ferand, I know - God help us. I have a debt of honor to pay this man."

They turned a corner and skirted a cart, jumping over the pools of refuse. Ferand pulled a cloth from his sleeve and covered his nose. Alcadio turned back closer to the building walls and kicked a rat away with the side of his boot. Ferand glanced at the rat as they passed; it was dead. He leaned forward. "For what do you pay this barber; taking some of your bad blood?"

Alcadio glanced back. "Not a barber, good friend, a physician and a man of learning or I have no whiskers to tickle a wench."

Ferand grinned. "You pay enough, Alcadio. Why should you be so generous?"

They had left the squalor of the center of the city market and were passing a monastery. On the opposite side, as the street turned, was a wall and a gateway. Beyond, through the gate opening, Ferand could see a large house. The open space now allowed Alcadio and Ferand to walk side by side. Ferand waved a finger ahead. “Is this the simple hovel of your physician?”

Alcadio grinned. “Yes, you may wonder. If not a noble, only the learned may live so well.”

Ferand appraised the house as they passed through the gate and into the grounds. “The physician must have a patron of means.”

Alcadio looked at Ferand. Ferand returned the look sheepishly.

“Yes, Ferand and the river is brimmed with water.”

As they approached the doorway, a small bald man in a leather apron stood up from a bench. He was holding a boot in one hand and a stiff brush in the other. His mouth opened in surprise. “Senor Alcadio! Monsieur is not aware...”

“Calm yourself, Simon, I have God’s news. Can you carry my presence to your master?”

Simon dropped the brush and carefully laid the boot on the bench. His head went from one to the other as he wiped his hands on the apron. “Yes, Senor, yes, wait, I must...”

Ferand’s eyes suddenly looked at the doorway. Alcadio glanced at his friend then turned, following his glance. De Chauliac was standing in the doorway.

Alcadio bowed. “Monsieur, forgive my surprise to your household.” Ferand, watching his friend, bowed but said nothing.

De Chauliac bowed. “You need no forgiveness, Alcadio. Your errand?”

“When last you invited my company, I was overpaid. I feel the debt and wish to clear my obligations.”

De Chauliac smiled. “Alcadio, you are a man of honor. I see no overpayment. You gave all, and more, of the knowledge I desired.”

Alcadio's face was solemn and set. As de Chauliac saw Alcadio's expression, he felt a chill. Alcadio took a deep breath and pulled his chin down. "Monsieur, the pestilence is in Avignon."

He looked at the two seamen. "Have you witnessed this? How long past? From whence did you just travel?"

Alcadio and Ferand looked at each other. Alcadio blurted, "Yes, physician, it progresses as we speak." Ferand put his hand on Alcadio's arm and looked at De Chauliac. "Physician, on the river bankment. No doubt brought from the south in a barque du Rhone. My cargo may have carried its foul air. My eyes suffered the sight of black eggs on the body of my own seaman, Pietro. How long? The length of our walk to your door."

De Chauliac shivered and straightened; his eyes widened and he held his hand out to Simon. "Simon the boot brush." He took the brush from Simon's shaking hand and began to slowly look over the two men. He stepped forward. Alcadio stepped back, puzzled, and de Chauliac held up his hand in reassurance. "Stay Alcadio, I but look to see if there be any objects amiss on your person."

Alcadio blinked, but he stood and straightened, holding his arms and hands level.

As de Chauliac searched, he occasionally brushed Alcadio's clothing. Finishing Alcadio, he turned to Ferand. "Senor?" "Signore Ferand, monsieur."

"Ah," de Chauliac waved the brush. "You object?"

Ferand smiled and held up his arms. "God guide your hand, monsieur." He looked at Alcadio with a smile. "and your brush."

As de Chauliac's eyes concentrated on Ferand, he glanced up at Alcadio. "I would ask another service from you senor, and your companion - if agreeable."

Alcadio looked at Ferand, raising his eyebrows. "Ask what you will, monsieur."

De Chauliac finished with Ferand and stood back, thinking. As he appraised the two men, he seemed to decide on his thought.

"Accept the comforts of my house for another day. You will have better care than any inn."

Alcadio was surprised; "A gracious offer, monsieur. You may recognize my puzzlement. The storm brews on the river landing. The hours of safety are few. What purpose may we serve in sailing so close to the rocks."

De Chauliac stared at them intensely. "You have seen the pestilence and its evil work. You both are books I may profit from. I am a physician, sworn to aid my fellow man. Your minds may save the lives of many. I would learn from you, that I may gain weapons with which to fight."

Alcadio considered, his sunburned face hard and grim. He shivered and nodded at the physician then addressed his friend. "Ferand, we need time to arrange a departure. What do you answer to this?"

Ferand stroked his chin. Dropping his hand he looked at the clouds, judging the wind direction. "If this weather be trusted, we may be blessed by God. We roll our own bones, with a long chance, should we turn south by southwest. The wind is clean for now and, on my mother's rosary, I'll vow it will hold for two days."

Alcadio nodded in agreement. "I also would so wager, Ferand. But we must face our fate in two days time. To take a cargo north under oar would be death."

Ferand considered then faced de Chauliac. "Physician, we cannot stay without the assurance of two good horses on the second morning."

De Chauliac pursed his lips and began to pace as he thought. The seamen watched him. After a few minutes, he stopped. "I shall so assure you both."

Ferand stared hard. "Will you swear this on the blood of the Savior."

De Chauliac nodded. "On my oath, Ferand."

The Papal Palace Avignon

As the door opened and the sound of steps broke his sleep, Clement rose groggily and rested on one elbow. "Marceau, you know well enough not to disturb our person after midday meal."

Marceau bowed. "Forgive my intrusion, your Holiness; Monsieur de Chauliac insists. He vows you would be angered at any delay." Clement turned on his couch and slid his feet into his soft apartment shoes. He brushed invisible specks from his robe and straightened his surplice as he stood up. Taking a long breath, he walked to his receiving table and waved his hand at Marceau as he sat. "Show him to me Marceau and pray his anticipations are true." Marceau, hid a wry smile, bowed and went back to the door. Clement gazed at the wall and blinked; trying to clear his mind and refocus his eyes.

"Monsieur de Chauliac, Holiness." Marceau stood to the side of the doorway and de Chauliac rushed into the room and bowed.

"Holiness, forgive my intrusion."

Clement looked up with an expression of exasperation. "I shall wait on my good nature until you have explained, physician."

De Chauliac's eyes flickered. Regaining his composure, he leaned forward earnestly. "Holiness, the pestilence has arrived in Avignon. Already a number of porters and boatmen lie dead on the river docks."

Clement's head jerked up to stare at de Chauliac. "You have seen this?"

"No, Holiness. I came to prepare you as I travel to witness what I may."

"NO...Guy, do not continue. You are needed by God and the Church; I will not permit that you risk your person in the foul air. Attend now - from whence did the tidings reach you?"

"Seamen from the south came to me. I have an acquaintance to support my trust."

Clement was staring at the floor; deep in thought. He appraised de Chauliac and decided that the physician would be discerning. The tale was true then. He held his lower lip in his teeth, then leaned back and spoke to the ceiling. "We must prepare. Have you the physick of the Greek?"

"There are two, Holiness. I have prepared but one. The other is fermenting according to instructions."

Clement looked puzzled. "How do they differ, Guy?"

"I know not, Holiness. The Greek specifies one should be administered when the indications evidence themselves."

"And the other?"

De Chauliac looked confused and self-conscious. "On my faith, Holiness. The Greek writes that the other be taken on news of the advance of pestilence. I wonder at the translation."

"News of pestilence? I wonder also. The translator?"

"Your own, Holiness, Aristo of Ithaki."

Clement shook his head. "Then it must be so, old Aristo is a Greek of fine learning. The text may be doubted - not he."

De Chauliac bowed. "As you say, Holiness."

Clement stood and placed both his hands on the table. His face grim, his lips pressed together, he leaned toward de Chauliac. "You have your news, Guy. The pestilence advances. Waste no more of God's time. Return to your labors. You must hurry the physick to readiness and bring it to me."

De Chauliac stepped back, horrified. "Holiness! But if it be harmful."

With a sarcastic smile, Clement slowly sat back in the chair. "Have you, then, a more sure shield for your Pope?"

"I trust God to save his vicar on earth, Holiness."

"I trust God also, Guy. I trust He provided a Greek physick, unknown for a millennium, to be of service, with death walking to our door. Leave us and stay within your own walls til the physick is prepared."

De Chauliac bowed. Turning slowly his thoughts were scattered. How to avoid the Pope's demand? Could the Greek potion be poison? And if it pushed his Holiness into the grave?

Marceau watched de Chauliac pass through the door. The physician was so deep in thought he was stopped by the corridor wall before, looking up and around, he turned to the stairs. Still holding the door, Marceau looked at Clement, puzzled.

"Yes, Marceau, you may well question. The pestilence has been at its work here in Avignon. You must stay within the palace. Your good health is the demand of your Pope."

—####—

Giuseppe

Giuseppe walked around the old wall. *Through the city streets? Ferand would avoid that. Where would he guide himself? North by Northeast, into the wind. Ferand was old in navigation; he would want the bad air behind him.* He looked at the sky as he walked. *High mare's tails, a change ahead but some few days yet.* A group of Nuns passed and he blessed himself. *Should I announce death's air at the river? Nay, they would hurry all the sooner to bring God's mercy to the drunken knaves dying in the river inns,* he grinned to himself, *with the cup still in their hands. Better to be in eternal peace, than eternally nursing their aching broken bodies.*

Giuseppe's eyes were everywhere; his head turning from left to right and up at the walls and towers of the palaces and monasteries. *The Templars, groaning under the weight of the wealth they gathered in the Holy Lands. The Dominicans, a larger presence than the Templars. Were they not the proselytizers of poverty? There ahead, between two Benedictine nunneries, Austins, Cistercians and Carmelites. The Franciscans down to the Southeast and outside the wall. A puzzlement - how many nunneries there were.* Giuseppe stepped aside and stood as a cart and two horsemen rode past to the river landing. As he turned to resume his walk, he saw the Synagogue of the Jews and the ghetto beside. *A fair place where all have a place, I'll credit that,* he thought.

As he approached the end of the old Roman wall by the palace of the Commune he gained on an old pilgrim. The pilgrim's staff had two pouches swinging from its iron hook and one fell to the ground.

Giuseppe shouted, "Hold man, you lose your day's meat."

The old man stopped and turned as Giuseppe picked up the leather bag and pulled the drawstring tight. The leather thong was frayed. The pilgrim held the staff end on the ground and lowered it to Giuseppe. Giuseppe took a leather lace from his own sleeve and added it to the pouch string. Then he tied the pouch back to the iron hook as the man held it still.

As Giuseppe finished, the old man raised the staff and, in a surprisingly strong voice, said, "I meant to use that hook on your arm, good sir. God be thanked my time has slowed so much."

Giuseppe grinned, as he towered over the pilgrim. *I quiver with fear,* he thought. Then he noticed the pilgrim's belt; it held a sword. *Ah, perhaps I overgrow my confidence. This man is an aged knight. His tricks may have taught me caution.* He bowed. "Forgive my hasty approach good knight. I thought only of the loss of your goods."

The old knight returned the bow. "And may God dull my suspicions of men. Your example is a lesson." Giuseppe pointed up the road. "I seek two men, Sir Knight; commoners and seamen. They would have leather surcoats and no cloaks; have they passed you?"

The knight's tone was sarcastic, "Many passed me. Two, such as you describe, some time past. They turned toward the Hospitaliers a hundred paces back." He pointed behind Giuseppe.

Giuseppe's head followed the knight's direction, then facing the old man, he bowed. "God's speed, and my thanks, be with you on your journey."

Giuseppe turned and quickening his steps, walked back to the side road. *I may yet overtake them,* he thought. He slowly realized he must find Ferand this day. If he could not, he would be forced to walk north with little hope of outpacing the pestilence. He shivered at the grim truth; no amount of great strength would stay death should the foul air reach him. As he turned onto the road the old man had shown him, he stopped to take his bearings.

De Chauliac was so lost in thought, he was unaware of his surroundings. As he walked to his home, he wrestled with the multitude of interconnected puzzles. *How to know if the Greek's potion was safe. And then, how to know if the Greek's potion would be of any effect. Yes, he could take it himself. But his Holiness was correct in one regard. If he, de Chauliac, was incapacitated or dead, he would be of no use to anyone. His Holiness was a great responsibility - and burden. He dare not risk himself. How to overcome the doubt?*

As he mused, walking the path on his unconscious memory, he was not in time to stop himself as he collided with Giuseppe.

De Chauliac's cloak slid to the ground as the clasp brooch was shaken loose. Giuseppe turned. He felt the collision but his bulk was such, even his balance was unaffected. De Chauliac had rebounded and fallen to the ground. Giuseppe, reached down and picked up the cloak and brooch, he held out his hand. "God grant you are not injured, good sir. I am a hard object to strike unaware."

De Chauliac looked up at the enormous man over him and smiled. "I see the truth of that; would I had seen so earlier."

He took Giuseppe's open hand as Giuseppe helped him to his feet. Giuseppe held up the beautifully woven cloak and shook and brushed the dust from it. "A fine cloth, fit for a nobleman." He handed the cloak to de Chauliac. De Chauliac took the cloak, noticing Giuseppe's hands were twice the size of his own. He looked up. "No, not a nobleman, a physician and a commoner as yourself."

Giuseppe grinned. "Not as myself, physician, I might exert myself a year to have such a cloak. And this besides."

He handed de Chauliac the brooch, as de Chauliac swung the cloak over his shoulders.

De Chauliac pinned the cloak in place and he looked at Giuseppe carefully. "Are you a porter, good man?"

"Nay, a seaman, sir, but a boatsman these days." He nodded at the river.

De Chauliac took the chance. "Do you then have the acquaintance of a Ferand or, perhaps, an Alcadio?"

"Giuseppe's faced cleared and brightened. "I do so, sir; I am in search of Ferand. Do you know his whereabouts?"

De Chauliac looked at Giuseppe carefully. He could see no sign of fever in his eyes or moisture on his forehead. He smiled, extended his arm with an open hand; inviting Giuseppe to walk with him. "He stays with me. Come, we shall reunite you."

Giuseppe paused and frowned. "Ah, monsieur physician, have you conversed with my friend?"

De Chauliac looked up at the huge man from the corners of his eyes. He waited until a Friar passed by and, lowering his voice, he said quietly, "I am aware of the pestilence good man. We must needs quicken our pace. I would not frighten fellow travelers."

Giuseppe turned and walked beside the physician. "Have you no fear of myself, monsieur?"

De Chauliac was striding as far as his legs would stretch, still Giuseppe took one step to de Chauliac's two.

"What may I permit myself? You have looked into my eyes. We are both in clear air." He shrugged. "We must leave ourselves in God's hands."

Giuseppe nodded sadly. "As you say monsieur. Still I would use the hands God gave to me. Are they not the tips of His fingers?"

De Chauliac looked up as he walked. How strange, he thought, much the same view as His Holiness spoke this same day.

—####—

An Inn, Avignon

Michel and Gerard leaned on the rough wooden table, opposite each other. Michel waved the glass cup in his hand. "You see, real glass. An orderly custom frequents this inn," he laughed, "how else would they dare such delicate wares?" He set his cup down on the table. "I know you sought me as an old friend, Gerard. Was that the only reason?"

Gerard smiled and sipped his wine. Setting his cup down, he cocked his head. "I pray you do not doubt my affection for you Michel. I could not travel without your knowledge."

Michel nodded and took another drink. "Do not concern yourself; I have full confidence. The question remains in the air between us. How are you to make such a journey without your own good horse?"

"Ah, I see. Your mind never walks far from your horses, Michel." Michel grinned and spluttered. "God stunt your wit, Gerard; you have cost me a good swallow." Michel took a cloth from his belt and looking at it critically, wiped the wine from his chin. As he wiped his tunic, he looked up through his eyebrows. "So you have a good animal? Say so and I will call you a liar."

Gerard sighed and leaned on the table. "No, Michel, I do not. I have coins enough and trust to find choices enough."

Michel leaned back. "Fagh! You may ride well but you are as poor a judge of horseflesh as I am a judge of women. My conscience would prick me all my days, should I let you care for yourself."

Michel shifted in his chair. "You should know, the Cardinal's stables are too well stocked. I have been commanded to sell off some number of fine riding horses - not the cart or millstone pullers - mind. You may have choices enough indeed; and for a fair price. To the point Gerard, I will be sure they are what they are said to be."

Gerard looked at Michel and thought, *God's hand again, what better than the man before me. At the time most needed, my friendship pays more than any could imagine.*

Michel could read Gerard's thoughts on his face. "Say nothing good friend. You will return the boon and soon enough." He turned and looked for a serving wench. "Another cup, Gerard, and I would hear of your journey to the strange land of Hibernia."

—####—

The House of Guy de Chauliac

"...as I fended off the miller, I chanced to look to Giuseppe. He was quietly leaning his back against the wall, his cup still in his hand."

"But the miller's friend?"

Ferand held up his hand. "Was behind Giuseppe, flattened on the stones, still standing! I looked hard, my mouth open. I took a few paces to look aside," Ferand acted out the scene, "I thought Giuseppe might need be warned of a knife. When I could see behind Giuseppe, the poor small man - small man! - he was the size of any of us," he pointed at himself, Alcadio and de Chauliac, "was so held, his arms were frozen helplessly."

Giuseppe looked self-conscious. He held up his glass to Ferand. "And so, did you come to watch him, that I might move - no. You took a drink from the table and toasted me instead."

Ferand laughed. "You had no need of aid, when you stepped away, he collapsed as a knob of old rags."

"God's luck," said Giuseppe.

Simon had stood in the doorway, listening to the tale, holding a pitcher of wine. He laughed along with all there and then came over to the table and refilled the cups.

De Chauliac leaned his chair back and held his cup for Simon. He grinned at Simon. "Come Simon, your sense of duty does you credit; find a cup and have a drink with good company." He waved at the men around the table. Simon pulled a cup from under his tunic. "I had hopes, master."

De Chauliac laughed as Simon filled his cup and took a sip, and turned back to the table. He looked at his guests, smiling. *I like these men,* he thought. *They are rough, but clean. They brook no pretensions and have no fear.* Then his face turned solemn. *Except of the pestilence; God help us all.*

Alcadio and Ferand were reminding each other of old stories, laughing and slapping each other and the table. Then Alcadio glanced at de Chauliac and saw his face. His laughter faded. Ferand, following Alcadio's look, turned to de Chauliac, puzzled. "What foul weather disturbed your thoughts, physician?"

De Chauliac smiled sadly and let his chair down to the floor. "Please excuse my rudeness and continue." He waved at Ferand. "I allowed myself distractions that have no place in such a time and such a company."

The men nodded in appreciation of the grace of de Chauliac's answer, but the cheerful spirit had gone. Alcadio looked into his cup and then at the physician. "You thought of the death all our thoughts avoid." He swept his hand around the table.

"Since you tax me with it, Alcadio, I admit it. I am a physician. I live with death in my trade."

Ferand smiled grimly. "Not such a spectre as this, I vow."

De Chauliac returned Ferand's look. "No, not such as this. My thoughts are troubled. They are not of death but brought to the boil by its presence."

The seamen looked at each other, puzzled.

Giuseppe spoke first. "His Holiness is afraid and demands you see to his safety?"

De Chauliac stared. "Your arrow is true to the mark Giuseppe, but you could not know how I am placed. No choice presents a safe course."

Alcadio slapped Ferand's arm with the back of hand. "A storm Ferand. Your ship to sea and into its teeth or stay in the cove and pray not to be driven on the rocks." Ferand glanced at Alcadio and nodded. Then he looked at De Chauliac. "Expose your thoughts to us. We may not be learned in the craft, but here are three good minds. We may not be the edge to cut the knot, but whetstones to sharpen your own blade."

De Chauliac held his cup in both hands. He took a sip, then set it down and turned it on the table with his finger. As he raised his head, he smiled. "A fine offer and your knowledge of the world may be more to the task than the college of Paris."

He told them of the Greek codex, the potions and the Pope's determination to take it. Then he took a long drink. "You may tell my thoughts. I dare not swallow the potion myself, lest it be harmful. I dare not allow His Holiness the potion." He leaned back and looked at the ceiling. Then he lowered his head and looked from one to the other. "And, to close the box, I dare not risk to leave the potion unused."

A silence fell as each in turn thought and slowly sipped his wine. Ferand looked into the air and said, "You do not trust this Greek?"

De Chauliac thought then lifted his cup to Ferand. "He is not a Christian. Does God provide such blessings from a pagan? But no, it is not the absence of a trust or my faith. I wonder at my own failings. Is this potion matched to the pestilence or some eastern scourge I know not."

Alcadio pointed at De Chauliac. "Ah, when first you called for me. You sought to make a match - my memory against the words of the Greek."

De Chauliac nodded. "Yes, you had seen this death. I hoped to confirm my judgment."

Giuseppe frowned. "Was the match made?"

De Chauliac looked uncertain. "It seemed thus to me. Am I so infallible? All my reputations say this. In the quiet of my own mind, I have doubt."

"As do we all," said Alcadio.

Ferand spoke as if to himself. "A potion swallowed upon news of the advance of the pestilence. How can the Greek effect a cure before the malady arrives?"

De Chauliac watched Ferand. "This question would vex the intellect of Aquinas, Ferand. Would that God gifted me with the wits of that man."

Ferand chuckled. "I am encouraged in my admiration of your talent, monsieur. Were you to vaunt your knowledge to us all - as some present a relic - I would trumpet that Avignon throw your potion in the Rhone."

De Chauliac flushed, lowering and shaking his head. "You have a tongue, Ferand."

Ferand grinned. "As to the deed..."

De Chauliac frowned "Deed?"

Ferand looked to the others. "Is this not truth? 'In what ways does our fine friend act' is the task we set ourselves upon."

Alcadio and Giuseppe nodded. Giuseppe looked at Ferand. "How do you say?"

Ferand turned to de Chauliac and pointed his thumb at his own chest. "I shall swallow your Greek's potion." He lifted his cup. "I swallowed your potion this night; God grant the one is as good to me as the other."

De Chauliac, his mouth open, stared. His face was a mixture of surprise, relief and concern. Alcadio watched the physician closely, then raised his cup. "Ferand leads well, I have no want of courage. I shall also taste your potion, monsieur. The chance of the potion against the air of death is a worthy wager."

Giuseppe raised his cup. "The pestilence followed from Sicily to Genoa to Marseilles to Avignon. I weary of the chase. What more may I ask of God than to join my companions."

De Chauliac leaned toward them. "I entreat you to reconsider; you may all be far to the North in two days."

Alcadio snorted, "Spare yourself, monsieur. We are not men to talk our deeds to improve our height. The moment of death could be delayed, as you say. Better to wager from this strong and pleasant room, than throw the chance away to purchase a few more days."

Giuseppe hunched over toward De Chauliac. "What does the Greek say?"

Alcadio echoed, "Yes truly, does he offer us safe passage?"

Ferand was sipping from his cup. He set his cup down and turned in his chair.

"Mmmm, set aside your fear monsieur, we'll not tax you on it. Say just what the Greek did scratch on the page."

De Chauliac looked up, gathering his memory. He took a sip then rested his elbows on the table; the cup in both hands. "He begins telling of a fearful pestilence of centuries past. Centuries before his time - mark that. He places a scene in your mind; a scene from Hell."

Ferand mumbled, "Marseille was a scene from Hell." Giuseppe nodded, silent.

De Chauliac went on. "The Greek's eyes saw all the ones who died appeared the same, first hot with fever, then black eggs in the groin and armpits. Last, when death was on their face, splashes of black and purple in the skin. And blood, urine, vomit - even the breath - foul beyond enduring."

Alcadio looked at Giuseppe and Ferand. "This was as we saw. The Greek may have as well walked among the Genoese; may their souls rest in God."

Ferand nodded to the physician, "and then?"

"He tells of a great physician - a god - who took pity on the Greeks. He gave them the makings of two potions - physicks. To stop the death of this curse. The first to take at first sight of the black eggs or smell of its foul perfume."

"The other?"

"The other taken on news of its arrival."

Ferand sat back and sipped his wine; with a wry smile he looked around at the others. "You hear, it may so fall we needs must swallow *two* potions." He lifted his cup. "I would sooner drink from this flask." Alcadio laughed. "Between draughts of Greek elixir - to freshen my mouth."

Ferand laughed in return. "That we may better relish the second and discern the subtle differences."

De Chauliac smiled. *These men know the way to settle the fears in the mind,* he thought, *I should be taught from their example.* They stopped laughing and faced him. Giuseppe said, "Is that the end, monsieur?"

De Chauliac shook his head. "No, the Greek..." he paused and smiled sadly with his eyes, "vows no man shall die that has the potion in the proper time."

"Proper time?" said Giuseppe, looking at the others, "I cannot grasp the meaning."

Ferand looked at Giuseppe grimly. "Soon enough, Giuseppe, soon enough."

De Chauliac nodded.

Giuseppe's eyes went from one to the other. "How to tell?"

De Chauliac sighed, "We cannot."

Chapter 25: Where is the Book?

"Sir?"

"yes, Robert."

"Jimmy has called again; his third call in as many days. I think he is growing more and more impatient."

The old man chuckled. "Of course he's impatient, Robert. Surely you expected that; I did."

"Yes, sir. Could he become dangerous?"

"I suppose he might in some sense but he isn't stupid. He realizes we are the key to the solution."

"Solution?"

"Oh yes, where is the book. Or, more to Jimmy's mind, where is the $250,000."

"Yes sir, I see."

"I apologize Robert. I have kept you out of my thoughts. I have a new factor in the problem."

"Sir?"

"Mr. Cash."

The old man placed his book on the table and leaned back in his chair.

"It would be simple to give Mr. Cash to Jimmy. Although, I suspect Jimmy would have more trouble there than he might expect. The difficulty I face, now, is that I rather like and even admire Mr. Cash. I cannot bring myself to expose him to Jimmy."

"You expect Jimmy would do him some harm."

"Perhaps, but, Robert, there may more risk than that; Mr. Cash may do Jimmy some harm. It would produce some noise and that noise could very well reach here; to our quiet room."

"How, sir?"

"I think I read Mr. Cash well enough. He would connect Jimmy's sudden appearance to me. After he disposed of Jimmy, of course."

"Mr. Cash seemed a very pleasant civilized man, sir."

"Oh he is, and more than self-sufficient, Robert. I saw a few glimpses of his mental edge in our conversation. He tested me Robert; and, so well and so smoothly, I was completely unaware; until I thought about it later. I am certain he has the physical skill and the mental wiles to be more than a match for Jimmy."

"What should I do, sir?"

"Find out what you can about Mr. Cash, Robert. Quietly of course. You should start with your contacts in Ireland. His accent is fresh. Do not confine your research to the usual facts. I wish to know what sort of man he is; most importantly, can he be trusted."

"Yes sir." Robert turned to leave.

"And Robert?"

"Sir?"

"Pursue this as quickly as you can; we need to defuse Jimmy."

"Yes sir."

—####—

"Sir?" The butler walked into the room and stood behind the old man's chair.

"Yes Robert." Robert walked around the chair and stood to the side. He was carrying a large stack of papers and photographs in a folder.

"I have a, rather lengthy, report from Liam."

"Dublin Liam; what does he tell us?"

Robert opened the folder and looked at a hand written sheet on top.

"I have prepared a rough synopsis, sir. Mr. Cash is a detective."

"Interesting, we may have surmised as much ourselves."

"Yes sir, he is a very good detective and very much admired and respected."

"Good, good; go on."

"He is in his fifties; a widower and completely inactive since his wife passed away. His sister lives here, in Cincinnati."

"Wait a moment, Robert. When did his wife pass away?"

"Umm, a little over three years ago, sir."

"Long time to be unoccupied; I would assume his grief dampened his energy."

"Yes sir. Particularly since her death was premature and violent."

The old man started and looked up at Robert. Robert looked up from the documents.

"Does Liam tell us what happened?"

Robert looked through the papers while he spoke. "Yes sir and it appears you were correct in your appraisal of Mr. Cash."

He found the paper he was looking for and began to read.

"The couple were surprised returning from a restaurant dinner. The time was shortly after ten in the evening. There were two criminals associated with an English organization. They opened fire on the Cash's."

"Good Lord and Mrs. Cash was killed?"

"Yes sir and both of the gunmen." The old man looked up.

"Wait Robert. Who killed the criminals?"

"Mr. Cash sir."

"Indeed! *two* of them - in the dark?"

"Yes sir, with a pistol at a distance of approximately thirty yards."

The old man and Robert stared at each other. Then the old man shook his head.

"Robert, I'd rather not be one of our Mr. Cash's opponents."

"Nor I, sir. Shall I go on?"

“Ah...one moment; does Liam remark on this?”

Robert turned over two pages. “Yes sir, he notes that Mr. Cash has a very cool head and is a superb marksman. He also comments that the two gunmen were, doubtless, uninformed on this point.”

“They were painfully disappointed, I would think - however briefly.”

Robert smiled. “Yes sir.”

The old man thought for a few minutes. Robert waited. Finally, the old man looked up.

“Robert, I think I would like to see Mr. Cash again.”

“Yes sir, I could arrange it for tomorrow.”

“No, Robert; thank you, but I cannot request such a meeting without very good cause. Remember he is a detective. His mind lives in suspicion. He may well come to the conclusion that I am responsible for his possession of the book. Although I may take him into my confidence; I want to be confident in him before doing so.”

Robert was startled. “Take him into your confidence?...sir?”

“Yes, I have thought on this since Mr. Cash left. As the matter stands I feel I have no choice.”

“I’m sorry sir, I don’t understand.”

“Think about it for a moment. There are only two paths available to me. One is to tell Jimmy about Mr. Cash. If I make that choice, I invite spotlights shining from God knows where. It would be likely they would reach me. Either Jimmy would produce the disruption or Mr. Cash. After what we have learned, surely we would expect Mr. Cash to follow up and follow through.”

Robert blinked. “I see, sir. The other choice would be to tell Mr. Cash your situation and, presumably warn him about Jimmy. But could you, ah, misinform Mr. Cash and Jimmy and let it go away?”

“I don’t think it will go away, Robert. Mr. Cash is obviously curious and determined. On the other side, we both know Jimmy is not likely to just quietly leave Cincinnati without his $250,000."

"Indeed, sir, highly unlikely."

—####—

Jimmy hung up the phone and looked at Jock. Jock got up and walked over to him.

"Well?"

Jimmy shook his head.

"Ah, same old shit. The butler grabs all the calls."

"And?"

"'Thank you for calling, sir. I'll be sure to give him the message'."

"So you think he's stalling us."

"That's too simple Jock." Jimmy paced pulling on his ear and thinking. Then he stopped and faced Jock. "You know, it may be a good sign, not a bad one."

"Blather."

"No, really. If nothing had happened. No action at all. I think he'd just say that. 'Sorry Jimmy, nothing's turned up so far; be patient; give it time - blah blah'. But I'm getting nothing, right? I think something's shak'n and he's close."

"Hope you're right. We can't idle 'round here forever."

"It's ok, Jock. I'll keep giving the old man's butler his wake up call. If it lasts much longer, I'll drop in again to fix his refrigerator. If I smell there's no effort, we'll move on it ourselves. We found the old man - maybe we can find this guy, too. Either way, I'm antsy myself, we'll do something - count on it."

Jock looked tired and disgruntled.

"Damn Jimmy, I do and I have been - for too long. Steve's driving me round the bend. Whatever you want to do, give Steve something now. I need him off on a works project and well away from me."

Jimmy looked up at Jock and his face set.

"You want Steve to do something? Well, you'll do it, too and you'll keep your ass under control.

I'll tell you what, you and Steve want to keep checking the old man? OK, here's the deal, stake him out."

"What?"

"You heard - you and Steve get your butts over and park where you can watch the old man's front door. Take a pad and pen with you."

Jimmy stood up and looked into Jock's face.

"I think you're right and you need an occupation. I want to know what cars and what people are going in the old man's front door between six in the morning and - let's say - eight at night - every damn day."

"Why do I have to go?"

"Because I don't trust Steve to write it down; never mind get it right."

"Well enough. I'll go find Steve. It'll give me chance to catch up on my reading."

Jimmy grinned. "It's important Jock. You may well find out everything we need; so keep your eyes open."

"Yah, like the lallan in the tweeds that took the book."

Jimmy looked up quickly and frowned. "Listen close, if you do see anyone that you think is that guy, you sit tight - don't do a damn thing. Got it?"

"I could cobble him and why the hell not?"

"First, he may not be the right man and you'd blow everything. Second, he might cobble you, mate. That'd be good. I get a call to bail you out of the justice center or pick you up at a hospital. Jimmy paused and stared at Jock.

"Now get this - if I did get a call like that, I'd let you rot."

" Ah right, right; I'll not touch a sweet hair on anyone."

"Good, I'll see you later tonight."

Jock walked out and Jimmy sat on the couch, thinking.

He's right and this's a good move. Even so, I should go tweak the old man. I need to goose some action here. The guys are getting wound up and that's not good. I wonder if I should have insisted Jock go along. He's smart enough to be dangerous and he might get Steve hopped up. Ah shit, don't even think about it; just get moving.

Chapter 26: Something is Wrong

Seamus sat on the porch sipping his beer. Something was wrong, he knew that. What he didn't know was what it was and why it was at him just now. *What's the worry? I found more than I wanted to know about the book. I know where it came from...ah, originally... at any rate. All the grist me mill could grind and the mill wouldn't grind. T'was as if it stuck on a stone and the wheel wouldn't turn until it was pulled out.*

P.J. drove into the driveway, waved and disappeared past the side of the house. A few minutes later he walked around the end of the porch. "And how's my favorite brother-in-law this fine day?"

"Cheers P.J.; not so good; I'm stuck on something."

"Oh, well let me fetch some lubricant and well see if we can push you off."

Seamus smiled, "good on you. I'll be patient." P.J. went in the house and Seamus stared at the trees across the road. *They are beautiful, too bad I can't take them home with me.*

A few minutes later, P.J. came out and handed Seamus another beer. "So what's the problem?"

Seamus looked over at him. "Well that's it, you see, I don't really know. Something odd or wrong is stuck in my head. Something I can't identify."

"I've been there before."

"As have I. 'Tis a good sign, usually. It points to a break in the game. But this is a stile I can't get over."

"So no way forward? Is that the way?"

"No way forward is never new; this has my coat tails and won't let me go the way I clearly see before me."

"So stop."

"Ah yes, let it all come to rest."

"Best, sounds like the only choice you have."

"You're a wise man P.J.; I've always done that before. I suppose I'm a bit long out of harness."

P.J. took a sip then turned to Seamus.

"Wait a minute, when did this start?"

"A day or so back."

"What was that day?"

"The day Maeve and I went over to the see the millionaire." Seamus froze then looked up at the porch ceiling. *Of course! It had to be something about the talk with the old man.* He looked at P.J. "Now you've ruined it. Now I'll be wracking my head on that talk. How am I to let it rest?"

"Sorry Seamus."

"You're fine, P.J. I have more than I started with."

P.J. stood up and walked over to the porch rail. He turned and looked back at Seamus. "Maeve told me we're having Father Schmidt to dinner."

"So she says, tomorrow night. He called and asked about my trip. She put her nose right into it."

P.J. laughed, "She likes to entertain and he's a very interesting guest."

"Oh, I don't mind at all. It'll be good for me to go over it all. He is interesting and he may turn over something for me."

"You think so?"

"Oh yes, if he doesn't bring something fresh, he will likely help me turn to a spot I missed."

"OK, I follow. Like teaching a class to learn the material."

"Exactly right."

The next night, dinner was as much talking and joking as eating. Seamus and Father Schmidt had a good round of comparative religion and Maeve was, by turns, shocked and delighted. After dessert Maeve stood up.

"Alright, all of you out and into the front room. P.J. will bring in the coffee and I'll tidy up here. Now, not one word about the book until I'm there. I want to take it all in at first hand."

Father Schmidt and Seamus walked toward the lounge and Father Schmidt turned to P.J. as he was going to the kitchen. "Not Irish coffee? I was sort of looking forward to that."

P.J. chuckled. "You'll have it Father. Seamus?"

Seamus turned around. "Thank you, no I'd best not. I'll be dozing off."

After Seamus and Father Schmidt were sitting down chatting about the weather. P.J. came in with the coffee.

"Here we are. Father, yours has the cream on top. Weather? Is that all you two could think to talk about?"

Father Schmidt made a face. "Well, Maeve gave the orders. I'm being careful. I can't wait to hear what Seamus found out."

Seamus smiled. "I pray you won't doze off as I threatened to do. It is more than a bit cerebral Father."

"I like cerebral. I was trained for it but it's a natural inclination, anyway. That's why I chose the Jesuits."

P.J. shouted at the kitchen. "Maeve, what's keeping you. They've started."

Maeve appeared in the doorway waving a spoon. "Now what did I say?" she pointed the spoon, "P.J. regale everyone with some doings at the book shop."

P.J. grinned and looked at them. "Don't worry, I'll ignore that."

Father Schmidt sipped his coffee. Then looked over at Seamus.

"Well, Maeve gave you my message, right? About my friend's find in the Vatican Library? I should say, not found in the Vatican Library."

"Yes, she did. I have no more explanation than you, Father."

Father Schmidt shifted forward on the couch. "Well, we have reason to believe there were four books. They would be the original, yours, the one the monk did for the Pope and the last one...number four...which should be exactly like yours. Now, my friend tells me the only thing he found like any of them is an unbound fragment. How does that fit?"

Seamus sat back. "Well, in the absence of more knowledge there are only two possibilities. The first would be that the copy in the Vatican is all that was ever done for the Pope. That would leave us with two and half books to uncover. The other choice would be the fragment is more on top. That would make four and a half books together."

P.J. leaned forward. "But can we know which is which?"

Seamus looked at a spot on the ceiling. Then he took a sip of coffee.

"Father, did your Monsignor friend say if his fragment was Latin and Greek or just Greek."

"Oh, I thought of that. I asked specifically. He went through every page, it was all Greek."

"So then, it was the copy for the Pope or another partial copy, not part of this at all."

"Correct."

P.J. looked disappointed. "Doesn't tell us much."

Seamus laughed. "It, assuredly, does not. Still, we know there were two of the versions I have. There's not a change in that. As for the other, we cannot say."

P.J. grinned at Seamus. "Yes you can. Let's have the conjecture, Seamus. You're known to be good at that."

Father Schmidt put his coffee on the table and sat back.

"Come on Seamus, you are a detective."

Seamus grinned back and then sighed and nodded his assent.

"All right, here we are balancing probabilities against possibilities, as Sherlock would say.

We can dismiss the other version like the one I have, as the fragment has no Latin preface. We are left with the original and the copy intended for Pope Clement. It cannot be a fragment of the original, since the original was, undoubtedly, bound. It must be a fragment of the commission our monk was given or it could be a fragment of another commission separate and unrelated."

P.J. and Father Schmidt nodded and Seamus looked up, thinking.

"Why would the first be left incomplete? Even if our monk died, the Abbot would certainly assign another to finish the job.

Seamus looked at the doorway.

"Since Maeve still isn't with us, I'll hold back the fruits of my trip. Let's go on."

Father Schmidt interrupted. "Suppose the commission was completed and lost on the journey back to Avignon."

"Excellent Father. Let's pursue that. The bag with the finished copy and the original are lost at sea. The Pope is told of the accident."

P.J. was excited. "And then ordered another."

Seamus smiled at P.J. "Why?"

"What?"

"Why would he do that, P.J.? He gave explicit instructions that only one copy was to be produced. The good Pope Clement would assume that all was lost."

Father Schmidt clapped his hands. "Yes that's true, but we know he made more copies. How about the monk confessing that and the Abbot then tells the Pope."

Seamus leaned forward. "I shall presume you don't mean in the confessional Father."

Father Schmidt looked chagrined. "No no, he hears about the loss and tells the Abbot they can still save the day. That kind of thing."

"All right, let us follow that thought. Then why would the monk even bother with the preface. The need for his apology and explanations would no longer exist."

P.J. and Father Schmidt both frowned and sat back in their chairs. "Hmm, then what does explain it?"

Seamus held out his hand and started counting on his fingers. "First, it couldn't have been lost in shipment or, so far as was known, no version would have been available to sponsor our fragment.

Second, the surreptitious copies remained hidden or there would have been no need of a preface. What could be left?"

"They all dissolved over time." It was Maeve standing in the doorway. She walked in and sat down. Seamus looked up at Maeve.

"Very good Maeve. I believe you are partially correct. Unfortunately, this is, likely, a multipart answer. Let's start with the original book.

The original was old when my book was new. The original may not have stood another six hundred years or so. But what of the copy?"

Maeve blurted, "That was lost in shipment."

"Only the one?"

Maeve thought a minute. "Umm, yes."

Seamus shook his head. "No, I think they would have both survived. That is most probable. They were packaged together; you can trust that." Seamus held up his hand.

"Hold on. Now that Maeve is with us, I can introduce more information."

Everyone settled back and watched Seamus expectantly. Seamus looked from one to the other.

"The one point that would seem most significant is the one often overlooked. Why was the book copy commissioned?"

Father Schmidt looked confused. "But that was done all the time. To preserve the knowledge and to disseminate the knowledge, they copied any book as often as possible."

P.J. looked at him. "Then why only one copy Father?"

Maeve nodded. "And more, why send it all the way to Ireland from Avignon?"

Father Schmidt grinned. "OK, I bow to superior intellect."

Seamus chuckled. "Don't take it amiss, Father. You are completely correct - usually. This is a little out of way, I think. All of us here... couldn't know.

I was enlightened while in San Francisco. There is a small portion of the book with annotations in the margins. The notes are in Latin and by someone intensely interested in those few pages. The great minds I learned from during my visit, told me those pages were, likely, describing a cure for Bubonic plague."

Everyone stared in amazement. Father Schmidt spoke first.

"Good Lord above, Clement VI was the pontiff when the Black death first arrived."

P.J. was thinking, then he turned to Seamus. "So we should assume this was commissioned so as to have the cure?"

Seamus squinted. "We cannot be sure. The timing is unknown and the death toll in Avignon was extremely high. If this cure was available before the plague struck, it didn't work. Wait a bit, that's me going too far. It could have been a valid cure and was suppressed or otherwise not available in time."

Maeve pointed at Seamus. "What does your doctor believe or, again, what do you believe?"

"I'm happy to say, I have to plead ignorance. The good doctor Meg is more than convinced it was impossible that this...um...prescription... would have any effect at all."

P.J. stood up. "I'm for more coffee and since I interrupted, doesn't this take us away from the point? Why should this be a help in deducing," he winked at Seamus, "where the fragment came from?" He walked to the kitchen and over his shoulder he said, "keep talking I can hear you, Oh, anyone else for coffee?"

Seamus stood up. "I'll have a little more P.J. and... you're quite right. It does appear to take us from the point; it doesn't though. Think on it a while." He walked out behind P.J.

Maeve looked at Father Schmidt. "I don't see the relevance Father; do you?"

"Well, Seamus said the important issue was why the book was commissioned. Where does that fit in?"

Maeve frowned, "I suppose he meant 'to cure the plague'."

"So how would that explain the fragment?"

"Aagh, my brother enjoys being obtuse."

Father Schmidt grinned.

P.J. walked back with his coffee. "Have you two figured it out?"

"We have not and Father is being patient. I would like to wring his neck."

"Father Schmidt's?"

"No, Seamus'"

"Now Maeve."

Seamus walked into the room, stirring his coffee. "She's right P.J. I do enjoy leaving a gauntlet on the table."

"All well and good, Seamus, but no one is picking it up."

"Let me shatter the suspense then. How long do you suppose it might take to copy such a book?

P.J.?"

"Oh weeks and weeks."

"Maeve?"

"I have the advantage of the talking with you and Sam. It would have been many months."

"Father?"

"My understanding is that a work this large with the additional illustrations could have stretched over a year."

"Good on everyone. We all agree, a great long time. I would think it could well have been even more than a year. Why? Only one monk was allowed to do the work, remember? Far worse was the need to prepare the pages and bind the whole work. Then add the time to send it from Avignon and then back."

"But we know the monk had the time."

"No P.J. I don't trust that. Yes, he had the time to do his copies, but when?"

"I'm balancing the probabilities again. You see it seems, from our view today, certain that the commission wasn't ordered without reason. The reason would be the old Greek cure for plague. Why would the Pontiff order it unless he knew the plague was coming to him? So how much time does that give our patient monk? Not enough! - is my thought."

P.J. leaned his hand on his chin. "So he didn't have time to finish it?"

"Not finish it and send it back to Avignon before the plague arrived, no."

Maeve jumped up. "I have it. The Pope realized it wouldn't be back in time and sent for whatever he could have."

Father Schmidt slid to the edge of the couch. "Of course, and that is why it wasn't bound; there wasn't time."

"Precisely Father. We do still need one more detail to help support the conclusion."

"What's that?"

"Does the fragment contain the margin notes."

P.J. looked at Father Schmidt. "Of course, there'd be no reason without them."

Seamus smiled. "Now that we have the key, we can say so. Even at that they only serve to mark the passages that pertain to the plague cure. The good Clement or his physician would have known what pages would be needed without the notes, of course. He looked at Father Schmidt, you'll have to ask your friend the Monsignor, Father."

Father Schmidt was looking at his hands, deep in thought. He shook his head and looked up.

"No I won't. I asked him if the fragment had the Latin preface. He replied, 'no, the only Latin are some notes in the margins towards the end'."

Maeve sat down looking smug. "So that's that, we know how the fragment came to be."

Seamus smirked. "I won't recant, but we'll never really know. This is our best use of logic and conjecture. I'll wager it's the answer, he said in all humility."

P.J. grinned, "Humility indeed, Maeve had the answer."

Maeve looked at P.J. "Oh yes, he has this way, luv. Seamus had the answer before we sat. He led us to it. He'd rather we found it, than just tell us - no sport otherwise."

P.J. looked to Seamus, "Is that so?"

Seamus looked sheepish. "Fraid so, it's a good job this fragment didn't have...the...Latin...preface." Seamus froze and stared into space unseeing. Everyone looked at him. For a very long couple of minutes, no one spoke. Then Maeve leaned over and waved her hand in front of Seamus' eyes. "What is it now? Have you seized up then? I won't be taking care of you."

Seamus blinked and smiled. "Now Maeve, I just had a thought."

P.J. squinted and said, "What is it?"

"Sorry, P.J. I want to work it through a little. I may have a grip on that niggle we talked about yesterday."

"Ah, well I hope you loosen its grip on you."

"And I hope I don't lose my grip on it."

Chapter 27: Lies

The next morning Seamus blundered into the kitchen at eight o'clock. Maeve was at the table sipping coffee.

He looked at Maeve, "I know, I know, P.J. off to his labor camp and I'm just working my knees."

Maeve smiled, put down her cup and went to fetch Seamus a cup.

"You have your time to fit, at last. I would imagine it was the San Francisco visit"

Seamus sat down and Maeve dangled the cup on her finger. "You can pour your own wake up; I don't trust myself to mix it."

Seamus stood up and took the cup. As he poured his coffee, Maeve sat and looked at his back.

"So and what do you have churning in your mind today?"

"I need to thank you and the good Father Schmidt for last evening's revelry."

"It was a pleasant time."

"More so than you know. I tripped over the rock that blocked my path for a few days." He sat down and took his first sip. Maeve tilted her head. "What was that then?"

"I was stopped on a puzzle. Some wrong bit in the head. You must have had such yourself. Not knowing what it was but not thinking on anything else."

"But you say you tripped on it. You know what it is?"

"Yes, or so I think. It was the talk with the old man. Something he said that wasn't right. I didn't realize it was that talk until last night. Now I have to gather my wits and remember what struck me."

"Last night?"

"Mmm, and exactly what and when in the conversation."

"With the old man."

"Yes."

"You'd best finish the coffee first."

"Agreed and perhaps a little more."

Maeve smirked. "If I'm to find some entertainment in you I'll fetch your second cup."

"Bribery, why didn't I think of that before?"

He finished the cup and held it up to Maeve. Then rested his head on his hand.

"You look like you're the worse for drink and haven't had a drop."

"Good thing, I can't handle my drinks."

"As I remember, you can handle them all right; you can't keep them down."

"That too."

Maeve put the second coffee in front of Seamus and slid into her chair. "Take that a little more slowly or you'll have an upset stomach."

Seamus nodded and sipped. "What you don't know Maeve is that I lay awake, grinding the talk through in my head, until about three this morning."

"Ah, so that explains the look of illness and more than usual ugly face."

"And the same to you."

"And after all that, you don't have the answer?"

"I do but I can't be dead certain."

"So?"

"Sometime toward the middle of our chat, I found myself testing the old man. I didn't suspect him; I think it was reflexive habit."

"How did you test him?"

"I asked if he knew where I might have it repaired."

"It's in no need of repair."

"No, but I wanted to know if he would react to that."

"Did he?"

"He was quite amenable and suggested some local college."

"So, you wasted that one."

"Ah, but then I told him there were pages missing."

"You devil."

"It was years of this that prompted the thought, Maeve. I had no reason to wonder at all."

"It wasn't a polite way to speak to the poor old soul, all the same."

"Poor old soul? He could buy you and I and the rest of Kenmare, if he liked. Nevermind that, he has no sign of age, Maeve. His mind is as clear as air after a western gale and as strong as the gale itself."

"It's your case, Seamus. What did he reply?"

"That's it, he suggested the Vatican library to replace missing pages."

"Well he might, I would have said the same."

"As you said, but I said 'except for the preface' and he, I'm convinced of this, said, 'yes, except...for... the... preface'."

"Maeve stared at Seamus. "I don't understand. Why would that be odd? Its true enough. There would be no preface in the original. The old man had no way of knowing the original is lost."

"All correct, just as you put it. But, you see, he told me he had never read it. He mentioned early on he didn't read Latin or Greek."

"I still fail to see your point."

"Maeve, he couldn't know there would be no preface unless he had read the preface," he paused, "or someone told him what was in the preface. The preface is the only evidence anyone could have that this copy was different from the original book."

"Different in that no other copy would have the preface."

"That's it, Maeve."

"Doesn't seem so much."

"So you would think, but it means very much. The only explanation I can conjure up is - he has read the book or has had the preface read and explained to him. Something is not right about your poor old soul, Maeve."

"He may well have drifted off and was being agreeable."

Seamus sighed. "Regrettably, you could be correct. I don't believe that is the case. He is not senile or even a slow thinker, Maeve. He is very quick in his head."

"Now what would you do."

"Pay him another visit and sort it out."

"Oh, to be sure, something such as, 'hello again, I just remembered you lied to me and I'm here to say so'."

Seamus chuckled, leaned back and sipped his coffee. Then he leaned forward and rested his arm on the table. "Yes, you have grasped my dilemma. I must work out how to catch him out; without him catching me at it."

Maeve looked over her cup. "Fine, fine, and when you've done that, I'll take you over and wait in the car."

Seamus frowned and looked at Maeve. His face was hard and ernest. "Maeve, when that happens, be sure to lock the car doors."

"Whatever for?"

"It will strike you soon enough; so let me say it now. If my suspicions are true, the old man could very well be the man who sent the book to the sale."

Maeve's face went blank. "You feel this is dangerous?"

"Oh yes indeed, dear sister. I wasn't meant to have this book and those who were will want to find me."

Maeve suddenly looked frightened. "Mother Mary, the old man knows who you are!"

"And, by now, who you are and P.J. and Father Schmidt and Sam and, above all else, *where* we are Maeve."

"She stood up, "I should have all the doors and windows locked and barred."

"Now Maeve, I thought it through. Even supposing I'm right, if the old man was set to do me an injury, he would have so, then and there. I don't understand his game but he has one."

—####—

The butler walked into the study and stopped by the old man's chair.

The old man closed his book on his thumb and lifted his head. "Yes, Robert?"

""Sir, Mr. Cash has called and requested he pay us a visit."

"Ah, how convenient. Did he say if he had a reason?"

"No sir. In his words, he's 'calling your bluff' as to his intelligent conversation."

The old man chuckled. "I must admit, I like him. The fates are on my side, Robert. This removes any need to concoct a story to pull him back."

"Yes, sir. When would you like to schedule his arrival."

"I should think tomorrow morning at ten. That will give my courage and resolve time to build."

"You intend to enlighten him sir?"

"Yes, Robert, I think so. As I explained, I see no other course."

"I'm sorry, sir, I don't understand the value."

"Frankly Robert, there may not be any value; apart from easing my conscience. However, at the least, Mr. Cash will have reason to leave the premises and avoid Jimmy and his more dangerous associates."

"I see, this would prevent Mr. Cash's possible murder but what of yourself, sir? It worries me that you are left with no resolution for Jimmy."

The old man's face softened. "Thank you Robert. Your concern is appreciated. I do have a resolution for Jimmy; simply pay him the money and hope the transaction remains secret."

"Yes sir, a very difficult move in these days of technological law enforcement."

The old man sighed. "I know, Robert. I could very well get nabbed, as they say. I wouldn't be arrested though. I would be embarrassed."

"But sir..."

"No Robert, let's not continue in this vein. There will be time enough to wrestle with the problem when I must."

—####—

"Mr. Cash, sir."

Seamus walked into the study as Robert held the door. The old man was standing holding onto the back of his chair.

"Mr. Cash, an honest pleasure to see you again. Please have a seat. Robert would you mind staying for a moment?"

Seamus walked over to the chair and shook the old man's hand. Then he looked at Robert quizzically, nodded and sat down. The old man sat and nodded. "So, what brings you back? Surely, it isn't my scintillating conversation."

Seamus smiled. "You are quite wrong, sir. It is indeed your conversation that prompted my return." Seamus' eyes had a friendly glint but his smile turned sardonic.

The old man looked over his glasses. "Ah, I rather thought you were a little quick for me. What was it?"

"The book, of course."

The old man looked up remembering the previous talk. "Hmm, the damage you spoke of?"

"Yes and a little more."

The old man looked down. "I recommended Hebrew Union College and," he paused, "my memory says you claimed missing pages."

Seamus leaned forward and put his hands together. "Yes sir, that's right."

The old man's eyes looked up. "I believe I said you should go to the Vatican Library."

Seamus nodded, smiling. "Yes you did, and then?"

"You agreed with me."

"Yes I agreed, except..."

The old man looked up as he remembered. "Ah curses, except for the preface."

Seamus sat back. "There sir, you have it."

The old man shook his head. "I'm not as fast a thinker as I once was."

Seamus chuckled. "And a good thing, it helps the rest of us catch up to you."

The old man sat down and relaxed back in his chair. "So you found me out. What meaning can you derive from that."

Seamus took the implied challenge with good grace. Looking up at Robert, he stood up and walked around his chair. With his hands on the chair back, he leaned toward the old man.

"How long did you have the book in your possession?"

"The direct approach. Well, I think that's best. I will be completely candid with you Mr. Cash."

"Seamus."

"All right... with reservations... Seamus."

"How long sir?"

"Years and years, ah...Seamus."

Seamus grinned. "Good enough. Do you read Latin and Greek sir?"

"I read Latin, not Greek."

Seamus walked around his chair and sat down again. "You have read the preface, then."

"Oh yes, many times."

Seamus crossed his legs and leaned on his hand. "That was the conclusion I reached. Only then could you have known there would be no such preface in the Vatican."

The old man sighed. "Of course, now that I realize how I was tricked. Only someone who knew the contents of that preface could possibly know."

Seamus stood up again, walked over to the bookshelves, turned and looked back at the old man. "Were you about to tell me all this sir?"

"Yes Seamus, I was and a great deal more."

"I felt, rather than thought, you might. I would appreciate the 'great deal more' and I have a reward for that."

"A reward? I certainly have lost any interest in rewards, Seamus."

Seamus chuckled and walked up to the back of his chair. "No, I doubt you would have interest in the usual rewards. You see, I believe I have uncovered much about your book you do not know."

The old man leaned back and put his finger to his chin.

"Ah, now that reward piques my interest. Fair enough. You had better sit Seamus."

He looked around at Robert, "Robert, we come to the reason I wanted you present." Seamus sat down and glanced at Robert before focusing on the old man. "When you like sir."

"You are probably in some danger."

Seamus shifted in his chair. "Yes sir, I know."

"You do?"

"Oh yes, I assume that some other...ah...party, was the intended recipient of the book. They would most certainly want it. I am aware it is intrinsically valuable. So it follows..."

He let the word hang.

The old man smiled. "Very impressive Seamus, I expected no less. What you couldn't know is that they are young and criminal and potentially violent."

Seamus expression became serious. "Sir, how did you come to this position?"

The old man's face was sad. "I am paying today for the haste and indiscretion of my youth. Indiscretion! How poor a word. Stupidity, would be more accurate."

Seamus waved his hand. “Pass that, my youthful stupidity is more than up to any man.”

“Perhaps so, but you didn’t arrange a burglary.”

Seamus hands dropped to his knees and he leaned forward.

“The one I found, in 1920- something?”

“Yes.”

“This book was part of that; what of all the other priceless antiquities?”

The old man looked chagrined and looked up at Robert. “Robert?”

Robert glanced at the old man and then addressed Seamus. “As you are doubtless aware, sir, there are many wealthy collectors who may be approached, shall we say, discreetly.”

The old man interrupted and went on. “Some of these...ah...collectors, are actually public museums, Seamus.”

Seamus’ surprise showed in his expression. The old man continued.

“Oh yes, and at these levels, a fervor, almost a righteousness, excuses any ‘unknown’ source difficulties.”

Seamus put his hand to his mouth. “I understand. The public interest and preservation are above such concerns. Is that the way?”

“That’s about it Seamus.”

“Is that why you were, um, ‘indiscreet’?”

The old man grinned. “That is what I told myself. His face went solemn. “But it was a mistake and a crime, Seamus. I have since realized such mistakes have a price; however long it may be before the bill comes.”

Seamus was watching Robert as he looked down at the old man. It was obvious that Robert was more a friend than a servant. Not so surprising, he had probably been with the old man for decades. He frowned.

“Pardon me sir. I am not so quick as you may credit me. What is the connection to these young and dangerous?”

"Oh, my apologies. I had drifted into the assumption you knew everything. It is all too simple. The leader of this band is the son of the man who performed my burglary. "

"Lord bless me."

Seamus started to think and the old man watched him. A few minutes passed and suddenly, Seamus shook his head. "Sir, I can make a logical leap to what this all means. Correct me where I'm wrong. You saw the chance to give this young man the book and thus, rid yourself of the evidence. I do not know two important bits.

The first is why you felt the need to pass him the book.

The second is why you didn't dispose of this in the same way as all the other...ah...loot."

"The second question is easiest. I couldn't bear to part with it.

When I realized it was a problem, most of my former contacts had died or been placed in nursing homes." A resigned smile appeared slowly.

"The first bit was an accident. The young man, his name is Jimmy by the way, contacted me. He's a drug dealer, Seamus and he needed to launder a large sum of money."

"And you took the money."

"Yes, God help me and the rest you know."

Seamus nodded. "Now we arrive at the crux of it all sir. Umm, 'Jimmy' will want his money or its equivalent. And the book is now comfortably ensconced in my dresser drawer."

The old man looked tired. "I realize it is unfair, Seamus but could we just give Jimmy the book and be done with it?"

Seamus stood up and walked around behind his chair - pacing.

"Ah well sir. I don't believe you will want to when I finish giving you your reward."

"Is that so? Good grief, I had forgotten your reward."

"Well then, you already know that the book is of great value."

The old man blurted, "It's priceless."

"Yes, as a peculiarly rare manuscript of the middle ages. What you may not know is its contents may be even more valuable."

"This would be the portion in Greek. I am aware it is a Greek medical treatise of some sort."

"That's quite true, it is a Greek medical text. However, it is not one of the many known medical texts. It is almost certainly - um, I'd best come back to this - unique, I was about to say. It is, so I'm told, a Greek medical family's workbook. The knowledge is accumulated over many generations. I don't really know how many. Here is the most interesting part. A portion of the book contains a cure and a vaccination for Bubonic plague."

The old man was fascinated. "I know nothing about medicine Seamus. I thought the plague was long since gone."

"You would think so - I did; apparently not. There have been cases recorded, in the last few years, right here in the United States."

"But they no longer die of it."

"Yes they often do. More often because it isn't recognized soon enough. India has fought some major outbreaks and lost high numbers of people."

"All right, the cure is available, even if not administered promptly. The point you make is that there is no vaccination."

"Not as far as my doctor friend knows."

"Should we actually pursue this Greek potion? It seems a bit fantastic."

"Yes it does sir. Nevertheless, I would be uneasy in my conscience if I didn't try."

The old man thought for a second. "I think I would too, Seamus."

Seamus sat back and thought. *Lord, indeed, what if the Greek's potion actually did work - how? More to the point, how to find out... Nigel!! I have his e-mail address, it's worth a go.*

—####—

Maeve saw the door of the mansion open. She gathered her books and papers and, reaching around, put them on the back seat. As she saw Seamus walk out, she unlocked the car doors and waited. Seamus turned back to the butler and shook his hand. Then he walked down the steps towards the car. The butler stood and watched Seamus until he reached the car.

As Seamus opened the car door and slid onto the seat, the butler closed the door.

“What was that about?” She pointed at the mansion.

“What was what about?”

“The valet watched you all the way to the car. You’ve become quite chummy with this lot.”

Seamus grinned. “Yes I have. As to Robert, he was looking out for my back. You did have the doors locked, didn’t you?”

“Yes, I did.”

“Did you notice anyone or anything odd?”

“I did not.”

He sighed. “That’s a relief. Now I have a question. May I send an e-mail from your computer?"

"Yes, you can. I'll show when we get home."

"Oh goodie, let’s go home.”

When they got back Seamus followed Maeve into her office. She poked a few buttons.

"Here you are Seamus, put the address here." She clicked and Seamus said, "Hold on a minute and I'll get my address book."

He ran upstairs and came back with his address book. He opened it to the right page and gave it to Maeve.

"It’s right at the top, Nigel."

Maeve looked and keyed it in.

Then she got up.

"Have a chair Seamus and just type it in. I suppose you'll want me to tell you if he replies."

Seamus settles into the chair and as he looked at the screen he said, "That would be good Maeve and he will reply. This is right up his alley."

Maeve was curious.

"So, who is Nigel and how does that apply to your...umm...new life."

Seamus looked into space.

"Nigel is an old acquaintance of mine. When I first met him he was working for a large pharmaceutical firm. I think it may have been Glaxo. Some years later, I met him again. He and I had 'hit it off' so to speak. By then he was with the research labs at Porton Down."

Maeve looked slightly amazed.

" What does he do? For that matter what do they do at Porton Down?"

Seamus sighed.

"Well, I think he's a biochemist. But I'm really not sure. As to Porton Down. They are mostly trying to find ways to fend off terrorists with biological weapons. Between you and me, though, I think they may be working on some biological weapons of their own."

Maeve made a face.

"Eeww, thank you for that cheerful thought."

Seamus went into the kitchen, had a sandwich for lunch and went up to his nap.

Well, the ball is still in play, he thought.

Chapter 28: The Stakeout

Jock and Steve rushed through the door and slammed the door back against the wall.

Steve was yelling, "Jimmy!"

Jimmy jumped up.

"What the hell! Keep your voice down - What are you doing here?"

"We have big news."

"You're supposed to be watching the old man's house."

"That's it. We watched a guy go into the house and - swear to God Jimmy - he's gotta be the one we want!"

Jimmy looked at Jock, "Jock?"

"Ah think he's right, Jimmy. He was an old guy, but he had the jacket and cap."

"Like yours?"

"Too close to be a chance. It was a different color than mine, but Gladys said that."

Jimmy turned around rubbing his chin. "Shit, if you're right, we've got a real problem."

Steve almost shouted, "Whatta ya mean? Let's go grab the asshole and get our book!"

Jimmy looked at him hard. "Did you follow him?"

"Ah, no."

"Then where is it you're going, stupid?"

Jock mumbled, "We did see the car. Some skirt was driving it."

"Did you get the license number?"

Steve looked at Jock and Jock shook his head. "Umm, no," Steve said quietly.

Jock turned and shook his head. "Ah God damn it, why didn't I think of that."

Jimmy looked disgusted. “You two are a coupla idiots. You see the guy walk in and do you stay and wait and follow him? - noooo. You come racing over here and wake up my neighbors and their dogs. Jesus Christ! what morons.”

He walked over to the couch and slumped down. Then he looked up at them both.

“Well, maybe it's just as good. If you had followed him he’d probably have spotted you and called the cops. That would have been more of a mess. Besides, he may not be the right guy anyway.”

Steve blurted, “Ah Jimmy, he’s gotta be.”

“NO! - he doesn’t. There’s lottsa people with tweed jackets and caps. They’ve gotten very popular. Or haven’t you noticed?”

Jock looked tired. “So, you think it's just a coincidence, huh?”

Jimmy was thinking. He looked up at Jock. “How many visitors does the old man get?”

Steve turned around. “Shit, nobody ever goes there. What did we count Jock? three? four? all week?”

Jock glanced at Steve and then stared at Jimmy. “He’s right and the only people we saw were dressed in Armani suits and driving very classy cars.”

Jimmy pursed his lips. “So, this guy looked like just one of the unwashed, huh?”

“Well, not that bad. He wasn’t pushing a shopping basket. But he wasn’t stopping by from a museum or on his way to the Banker’s Club either.”

“OK guys, this may be just enough. I think it worked out right. I should be happy you’re both incompetents. You know what? I think he *was* the guy.”

The others stared at Jimmy. “Wha’?” “Say again?”

“You heard me. Not only that but I think the old man found him and he’s trying to get our book for us. I thought about this. Listen.

“Suppose you were the old man and you were trying to find and get the book back. If you had a brain,” he frowned as he looked at them, "you'd know that the best would be to just make up something. For instance, he might say to this guy, 'I heard you got this book and I collect them, how about selling it to me for...say, a thousand bucks'." The poor slob isn't likely to be an antique dealer is he? He'd figure he just won the lottery."

Jock was thinking. "Yes yes, I see where you're going. What's a grand to the old man. He could charge us that as a finder's fee."

Jimmy nodded. "Damn right, and I'd pay it too. What's that to the book?"

Steve looked hopeful, "so does this mean we can stop watching the place?"

Jimmy looked up and made a face. "Let me think about that." He thought for a few minutes and then stood up. "Yeah, I guess you can lay off for a little bit." He walked over to them, "but I think I'm going to drop in on the old man; just to see what's going on."

He waved at them, "OK get outta here. I've got things to do."

Jimmy walked over to the couch as Jock and Steve walked slowly to the door. They turned and looked sheepishly at Jimmy's back and Jock pulled the door closed. Jimmy turned and shook his head, then sat down putting his hands behind his head. He stared at the ceiling.

Maybe they were right. It looked that way but the important thing was - was he right? It sounded good - so what. Could the old man be pulling a fast one? Getting the book back for himself and shrugging it off? Jimmy could hear the butler's voice. 'I'm terribly sorry, sir. There's nothing more we can do.' Jimmy got up and started pacing as he thought. *I don't want to believe that possibility. I prefer my first take. Still, it's been a while; I better go talk about things with the old man. If there's something screwy, maybe I can sniff it out.*

He walked into the bedroom, took his coveralls out of the closet and put them on.

—####—

Robert walked into the study, stopped by the chair and coughed.

"Yes Robert?"

"I apologize, sir. It's Jimmy."

The old man closed his book and turned his head without looking up.

"Well?"

"He's here, sir, in his coveralls; insisting he speak to you. I tried to suggest he arrange a time but he refuses to leave."

"Don't be concerned, Robert; show him in. I have plenty of time."

He turned his head and looked straight ahead at the bookcases on the far wall. "This may be for the best. I would like to know what our Jimmy has in his head."

"Yes, sir."

Robert turned and walked out. The old man put his book on the table and sat back with his hands in his lap. After only a few minutes, the door opened and Jimmy walked over to the chair opposite the old man's. He sat down defiantly and folded his arms.

The old man chuckled and smiled. "You really have no reason to put up your guard Jimmy. I have no interest in doing you harm. Now, why are you here? I told you to be patient."

Jimmy unfolded his arms, put his elbows on his knees and clenched his hands together. "I've been damn patient and your butler," he glanced up at Robert, "has been standing me off. I want to know what the shit's going on."

The old man considered Jimmy for a second; then sighed with an expression of resignation. "Jimmy, nothing is going on. The project is still in progress."

Jimmy forgot himself. "What about the guy in the tweeds the other day. What was he about?"

The old man's mouth opened. The surprise was genuine but his mind turned quickly to fending off Jimmy's implication. The old man leaned toward Jimmy. In an indignant and slightly amused tone he said, "You're watching my house?"

It was more an accusation than a question. Jimmy was flustered for moment and then recovered and turned defiant.

"You're damn right I am. Why should I trust you?"

The old man sat back. "Well Jimmy, if you don't trust me what can you do? I helped you, don't forget and, as you pointed out, I didn't have to."

Jimmy was silent. The old man's expression relaxed as he said quietly, "Do you think I wanted your money?"

Jimmy shook his head. "No no, I sure as shit know you don't need my money."

"Well then, relax and hold on for a while. There are possibilities emerging that will be of benefit to us both." The old man was thinking furiously and appeared completely calm. Indifference was natural to him. He was tired in every way except his thoughts. This visit from Jimmy was a warning - time was running out.

Jimmy stood up and looked down at the old man. "OK, I'll hold on for a while." He looked at Robert. "At least tell your man here to keep me informed when these 'possibilities' break. I've had it with sitting in the dark."

The old man glanced up at Jimmy from the corners of his eyes.

"Very well, Jimmy. Robert will let you know as soon as we know. However, you must stop calling the house continuously. We will get in touch within a week."

Robert's eyes flicked to the old man and then returned to Jimmy as he turned towards the door. "I'll show you out sir."

"Yeah right."

Jimmy walked out first with Robert following.

Chapter 29: Sailors leave Avignon, 1348

Clement paced the room, alternately holding his hands behind his back then unconsciously wringing them. The door opened and he spun around to it.

"Marceau? What news?"

The grand butler walked into the room a few paces and bowed. "Your architect has been delayed, Holiness. He would have me beg for another time."

Clement's mouth opened, then closed, leaving an expression of disgust on his face.

He looked at the floor and shook his head. "Marceau, Marceau." He looked up. "My disinterest in the architect is only matched by my disinterest in Rome's most recent debauchery. I expressly instructed you to discover the state of the pestilence in Avignon. Have you no sense of immediacy?" Clement turned and resumed pacing, talking and waving his arms as he walked. "By my faith - which is reaching a height of dizzying proportions - there must be some recognition among the peasants of the kitchen, of the flood of benefice seekers, of the couriers, of the creeping hierarchy of the church politic. Someone must have eyes to see or ears to hear - Marceau?"

He stopped and turned accusingly to Marceau.

"Have you received word from the physician?"

"Not after the end of this day's sext devotions, when he took his leave, Holiness." He bowed.

Clement smirked.

"Your sarcasm is noted, Marceau."

The Pope sighed and slowly walked back to his chair. He pulled up his cassock and sat down. Looking up at Marceau, he played absently with a large solid gold cross on the table in front of him.

"So, no grist for my mill, Marceau. God gave me many gifts; unfortunately, patience was not among them."

Marceau relaxed. "I do have some tales to repeat, Holiness. I held to my silence to be sure of their truth."

Clement's eyes flicked up to Marceau. "Marceau! permit my own judgment of veracity. I judge men and their tales with all due cynicism."

"Marceau's expression grew grim. "Thus far, in less than the span of Lauds, Holiness, more than a centum of souls have gone to God. Most of their remains, lay where they fell - unshriven. The clergy hurry to perform the rites but are being overwhelmed."

The Pope's face was blank as he thought. *When would Guy's physick be ready? At this pace the pestilence could well kill all. The physician's potion would be a joke of the devil as he rushed to the bedsides of corpses.*

He nodded at Marceau.

"Is there more?"

Marceau sighed.

"Yes, Holiness. I pried carefully to ascertain the thoughts of the populace. Most are unaware. Those who know of its work, have no imaginings of the immensity. They seem not to think on it as a death that moves. A small number avoid the river. It has been said there is a bad air passing with the current."

Clement stared into space. *No fright as yet; that is good,* he thought. He re-focused on Marceau. "Do your investigations hear of any blame?"

Marceau thought.

"I have heard none, Holiness."

Clement turned away.

"You have performed well, Marceau. I will forget my early words. Inform the architect he may see my secretary and arrange another day."

Marceau bowed, turned and left; carefully closing the door.

Clement thought, *but there will be blame and fear and violence; more so than commonly occurs. How to prepare?*

He walked over to the window and gazed down across the city of Avignon. A haze of steam and smoke rose from the filthy streets. Some few open fires burned with small flickers. What streets he could see between the buildings were black with a squirming, shifting mass of people. Each one had a purpose, an errand or a labor, even if the goal was drink or a woman. He smiled grimly to himself and his eyes were cold and sad. *If they but knew what creeps, or races, up from the river less than half a league away.*

—####—

Avignon: the horses

Gerard and Michel walked slowly through the door of the inn. They squinted and shaded their eyes against the bright sunlight. Michel turned to Gerard and chuckled. “I would believe our efforts took more of God’s day.”

“And I, though the sun is lowering.” Gerard lifted his arm and pointed west toward the river. As he held his arm out a shrill scream drifted up to them from far off. They stopped and looked at each other. Looking back in the direction of the scream they could hear other shouts and shrieks. The noise was muffled by the other constant sounds of the city but it was pitched high enough to be distinctive.

Michel’s face went hard and white as he turned to Gerard. “So soon? Could this be as we feared and you warned?”

Gerard didn’t move. His ears were straining to make out something he could recognize amid the roar. He nodded his head slowly, his lips pressed. “So may it be, Michel. Whether yes or no, time is precious. How may we gain two of the fine horses you spoke of?”

“Quickly? I must work it out.”

Michel put a knuckle to his mouth as he thought. Then he raised an eyebrow and looked at Gerard from the corner of his eyes. “I have a commission to lead a selection of mounts to a physician I know. He is a great man, he attends the Pope. But he is also a good man, if God made one.”

Gerard looked at Michel. "When, Michel, when?"

"Lauds tomorrow."

Gerard smirked. "When, Michel?"

"Before the end of Prime devotions - Terce."

"What are you suggesting, that we take them from the physician's review?"

Michel looked hurt. "Should I suffer such an implication? I am an honest man. But mark, the physician will not take them all, though all be worthy. I intend that no choice be awry."

Gerard smiled. "Pardon my words, Michel. You think to choose from the number that remain."

"Yes, should you perchance to be at that place, at that time, surely all bargains are desired. My master, the Cardinal, would be pleased."

—####—

The dawn was cold and the light thin. Although the sky had only wisps of clouds, the haze that always rose over Avignon blotted out the sky for those on the ground. A mist covered the river and crept part way up the banks; covering the docks and trader merchant warehousing. As the slope increased up toward the city streets, the mist was left behind and lapped across the streets. Some streets seemed to sink into the mist; as if sinking into the river. The people of Avignon rose before the light and stumbled from their beds to the closest drink. In March the drink preferred was hot; warmed over the fires in pots and ladled into clay and wooden cups for the customers or the master of the house. By daybreak, a strange drone was heard from many directions. Most peasants beginning their labor, stepping out in the streets, ignored it. They heard the sound each morning. It was from the nunneries and monasteries; the prayers of Prime devotions, the dawn of a new day and the beginning of Lauds - the sunlit portion of the Divine Office. Some few looked to the nearest religious enclave, blessed themselves and hurried on. Most did not; too absorbed in their daily hopes or fears. The noise of the city began as a mutter and rose in pitch and volume as the day progressed. As it peaked to a deafening roar, as if by prearrangement, all lowered their voices and took more care in placing, moving or hammering. The din subsided, only to begin the rise once more.

As in all cities, the larger part of the populace was peasant worker. Unlike most cities, the wealthy were numerous and visible everywhere - walking with an entourage, riding slowly through the streets with a cloth to their noses or young and strong, striding alone with one hand on the hilt of a dagger or short sword. To complete the mixture, countless friars, nuns, priests and monks bustled amongst the crowd, most, particularly the nuns, in small groups of three or four. Some on the errands of the church were individually searching for a house or shop to buy some necessary for themselves or, perhaps, to see to the Holy needs of the sick, the injured or the dying.

—####—

The House of de Chauliac

Simon opened the door and, glancing quickly, threw a bucket of old water out into the open. He retreated, closing the door, and went to the scullery. Setting the bucket in the corner, he picked out some small logs for the fire. As he knelt to add the logs burning under the pot, he heard steps behind him and turned, startled. It was Alcadio, yawning. "Hold Simon, I had no intention to make you start."

Simon smiled and stood up. He reached to one of the hooks on the mantle and, taking a cup, he ladled some spiced wine from the pot and handed it to Alcadio. "This should stanch your yawns, sir. I prepared it at the shank of the evening and it has simmered until now." Alcadio took the cup and sipped, then recoiled and blew on the hot liquid. "God bless you, Simon. May I humbly say, you could have the fire some lower. Its ferocity has bitten my lip." Simon's face fell and he turned and spread the fire with an iron. "Agh, I only sought to warm the company; some water, sir?"

Alcadio laughed, waved his hand and sipped again. "Do not fear, Simon. My lip and your fine drink will cool soon enough." He walked to the window, looked out at the early light and the haze and turned back.

"Am I risen before the house? I must mark this as an accomplishment."

Simon relaxed.

"You are sir, and well before; devotions have just begun." He tipped his head to listen and Alcadio lifted his head as he heard the monks nearby. "As you say. I have been on land too long. At sea, I would be facing into the wind before God's light struck the water."

"God's truth, Alcadio, as you would better face with the wind." It was Ferand. He had stepped into the room and stopped, stretching his back. Simon took down a cup for Ferand, as Alcadio laughed. "Not before my eyes awakened, Ferand."

Ferand sat at the table and Simon set the hot drink in front of him. He nodded his appreciation to Simon as he picked up the cup and took a sip. There was a thump at the doorway and all looked over. Giuseppe was leaning against the jamb rubbing his eyes. Standing just behind him was de Chauliac. De Chauliac leaned his head around Giuseppe, slapped him on the shoulder and winked. "I would not expect a man of this size to suffer as we smaller men might." He squeezed by and walked over to the table opposite Ferand. As he sat, Simon gave him his drink and took another to Giuseppe, still standing at the doorway.

Giuseppe smiled and sipped; he raised his cup to the others. "This will gain God's cure. I thank Him for the forgiveness I hold." He waggled the cup and took another drink.

Ferand chuckled. "Your forgiveness was helped by good Simon's labor and our host's fine cellar."

Alcadio made a wry face and held up his cup. "Would that I could trust the Greek's draught to please my taste so well."

Ferand looked at de Chauliac over his cup. "Tell us we may sip the potion from a smaller cup, monsieur."

De Chauliac smiled but his eyes were sad. "As I fell on my bed, my mind was set that your memories would fail you before this dawn."

Ferand looked over his head at Alcadio. "You broke a worthy silence, Alcadio. We had slipped the moorings and headed for open water!"

De Chauliac looked up. "You may well. I have no grip on your intent. Such a moment expands a man's courage."

Alcadio walked around to the table end, set his cup down and leaned on the surface with both hands. "And loosen's his tongue, monsieur. But I hold to my words. They were thought out. Your Greek offers the only shield with a chance worthy of the risk."

Ferand nodded. "As he says, physician, I see no safety in our flight. Before the Greek, we had no other course."

Giuseppe had walked up behind Alcadio. "When the wind turns we are lost; we cannot ride so fast."

De Chauliac sipped his hot wine. "I may not ride at all," he said grimly.

—####—

The Papal Palace

Marceau stood on the flagstone esplanade, gazing over the wall at the city. A strange procession started down by the river and threaded its way through the streets, past the lower roadway toward the convent of the Benedictine nuns to the south of the Papal Palace. Small groups, interspersed with occasional carts, made up the crowd. Men and women, some weeping, some grim faced matched the gait of the horses. The carts had one or more shrouded corpses laying in their beds; stacked like faggots of wood. Some groups had men carrying a wrapped body on a board between them. Marceau turned to the sound of boot steps climbing the ramp. As they approached, he saw a sword hilt and long hat emerge from behind the wall. A young knight stopped as he saw Marceau and, walking to within a few paces, he appraised Marceau's dress. He looked puzzled, then, putting his heels together, he bowed. "Am I addressing the Grand Butler of His Holiness?"

Marceau bowed and answered, "Yes, sir knight, I have that honor."

"I feel constrained, good man. I have observed a difficulty and know not the proper personage to inform."

Marceau smiled and nodded. "I understand fully. The functions of the Papal City are numerous and ever changing."

The knight's tense formality vanished. "I was directed to the Palace, to seek the proper department. Would you direct me?"

"With pleasure, sir knight. Describe the difficulty you mention."

The knight replied by walking over to the wall and, with his arm, he indicated the flow of people below. "You observe? A Mass has been said for all. They sought to be buried in the cathedral plots and the space was inadequate. They have been granted room in the shadow of the Benedictine's walls."

Marceau walked over and looked at the throng. Almost to himself Marceau muttered, "so many."

The knight looked at him quickly. "More than you may tell, watching. I spoke to some few priests recently. Their voices cracked as they counted. As they summed the rites performed - among themselves - they numbered more than one hundred. I marveled they could still stand. All were worn with the sadness and labor."

Marceau eyes opened. "Over one hundred?"

The knight turned away from the wall and rested his hands behind him on the edge. "I so vow, good man; within the span of only one of God's days."

Marceau frowned. "The difficulty looms clear, sir knight. The gravediggers are not prepared for such sudden work."

The knight pushed away from the wall. "Thank God and the Good Father of Avignon that we have consecrated ground in abundance. Where would you have me express my concern?"

"Sir knight, your interest does you credit. You may leave this with myself."

The knight was surprised. "The grand butler of His Holiness? Surely you have more matters to tax your time."

Marceau bowed and said softly, "My judgment informs me, sir knight. His Holiness will be desirous to hear of this." He dropped his voice as he looked over the knight's shoulder at the stream of people still passing. "The immensity may exceed our imaginings."

The knight studied Marceau and then shrugged. "As you wish, good man. I cannot send my worry higher than the Holy Father of Avignon." He bowed, turned and walked away. Marceau watched his back and fought within himself. *Should I warn this good knight? No, I may not. This is a man of action. He would carry my words throughout the city. A great rabble would flee and a great rabble would storm the palace.*

He sighed and hurried to tell the Pope.

The Potion

De Chauliac carried the glass jug into the scullery and stopped. Alcadio, Ferand, Giuseppe and Simon sat at the table with somber faces.

"Simon? You also intend to risk the Greek's physick?"

Simon looked up, swallowed hard and opened his mouth then, closing it, he nodded. Alcadio, sitting next to Simon, grabbed his shoulder and shook him lightly. "Your Simon has the wit and follows good counsel."

De Chauliac frowned. "These things I know; I trust Simon appreciates the risk he forces on me, as on himself."

Ferand turned his head and smiled at de Chauliac. "This company trusts the Greek, monsieur and, more to the moment we face, we trust you - more than you trust yourself. Match our courage; it is as God wills."

Simon had placed four small glass cups on the end of the table, according to de Chauliac's instructions. De Chauliac carefully filled each in turn from the jug. As he set down each one Simon and Giuseppe handed the first two over to Alcadio and Ferand until each had a cup in front of them.

De Chauliac straightened up and stepped back. The four sat with their hands on the table, staring at the cups.

Giuseppe leaned over and sniffed the cup. He looked at the others with surprise. "It has no perfume." Ferand sniffed at his but said nothing.

De Chauliac broke the silence. "This may be passed over. Before sext has well begun, an ostler brings horses for my review."

Alcadio looked up sharply and then turned to Ferand. "Ferand?"

Ferand shook his head. "My reasoning still pertains; whether there be fine horses tethered at the door or a good ship with a beating wind."

Alcadio smiled at de Chauliac, picked up his glass cup, toasted the company and tossed it back in one gulp. "Fagh! No perfume but taste enough." He stood up, spluttering. "You can consider some sweet in your next brew, monsieur."

De Chauliac went to the mantle and, taking down four cups, began filling them with spiced wine. Alcadio took a cup and drained it. Taking the other cups from de Chauliac he placed them next to the others on the table. The other three had sat and watched. Now, Ferand tossed back his potion and Giuseppe followed. Then they each drank the wine.

De Chauliac and the others turned and looked at Simon. He smiled weakly, picked up the physick and the wine - one in each hand. Looking at the others, he tossed back the potion and then drank the wine immediately.

De Chauliac walked over and looked into the jug. "Enough more for four, perhaps five, men." He turned and waved at the door to the apothecary. "The remainder awaits."

He went from one man to another, studying them. He looked in their eyes, felt their muscles and listened to their breathing. Then he stood up and his face cleared. "Time must pass for certainty but I detect no effects as yet."

Ferand stood, stretched his back and walked over to look out the window. He turned to the rest. "I feel no trouble but the taste the Greek left behind." He made a face.

Simon looked up at de Chauliac. "Master may I speak?"

"Freely, Simon."

"Would not all surrounding us be better served, should you have the safety of the potion."

Giuseppe looked at Simon and De Chauliac. "He speaks with God's tongue, monsieur. Your safety is the more advantageous." He waved at the rest and himself. "What matter to the world should we succumb. The loss of the talent of de Chauliac harms all."

Ferand grasped de Chauliac's shoulder. "You hear the truth, monsieur. Your life is the concern of many. Our's? - only ourselves."

Alcadio walked and waved his hand. "We are well, as you see. The potion may preserve us or not. It does not harm us, you are witness to this."

De Chauliac thought and looked from one to the other. He stepped over to Simon sitting at the table and put his hand on his shoulder. "Simon you are well liked and well respected. I will take your good judgment and follow your courage."

Simon blinked and looked uncomfortable under de Chauliac's gaze. Ferand rinsed a glass cup in the spiced wine and threw the excess into the fire. Then he filled the cup from de Chauliac's jug. Handing it to the physician, he nodded and said, "it is as well that you may tell His Holiness you precede him." He chuckled.

De Chauliac chuckled in reply, tossed back the potion and took a long drink of wine from the cup Giuseppe handed up to him.

Alcadio slapped and rubbed his hands together. "This day, we defeat the pestilence that scourges the world." He stopped and looked at de Chauliac. "Wait, physician, there were two elixirs." He pointed at the jug. "Which did we all risk?"

De Chauliac's tongue was washing his mouth. He took another sip of wine and looked at all of them as they waited. "That to be used upon news of the pestilence."

"And should we, any one, have the pestilence today?"

De Chauliac shrugged. "I cannot tell."

The Papal Palace

As Clement listened to Marceau his shoulders sagged. As Marceau completed his description, the Pope's expression was resigned and sad. He thought, then shook his head and stiffened.

When he looked up at Marceau he was determined and irritated. "See to the assignment of grave diggers, Marceau. Arrange that they labor the more at night. I would not wish this effort of preparation to be too visible to the populace." Marceau nodded, "Yes, Holiness."

Clement stood up and began pacing angrily. "Where is the physician? My foresight will all be fruitless without the Greek elixir - in a bottle - in my hand!"

He stopped and glared at Marceau. "Send a courier to de Chauliac. The courier is to insist on the potion."

Marceau looked worried. "How may the courier be instructed, Holiness? I must need to explain the significance. Should a courier be so informed?"

Clement stared, then resumed his pacing as he thought. "Your caution may be wise, Marceau. We must forego or choose carefully." He stopped and twisted around to Marceau. "De Pont Saint Esprit is the man. He may be entrusted with so delicate a charge. Now that he is returned from Hibernia we have the Greek's pages to check de Chauliac's memory."

Marceau looked at the floor and said softly, "Gerard has departed your service, Holiness. He was to journey to his home this very day." As he spoke, he knew what the Pope would reply.

"Find him, Marceau. Find him and command he return, in my name."

Marceau choked off a sigh and bowed. "Yes, Holiness; I shall try."

As he turned to leave, Clement's voice came from behind. "We cannot permit the loss of any so useful. These times are trial enough."

Marceau strode hurriedly from the apartment. How to find Gerard, he thought. He may well have escaped the city by this late hour. He headed for the armory, seeking the garde du chateau and the constable. God smooth the way, he muttered to himself. With a wry smile he realized, he would rather trust to God's mercy than His vicar Clement VI.

As he passed under an archway, he heard the constable's voice. It was coming from a corridor leading toward the kitchens. He turned and stopped.

"God's blessings Marceau; you labor your breathing."

Marceau chuckled. The constable and the garde du chateau were together. They explained they were told of some preparations in the kitchen that must be tested to ensure they were both safe and worthy. Marceau laughed and joined them, explaining that he believed his approval was also warranted.

As they walked, Marceau told them of the commands Clement had issued.

The constable stopped. "My squires are in need of exercise. You may use them for your search - one full day." He held up one finger. The garde du chateau nodded. "I shall also so instruct my pages; they are fit enough."

Marceau turned and bowed to both. "May God smile upon you both. Dare I hope to send them on their errand this same day?"

They both grinned. "The messengers we seek may be found in the scullery," said the constable. "As you are aware, Marceau, the kitchen immediately precedes the scullery," said the garde du chateau. "No moment shall be wasted," said the constable with a grin.

They continued walking.

The Horses

A stream of young men poured from the Papal Palace. As they reached the street, they scattered in the four directions of the compass by prearrangement. All were intent on their goal. The grand butler had offered a reward for whosoever found and returned with Gerard de Pont Saint Esprit.

As the search began, Gerard and Michel rode to the house of de Chauliac. Each man leading a string of other mounts for de Chauliac to review.

Alcadio stood at the window. He pointed and raised his voice. "The stable master arrives and with fine animals, if I am any judge." Ferand walked over and looked out. "God and myself shall judge the choice I ride." He turned to De Chauliac.

"Do we choose, physician? I heard your words. The effects may not be told before the passage of two full days."

De Chauliac nodded. "I believe so, Ferand. The potion aside, I vowed these animals as the condition of your stay."

Alcadio spoke from the window. "One of those riders is no ostler." Ferand looked over Alcadio's shoulder. "You judge well, Alcadio. He appears of higher station to my eyes."

De Chauliac came up behind the two and peered between them. "Odd, he is a man familiar to me."

They turned and looked at him. Ferand said, "You know this man?"

"I do. He is a courier for His Holiness; one with a high place in the Pope's esteem. I wonder at his presence here."

De Chauliac turned and walked to the door. Alcadio and Ferand followed. Simon passed before de Chauliac to open the door and greet the visitors.

Michel pulled up and started to dismount. As he did Simon opened the door.

"Ah, Simon, I missed your company these last weeks. Your master has you roped to your duties?"

Gerard stayed in the saddle as Michel handed the rope of his string of horses up to him.

De Chauliac and the two seamen walked out into the light. Michel bowed. "Monsieur, as promised. God's blessings to you." He turned and looked at the sun. "Forgive my arrival at a shade past the time."

De Chauliac bowed. "Prompt as you are, Michel, your tardiness is too soon for other men." He smiled at Michel and looked up at Gerard. He gave him a short bow of his head. "De Pont Esprit, is it not? His Holiness' preference in all missives of importance."

Gerard bowed his head in return. "Monsieur. I blush at such praise; I am a simple courier as much as any other."

De Chauliac walked over and looked at the horse and then up at Gerard. "You understate your talents, sir."

Michel walked over and motioned for the ropes. Gerard handed the ends to Michel and dismounted. Alcadio had taken the reins of Michel's horse and was admiring it.

As Michel and de Chauliac slowly inspected the horses. De Chauliac said. "Do I impose with my curiosity, monsieur? I wonder what event brought you on this errand. Michel's company is pleasant, yet even that seems short of the need."

Gerard laughed. "As you perceive, monsieur, Michel and I are long comrades." De Chauliac looked sideways at Michel. "The horse would be the common element, I'll warrant."

Michel looked chagrined. "Am I so clear to all?" Alcadio and Ferand were grinning at the conversation.

De Chauliac turned to Alcadio and Ferand. "The choices are for you to make. Each of you will require two mounts." Alcadio and Ferand looked at each other. Giuseppe had appeared in the doorway and heard De Chauliac's comment. He tapped Ferand on the shoulder. "Ferand, my purse is not so full, that it may stand the burden of two old horses. I doubt it will stand one of these animals." He nodded at the horses.

Ferand patted Giuseppe's hand on his shoulder. "Do not concern yourself, Giuseppe. I do not forget your share of my last two cargoes." Giuseppe let out a breath. All three began to review the horses.

Michel frowned and looked worried. He turned to de Chauliac. "Monsieur, I believed you were intending to purchase, at most, four. How must I adjust my count?"

De Chauliac was looking at one of the horse's hooves. He looked sideways at Michel. "I thought to find four good mounts, Michel. The arrival of Giuseppe raised the need to six, no more."

Michel looked confused. "But what of yourself, monsieur?"

De Chauliac stood up and walked over to Michel. He placed his hand on Michel's shoulder. "I have no need of a good horse, Michel. I am not permitted to travel."

Michel glanced over at Gerard and Gerard raised his eyebrows. De Chauliac caught the exchange. "Does this impress your thoughts, Michel?"

Michel looked down and muttered. "Monsieur, you above all, must be aware of the pestilence."

De Chauliac was startled. "You have knowledge of this?"

Gerard walked over to the two and bowed his head briefly. "I am at fault in informing Michel, monsieur. I seek to leave and return to my family to await my fate amongst those endeared to me."

Alcadio, Ferand and Giuseppe had stopped and stood, listening. Simon was listening in the doorway. De Chauliac's face cleared. "Ah, understanding comes to my mind. You proposed to purchase the mounts left unchosen."

Gerard nodded. "Truth, monsieur, we…" he nodded at Michel, "would be on the roads north this very day. But what of yourself? Your death would serve His Holiness poorly."

Ferand and Alcadio walked up behind De Chauliac and Alcadio whispered in his ear, "These are good men, monsieur. Would you offer them the Greek's safety?"

De Chauliac sighed and turned to Alcadio, then back to Michel. "Hold a moment, I must discuss a thought."

He and the two seamen stepped a few yards away. Giuseppe walked over and stood listening. De Chauliac looked at the ground slowly shaking his head. "My friends, as I know you so. What may I decide? Must I judge the quality of each man I meet? It is God's work to mete out life and death; I am unable to carry such a burden."

Alcadio nodded somberly. "All know the weight this burden presses on your mind, monsieur. But are you not a physician - a great physician? Do you hold yourself and reflect as you stand before a stricken man?"

"These are not stricken men, Alcadio."

Ferand leaned between the two and turned his head to de Chauliac. "True enough, monsieur. But when God sends a wind to drive my ship against the rocks. I dare not say, 'this is God's will' and be dashed to pieces. I reef or furl my sails, haul out my oars and grapple to change my course. That is God's will; that I have His gifts to save my ship and my men."

De Chauliac nodded sadly. “I hear your words and they are welcome to my ears. And what of the limit of the potion? I may allow, at most, a dozen men to take this hope. For hope it is. I know not if it is more than an unpleasantness in the mouth.”

Giuseppe chuckled behind them. De Chauliac turned his head. “What say you Giuseppe?”

Giuseppe shrugged. “My mind is not so keen nor is it filled with your knowledge, monsieur. My way has always been a simple one.”

De Chauliac turned around to face Giuseppe. “Tell what you see as a simple way.”

Giuseppe smiled. “To do what can be done as it comes to possibility, monsieur. Let God decide from that.”

De Chauliac thought a moment, then walked over to Michel and Gerard. He looked at each in turn and said, “God’s plan is seldom known to us. He has sent you here this day, I vow.” he turned and pointed at the seamen. “And those good men to, ah, 'set my course'.”

Ferand grinned at the sea-faring allusion.

Turning back he explained the discovery and the creation of the Greek’s physick; taking care to warn them that no promise could be made. They listened in growing astonishment. Finally, he asked, “What say you? You have the knowledge and my offer. I promise hope - no more.”

Michel and Gerard conferred. Then Gerard turned to de Chauliac with a grim smile. “Only a fool would refuse your hope. Without it there is nothing.”

“There is God’s mercy.”

Gerard gazed at the physician. Michel looked up as he said, “Your offer may well *be* God’s mercy, monsieur.”

—####—

The Papal Palace

“His presence was assured, Marceau. I trusted no error in allowing the physician to leave his apartment. You are charged to ensure the physician stands before me - with the potion - sooner than vespers tomorrow.”

"Yes, Holiness. No word has been received of de Pont Saint Esprit. Shall I dispatch a delegate to his origins in the North?"

Clement waved his hand, "I wish no waste of men in this crisis. The courier may survive to be of use," he looked at Marceau darkly, "or not - God's will be done."

He walked over to the window and stared at Avignon. It looked as it always had. He knew death rode the air - drifting across the streets - but no sign was visible.

As the Pope stared through the window and mused. Marceau spoke behind him. "Holiness?"

He answered without turning. "Yes, Marceau."

"Do I engage another courier and so inform him?"

Clement turned his head. "Engage a page or whosoever you may trust, Marceau. Do not inform them; merely direct them to de Chauliac's abode and deliver the Greek pages and my summons. The physician will be aware of my intent."

"Yes, Holiness."

Marceau turned to leave and Clement turned around quickly. "Marceau!"

Marceau turned back. "Yes, Holiness."

"Ensure that no matter the person you select, they are instructed to avoid the city streets. Upon their return, do not permit that they enter the palace grounds for three days."

Marceau blinked and bowed. "Yes, Holiness."

—####—

The Sailors Leave

Giuseppe, Ferand, Michel and Gerard sat on their horses. Each had a lead to another fresh mount. De Chauliac, Alcadio and Simon stood in front of them just outside the doorstep.

Ferand motioned to Alcadio "You have chanced upon courage recently. Have you no concern for who misplaced it?"

Alcadio laughed. "Having misplaced his courage, I trust he has already fled."

Giuseppe leaned over his saddle. "Will you explain prolonging your presence here. The pestilence ignores your bravery, if such it is."

Alcadio looked at De Chauliac and smiled. "There is no puzzle, Giuseppe. Late into the night the good physician and I discussed the world at length. I stay to assist his efforts."

Gerard looked at him. "You cannot assist monsieur with the Pope; what remains?"

Alcadio looked up and nodded. "You speak the truth, Gerard." He raised a finger. "I can assist Simon in the preparation of more elixir."

"Ah." The men sat back in their saddles. De Chauliac walked over beside Gerard's horse and handed up a leather bottle. "Here Gerard, an amount as if a finger of spirits. Be sure they have some honeyed water to follow."

Ferand laughed. "And soon."

Michel looked at Gerard. "What gift is this?"

Gerard looked back at Michel but de Chauliac answered, "Greek gifts, Michel; we pray they are not as some Greek gifts have been."

"God's blessings on you monsieur," said Gerard.

Giuseppe looked at De Chauliac. "But what of His Holiness?"

De Chauliac smiled. "I have the sum of four men more, Giuseppe."

Michel turned his horse and looked at Alcadio. "You retained two fine mounts; I, now, cannot puzzle why."

Alcadio walked over and looked up at Michel. "Think on it, Michel. Should the Pope die?"

He nodded. "Ah, you would need to ride." He raised his hand in parting and looked at the others. Gerard turned his horse and looked down at the two men standing. "May God keep you in His hand."

Alcadio and de Chauliac held up their hands. De Chauliac grinned. "When God is this close we cannot but feel His presence, Gerard. Ride with God and the wind."

Ferand looked around and shook his head. "*Against* the wind monsieur; ah, landsmen."

Alcadio chuckled. "God with you Ferand; keep all on their course."

Ferand nodded. They all turned and rode away.

De Chauliac turned slowly to the doorway. Alcadio took out his dagger and cleaned his fingernails. Standing next to Alcadio, Simon sniffed. Alcadio looked around. "Ah Simon, I too shall miss my friends." He smiled. "God will allow us to meet again."

Simon looked embarrassed and went into the house. De Chauliac walked slowly over to Alcadio and stopped, watching the dust as the rest rode out of sight. He turned to Alcadio and Alcadio's eyes looked up from cleaning his nails. "You can do no more here, monsieur; best you prepare yourself for His Holiness."

Suddenly, Alcadio looked up over De Chauliac's head. De Chauliac turned around. A courier walking at full stride was approaching. He wore the tunic of the Papacy.

De Chauliac turned his head to Alcadio. "You appear prescient, Alcadio. I must guard myself." He grinned.

The courier strode up to de Chauliac, stopped and bowed. "Monsieur Guy de Chauliac?"

De Chauliac bowed. "You have found him, courier."

"God be with you, monsieur."

"And also with you."

"His Holiness requests your presence, monsieur. Ah...at the earliest opportunity. He also instructed that you be given these pages." The page handed the pouch to de Chauliac.

De Chauliac smiled and looked at Alcadio. Alcadio raised his eyebrows then his eyes squinted.

The courier waited as de Chauliac pondered. Then he looked up at the courier. "Was there a time specified by His Holiness?"

“No, monsieur. Do you send a reply?”

De Chauliac nodded. “Please convey God’s blessings and inform His Holiness I shall stand before him this very day.”

The courier bowed, turned and walked away without a word.

De Chauliac sighed and turned back to Alcadio. As he walked past him through the open door, he muttered. “I must gather the remaining potions and something to please His Holiness’ palate. The joy in this is in this pouch.”

He opened the pouch as he walked and , seeing the pages from the book, his face brightened.

"Alcadio, I have the Greek's potion in my hand. I must compare to what has been done and hope it is correct."

Alcadio nodded. “As you say, monsieur.”

A while later de Chauliac appeared in the doorway. Alcadio looked around. De Chauliac's was smiling.

Alcadio looked relieved. "All is well?" he said.

De Chauliac smiled back, "All is well. We have not spent all these days in vain."

Alcadio was relieved.

"Or those to come,” he said.

—####—

The Papal Palace

Marceau held the door. “Monsieur de Chauliac, Holiness.”

Clement stood up and glared as the physician walked into the apartment.

“You dare remain absent for three good days without my leave? I instructed that the Greek’s physick be in my hands all that time past.”

De Chauliac bowed. “Forgive me, Holiness. The potion was not complete and required that span of time. I cannot hurry God. I dare not hurry the Greek’s formula.”

Clement stared, then relaxed. “Do you inform me the potion is prepared?”

De Chauliac bowed again. "Yes, Holiness. I do caution that there is no promise in it."

The Pope nodded briefly. "Yes, yes, I am aware we are all in God's care. The Greek is not so worthy of trust." He smiled thinly. "The Church must be more tolerant in these times," he paused, "and I am the Church."

Clement turned and walked quickly over to his receiving table. As he lifted his robe and sat down, he motioned to de Chauliac. "Prepare your physick for myself and Marceau; we may not delay."

Marceau looked surprised. De Chauliac looked around at him and then walked over to the table. As de Chauliac reached into his leather bag and began placing glasses on the table, Marceau slowly walked up beside him and bowed to Clement. "Holiness?"

"Yes, yes what is it, Marceau?" Clement was watching the physician.

"My need is not so great. Must so precious a treatment be spent on such as myself."

Clement's eyes flicked to Marceau's face. He saw the nervousness, if not outright fear. He smiled to himself. Then he turned to de Chauliac. "Physician are we at risk to our person?"

De Chauliac was about to pour; he stopped and bowed his head briefly. "Holiness, I have myself ensured there is no harm."

Clement looked at the, obviously relieved, Marceau. "You hear, Marceau? I have the Church in my hands. I must not falter. Your services are the extension of my will and cannot be lost." He glared at Marceau. "You are commanded by your Pope."

Marceau blinked and bowed nervously. "As you require, ah... forgive me, Holiness. Yes, of course."

Clement's face acquired a satisfied smile. He turned his head to de Chauliac and looked at the table. The physician had arrayed two small glasses and two larger glasses on the table. One of each size were in front of the Pope; the other pair were on the outer edge, where Marceau stood.

De Chauliac straightened up, bowed his head and said, "you are to swallow the contents of the smaller glass - that is the Greek's physick. As rapidly as possible, swallow the honeyed water in the larger glass. The potion is...ah...rather distasteful, Holiness."

Clement looked up at de Chauliac. "God should bless you, Guy. After my temper, you may have well overlooked the honeyed water."

De Chauliac bowed his head. "Holiness."

Clement reached out his hand, picked up the potion and tossed it back. Then he picked up the honey water and drained it, tasting it, he rinsed his mouth with the water. Setting the glass down, he made a face. "You are a truthful man, physician - ugh, more foul than Avignon air after the rain." He looked around and up at Marceau. Then motioned curtly to the glasses. "Marceau!"

Marceau did as the Pope had done while Clement and de Chauliac watched him. When he finished, with an expression of disgust, the Pope sat back in his chair and waved at Marceau with the back of his hand. "You may go, Marceau, but bring back to your mind my injunctions. The Greek potion is not a promise from God. You must remain in the palace grounds."

Marceau bowed, "Yes, Holiness."

As Marceau left, de Chauliac was placing the glasses back into his bag. Clement leaned forward. "Guy, what supply have you prepared?"

"Holiness, I have but sufficient for two more men...ah...at present. More formula is beginning the series of fermentations according to the Greek's instructions."

"To be ready...?"

"In sixteen days, Holiness."

Clement slumped back in his chair. His face was grim. "To provide for how many men, Guy?"

"Twenty-four, Holiness."

The two men stared at each other without a word for some time. At last, Clement nodded sadly. "Go with God, Guy de

Chauliac; go to your alchemy and labor long and quickly. As you succeed, so do men have hope to live."

Chapter 30: The Plan

”Seamus” Maeve was standing at the bottom of the stairs smiling, her eyes twinkling.

Seamus was just laying down for his afternoon nap; his shoes were off.

“Yes, Maeve.” *Now what?* he thought.

“You have a phone call” *She sounded a bit, what? excited?*

A phone call? Who could be calling me? Seamus thought.

“It’s Doctor Farrell; we had a chat; she’s coming to Cincinnati.”

Seamus’ heart jumped. *Meg, coming here, ohmigod.* “I’m coming Maeve.” Seamus leapt off the bed and ran down the stairs in his sock feet.

Maeve dangled the phone a minute, then gave it to Seamus as she turned around. She rushed back into her office. Seamus took the phone and slowly walked after Maeve as he put the phone to his ear.

“Meg? What’s this? You’re coming here?”

“Yes Seamus. By sheer fluke. There are two reasons. One is a meeting of some of the AAMH members. The ones focused on ancient Greek history. The other reason is a seminar on handling the health care insurance companies. They are both important to me and both on the same day in Cincinnati next week.” Seamus smiled as he thought *Lord it’s good to hear her voice.*

“That’s wonderful. Can you stay longer? I can tell you what happened since I got back.”

“I’d love to Seamus. I’ll be coming in on Wednesday night. The meetings are on Thursday. Can your sister put me up until the following Sunday? I’d be flying out at about 2 o’clock Sunday afternoon.”

Seamus walked up to the doorway to Maeve’s office and leaned through.

“Maeve can you give Meg a place to stay next week?”

Maeve looked up from her desk and frowned.

"I suppose so. When? I mean what days?"

Seamus talked into the phone.

"Hold on a minute Meg." Then to Maeve.

"From Thursday night til Sunday about noon."

Maeve thought for a few seconds.

"Of course, she can have Conor's room he can spend a few days with one of his friends. I think he'd rather do that than stay here."

Seamus turned around and slowly walked toward the front door,, talking to Meg.

"Yes, Meg. No trouble at all. You'll have my nephews room; is that all right?"

"Of course, as long as I'm in the same house, anywhere would be more than all right. Sorry, Seamus I have to hang up, I'm in my car and the traffic is getting messy."

"All right Meg, call when you get in and we'll sort out how you find us."

"Thanks, Seamus, I will; it will be great to see you again, bye."

"It will be wonderful to see you again as well, Bye Meg."

Seamus carried the phone back to Maeve and went back up to take his nap. *What a good day this has turned out to be,* he thought, *I never thought I'd see her again.*

He was halfway up the stairs when the phone rang. He heard Maeve answer but couldn't hear what was being said. Then.

"Seamus" Maeve's voice was much louder than he expected. He sighed and, turning around, started back to her office.

"Yes, Maeve. I'm right here."

Maeve had her hand over the phone mouthpiece. She whispered, "It's the butler of the old man. He wants to talk to you."

Seamus took the phone and said to Maeve, "Robert? Interesting. He's a very intelligent and likeable man, Maeve. You sound as if it's a plot for a murder." Then into the phone as he turned and walked toward the front door, again.

"Robert, good to hear from you. To what do I owe the honor?"

"Mr. Cash, my pleasure. I'm calling to request you visit us tomorrow morning, would that be convenient? Knowing of the short notice and you being somewhat dependent. I can arrange for a car to pick you up."

Seamus thought for a few seconds. *Well, why not? But what occasion could be prompting this, I wonder?* Then to Robert.

"Of course Robert and, thank you, the car would be a great convenience."

Robert voice was audibly pleased. "Excellent, Mr. Cash. You may expect the car to arrive by 9:30 in the morning. Could you provide directions?"

Seamus blinked. *Good lord, I am slow this morning. Of course, he doesn't know the address. How did he find the phone number?*

"One moment Robert, I'll give you to my sister." He cupped the phone and shouted toward Maeve's office.

"Maeve, can you give Robert directions to us?"

Her voice came from the office.

"Surely Seamus, bring me the phone."

After handing the phone to Maeve, Seamus walked to the front door and thought, looking out at the street.

I hope this isn't a mistake. Still, if he worked out the phone number the address should be simple. What a minute, why ask for directions? He shook his head. *Well, I can't fathom it and, with luck, it doesn't matter anyway. Likely he thought it prudent to ask for directions so that I wouldn't think he was snooping on me.* He chuckled to himself. *If that's it, it's too late, Robert. Hummm, it might be entertaining to bring it up and catch him out. Now Seamus, that wouldn't be nice. But it may well be worth knowing why.*

Maeve's voice came from the office.

"Well, Seamus you have developed a busy life lately. What are you going to do next."

He grinned.

"I'm not going to Disneyworld. I'm going to try again to have me nap."

"Well, you'd best get to it, you're running out of time."

Seamus smiled and started up the stairs. *What could happen next?* he thought.

The next morning Seamus was up early, had breakfast and was dressed and, rather anxiously waiting at the front hall with his second coffee when he saw a huge, old, but in perfect condition, black Mercedes pull slowly up to the front of the house. A driver, again in a rather old fashioned uniform, got out, looked at the house, hesitated, then closed the door of the car and started up the path.

Seamus shouted back to Maeve.

"My car is here, Maeve, I'm on my way." He heard her voice from the office.

"Right Seamus, see you later"

He opened the door and stepped out before the chauffeur reached the porch. The chauffeur stopped.

"Mr. Cash?"

Seamus smiled as he closed the door.

"That's right, ready to go."

The chauffeur turned and went back to the car opening the rear door and holding it for Seamus.

"I'm not used to this sort of elegance," he said as he got in.

The chauffeur just nodded and closed the door.

A few minutes later the door was opened for Seamus in front of the old man's house. As he walked up the stairs, the door opened and Robert bowed.

"Nice to see you again Mr. Cash."

Seamus nodded.

"I'm not used to this treatment Robert. I feel like royalty and please just call me Seamus. "

Robert chuckled as he said "we just try to ensure you won't refuse our requests...ah...Seamus."

Seamus thought. *Well, now's as good a time as any.*

"Robert, something has been puzzling me since yesterday. Why did you bother asking me for directions?"

Robert looked chagrined and then sheepish.

"Well, ah, Seamus. I should keep in mind that you are a detective. I realized after you answered that I shouldn't know how to reach you and tried to put you off the thought that I had done a little snooping."

Seamus took Robert by the arm and they started walking through the vestibule toward the library.

"I thought as much. Was tracking me down very difficult?"

"Oh, no sir. A few minutes on the computer unearthed a rather rich biography, complete with the fact that you had a sister in Cincinnati."

Seamus nodded and thought, *Lord the computer has eliminated any secrets.* He sighed out loud and laughed.

"Well, no harm but I should have known my whereabouts would be obvious. Should I worry?"

"I don't think so, sir. I knew who you were. The ones we have to worry about do not, thankfully. I believe that is why you have been invited here today." Seamus' eyes flicked to Robert.

"So, things are coming to a head?"

"Yes sir, I must leave you there and he will explain everything to you shortly."

Robert opened the library doors and Seamus walked in. The old man turned in his chair and looked up at Seamus.

"Mr. Seamus Cash, sir." Robert said and then backed out, closing the doors.

The old man smiled and waved at the chair opposite.

"Welcome Seamus, please sit down. We have something interesting to talk over."

Seamus sat down, leaned forward and stretched out his hand. The old man shook his hand and leaned back.

"I have had a visit from our...ah...mutual acquaintances. The young ones who desperately wish to know who and, more importantly, where, you are."

Seamus grimaced but his eyes showed his sense of humor.

"I assume you have some thoughts about the situation, sir."

"I do indeed. We must construct a wheeze to divert them and the increasingly annoying threat they remind me of. The threat is becoming more likely as their patience wears thin."

"Do you believe they are likely to turn violent?"

"Well, Jimmy is not the violent type. He has a high opinion of himself and thinks, as a businessman, he should avoid such crude behavior. Nevertheless, he has very violent , um...employees and they would not care, should he even suggest it."

Seamus thought, *Hum, this could be tricky, if not impossible.* Then he said, "What sort of wheeze do you suggest, sir? Whatever we might concoct, it must be long term. They will not likely forget their missing money."

"Well, I have thought this through and, interestingly, our medieval Irish monk, I believe, has given us the solution."

Seamus sat back in his chair his thoughts racing. *The Irish monk? What? Oh, of course, you clever old man. There are two books.*

Seamus couldn't help grinning at the old man.

"I think I'm starting to see what you are up to sir and I like it very much. We do have a lot of details to iron flat, however."

"Yes we do. Which is the very reason I have asked you here this morning."

About a half hour later Robert came noiselessly into the library with a tray. He walked behind the old man's chair and set a half full brandy glass on the side table then a full old-fashioned glass with ice on Seamus' table. As he straightened up, the old man was just sniffing and sipping his brandy. The old man looked startled and stopped Robert as he was about to leave.

"Robert, this is my best brandy!"

Robert looked both chagrined and defiant.

"Yes, sir. There do not appear to be sufficient occasions to encourage your pleasures these days. I would rather your brandy did not outlast you, sir."

The old man nodded and looked almost chastened.

Seamus smiled and sipped his drink. Then he looked almost as startled as the old man.

"Robert, I can assure you that if I could afford this," he waved his glass, "I would most definitely not outlast it. It's Cooley's best or I miss my guess."

Robert bowed. "Yes sir, I thought it the right choice for your visit. Should any refills be required, please ring for me." He walked away.

The old man pursed his lips and took another sip.

"This should help lubricate the wheels a bit."

Seamus sipped his Irish and took a deep breath.

"Indeed, sir."

It was another two hours when the bell rang in the butler's pantry. Robert glanced at the bell and started for the library.

—####—

Maeve heard the screen door slam.

"Seamus? Is that you?"

"Yes, Maeve."

"Well, how did it go? What was it all about?"

Seamus was hanging up his jacket. He stopped and thought a moment.

Do I give her the story? No, I think not. It's complicated and she would be worried and give me a hard way to go. He said, "Maeve, I think I'll just keep it quiet for the while. You'll know all the details soon enough."

Maeve's voice was a little peevish.

"So, I'm to be kept in the dark?"

"Now, Maeve. Just for a short time. It's rather involved and confusing. I don't have my own mind clear on it yet."

"All right, then. I should keep you in the dark but I won't. You have a reply from Nigel. Tell me what you need to do next."

"Great, what did he say?"

"He apologizes for the delay but he was on a project. Now he's through with that and has a break. He wants you to send him a translation of the Greek formulae and he'll give it the full treatment."

Seamus smiled to himself. *Umm, I'll have to wait for Meg to get a translation. That's soon enough. Well, I may as well check on all the wheels turning now as later, he thought.*

He raised his voice down the hall towards Maeve's office.

"Actually, I do need to talk to Sam again. Would you give me his phone number?"

Maeve appeared in the doorway.

"You've the luck, Seamus. I have to call Sam myself about a campaign we're working on together. I'll just hand him over to you when we're finished."

Maeve was talking to Sam for almost an hour and Seamus was getting impatient when she walked into the kitchen and handed him the phone.

"Just bring it back to the office when you're finished, Seamus," she said.

"of course," said Seamus. Maeve smiled.

After the conversation with Sam, Seamus took the phone back Maeve.

"I think I'll have my delayed nap now, Maeve," he said.

"Don't sleep too soundly, Seamus, you could have another rash of phone calls."

" I shouldn't think so, Maeve - I've been called by everyone I know already."

—####—

The next morning Seamus slept a little later than usual. *I suppose the trip to California did this,* he thought as he looked at the clock. The morning was slow. He had his coffee and some toast. Then he took a short walk. He was aware that the walk was a good thing and very different from just a few weeks ago. Back at the house, he read, well, looked, at the book. *Lord, I wish I could read Greek,* he thought. By noon he was thinking of the next few days. *It would be good to see Meg again. I wonder if Tony has played any matchmaking games since I left,* he thought and then shook it off. He didn't know whether he preferred a yes or no. Then he realized he hadn't heard from Sam. *Time to push the ball along,* he thought.

He went into Maeve's office and stood, waiting until she stopped thrashing away on the computer and looked up at him.

"Well?" she said.

"Um... Could you call Sam for me?" Seamus said sheepishly.

Maeve gave Seamus a warm look.

"Not a problem - I need to talk to him again myself."

Maeve was much friendlier these days. I suppose I can claim credit for that, he thought. I was enough to ruin anyone's mood before.

As he was talking to Sam, there was a beep in the middle of Sam's words. *What was that?* He turned to Maeve.

"I just got a 'beep' Maeve what is that?"

She frowned. "Ah, someone is trying to call in. It's probably a telemarketer, just ignore it."

Seamus finished talking to Sam in the kitchen. He didn't want Maeve to overhear. Then he took the phone back to Maeve and laid it on her desk. Maeve picked it up, looked at it and pushed some buttons. Then she looked up at Seamus.

"Hold on," she said, That was your friend the butler at the old man's. Wait a bit and I'll see if he left a message. She pushed some more buttons and listened, Then she looked at Seamus with a, what? - worried expression?

"Seamus, he wants you over there right away and he sounds rather worried; even downright upset. I hope the old man's all right."

"Lord, how do I do that?"

Maeve shook her head.

"Seamus, I'll take you, but you need to call him back and tell him you're on your way."

She pushed more buttons and handed Seamus the phone. "That's Robert's number ringing; tell him you're coming."

Seamus recognized Robert's voice. "Robert, its Seamus, I'm on my way."

Robert's voice sounded relieved. "Thank you very much sir, I'll see you then."

Chapter 31: Attacked

Jimmy, Jock and Steve stood in the vestibule at the tradesmen's entrance. They looked around nervously; shuffling their feet, staring out the window and putting their hands in and out of their pockets.

Jimmy growled. "What the hell is this? Robert sees some damn light on the wall and disappears."

Steve adjusted his shoulders, glanced at Jock and wanting to be tough like Jimmy, he lowered his voice, "Yeah, he didn't even say how long he'd be gone."

Jock watched Steve perform and scratched his head. He sighed, "What do we do?"

Jimmy had gone from frustrated to very annoyed. "We'll give him five minutes. If he's not back, we go looking for him."

Jock grunted and Steve grinned.

—####—

As Seamus reached for the bell, the door opened; it was Robert.

"Welcome back , sir."

"Thank you Robert. Do you know what it's about?"

"I do sir. I took the liberty of calling you."

Seamus walked through the door and Robert closed it behind him. They stopped and Robert lowered his voice. "I haven't yet awakened the master from his afternoon nap. I received a phone call from Jimmy this morning. For the first time, he struck me as dangerous."

"Dangerous? Robert you strike me as a level headed man. Is this truly serious? What do you expect?"

"I suspect the pressure from his...uh... henchmen may be encouraging Jimmy to rashness, sir. I felt it would be best to enlist your presence and support."

"Only too glad to help. What should I do?"

“Events have outpaced me, sir. At this very moment, Jimmy and his men wait in the house. I left them in the mudroom just inside the tradesmen’s entrance. They arrived unexpectedly moments before yourself.”

“I see. May I suggest you wake the master. We may want his guidance in all this.”

Robert nodded and smiled. “I agree, sir. It’s good to have you here. I will arrange for the master to receive us in the library. It will take a little time. Would you mind waiting?”

“Not at all. I have wanted the chance to enjoy the art work and this presents me with the opportunity.”

Robert smiled and, bowing, turned and left Seamus alone in the foyer.

Seamus watched him leave and then glancing around at the walls, walked over to the nearest painting. *Good Lord,* he thought, *this looks to be a Rembrandt.*

After a few minutes, Seamus was admiring his third masterpiece. Behind him a door opened without a sound. Jimmy’s head came through the open doorway and he looked around. As he saw Seamus’ back, his eyes widened and he disappeared back through the door. The door closed partially.

In the adjacent room, Jimmy turned around and put his finger to his lips. “Ssssh,” he whispered. “You’ll never believe this. The guy you saw in the tweeds is right through that door; and he’s all by himself!”

Jock’s jaw dropped. Steve reached into his jacket pocket and pulled out a pistol. “Well, c’mon, let’s go get him.”

Jimmy grabbed Steve’s arm and hissed, “Hold on, we don’t want him hurt, you idiot. He’s the only one who knows where the book is.”

Jock leaned over to Jimmy and said softly, “So, what do we do? This chance is too good to miss.”

Jimmy stroked his chin, then leaned close to the other two. “OK here’s the deal. He’s got his back to us. If we can be quiet enough,” he leaned forward and looked significantly at Steve, “we can get behind him before he knows we’re there. Then Steve clips him on the head and, when he slumps, Jock and I grab him by the armpits and drag him in here. Got it?" The other two nodded.

Steve changed his grip on the gun; holding it by the muzzle. Jimmy turned and slowly opened the door. As he peered through, he could see Seamus had moved to another painting. He still had his back to the door.

The three crept into the foyer. As they approached Seamus, Jock and Jimmy arranged themselves on either side of Steve. Seamus was completely engrossed.

No more than three feet away, they stopped and Steve stretched his arm back and to the side. The intent was to hit Seamus a glancing blow from the side with the butt of the gun.

As Steve swung, Seamus noticed his shoelace was loose and bent over to tie it. Steve's gun, missing Seamus, clipped Jock on the head just above the temple - Jock crumpled to the floor.

Jimmy stepped back in horror and Seamus, hearing the thump of Jock's fall, straightened up.

Steve was off balance, in forward motion, toward Seamus' back. As Seamus stood up, the back of his head smashed into Steve's face. Steve went over backwards and fell hard on the marble floor; he was unconscious.

Seamus had turned in time to see Steve fall. He held the back of his head and looked at Steve and then Jimmy. Jimmy's face was a blend of consternation and fear as he returned Seamus' look.

Seamus pointed at Steve on the floor. "I'm terribly sorry, did I do that?"

Jimmy looked blank. The attempted attack had lasted only a few seconds.

A door opened further down the hall and Robert appeared. In his hand was a small automatic pistol. As Jimmy and Seamus both turned toward Robert, he raised the pistol slightly and said quietly, "Master Jimmy, raise your hands, if you please."

Jimmy raised his hands and Seamus bent down to retrieve Steve's gun. He slid the gun into his jacket pocket and carefully stepped away from the two men on the floor.

Robert smiled at Seamus. "When I discovered these three were missing, I worried this may happen. May I express my admiration, sir."

Seamus looked chagrined. "Some time may pass before I explain this to you Robert."

Robert handed Seamus his pistol. "Would you be so kind, sir. I have never been comfortable with firearms."

"No trouble, Robert." Seamus took the gun and casually pointed it at Jimmy.

Robert went over to Jock. Jock was groaning but he had recovered enough to sit up. Robert helped him and propped him against the wall carefully patting him down. After satisfying himself Jock had no weapons, he turned to Steve. He knelt on the floor and checked Steve for weapons; Steve remained unconscious. Then he reached in his own inside pocket and brought out a vial. Snapping it in his fingers, he waved it under Steve's nose. Steve's head rolled back and forth at the smell and he opened his eyes. "What? Where?...oh...oooh."

Steve sat up and looked at Jimmy sheepishly; his nose was bleeding. Jimmy glared.

As Seamus was marveling at Robert's good health, the butler stood up and rubbed his knees.

He noticed Seamus watching him. "My knees seem to be holding up somewhat better than my other parts." He stepped over Steve's outstretched legs and stopped next to Seamus. "The master waits in the library. I have explained the situation. He knows nothing of this, of course." He waved the back of his hand at Steve and Jock.

Seamus nodded. "Suppose you inform him of the news. I shall wait until these two are a bit more able to walk."

Robert glanced at Jock and Steve, nodding he said, "A good suggestion. I'll return as soon as possible." He walked down the hall and through a door on the far end.

Seamus waved the pistol at Jimmy. "Suppose you sit on the floor and see to your friend."

Jimmy sidled over to the wall and sat down next to Steve. Jock had staggered to his feet, holding his head.

Seamus pointed the gun at Jock. "I'd prefer you sitting as well, sir."

Jock slid down next to Jimmy, still holding the side of his head.

Seamus, keeping a wary eye on the three, resumed his admiration of the paintings. He was almost to the main door when the corner of his eye caught Robert walking up the hallway toward him.

"Sir, the master suggests that everyone be brought to the library to discuss matters." He smiled, "He expressed regret that he missed 'the action' as he put it."

Seamus chuckled. "A pity. Lead on Robert; I recommend you move slowly. I will follow behind."

He waggled the gun at the three on the floor. "You should all be well rested; up you get with your hands behind your heads and follow Robert. Stay well back and walk abreast."

The three stood and, following Seamus' instructions, slowly started off behind Robert.

Robert walked slowly and carefully, now and again turning to judge how close they were.

As they reached the end of the hall, Robert opened the double doors and stood back to allow Jimmy, Jock and Steve to pass. The doorway was wide enough for all three.

Seamus followed and as he reached Robert he heard a voice from inside the room.

"Ah, Jimmy, truly unexpected pleasure. May I suggest you have a chair and your healthy young friends can stand alongside. Oh, you may put your hands down."

Seamus looked at Robert. "He doesn't fluster easily," he whispered.

Robert whispered back, "Ah... no sir."

He handed the gun back to Robert. "Perhaps it would be as well for you to have this back." He patted his pocket. "I have the one I fetched from the guests."

Robert nodded, took his pistol from Seamus and put it in his inside pocket.

Seamus walked into the room and carefully chose a spot to allow a clear view of everyone and stood with his hands behind his back.

The old man turned his head. Acknowledging Seamus with a smile and a nod, he said, "Robert, could I have a word."

Robert walked over to the old man and bent down at the side of the chair. The old man spoke in a whisper. After a conversation of a few minutes, the old man nodded toward Seamus and Robert straightened up and walked over to face Seamus.

Robert's back was to Jimmy and as he spoke, Seamus watched the three over Robert's shoulder and listened carefully.

The old man turned back to Jimmy. "Jimmy, you surpass yourself. Rash action is not what I expected from one who has so much to lose."

Jimmy was nervous but with his two men behind him, he had to play 'boss'. If only for their benefit. "Bullshit, I spotted a double-cross and I had a chance to cut my losses." He pointed at Seamus. "He's got the book and I want it back. That's the bottom line."

Seamus kept his face impassive, didn't move or say a word. The old man shook his head.

"Jimmy, Jimmy. You leapt before you looked. Mr. Cash is a detective; an Irish detective. I hired him to help me."

The old man paused to watch the effect of his words. He was rewarded as Jimmy's expression changed from confident to confused.

The old man went on. "You see the book was originally from Ireland. I knew of Mr. Cash and felt he was appropriate. We have done business before."

Jimmy recovered, "All right, I don't give a shit; all I want is the book. Do you have it or not?"

"No Jimmy. I do not have it. Nor is it ever likely I will." He glanced at Seamus.

Jimmy was silent.

The old man took a sip from a glass on the reading table and then slowly and deliberately replaced the glass.

"Don't worry about it Jimmy. It's not the book that matters to you. As we all know, it's the money."

"Damn right it's the money; it's my money."

The old man sighed. "I have a proposal, Jimmy. Are you interested?"

Jimmy looked unsure; then blurted, "Propose whatever you want. I don't have to take it."

"You're quite correct, you do not have to accept. Robert?"

Robert walked over to the side of the old man's chair. And faced Jimmy.

"The master is prepared to fund you Master Jimmy."

Jimmy looked as if he'd just won a pinball game.

Robert continued, "But…"

Jimmy frowned.

"The funds cannot be a simple exchange of cash. The authorities would be far too curious."

Jimmy blurted, "What the hell else is there?"

The old man waved his fingertips at Jimmy. "Now now, Jimmy, calm yourself."

Robert continued. "There are a few conditions you may even enjoy."

"Oh yeah, the catch. OK, What's the catch?"

"No catch. You will be, ah, shall we say - sponsored. This is a cover to confuse investigation."

Jimmy glanced to the right and left at Jock and Steve. Then he stared at Robert.

“Sponsored to do what?”

“You and your cohorts are going on an archeological dig, Jimmy.”

Jimmy’s eyes widened. Jock said, “again?” Steve looked at Jock and said, “a what dig?”

Jimmy muttered to Steve, “Archeological, Steve. I’ll explain later.” He was intrigued but tried to hide his thoughts. Stressing his disinterest a little too strongly, he answered Robert.

“Why would we do that? We’re not archeologists.”

The old man smiled as Seamus’ chuckled. Robert nodded.

“We understand that Jimmy but the master believes you will be pleased when we explain.”

The old man interrupted. “Listen carefully, all three of you. This could solve all of your difficulties.”

Robert continued as the old man took another sip from his glass.

“You are currently under scrutiny. This would send you out of the country on legitimate business.

You want the return of your money. This provides an account with the full funds on deposit.

Although you may only pretend to the project, the master feels you will be delighted to follow through.”

Seamus walked up next to Robert and Robert turned to him. “Mr. Cash?”

Seamus looked hard at Jimmy as he said, “You see, there is another book.”

Jimmy fell back. Jock and Steve stared.

The old man smiled broadly and decided to push the news even harder. “Yes, Jimmy. Mr. Cash informed us another book, identical in every respect - exists - in Ireland. It only remains to be discovered.”

Jock tapped Jimmy on the shoulder. “We could pop in on my uncle; he keeps a good crock Jimmy.”

Jimmy brushed Jock's hand away. "Give me a break. We don't know where to start."

The old man glanced up at Seamus. "Mr. Cash?"

Seamus was warming to the idea. The more he played the impromptu part, the more he was beginning to believe it would work.

"I can help you there. There is enough evidence to guide you to prospective sites. More than that, your proofs would be welcomed by the Irish Archeologists. The Government of Ireland might well help."

Jock and Steve both wondered what Jimmy's reaction would be; they liked the idea of leaving the country. Jimmy was staring at his hands, thinking.

The room was quiet for a few seconds. Finally, Jimmy looked up at Seamus.

"OK, I'll think about it." He twisted around to Jock and Steve. "What do you two think about it?"

Jock was surprised, and pleased, that Jimmy would ask. He wasn't used to Jimmy being uncertain about anything. As he continued to wonder, he said, "Sounds fine enough to me. Hell, Jimmy; we might have the money and the book...uh sort of."

"Steve?"

"I dunno, yeah, I guess. Shit Jimmy, this kinda stuff is up to you."

Jimmy was still trying to work it out. It sounded like a great idea; so good he couldn't figure out why the old man offered. "OK, um, you're lettin' us go?"

The old man nodded. "Of course, Jimmy. Let Robert know what you intend to do but don't take too long. I want this resolved."

Jimmy stood up. Suddenly he wanted to get out and go have a drink.

The old man leaned back and said quietly. "By the way Jimmy, no more shenanigans or I will withdraw my offer."

The old man's tone was hard and dry. Jimmy noticed and blinked. *Was that the reason?* he thought, *just to get me out of the way?* He mumbled, "Yeah, all right, I'll call in a coupl'a days."

Seamus stepped back, then walked around behind Jimmy and Jock, his hand in his pocket. Robert was watching and realized Seamus intended to cover the rear. In a voice like ice, he told Jimmy, "Follow me please."

Robert, followed by Jimmy, Jock and Steve, walked out. Seamus followed a few steps behind, keeping his hand in his pocket.

As they reached the front foyer, Steve turned around to Seamus. "What about my gun?"

Seamus removed his hand from his pocket and looked at the gun. Then his eyes darkened. "I think I'll keep it for the moment. Perhaps, after some understanding is reached, I'll arrange for Robert to return it you."

Steve heard the quiet menace in his voice and backed up a step. "A...all right, I guess we can settle that later." Subdued, he turned back and followed the others out the door.

After some minutes, Robert and Seamus returned to the library. Seamus walked over and took the seat formerly occupied by Jimmy.

He smiled at the old man. "Full marks, sir. That was brilliant."

The old man chuckled. "What would you say were I to tell you I meant every word."

Seamus leaned back, resting his head on his hand. The old man's eyes watched Seamus carefully.

Seamus mused a moment. It *was* a very likely plan.

"I haven't settled my mind on that lot in my country."

Robert was thinking Ireland was too pleasant a land. He would rather have Jimmy and company suffer. Almost unconsciously, he said, "I hear Ireland is the land with forty shades of green."

Seamus caught Robert's tone and at the thought behind it. "It is a pretty place but it's not the Costa del Sol. After a taste of the weather, I would think the Jimmy gang would bring the number up to forty-three."

Robert was satisfied. The idea of Jimmy in a cold, hard rain was very appealing.

Seamus enjoyed the joke for a minute, but the serious issues pushed the joke aside. His face was serious as he pointed out, "Ensuring they stay away from mischief might be difficult."

The old man considered. Then sighed, "Too true, Seamus. I must surround them with an invisible net to keep them well contained. I can afford it and, with your knowledge and expertise, it could be done. I suspect it would be much more effort here - than there. Still, I will leave this decision in your hands. If you say no, we shall return to the drawing board."

Watching the old man as he thought, Seamus wondered about his age. He thought the old man looked tired for the first time in their brief association. *And why not?* He was well into his nineties; how far in was trifling at that stage. He realized that the problem of Jimmy and company was wearing him down and ethics were becoming softer in the hope of being rid of it all. *Still... What did the old man foresee?*

Seamus had to ask, "Jimmy and his gang would be safe from the law. Shouldn't they have more punishment than the Irish weather?"

"They have done damage but the damage is done. It cannot be changed now. This stretches my responsibility to the law, yes. Still, consider the points. Jimmy's greed will likely drive the pursuit of the book. He, and his parasitic friends, will be working - and working hard - at a worthwhile task. They will suffer more at their own hands than prison. The probability is high that they will be bending their backs and tearing their hands for many years longer than any sentence they might receive. They must involve the legitimate Irish archeologists and even the Irish Government; we will see to that."

"And they may even actually find the book." Robert breathed softly.

The old man glanced up at Robert and went on. "Yes, and good will come out of the labors of three of the laziest dregs."

Seamus was won over. He grinned and raised his hands, palms outward. "Enough, I must agree. The weight of your argument has crushed my objections. What instructions have you for me?"

The old man was quiet for a moment, then, "I move too quickly, Seamus. Jimmy must accept my offer. There is nothing we can do now but wait."

Chapter 32: Death in Avignon

The morning air was chill but clear. Just before dawn a brisk wind had pushed the smell and smoke to the west and south. The people of Avignon woke with a stiffness in their bodies and stumbled from beds or pallets, crablike, in search of warmth. Those with means called for their servants and hot drink. Those without, fumbled with small sticks of wood and bits of candle wax to rouse the dormant embers. Some calls returned no answer; some did not arise. Others wondered at the cold they felt; *the air was not so cold,* they thought.

Many labored to their feet from a mat of rushes in the shops and merchant storehouses. They stretched, shrugged on their tunics and surcoats, if they had them, and hurried to the nearest inn for a fire and something hot besides. Those already walking the streets could see the flickering candle and firelight from windows and doorways. A low murmur of voices and the scattered clink of pots, kettles and ladles drifted out into the air.

Slowly a different voice was interspersed with the usual. A more excited, higher pitch than the time warranted The wail of a woman and the abrupt and tense reply of a man. The number of these grew as more people awoke to begin the day. Those already out of doors found themselves slowing their pace in curiosity, then confusion. Some doors slammed open against the walls as someone ran into the street and the darkness.

The light of dawn began to creep across the city. As if water, it flowed around the churches and large convents and monasteries and shot down the thin streets only to stop against a house or shop wall and slowly press against it - rising. The light exposed early travelers, not walking, but frozen or in underwater motion; looking about as others emerged from the doors in fear and shock.

"The master's foully murdered...he burned... God save me...the devil's stench...make way...fetch a barber...hold up man...run, run as far as God allows...he is yet unshriven...go to the sacristy...a priest, a priest...gone, not so soon...so rapid...it cannot be."

Then a reaction began. Houses and shops began to shutter their windows and close and bar the doors. Many after rushing into the street stopped, looked about quickly and, turning, rushed even more quickly back into the houses. The slam, thud, clank and thunk of wooden and iron bolts was heard - and the streets were quiet again.

The homeless peasant, porters and migrant laborers stood, their faces blank, slowly looking about as if inspecting the architecture. As they looked, they looked at each other and then, congealing into small groups, began talking in hushed voices. Many of the inns had barred their doors. Those hoping for a fire and a drink stared, unbelieving, as the dream was blocked. Some stayed close, in the hope the door would be opened; others sadly walked away to seek another or return to the mat they had left only minutes before.

Gervais and Alard had watched with consternation. "And you make – what? - with this, Gervais?" He waved at the inn.

"I make nothing with it, and you?"

"That we shall load the carts cold and dry, my friend. Come, rather on my mat and out of the wind, than this inhospitable street."

They walked back toward the river. "Alard, the river bank is damp and foul. Let God warm it some before we arrive."

Alard turned his head. "As you say, we have a sunlit side from here to the open." He waved to the south. "Let us go to the end and turn back to the next below. The time is fat before the work begins."

As they walked, the sun, and the walking, warmed them. Crossing a narrow alley Alard stopped and sniffed. Gervais turned. "Deny you smell a wench this early." Alard grinned, then looked into the alley with a frown. "The air has blown the stench from the street and still I smell foulness." Alard walked back to him and looked. "Gervais, you will lose your humor for the full day without the answer. Come, let us see the dead horse or dog and, then, make up the time."

He walked into the alley a few yards and put his hand to his nose. "Pugh, you say less than the truth, I say go on and..." He stopped. Gervais had slowly followed a few paces behind. Alard turned to him with horror on his face. "Back, back Gervais. I must have air."

They stumbled out of the alley and Alard bent over and held his knees. He looked up at Gervais. "We are at the edge of Hell, I vow." Gervais stood with his mouth open at his friend. "Wha, what do you see? My eyes saw not so far."

"Human corpses, three, four, I know not if there be more. Not long gone but, black, black, as in the grave. The rats were dancing on their faces." He turned to the wall and vomited. Gervais looked uneasily at the mouth of the alley. Then back to his friend. "The devil has come to Avignon. I say leave him to his work and go."

Alard, looked up, coughing and spitting. "And the means with which to travel?"

Alard looked back grimly. "Steal what is needed. He nodded at the alley. "Their needs are done."

Alard stared at Gervais then shook his head. "I cannot, my stomach would leave me." Gervais looked around, then lifted his own tunic and tore a length of cloth from the tail of his shirt. Walking across the street he squatted down and rubbed the cloth in some spilled tar. He stood up, turned around and, putting the cloth to his nose, he nodded to Alard and slowly walked back into the alley. Alard leaned against the wall and looked up and down the street - it was empty. He heard Gervais coughing and choking and scuffling in the alley. Suddenly, Gervais, ran out of the alley and around to the wall beside Alard. He pulled the cloth from his nose, took a deep breath and coughed. In his hand he had four leather pouches. He handed them to Alard. "See what God paid me for my labor."

Alard opened each hurriedly and as he lifted the coins enough to see, he looked up quickly. "It is enough and more." He looked around nervously. "Find your legs and your speed, Gervais. We have no time to ponder."

They began to walk. As they quickened their pace, Alard counted out coins and handed them to Gervais. He brushed the back of his hand. Gervais took the coins and slapped at his hand. "The devil take these Avignon fleas."

Alard grinned. “They are behind us, Gervais, we are away and soon.”

“Ah, a flagon of good wine and a wench for each knee.” Gervais slapped his friend with the back of his hand and grinned.

—####—

Fouinon- the cutpurse

Fouinon walked slowly through the streets. The building doors and windows were all barred and shuttered. The streets were empty. A few cats and dogs wandered, as puzzled as Fouinon. A horse walked slowly out from a side alleyway and stopped. Fouinon watched. When the horse saw him, it twitched up its tail and cantered in the other direction, enjoying its freedom. As Fouinon watched the horse, the door of an inn opened and a man’s head emerged. The man turned his head to the right and left as if fearful he was watched. He saw Fouinon and stared. Fouinon stared back. Deciding Fouinon was not a threat, he went back into the inn, then slowly backed out the door. He wore a leather apron, such as a smith would wear in the forge. He was carrying a man’s body. Another man held the body by the legs and followed out the doorway. The two men carried the body to the next alley up, away from where Fouinon stood, they turned and disappeared. Fouinon stood still, then slowly started toward the inn. After only a few steps he stopped. The men were walking from the alley - without the body. They watched Fouinon as they walked back to the inn door. He began to walk, they quickened their steps. He paused, then started to walk again even more rapidly than before. They slowed their pace when Fouinon paused, then rushed for the inn door when they saw his intent. They ran through the door and slammed it; Fouinon could hear the bar being lowered into place. He stopped and shook his head. *This passes a joke,* he thought, *has Avignon succumbed to madness?* He walked past the inn and up to the alley entrance. As he reached the end of the alley, he put his fingers up and pinched his nose, *God and all the angels, the smell, as there would be in the air after a thousand battles left ten thousand dead.* He recoiled and turned away.

He walked back toward the inn door and stopped, looking at the ground. There was a trail of blood and, ugh - something else, that followed the path of the corpse.

He stepped carefully to avoid it. Looking up he saw the door to another inn some way distant. It was open and the same strange event - two men bearing a corpse. His hair stood up. *Not the custom I would wish in any inn,* he thought. He turned and started to walk away up a side street. He could hear the noise he would expect; the bustle and roar of a city coming from ahead as he walked. As he walked, two priests and a friar were approaching him. As they neared, he raised his hand. "God be with you."

They stopped. "And also with you, good man. Where do you travel from?"

Fouinon turned and pointed down the street. "For the time, from just two streets away and glad I am to leave. What has befallen this place?"

The friar looked at the two priests in turn, then at Fouinon. "Sadly, the river streets have been under the curse of a profane air. Many have died. The populace is fearful to venture abroad." he turned and pointed back the way he had come. "God guide your feet to the higher ground, where the air is clean."

Fouinon bowed. "My thanks, good friar. Do you intervene?" He waved down the street. "We are but a few, of many, who seek to perform the last rites and see to Christian burial, good man." He turned and nodded behind him. Fouinon looked and saw a number of carts and men with carrying boards coming slowly down towards them. He bowed, "Go with God." The friar and priests bowed and continued past.

Fouinon turned and stepped back in a doorway to allow the men and carts to pass by.

After the, grimly quiet, group of men and carts had passed. Fouinon stepped out and started up the street. Looming over the houses and shops on his right, he could see the Papal Palace. He stopped and stared a moment, thinking. *The Popes must be on their guard in these days. The new home of the Church looks as a fortress. I may be at more risk here than I supposed.* He shrugged unconsciously. *But what else to do? Every man needs a trade. A cutpurse is an old occupation and,* he smiled to himself - *historic, if not admired.*

After a few hundred yards, he came to a busy cross street. It was overflowing with the people of Avignon. As he stopped, a few who had seen him come from the streets below, looked at him warily and stepped out of their way to avoid him. He noticed, *and the rest of those down below?* he thought, *are they not permitted to escape their fate?* He looked around. There were no knights or squires or lackey pages on a watch. He looked back the way he came. *It must be more effort for some to leave their homes and possessions.*

Fouinon walked with the people in the streets, not too quickly to pass one nor too slowly to be overtaken. Many had their pouches under their surcoats and capes; it was still chill. He approached an inn. He sighed as he thought, *I must wait until the sun warms them and melts their caution.* He turned into the inn for hot wine and a rest of his feet.

The inn was quiet. A small group of men sat together by the fire. A pair, long wed by their look, sat away from the door, pilgrims, their walking staffs against the wall behind them. He chose a good chair with a back, near to, but not familiar with, the group at the fire. As he gazed with a well-practiced blank look, his head reviewed the inn's plate on the far wall.

A serving wench came to him and handed him a cup. He looked up, if her tunic was cut any lower she would be undressed. He admired her as he raised his cup. She poured the hot spiced wine and put out her hand with an appealing smile. He put two coins in her hand. She held them up and inspected them carefully. He drank from his cup as he waited. She looked from the coins to his face and grinned - she had a tooth missing. He held up his cup again and she topped it up.

As she turned she cocked her hip at him and tilted her head. He shook his head, sipped and went back to gazing carefully. From the corner of his eye, he watched the group of men. One was sweating profusely. He must be too close to the fire, thought Fouinon. Suddenly the man slipped from the bench and looked surprised and confused. The others looked at him and then one rose and tried to help him to his feet. As he put up his arm he coughed and a trickle of blood ran out of his mouth. The friend took his arm and another stepped around to take the other arm. The two men lifted him and, with his arms on their shoulders, they took him to the innkeeper. The conversation was impossible to hear. It ended with the innkeeper pointing up and the three slowly climbed the stairs.

Too much wine? thought Fouinon.

A friar walked into the inn. He looked about and, seeing the innkeeper, he walked over. The wench approached the friar and he waved her away. He was excited about something. As he spoke to the innkeeper he was pointing behind and then at the back of the inn. The innkeeper looked patiently bored to begin and then he began to frown and nod. When the friar stopped, the innkeeper paused a moment and then said something to the friar, nodding up the stairs as he talked. At that, the two both walked up the stairs.

Fouinon sipped his wine and took it all in; his habit of observing kept him well fed. On a table against the far wall the wench was coupling. She was bent over the table holding the table edge in both hands while the man took his pleasure. She clenched a coin in her teeth. *Her payment,* thought Fouinon, *mayhaps that habit had cost her tooth. The tales of Avignon's debauchery were true.*

After a time, the length of a short mass, the friar came down the stairs and hurried out of the inn.

The serving wench had finished and walked over to Fouinon and lifted her pitcher, questioningly. He shook his head and stood up. Time to be at the task. He stretched and left the inn. As he stepped out into the street, a friar and four men strode up and he moved to the wall beside the door to let them pass. He followed them and, stopping at the door, watched them as they took the stairs, two at a time.

—####—

Three carts wobbled on the road below the wall. The track was still muddy from the recent rains. The river was running high and swift. The carts were carefully loaded with coffins, roped tightly. Still they shifted from side to side as the cartwheels climbed and dropped over the ruts. If anyone were to look carefully, they would notice the coffins were rough boards. No smoothing had been done in the haste of the coffin maker. A single cross was burned into each lid with a heated iron. Alongside the coffins were, even rougher, two-board pallets with extended frames to allow four men to carry a load. As they shuddered slowly toward the lower hillside of the city, a line of coffins passed in the opposite direction. These were full and carried by stone-faced men, interspersed with women and children. The two streams arced around the base of Avignon not far from the riverbank. It was a longer path but it was not as strenuous as climbing the hillside.

The last of the three carts had a half load.

Between the river and a point part way up the hill, the streets were filled with a continuous line of people. Clergy, porters and intermixed merchants, shopkeepers, servants and even the occasional noble - labored. From the doorways, men carried bodies, some shrouded, others not. Clergy knelt in the street, administering extreme unction. Men, and some women, wrapped the bodies in sheets and, where a coffin was available, placed the body in a coffin. Some bodies lay in their winding sheets against the building walls out of the flow of traffic and were ignored.

The noise was deafening. Hammers drove pegs into coffin lids. Men shouted above the roar. Carts creaked and scraped through the streets. Some carts were loaded with coffins, some shrouded bodies, some bundles of cloth, some coffins already sealed. Standing at the end of one street and watching quietly, was Simon. As he watched, men and women collapsed in the midst of their tasks. Those laboring alongside, turned and saw; then went back to their work. Slowly, one carrying a coffin, one a bundle of linen, one a body to the street - put down their burden, looked around with a strangely blank face, turned and walked away. More bodies were brought out, more people in the street collapsed and more walked away. As Simon watched a group of nuns passed him and went ahead of where he stood. As they walked, one of the nuns dropped; she looked like old clothing slumped against the wall of a shop. The others continued ahead and then, one-by-one, they stopped to help, until they were scattered down the length of the street. A cart rolled up the street and Simon stepped back against the wall to let it pass.

The driver, walking beside the horse, slapped the horse's rump. His eyes blinking and flickering with fear, he began outpacing the horse. The cart was filled with a few coffins and a number of shrouded bodies; a rope wrapped around all together. Simon watched the cart as it moved away; the bodies, jostled by the cart, were shifted and squeezed by the coffins. The bodies oozed, though they were dead no more than two days; the shrouds were stained and wet.

Simon turned back to the street, another nun fell as he watched. A priest saw the nun slump over, looked up and then fell on his back - dead. Simon heard a crash from overhead, looking up he watched a body fall from an upper window. As the body crumpled on the street, Simon looked up at the window. Bent over the window ledge was another man; he was dead.

Most of those left in the street all started at the sound and, watching, stood up, dropped their hands and slowly walked away.

A few priests, friars and the nuns were all that were left. An empty cart, left behind, began to move; the carthorse straying toward the scent from an open shop door.

Not one person made a sound. The rats came out from the alleyways, looked carefully at the, now quiet, street and scampered over the bodies and in through the open doors.

Simon walked away.

As he reached the first cross street, the street traffic increased. *A different person inhabits Avignon,* he thought, *far fewer and somber of face. A more determined stride and a pose of defense. A wary face, perhaps a brave face but not a face of confidence or a face of hope.* He turned around and looked at the bridge of Avignon. It was thick with people, horses and carts. Most crossed away from the city. Some few threaded against the traffic to enter. He squinted and stared. *Yes, there were bodies on the bridge.* They lay where they fell; the others walked around and over them.

He turned and tried to see to the south. A solid line of people and death carts left the streets below and wound around to the south and east of the Papal Palace; to the graveyards. He knew there was another such line moving to the north; not so full, since those parts had fewer and smaller burial grounds. He turned back to the bridge and winced in surprise. They were tipping the bodies over the edge wall into the river. Along the bridge, on both sides, he saw the bodies fall and splash. He leaned forward as he watched and noticed some bodies had cords and weights attached. He looked downstream and went cold. Not all were weighted. They floated, bright colored spots on the surface of the water.

—####—

The House of de Chauliac

Alcadio turned to the door as it opened. He grinned as Simon entered. "Simon, I missed your attentive service; the fermentation is advanced and needs skimming. Are you yourself?"

Simon recounted the horrors he had witnessed. As he spoke, Alcadio's face grew longer and sadder. At last Simon poured himself some wine and sat at the table. He looked up at Alcadio. "Our efforts are wasted, sir. There are too many and they leave us too quickly. Only God could prepare what is needed." He pointed at the door where the Greek's formula was being prepared. "The quantity needs be a thousand fold and in readiness before the morrow morn." He shrugged. "To continue would be fruitless."

Alcadio sat opposite and gazed at Simon sympathetically. After a long silence he spoke quietly. "Simon, you must find the strength inside yourself. God has given the gift, we must do as we can. Those few our labors save are saved. Despair surrenders without a struggle."

Simon did not look at him. "And should the Greek be mistaken?"

Alcadio smiled grimly. "Our feelings would be spared, Simon, since we would not be."

Simon looked up sardonically at Alcadio's humor. "Your fatalism thus insists we go on." Alcadio sat back. "How else should we squander our time." He waved at the city outside. "All my sinful pleasures are taken away from me. I am best filling my mind or I shall pity myself."

Simon laughed, sipped from his cup and walked to attend to the alchemy.

The door opened, followed by de Chauliac. He nodded at Alcadio and looked around. Alcadio nodded at the door of the apothecary. De Chauliac laid a large bundle he was carrying on the floor by the door, turned back, fetched a cup and sat opposite Alcadio.

Alcadio looked at him, then the door where Simon worked. Leaning forward he spoke quietly. "Simon visited the lower city. He told a tale of horror and his humor was crushed." De Chauliac looked at Alcadio for a moment, sipping, then put down his cup. Alcadio spoke again. "My humor, also, has sailed in better weather."

De Chauliac smiled wryly. "We agreed your confidence exceeded my own; to stay is my occupation." He nodded at the doorway. "The horses await your use, whenever you choose."

"And Simon?"

"Yes, and Simon."

Alcadio scratched his ear and looked at De Chauliac with one eye. "You have a healthy tongue, monsieur. I vowed I would stay."

"Not to me."

"To myself, much harder to escape." He grinned, "all the more so - I vowed sober."

De Chauliac chuckled. "God may intrude on your efforts, I shall not." Alcadio pointed at the bundle. "A strange parcel for a physician to carry. Where is your washerwoman?"

De Chauliac looked at the bundle. "I have arranged for a costume to protect me. I venture to the lower city to assist the stricken."

Alcadio's face was shocked. "You risk yourself? What of the injunction of the Pope?"

"I must learn; there is no other way."

"Clothing cannot stay bad air; you imperil yourself."

De Chauliac walked over and rummaging in the bundle he held up a strange masked hood of leather. A long bird-like beak projected from the mask. Round eyepieces of glass protected the eyes.

Alcadio recoiled. "As frightening as the pestilence. You may want for work, monsieur, you will hurry your patients along as you approach."

De Chauliac sighed. "Mayhaps the truth."

Alcadio stood up and looked at the beak. "What purpose demands this?" He tapped the beak with his finger. De Chauliac turned the beak over. There were two holes cut in the underside. "The beak is loosely packed with muslin. The length and the muslin will sift the air."

Alcadio sat down again. "Air it still shall be."

Simon came into the room and bowed to de Chauliac. He nodded. "Simon, Alcadio tells of your travels. Fetch a cup for yourself and sit. I wish that you recount all you observed."

Simon sighed and retold his morning. De Chauliac listened carefully without interruption.

Simon finished and waited. De Chauliac thought for a few moments. Then with a puzzled look, asked, "you say one of the nuns collapsed after they passed you?"

"Yes, master. The air struck her as she walked. I held my breath for very fear. When I could no longer, the current had passed."

De Chauliac shook his head, "This cannot be so. The pestilence is death, to be sure, still not so suddenly one has no time for a blessing." He looked at Simon. "What order of habit?"

Simon looked confused, "I...Cistercian I believe, master."

De Chauliac leaned back. "Then they must have walked from East of the Palace of the Pope." He turned to Alcadio. "Alcadio, is your faith so strong you will journey to the Cistercian nunnery?"

Alcadio sat up. "Away from the river? Though I have mislaid my armor, I shall persevere. What would you have me do?"

De Chauliac thought, then counted on his fingers. "Do not enter the grounds. Inquire at the gate. Have any of the inhabitants - any - sickened. Watch carefully for signs that all is not well.

"You would have me make no word of pestilence?"

"No word. Such may be thought a mark upon their sanctity; thus engendering silence."

"Pure of heart they must be, but subterfuge is not a skill you possess, monsieur. If they would mask the truth, we must be more sinuous. Allow that I use my own devices."

De Chauliac paused then smiled. "As you wish, doubtless you have the talent required."

Alcadio feigned affront. "Monsieur!" Alcadio's face grew serious. "Monsieur, to what purpose?"

"I must clear away this 'bad air', Alcadio. Should the nuns harbor this foulness, the air is not to blame."

Alcadio looked puzzled. "Then what transports it, monsieur?"

De Chauliac stared at Alcadio. "What lives and moves, Alcadio - ourselves."

Simon looked up. "Other creatures live and move, master."

De Chauliac looked at him. "Yes, Simon, those also."

—####—

The Papal Palace

"Monsieur Guy de Chauliac"

Marceau announced and then left hurriedly, closing the door. Clement stood up. His face was grim and his eyes expectant. "Physician, what have you?"

De Chauliac bowed. "Holiness, more physick is in readiness. Arrangements have been made. Marceau will provide the treatment for those you so indicate." The Pope sat down. "Go on."

"We redouble our proportions, Holiness. A further fermentation period yields a four-fold increase in quantity. But, I beseech you, do not trust in the potion and admit no other recourse."

Clement drily replied, “Present to me another recourse.”

“My observations and judgment indicates the pestilence is transported by the populace themselves. For the preservation of the Church, I propose you confine yourself in the protection of your own apartments.”

“My Church lessens day by day, physician. The number of penitents who remain have concluded the world has come to its end.” He stood up and walked to the window. He pointed at the river. “I have consecrated the river. That body of water is now holy ground. Hundreds of the faithful are...” he paused, “ah... ‘interred’ in its swirling depths. Requiescant in Pace.”

He blessed the river and turned around to de Chauliac. “To ensure an end of these watery burials, large pits are being dug to receive the dead. They shall be closer to their brothers now than ever they were in life.” He shook his head in anger and sorrow.

“Preserve the Church? My daily Mass is attended to overflowing. As I turn each morning to the faces of faithful , they are not the faces of the Mass before. Some stay after Mass, last rites are administered and they are carried to their final rest.”

He turned back to the window. “Those many who visit Avignon are exceeded only by those that leave.” He walked back and sat down. “I dismiss in my calculations those who arrive, only to rapidly depart,” he paused, “...this life.”

He sighed and looked up at de Chauliac. “What of the daily administrations of the Church? What of those who seek my counsel? Would you have me bar my doors?”

De Chauliac thought, then walked over to the fireplace. “Holiness, instruct Marceau to maintain a large fire throughout the day and night. Such heat would discourage the imposition of a foulness.”

Clement looked at the fireplace. “The days are turning warm; I shall be as a pheasant on a spit. A worthy example of the opinions of many. For those who doubt my holiness; they shall say, ‘Christ’s Vicar in this world, is being subjected to a small foreshadowing of his residence in the next.’”

De Chauliac looked uncomfortable.

Clement smiled. "As you say, physician. I shall so instruct Marceau. Though all the legions of Satan conspire, we shall strive to continue. You may go, should your words be true; you, yourself, are a risk to be avoided."

De Chauliac bowed, turned and walked to the door. As he reached it, the door opened. Marceau had overheard. Marceau bowed to the Pope. "Holiness, I shall arrange for the fire to be lit." Clement sighed and waved him away.

The Streets of Avignon

De Chauliac, wearing his protective cloak and beaked leather hood, pushed the door with his boot, it did not budge. He turned his head and, peering down from the corner of his eye, saw the latch hook projecting from a slit in the door. He lifted the latch and bumped the door with his shoulder. The momentum carried him in a step and the beak rapped against the doorframe. He backed up until the beak cleared and, turning his head forward, he rubbed his neck.

I must practice in this costume or my injuries will curtail my services, he thought. He strained to see through the glass lenses. Slowly his eyes adjusted to the dim light. The room was empty. A table and a bench had been knocked over. A bucket on its side had rolled and left a wide area still soaked. He looked across toward the back wall and saw a staircase. Some of the rough hewn balusters had been broken from the stair tread side. The jagged ends protruded outward. He climbed the stairs. At the top, a single large room matched the room below. Against the far wall, by a window, was a rope bed with a mattress bag of rushes and a body. He walked over. As soon as his steps could be heard, the body rolled over. He was still alive; his eyes opened in astonishment at the sight.

De Chauliac noticed a keg and slid it across to the bed with his foot.

"I am a physician, do not alarm yourself. Do you suffer pain?"

The man shook his head and stuttered, "C.c.c Cold." de Chauliac pulled a cover from the foot of the bed. The room was stiflingly warm. Before covering the man, he looked carefully at the man's exposed chest and upper arms. The chest was spotted with boils weeping blood and pus. Black and purple blotches covered much of his chest and stomach. Under his armpits were black growths, clustered, like bunched grapes but larger and of varying sizes. De Chauliac covered him up and looked at his face. He was glistening with sweat. The droplets ran down to his chin. His eyes were glazed and unfocused.

The man snatched the cover and pulled it tight under his neck. De Chauliac pulled the corners up and tucked them under the man's shoulders. The man smiled and nodded his thanks. The stench was overpowering. De Chauliac pulled a vial out from under his cloak and pulled out the stopper. "Here drink this." he held the edge to the man's lips and poured the liquid slowly into the man's mouth."

"If time allows me, I shall return to see to you."

The man nodded and his head rolled to one side as his eyes closed.

De Chauliac stood, trying to control his stomach and noticed a large reddish brown stain oozing from under the man - he could not control his bladder. De Chauliac walked away, down the stairs and into the street.

As he reached the open street, a dog ran past with a man's arm in his mouth. He stared at the dog as it turned into an alley. Then he noticed the rats, many clambered over the bodies but many were dead. The rats were scattered amongst the human, dog and cat corpses. He reached up to tear off the leather hood and caught himself.

God strengthen my mind and my purpose, he thought, *I dare not.*

The stench was debilitating but he was becoming accustomed to it. *I must sprinkle some pleasant scent into the muslin,* he mused. He sighed, gritted his teeth and advanced to the next house. His path was crooked as he avoided the bodies.

—####—

Alcadio stared. "You entered the houses! Many?"

De Chauliac nodded. "I set myself to the length of two streets. The very first taxed all my intentions."

Alcadio smiled. "The first house had destroyed mine; were I ever so foolish to intend."

De Chauliac returned a wry smile. "This day I envied you your occupation, Alcadio."

"And was your learning thus advanced?"

De Chauliac shook his head. "I cannot tell; horror still grips my thoughts."

Alcadio took de Chauliac's cup and refilled it from a flagon. "Forget this day until the morrow, monsieur. These suffer but a short time and after," he paused, "they have use only of the carts."

"You forget the Greek, Alcadio. I administered the potion to as many as I could."

Alcadio frowned. "The Greek elixir? My memory is not so faulty. Of what benefit to these," he waved his hand toward the city, "in this hour? They would need to have its taste two Sabbaths past."

De Chauliac raised two fingers. "The Greek directed two potions, Alcadio. The other was for the need of the afflicted. A need not pressing upon us," he pointed to the city, "but those presently in their beds."

Alcadio leaned back. "Ah, and was it with you?"

De Chauliac nodded. "And sometimes gifted to ones I supposed might save."

"Not all."

"No, not all." De Chauliac sighed. "Some were no longer with us. Some had only moments more. Some could not accept the potion; being too feeble to raise their heads. The volume available is small."

Alcadio leaned forward. "We must prepare as we can. The first elixir is too late but for those a week's ride North."

"Simon has been so instructed, Alcadio. You have labored these recent days on the very alchemy you say."

"Do you retain a supply?"

"I hold safe the quantity for six persons."

"So many. His Holiness consumes but one. That apart, the Pope has swallowed that same potion we all quaffed long past."

"I have no other to trust, Alcadio. Your faith in the Greek and myself I admire and envy. Should the one fail, I hold the other in extremis. I pray not to want its use."

Alcadio nodded. "I pray also, monsieur.

—####—

The steam still drifted from the city. The warming weather had reduced the quantity of smoke. The noise was softened. As if a number of animals muttered in the distance. The view from the upper walls of the palace showed the bodies scattered along the streets and roadways. A few death carts slowly clattered to the pits. Dogs and cats sniffed their way from alleyway to open squares and back to the alleys.

An unheard sound or unseen motion made ravens and magpies flap upward, only to settle quickly nearby. There were no bells. The Archbishop had forbidden the bells to toll. They had cowed the living who no longer thought of the dead. Many travelled North and East, not running but slowly walking without any destination. Straining the eyes, the dozens, no, hundreds, of bodies could be seen along the roadways and out in open fields. The human remains were intermixed with the corpses of dogs, cats, sheep and even horses and cows. Most wealthy nobles and many high clerics had left the city weeks before. They sought to escape by moving to their country residences or hunting estates. Some survived, others died on the journey or shortly after they arrived.

At the beginning of light, the sound of small groups could be heard at prime devotions. There were fewer, if louder, voices drifting thinly from the monasteries and convents. Some were completely silent or so sparsely occupied as to be unheard. A death cart, some men to carry or dig and at least one cleric to see to last rites made up hastily formed groups. They were deputations, cobbled together; visiting the cloisters, one by one. In the close quarters of a convent or monastery, most were already dead. The few that remained were so concerned with burials, they had only brief moments for their prayers. The visits often found only the dead; in the cells; in the chapel; some where they fell at their daily tasks.

As the gravediggers worked, their faces were wrapped with cloth to mask the smell and to protect against the pestilence. A watcher would have noticed the gravediggers searching the bodies of the dead, taking the purses and transferring the coins or jewelry to a larger bag. The larger bag usually hung around their neck. It was often so heavy it impeded the work but they would not set it aside.

Looting was common. Rough men and some ragged women wandered in and out of the houses at will taking anything of value, including spirits and flagons of wine. By late morning, drunken looters reveled in their riches as they staggered through the streets. Fights broke out and left more dead in the streets.

—####—

Simon has the Black Death

Simon stumbled and knocked against the table. Alcadio turned at the noise and saw Simon slide sideways into a chair. He dropped the wooden spoon in the vat, wiped his hands and squatted down to look at Simon's face. "Are you yourself, Simon?"

"A weakness passed over me; I felt it best to rest a moment."

Alcadio frowned and examined Simon more carefully. He was sweating heavily. He twitched and shivered, as he looked at Alcadio.

Alcadio rose and left to find de Chauliac. Simon felt dizzy and his eyes would not focus as they should.

De Chauliac came into the room and over to Simon. Alcadio stopped in the doorway.

After a brief look at Simon, De Chauliac stood and nodded at Alcadio. "Assist my efforts. Simon must be into a bed."

The two men lifted Simon by each arm and helped him walk from the room. After a few moments, they returned and sat at the table. Neither spoke for some time. At last Alcadio stood and went to the window. As he looked out, he shook his head. "The Greek has failed us."

De Chauliac looked at Alcadio's back. "We know not. Simon may be suffering with any illness. Many evidence such signs." Alcadio turned around. "Say the truth, monsieur, what do you believe?"

De Chauliac looked at and spoke to the table. "The pestilence has stricken Simon. The visit to the city exposed him."

Alcadio pointed at them both. "And our turn awaits."

"Perhaps." He looked up at Alcadio. "Stay your fear and your anger. We have not yet buried Simon. The test of the Greek is upon him; we must tend him and wait."

Alcadio smiled. "The Greek is a taskmaster. He tests us all." He shrugged. "Assign the duties then. What would you put me to?"

"You are the stronger of us. I know the method of it. We shall share both the work and the tending." Alcadio nodded. "Well enough. Pray that Simon is whole soon; that he may tend to me and repay the loan."

De Chauliac grimaced. "Myself also. But for this day we must clean. The Greek's instructions are specific; everything used or surrounding the formulae preparations must be washed."

"Yes - sadly four days have passed since the last scrubbing. Simon tired me that day."

De Chauliac looked up toward Simon in the bedroom above. "It may be well to wash poor Simon; he will need to be cooled."

"Do not expect his thanks for that."

The following day de Chauliac rose early and examined Simon. He still had a fever. There were swellings under his arms but they were the color of inflamed skin. A few small blotches of dull gray were near the swellings. De Chauliac gave him water, wiped his skin with alcohol to cool him down and left. As he walked into the scullery, Alcadio looked the question at him. He sat down and sighed as Alcadio pushed the morning drink in front of him. "He struggles. Only God knows whether he or the pestilence has the upper hand." Alcadio sipped and stared at the fire. "The black eggs?" he said.

De Chauliac nodded grimly, "They begin."

Alcadio crossed his legs, still staring at the fire. "Warm days for such heat in the grate; this is the protection you gave the Pope?"

"Yes, I sense the pestilence is consumed or repelled by the heat. I cannot say the reason."

Alcadio was in his shirt only. "It repels my tunic. We both have need of cooling down; no less than the good Simon."

Alcadio stood up and his shoulders drooped. "I have floor wood to wash this morning. The Greeks must have a longer day."

For two more days de Chauliac examined Simon morning and night. At midday he prepared him a meal of thin gruel and some mashed apples but only water to drink. De Chauliac started to apply a paste to the swellings on the second day. A mixture of mashed figs, yeast and butter in the hope to soften the swellings. De Chauliac abandoned the thought they would come to a head, burst and drain. Some few boils on Simon's chest did drain and De Chauliac wiped them off with the alcohol. Simon flinched and squirmed at that.

On the fourth day Alcadio and De Chauliac sat at the table nursing their aching muscles. A thump and dull clatter came from the stairs. They both stood and into the room staggered Simon. "My thirst overwhelms me, master, and I feel as in a fire. May I beg water?"

De Chauliac grinned and helped him to a chair. Alcadio filled a mug with cold water.

De Chauliac knew from experience that a man with a thirst and the sense of being heated was good; the fever was gone.

After Simon drank and rested, de Chauliac examined him carefully. The swellings were much reduced, the boils were healed and the dark blotches were barely visible. Alcadio was astonished and relieved. "The Greek has won the battle. His humor prevented him from informing us there would be a battle."

De Chauliac smiled. "He did so say that he who consumed the potion in a timely way would not perish."

"But only be sunk in such misery he wished to perish," said Simon.

Alcadio slapped Simon on the back. "Your loss was not to be permitted. Else I was to be in harness to a plow before long."

Simon smiled weakly. "My strength could not lift a harness, Alcadio."

De Chauliac looked at Simon with a soft smile. "As you say Simon. You needs be in your bed. Your strength may be found tomorrow." Alcadio stood up and waved at Simon. "Come stout fellow, I shall walk you the way."

As Alcadio returned, de Chauliac was at the window. He spoke, as if to himself. "We spend our hours in work and rest. The tasks are completed and the days become our past. A placid island in the midst of a roiling sea of suffering and death. God has blessed this small spot on which we stand. Yet His wrath and the Angels of death destroy all around us. What meaning can there be in this?"

Alcadio said softly. "That God distinguishes between all men. I see your place and God sees also. As to my place? God must plan a heavy tithe for me. I pray my debt be not above my ability."

De Chauliac turned. "And Simon?"

Alcadio smiled. "There was never a better man with a stronger heart. God arranged that he be in this place."

De Chauliac scratched his head then shook off the mood. "It must be so. Let us continue."

Chapter 33: Reunited

It was the day of Meg's arrival. She had landed the evening before and was spending all day at her conferences. The plan was for her to call when she was free. Seamus was up early - well, for him. He was nervous - pacing and fiddling with everything trying to distract himself. Maeve finally had enough.

"Seamus, go out and take a long walk, you're driving me crazy."

Seamus looked guilty and nodded. Maeve heard the screen door slam.

Lord, she thought, he might at least have found out when her meetings were finished.

Two hours later Seamus still wasn't back from his walk and Maeve was starting to worry. The phone rang; it was Meg. "Hi Maeve, I'm between meetings; I should be free in about two hours."

Maeve said, "Do you have a rental."

Meg answered, "No, I didn't think it made sense; I took the shuttle into town and I won't be driving around. I'll just take a cab after my last meeting. What's the address?"

Maeve gave her the address and told her Seamus was really looking forward to seeing her.

Meg giggled and said, "I am too. I don't know exactly how long I'll be, Maeve, watch out for the cab late this afternoon. Bye"

Maeve hung up.

Where the hell was Seamus? she thought.

She heard the front door open. *Aha.*

"Seamus?"

Seamus walked into the office.

"Hullo, I got lost," he said.

"Seamus, Meg just called, she's taking a cab later."

Seamus visibly brightened.

"Wonderful - She should be here in a couple of hours."

Maeve looked at him and sighed. *Oh Seamus,* she thought, *you're so excited. Bless you Doctor Farrell you have stolen my Seamus' heart - and his brain too from the look of it.*

"Oh Seamus, don't be so thick - she still has a conference to attend and then the traffic will get in the way. It could be three or even four hours."

Seamus looked crestfallen.

"Of course, I'll just go take my usual nap then."

More than an hour or so later, Seamus woke up, made sure he looked presentable and went downstairs, grabbed a couple of beers and headed for the front porch to wait. An hour and a half after that, the cab pulled up in front of the house.

Seamus squinted but the sun's reflection made it impossible to see who was in the back.

Then Meg got out and the driver went to get her luggage from the trunk. Seamus ran to Meg. They hugged and Meg kissed him again and again. She thought, *This was what my parent's called a 'clinch'.* She looked over Seamus' shoulder and saw the front door open. Maeve stepped out and watched them, grinning.

Meg whispered in Seamus' ear.

"Easy Seamus your sister might get the wrong idea."

Seamus turned his head to Meg's ear and whispered.

"I think she'll be sure to get the *right* idea Meg."

They broke apart and Seamus went to retrieve her luggage while Meg walked up to the porch.

"You must be Maeve," she said.

Maeve nodded and said, "And you must be Doctor Farrell."

Meg said, "Just Meg."

Seamus walked up behind with the bags.

"Where to, Maeve?"

"Conor's room. We'll meet you in the kitchen."

Seamus carried some bags past them and into the house.

"Come in, come in, Meg, and we'll sit and talk. I know we have a lot to talk about."

Meg tipped her head, questioningly.

Maeve went on, "You can tell me what Seamus has told you and I'll correct anything that needs it," she said.

It took Seamus two trips to carry all of Meg's bags into the house and up the stairs, He could hear Meg and Maeve talking and laughing in the kitchen.

Now, what could be so funny? he thought, then, he realized they were, most likely, talking about him. *Oh my, I hope this doesn't scramble Meg and me.*

He took a deep breath and walked into the kitchen. The girls were giggling over something he had just missed hearing.

"So, what's the joke?" he said.

Maeve looked up.

"I was just telling Meg how you mistook Robert for the old man."

Seamus nodded sadly.

"Oh yes, I felt a right eejit. I can see there won't be any blunders or failings Meg won't hear about on this trip."

Meg looked at Seamus fondly, "Oh, Seamus it makes you endearing and that's good."

Seamus gave her a crooked smile and asked, "So, how was your ride here?"

Meg sighed.

"It was strange. The cab driver complained about the traffic and kept apologizing for taking so long. I didn't think the traffic was bad at all."

Grinning, Maeve said, "That's the difference between Cincinnati and San Francisco Meg. The people of Cincinnati are truly spoiled."

She stood up. "I have a bit of work left to do yet today. I'll leave Seamus to keep you entertained. P.J. will be home soon enough. Seamus, you can make introductions and fetch the beers."

Meg glanced from one to the other and said, "Actually a beer sounds rather good."

Seamus brightened.

"Does it? Well then, we won't wait for P.J. I'll go fetch some now." He stood up. “I won't be a minute. The beers are in the cellar."

Meg chuckled, "Of course they are. I'll be on the front porch."

Meg and Seamus sat on the porch chatting about her trip and Cincinnati and sipping their beers for about an hour when a car pulled into the driveway and disappeared down the side of the house.

Seamus looked over at Meg.

"That'll be P.J. Maeve's other half."

P.J. walked up onto the porch.

"Hullo Seamus." He bowed to Meg.

"And you must be Doctor Farrell."

Meg held out her hand and said, "Meg, please."

P.J. took her hand.

"Very pleased to meet you Meg." Then to Seamus,

"should I fetch refills?"

"You're a good man, P.J."

A few minutes later P.J. returned and Maeve followed. Then, P.J. leaned over and looked Seamus square in the face.

"All right," he said, “I've been curious enough for the last week and I'm ready to pop. What's going on with the book?"

Seamus nodded and squinted up at P.J.

"Good enough P.J. I'll bring everyone almost up to date. I won't quite come to the end since there are elements that are moving now and I don't know myself what's going to happen next. Fair enough?"

Everybody turned and leaned into Seamus as he looked back and forth from one to another.

Seamus told everyone the story up to his last two meetings with the old man. Not knowing what Jimmy was going to do, he left out the old man's offer. He also left out his dealings with Sam over the last few days. *That would be obvious soon enough,* he thought, *I think I'll leave out Nigel, I'll have to enlist Meg's help with that soon.*

When he finished they all were thinking at once. Then Maeve broke the spell.

"All right, what about Nigel?" she said.

Seamus groaned.

"Well, yes, there is that." He turned to Meg.

"I'll need your help, Meg. I need a translation of the Greek's formulae to send to someone I know. He will be looking into it and may well find out whether it works or not."

Meg's eyes opened wide.

"Well of course. I'd be happy to but Good lord, Seamus, How can he do that?"

"Ah, Meg he's a biochemist. I don't know, but it's worth a shot."

Meg thought for a few seconds.

"Alright, the sooner the better. Where's the book; I'll get right on it."

Seamus held up his hand.

"Hold up Meg. It will have to wait a little longer. The book's not here."

Maeve's head snapped around.

"What! Where is it?"

Seamus looked guilty.

"I'm sorry Maeve, I didn't tell you. I took it with me the other day when I visited the old man. He's since sent it over to Sam. Sam will send it back to me when he's through. I expect it soon, probably by courier."

Maeve was staring at Seamus. Frowning, she said "So, that's what all the phone calls were about. What is Sam doing to it?"

Seamus patted the air down.

"Sam isn't doing anything to it. He's doing something *with* it. He's making copies. I told him he could make one for himself and he was very happy to take on the job."

Maeve and Meg both exhaled with relief at the same time and then looked at each other. P.J. Just looked a little confused and said, "So then, what's coming back here; the book and the copies?"

Seamus nodded.

"That's right. I think it's going to be a pretty large box."

Meg put on her best pleading face.

"Do I get one?"

Seamus smiled at her.

"Yes, of course you do - and me - and Tony - and even Father Schmidt."

"What about the old man?"

"Yes, him as well. There is one other copy I'll tell you about later. Then I can return the book to its rightful owner."

"And who is that?" they almost all said together.

Seamus was surprised, "Why the pope of course."

Maeve stood up.

"Well then, on that note, it's time for something to eat."

P.J. stopped her.

"No, no love. I'll grill. You sit and relax."

Maeve was very pleased. Seamus got up. "I'll help P.J."

The men left the women who had started up a conversation about something else - anything else.

After supper Meg excused herself.

"I'm sorry everyone, even though my clock is still on California time, I'm exhausted. I'm going to turn in."

Everyone nodded. Maeve stood up and walked over to her. "I'll come with you Meg and make sure you have all the linens and anything else you might need."

They went up the stairs together, chatting.

P.J. leaned back with his coffee.

"Well, Seamus she's wonderful."

Seamus grinned.

"I couldn't agree more but I don't know where to go next."

P.J. sipped his coffee, thinking.

"Leave it to her and don't worry about it."

Maeve came back down and walking over to Seamus she tapped him on the knee.

"Meg and I had a chat. Tomorrow we are going out for a tour of the sights. You are *not* invited."

The corners of Seamus mouth went down.

"So you can tell her all my secrets without interference?"

"Just so."

—####—

Maeve and Meg had only been gone an hour or so when a city courier drew up to the house and carried a large box up to the door. He rang the doorbell after setting the box on the porch and was walking back to his car when Seamus answered the door.

"Many thanks," he shouted to the courier. The courier turned and nodded. Seamus hefted the box and stumbled into the house. Hummm, a bit heavier than I expected, he thought. He took the box to the kitchen table and rummaged in the drawers for a sharp knife. Then turning he opened the box. After removing some packing bags, he pulled out a shrink-wrapped stack of paper and a note. Here you are Seamus, it read, I did the pages one-sided. This was a little tricky because of the bend from the binding. Lucky for us, the monk left a very wide gutter. *Gutter?* thought Seamus, *what's a gutter?*

He took out the remaining wrapped copies and then the original from the bottom.

He counted to himself as he looked at the packages. *One for me, one for Meg, one for Tony and...uh one for George. Oops, what about Nigel. He hasn't said he wants one yet. That leaves Sam's and - I wonder if the old man got one? Well, Sam can, no doubt, make more if necessary.*

Now, Meg can translate the potion for Nigel and Maeve can send it off. Seamus left it all and made a sandwich. After lunch he went up for his nap.

A couple of hours later he woke up to the sound of Meg and Maeve coming in; talking and laughing. He got up and dressed, then went downstairs.

"So, how was the tour?"

Meg grinned and gushed.

"It was wonderful. I had no idea Cincinnati was so interesting. Maeve showed me the city and all the beautiful parks.

There are so many of them. Better still they have so many hills with glorious views of everything."

Seamus mouth opened slightly as he thought, *Huh, once again I'm reminded of how much I've ignored since I've been here.* Then he said,

"well, I have the book...er... Books - back. So, I can put you to work on the translation for Nigel. If that's all right."

Meg was surprised. "Of course, I'll get it on it right away." Maeve tapped Seamus on the shoulder.

"And I'll send it off to Nigel as soon as it's done." She turned to Meg. "Why don't you sit at my desk and key it straight into my computer?"

Meg nodded and left Seamus standing as they both went into the office. Seamus with a blank face went into the lounge and sat down to read the paper. *Oh well,* he thought.

More than an hour later Maeve and Meg came in and sat down. Seamus looked from one to the other. "Well?"

Meg nodded.

“It's on its way. Maeve knows how to work everything."

Seamus sighed and leaned back. "Well, now we wait and see. Nigel is very good. He'll let us know as soon as he finds out anything."

Maeve coughed and turned to Meg. "It's well that you were here to translate."

"I was ordained for this. He likely arranged it all," she said, pointing at Seamus.

Seamus looked innocent. "I'm flattered but you give me too much credit. I couldn't have, even if I wanted to. Oh, by the way Maeve what's a gutter?"

Maeve looked blank then she had it. "Did Sam use that term?"

"Yes, he did. What is it?"

It's a print term. It refers to the space between the pages in a book or magazine. It's the gap in the middle to avoid losing the content where it's bound."

"Ah, the spot to help people read without bending the spine far back."

"Yes, and maybe break the binding. Well, P.J. will be here any minute and I'll just gather his tools so he can do the supper." She stood up and went into the house.

Seamus sat down next to Meg, staring across the street.

"So, how is the visit so far."

Meg looked amused. "It's been very nice. I like the quiet - and your sister."

Seamus turned his head to look at her.

"The quiet? What about the traffic just down the street?"

"Compared to San Francisco it's a low murmur."

The corners of Seamus' mouth went up. "Ah, yes, I suppose so. Meg? I knew I missed you but I didn't know how much until you got out of the taxi."

Meg's face was full of affection as she said softly, "Me too, Seamus. Worse, I only have one day left."

"If only you could have meetings in Ireland - perhaps every other day or so"

"Oh, Seamus, if only I could. There is a way though."

Seamus blinked and blurted, "How?" Then he thought, *That must have sounded eager. Am I so eager?*

Meg smiled. "Easy – I just retire from medicine. I *am* rather fed up with it all. I'd much prefer spending my time on my hobby - Medical history and then I could spend more time with you. You know, gardening, cooking, kissing."

Seamus melted and reached over to her. It was a long, sweet, tender kiss. So long they didn't notice P.J. pulling into the driveway and back to the garage. Just as they stopped and leaned back P.J. was standing in front of them.

"Well, I don't suppose I'll get much help from my brother-in-law with the grilling." He grinned and went into the house. Meg giggled and slapped Seamus arm with the back of her hand.

"So, you're afraid they'll get the wrong idea."

That was you. I think they already had the idea. Besides, Maeve is very happy about you - as am I."

Meg sighed, "and I only have one more day."

"Well, we'll make it a good one."

The evening was quiet and pleasant. P.J. grilled a good supper and everyone sat in the lounge and talked until late. Finally Meg stood up and stretched. "Well, my clock still hasn't adjusted and when the alarm goes off at seven it will be four o'clock for me. It's a shame I'm used to staying up late but I think it's time to call it a day. Good night all." Maeve, said "Me too." It wasn't long after, P. J. and Seamus turned in as well.

Seamus lay awake for a long time, thinking about Meg. *I really think I love her. This is a miracle. I never would have believed it could happen. Stop analyzing you dolt - just accept and enjoy.*

After about an hour the door opened silently and Meg stepped into the room and closed the door carefully. She stole around to the side of the bed, lifted the sheets and lay down next to Seamus. He whispered "Meg?!" She turned to him and whispered "sshhh." They made love on their sides slowly and quietly without a word and then rolled onto their backs. Meg turned back to Seamus and snuggled up to his side. They dozed off.

The next morning they woke early and Meg slid out of bed, putting her fingers to her mouth, she whispered "sshh, I'll see you downstairs." and went to her room.

Seamus got up, dressed and went downstairs. Maeve and P.J. were still asleep. He started the coffee and as he got out two cups, Meg walked into the kitchen. She stopped next to him and, leaning forward, kissed him on the cheek. "Well, my last day certainly started well."

Seamus hugged her with one arm. "I think it started even better for me."

She shook her head, "Don't be silly. If I'm going to start an intimate relationship to last the rest of my life, I want to know what I'm getting into."

Seamus put the cups on the table and turned around with his eyes twinkling. "So, that was an audition?"

“Of course.”

"Oh my, with no chance to rehearse. Did I get the part?"

She hugged him. "You did - a wonderful performance. I predict a very long run."

Seamus whispered in her ear, “I may even get better with practice.”

She giggled, "I promise to give you lots of practice." and then, "Let's sit on the porch until the coffee's ready."

"OK"

As they sat down, Seamus sighed, "The last day, sigh."

Meg frowned, "No its not, it's just the last day of this trip. I'm not moving to Madagascar, for heaven's sake."

Seamus grinned and nodded, "Of course, but when is the next? That's all I want to know. Wait a bit, I have to take the book back to the Pope. Unless my memory fails me, I think he's still in Rome. How about that for a next trip."

Meg beamed, "Ooo, I've always wanted to go to Rome. You'd better take me along or I'll hunt you down and take my revenge."

Seamus sat back in his chair, "Good, that's settled then" His expression was sad, "Still that's probably a month or so away. I'll be unhappy with the wait."

She touched his arm. "You'll be fine. Just look forward to us being together again. That's what I want to hear."

"I swear on St. Patrick's grave." He covered her hand with his own.

A noise came from inside the house. It was someone coming downstairs. Seamus jumped up. "I'd best go get our coffee before it's all taken." He went into the house. Back in a few minutes, he handed Meg her coffee. "It was Maeve, she's up early most days but I thought she'd sleep in on the Saturday."

"Do you think we woke her?"

"Lord I hope not. No... I don't think so. P.J. would wake before her if he heard any strange noises."

"Well, all right but I imagine I made some strange noises."

Seamus grinned, "Delightful is a better word."

They sat and chatted for a while. Meg stood up and reached over to Seamus. "Finished? I'll take the cups into the kitchen and then let's take a walk. It's very pretty here."

"All right, I've rather been in the habit of having a walk in the morning."

After a few minutes she came out and they started off on the walk. They walked a long time and by the time they returned it was time for lunch. P.J. and Maeve had reheated the leftovers from the grill the night before. Then Seamus stood up. "I'm still needing my nap," he announced. Meg thought for second and then stood up, saying," I think I'll do the same that sounds nice and I never have the luxury back home."

Maeve looked up, smiling, "If you spend time with Seamus, you'll never miss a nap."

Meg gave Seamus a crooked smile, "I believe you Maeve."

They both walked upstairs.

That evening P.J. grilled again. He liked to grill and preferred it to Maeve's cooking.

Of course, Maeve preferred not to have to cook.

Sitting in the lounge Maeve looked at Seamus.

"I almost forgot to tell you. Nigel sent a reply. He just said he got the formulas and promised to make them up and then start tests. But he also said the mixture took a couple of weeks so it would be a while before he could find out anything and you shouldn't think he was ignoring it all."

Seamus nodded, "Ah, well I must possess myself in patience."

Seamus went to bed about an hour after Meg. Maeve and P.J. were still up. He lay awake for a long while. Then he heard Maeve and P.J. go to bed. A few minutes later the door opened quietly and Meg came in, closed the door and climbed into bed next to him. She rolled over on her side and put her arm and head on Seamus' chest. They cuddled for a few minutes and went to sleep.

The next morning Meg woke up and got out of bed. She bent down and whispered, "I'm going to go muss up the sheets where I'm supposed to be sleeping," and left the room.

Seamus sighed to himself, *Ah, well, a very sweet last two nights.*

He dozed about another hour and then got up, dressed and went downstairs. As he was putting on the coffee Meg came into the kitchen. She kissed him on the cheek without a word and sat down. Seamus turned around. "So, coffee on the front porch?"

Meg beamed up at him, "Oh yes and I think I'll go sit there now until it's ready." She got up and walked out to the porch. Seamus followed.

Meg spoke first, "I have to pack and prepare myself for the mobile doctor role...and look. Last day and I really don't want to go back."

Seamus grimaced, "I don't want you to go back either but you're the one who said you're not moving to Madagascar."

"Yes, I know but right now it feels like it."

"Events will go quickly. As soon as a few pennies drop, I'll be calling you to come to Rome with me."

"Now that's something to look forward to."

They sat and looked out into the street without talking and finally, Seamus stood up and went into the house saying, "I think the coffee's ready by now. I'll bring it out."

He came out with the coffee and Maeve came up behind him in the doorway. "Good morning, Meg - sleep well?"

"Meg twisted her head to say, "Yes, thanks, it's so peaceful here."

"Ah, well by comparison to San Francisco I suppose so. I'll be right back, I need some coffee." She disappeared into the house.

When Maeve came back out P.J. followed behind her.

"So, Meg, you have to be at the airport when?" he said.

"My flight is at one thirty."

Maeve thought a few seconds. "Then we have to leave no later than eleven thirty. That will get us there by noon and you'll have time to go through the exciting security line."

Meg made a face and said sarcastically, "Oh goody, I suppose I should get the packing done."

She went into the house.

Seamus sat back and sipped his coffee and then, looking up at Maeve, he said, "May I come along?"

"Of course, I assumed you would."

—####—

Seamus was quiet in the car coming back.

"Well, Seamus, I don't want your depression coming back. The time will pass quickly and you'll be seeing her again."

Seamus, shook it off. "I know, and don't worry, so long as I have her to look forward to, I'll be fine."

The next day Seamus moped around. He didn't take his morning walk and he watched TV until lunch then went up to his nap.

Coming down the stairs he met Maeve standing at the bottom with a frown.

"Seamus you're back where you where you were before the book. You need something to occupy yourself while you wait for next steps."

Seamus looked at her sadly.

"Yes, Maeve but what?"

"Perhaps there's something you can do related to the book."

Seamus brightened.

"Maeve I think you may have touched the spot. Do you think Father Schmidt would teach me Latin?"

""I'm sure he would, I'll call him right now."

She turned and walked back to her office.

Seamus heard her talking as he went to the kitchen for coffee. After a few minutes she came into the kitchen.

"Well, you keep giving me work to do. Now we have to go buy a couple of textbooks. Come on, up you get. You can trade that coffee for a beer when we get back."

Seamus groaned and followed her out the door.

Chapter 34: The end of the Plague, 1349

De Chauliac sat at the table in the scullery. He was despondent. As he listened to Alcadio and Simon in the room adjacent he realized that no amount of effort would be enough. Alcadio walked in and, seeing de Chauliac, sat down opposite and looked at him, sympathetically.

"You are troubled, Physician or I cannot read a face."

De Chauliac looked up, sadly.

"Yes, Alcadio, I am dejected by my place in this time."

Alcadio with a puzzled tone, said.

"The Greek's potion works. You have saved your Pope. We prepare more to save others. Truth, the pestilence departs your door driven back by the cold wind. How many have gone to their God without your knowledge and intent? Why do you sadden yourself?"

De Chauliac eyes looked at Alcadio but he did not see him.

"Alcadio, my pride and fame misled me. I thought to save the whole of Avignon and thus, enrich myself in every eye. I was given a lesson from God. As we now know it would take a multitude of alchemists a stretch of time back before we arrived in this wretched city to gather enough of the Greek's elixir to save the total of needy souls."

Alcadio nodded. And replied,

"Yes, the need is too great for the time and we too few to defeat this eager death. But we labored as we could and we saved those most entrusted to our work. You cannot blame yourself for failure to save all."

De Chauliac protested "But I can so be blamed. Had I not been prideful, I would have thought to gather many more to work beside us and, thus, provide more and kept more from the grave."

Alcadio leaned back.

“Physician, could we have gathered enough and long enough ago to save all of Avignon? I think not.”

"Perhaps not, Alcadio. But on a future day I shall never see, there will be great guilds of Alchemists. These guilds will prepare physicks in quantities so large they will be available to every man."

Alcadio looked grim,

"For a price, physician, for a price."

De Chauliac looked at Alcadio with a wry smile and sighed.

"Ah yes, Alcadio, for a price," he said quietly, nodding.

A thought struck de Chauliac; he stared at Alcadio.

"Alcadio, a thought has entered my mind whether from an imp or an angel, I know not. The Greek's book - were it to become known to all. What might that portend?"

Alcadio pondered a moment and said "Mayhaps those guilds you spoke of."

De Chauliac shook his head.

"No, I fear worse than that. The world would be incensed. 'Here was the cure and the church kept it from us.' they would say. The populace would rise and attack the pope. The nobles would be excused their excesses and they, themselves, would seek to overthrow the papacy."

Alcadio was taken aback.

"Could that be true?"

"Ah, Alcadio, the politics are fragile enough. This could destroy the faithful's faith; which already shudders in the wind."

"But, physician, many saw you going into houses that contained the pestilence. You cannot be faulted."

"Making their anger a certainty, Alcadio, the populace will say, 'see, he was among the stricken and did not fall sick'."

"Say you did."

De Chauliac was startled. "Alcadio, say I had the pestilence?"

"Yes, then no hand would be raised to harm you."

"How did I escape?"

"Some physick that no man would wish to follow. You burned yourself. Destroying the black eggs with fire."

De Chauliac smiled.

—####—

The Papal Palace

Marceau opened the door.

"Holiness"

"Yes, yes Marceau, what or mayhaps who do you have?"

"Your physician, holiness."

Clement sighed.

"Does he say what purpose?"

"No, holiness, he seems, ah, concerned."

"Well, announce him. I trust it is of short span."

Marceau left and a few seconds later, returned.

"Monsieur de Chauliac"

De Chauliac walked in diffidently and bowed.

"Holiness."

Clement nodded.

"What is it Guy."

"Your holiness - the book prepared in Hibernia, has it arrived?"

Clement stared with his mouth open. *What could make this question, The Greek potion is long since prepared,* he thought.

"No, Guy, these copies take many Sundays to complete. "Why does this pertain? You have had what you desired for sufficient time."

De Chauliac wrestled with his thoughts and then blurted.

"Yes, holiness, may I request that when the book returns, it be destroyed."

Clement closed his mouth and thought furiously. *Why would the physician want the book destroyed? To keep it secret? From who?* Then he had it. *Of course, to keep it from anyone; to keep it from everyone. Should the knowledge that a physick was in the hands of the pope and not made useful to everyone. All would be fury. The nobles would be sure to tell the world and the uproar would destroy the church.*

He looked at de Chauliac with a grim smile.

"You have impressed upon my mind the strength of your eye, Guy. I see what you have seen. I am of the same view and it shall be done."

De Chauliac bowed, said, "Holiness" turned and walked away.

De Chauliac walked back to his house from the papal palace deep in thought. *Is this deed for good or have I been subjected to a demon's wiles? The Church will be spared the anger of the multitude. That cannot be argued. But the Greek's elixir, what of that? Should this pestilence return - what then? Hold! I still retain the copy not bound. The potion may be prepared again. I dare not destroy it. No help would remain for those to come. But then, what if those who could profit suspect the potion and seek to prove it. Where would they seek it? The Papal Palace of course - the Bibliotheca Secreta. Not discovering it there - what then? The Papal physician - myself. How to secure the pages thus that they could not be found? They must be removed to some place distant. Distant and not to be found soon. He stopped, Of course! Whence it came - Hibernia! Ah but how to have it delivered and where?*

As he walked and thought he entered his own courtyard. There were four horses in the courtyard. *What? What visitors may look to me?* he thought.

The door opened and Alcadio stepped out. A very large grin on his face. Behind him came Ferand, Gerard, Giuseppe and Michel. Alcadio waved.

"Monsieur you have your guests returned from the North."

De Chauliac bowed to all.

"But why? You were all safe from the Avignon air; how came you to revisit the city of the danger you had escaped?"

Michel went over to check the horses. Gerard came out to stand behind Ferand's shoulder. Ferand spoke first.

"The pestilence was squatting on Pont St. Esprit when we arrived, Monsieur. Gerard gave the potion to his kin. And, Monsieur, your Greek spoke the truth." He looked at de Chauliac intently. Gerard interrupted. "All my kin were spared, physician and the company you see assembled." He waved to Ferand and Michel and Giuseppe who appeared - filling the doorway. Gerard grinned and bowed.

"Knowing my kin were safe I felt the need to appeal to his Holiness' generosity and put me to the old service as courier. I felt the lack of his rewards."

Ferand laughed and explained further. "The rest of us, observing the peace and silence of Pont St. Esprit, chose to join Gerard and seek a place with some excitement - however risky to our persons. And, more, the cold season brought the wind from the north and northeast. I felt content that the pestilence had been driven to the south."

De Chauliac opened his eyes and looked at Gerard. My wits are slow, he thought. Gerard may be the courier of the Greek's book. He pointed to Gerard.

"Gerard, are you the courier who brought the book to Hibernia?"

Gerard nodded, surprised. "I am Monsieur. I was unaware you knew not."

De Chauliac gripped his arm. "And you know where the scribe is domiciled?"

"I do, Monsieur and as pretty a place as God ever made."

Alcadio had been following closely and interjected.

"Would you object to travel there once more, Gerard?"

De Chauliac's head spun to Alcadio and he continued. "Gerard, I have a manuscript I would have you take to this scribe. I will pay for your journey."

Michel walked up behind and spoke to de Chauliac's back. "Would you include myself, physician? I could see to the horses for Gerard. He has not the skill needed. I have a hunger to see Hibernia since Gerard spoke of it all these months ago."

Gerard held up his hand. "Hold everyone. I would intend to apply to his Holiness. His forgiveness is all that is needed to fill my purse. And more, the monk may well have finished the task and I must return his work to the library. This would provide two purposes for the journey."

De Chauliac blinked and thought. *Yes, no one knows of the intent to destroy the books, except Alcadio. Besides they must be here to effect the destruction.*

Alcadio looked at De Chauliac and thought. *The physician intends to keep his purpose secret. Then I must not divulge it.*

De Chauliac went into the house saying, "Gerard you will assist my cash box with his Holiness' largesse. But, whether or not, I will give you the pouch to leave with the monk. Hold before you go to the Papal Palace and I will give you the missive."

He came out a few minutes later with a papal pouch, the same he received from the pope. He handed it to Gerard.

"My thanks to you and here are some coins for the trouble you face." He handed Gerard a handful of gold.

Gerard nodded and put the coins in his purse. "You may trust in the completion of the task, Monsieur. I will visit before I depart and inform you of his Holiness' decision. Oh, and take my horse."

De Chauliac nodded and Gerard strode away toward the palace as de Chauliac waved at everyone and entered the house.

"Come all and enjoy some of Simon's fine spiced wine while we await Gerard's return."

Gerard strode up to the door. Michel and the others came out to hear the news. Michel looked at Gerard quizzically.

"Yes, Michel, I ride for his Holiness again. You and I will travel to Hibernia together."

Michel grinned as he said, "and I will only have to care for two good mounts. A rest and an adventure together. When do we depart?"

"As soon as may be, my friend."

De Chauliac bowed to Gerard and Michel.

"So soon as tomorrow is soon enough. Come in and rest for the journey." He turned and went into the house. Everyone followed.

—####—

As they rode, Michel asked, "Where do we cross to Hibernia?"

"Calais to Anglia. Across Anglia to the west coast and then boat again to Hibernia."

"Why not from Normandy in a line to Hibernia, Gerard?"

"I know not how your stomach travels on water, Michel but mine protests. I would make the time across the sea as short as I may accept. I fear there is no time short enough."

Michel nodded and thought for a spell. Then, "I know not Gerard, I have never travelled by water save the river."

Gerard looked at him. "Then we should both have care not to eat before we sail."

—####—

Hibernia

Gerard and Michel climbed out of the currach onto the stone ledge and looked up at the steps.

Michel looked at Gerard. "May St. Hippolytus protect me."

Gerard smiled at Michel. "Rather to ask a saint who protects mountaineers."

Colum walked over to Gerard and bowed. "Gerard it is a joy to see you."

Gerard bowed back. "And a joy to see you Brother Colum. This is my good friend Michel. On hearing my tale of Hibernia, he begged to join me." Colum bowed to Michel. "Michel I welcome you to our humble dwelling."

Michel returned the bow.

"Thank you Brother, may God be with you."

Colum nodded. "He never departs Michel. May you have peace here in this place devoted to His praise. And now we challenge the steps. Brother Bron will ascend in front and I will follow behind. You will have companions up to the top."

Michel looked up at the steps.

"I pray I will have angelic companions to add to my journey."

Bron, smiled and started up the steps. Gerard followed, then Michel and, finally, Colum. They ascended together, slowly but steadily.

At the top, Bron turned and held his hand out for Gerard who sprang up the last steps and turned with his hand out to Michel. Michel took his hand and pulled himself up to the wall at the top. Leaning on the wall he let out his breath. "God's mercy." He looked out over the cliff to the sea.

"It is a sight for the eye. And a cost for the legs."

Colum turned and walked saying, "after your exertions you should partake of our refectory, this way."

Gerard and Michel hurried to keep up. As they crossed by the yew tree, Fergus ran out to Gerard and rubbed against his leg. Gerard bent over and petted the cat. "Ah, Fergus, I missed you."

After some bread, cheese and ale, they walked slowly over to the scriptorium. The abbot walked quickly over to them and bowed. "Gerard, it is a joy to have you with us again."

Gerard bowed, thank you abbot I have always felt welcome here."

"And so you are, good friend. Colum has completed the book. I would believe that is the nature of your visit."

Gerard looked slightly surprised. "Well abbot I have another errand, to return the portion I collected on my last visit. Your words are more benefit to me. His Holiness will be greatly satisfied with my commission when I return."

Colum looked puzzled, "Gerard are there instructions for me?"

"No brother I was only told to give your previous pages into your care."

Colum shook his head, "Then so shall I do but I know not why."

Gerard had put the unbound manuscript on a table. The Abbot looked at it and frowned.

Colum walked to the back of scriptorium and came back with two books. One was obviously the exemplar. He handed them to Gerard. "Gerard, I will miss your visits."

Gerard smiled. "So shall I brother."

"You have survived the pestilence. God blessed you as a good man."

"Yes, I think I have more to accomplish. He waits for my efforts to be complete. I would He would say what those tasks may be."

Gerard put the exemplar in his satchel and picked up Colum's copy. He looked and turned a few pages, then turned to Colum.

"Fine work brother, did you also do the binding?"

Colum nodded, saying. "Yes, I have not the binding knowledge I would want. This was a useful lesson for me."

The Abbot looked at the book as Gerard was turning the pages.

He turned to Colum.

"Brother Colum the unbound pages are parchment, yet the book is vellum. How did this come to pass.

Colum looked blank, then,

"I consumed all my vellum Abbot and went to the pile in the back of the scriptorium for more pages."

"Please Colum show me from whence the parchment came."

They left Gerard standing, wondering. After a few minutes they returned. Colum looked worried and the Abbot looked puzzled.

Gerard asked the Abbot.

"Is all well?"

"Gerard I cannot tell. Brother Colum erased a manuscript that was old. He did not observe what the old manuscript recorded. We know not if it was of value. You must take it back to his Holiness and beg that his scribes with more skill uncover the original text. Only then can we know what has been covered. Colum did not scrape the pages. I am in hope that it can be done."

He handed the pages to Gerard and Gerard put them in his satchel.

—####—

Fouinon the cutpurse and Edwige

Fouinon walked slowly up the hill from the docks. It had been a profitless day. The pestilence had inflicted much harm on his efforts. The crowds were few and small. Without the crowds he was too easily noticed. He had been reduced to scavenging but that was dangerous. Other scavengers had surprised him and they would kill to get what they wanted. He sighed to himself. *How could a good man make a dishonest living in these times?* As he neared the end of the street he heard a woman weeping. There was a narrow alley in front and the sound seemed to be coming from it.

He turned into the alley and the weeping was louder. Only a few feet down the alley an opening in the walls led into a courtyard. He walked through the opening. The yard was full of refuse and the stench was almost overpowering. A woman was sitting on a wooden barrel, her face in her hands. She looked familiar. *What woman is that I would have met before?* He thought. *Oh, the girl I helped a year ago with the bale of cloth. What was her name? I have it - Edwige.*

He walked over to her and put his hand on her shoulder.

"Edwige, why do you sadden yourself?"

Startled, she raised her face out of her hands. She looked at him in fear and then she recognized him and grinned.

"Oh good sir!"

Her face went sad again.

"Oh, what am I to do, sir. I am a poor sinner, *mortal* sins."

It was Fouinon's turn to be startled. *What could this simple girl have done to believe that?* he thought.

He pulled over another barrel and sat on it.

"Explain it to me, Edwige."

"Oh sir, I have stolen. My uncle and his wife are dead. The pestilence carried them off All Saints Day last."

"How have you sustained yourself?"

"My uncle had a strongbox of coins. I have stolen from these when my hunger was too strong."

Fouinon thought carefully. *Wait, she is his niece and kin.*

"Edwige did your uncle have children?"

"No, he did not want to pay for them."

That fits the man, Fouinon thought.

"Then was your father his only brother?"

Edwige looked at him blankly, her eyes red and wet.

"Yes, he had no other."

"Are your grandparents still living?"

"No they have gone many years past."

Fouinon stood up and pulled her hand.

"Come Edwige, show me this strongbox."

She stood and walked to a door in the back of the courtyard's building.

Fouinon said to her back.

"You have fed yourself from the coins in this box?"

She turned her head and talked over her shoulder as she walked.

"Yes, not many, sir, I found that the Inns would give all that I needed for small parts of a single coin. But it has been many Sundays and a number of coins."

These must be coins of large value, thought Fouinon.

They went into the back of the shop. It was dark; the shutters were all in place. They could see by the light from the cracks. The strongbox was on the end of a long counter. Edwige went to it and opened the lid.

Fouinon looked and his eyes widened. The box was very large and filled to the brim with gold coins. It was a fortune.

After a minute he realized he was frozen in wonder. He turned to Edwige gathering his thoughts.

"Come Edwige let us go back out into the light. They walked back out into the courtyard as Fouinon thought, Can I take advantage of this simple girl? But then she cannot think herself a safe path and what others might ravage her for such a golden prize. I can resist that future and , with God's help, keep her from harm.

He took her shoulders and guided her back to the barrel.

'Edwige, sit and calm yourself. You have nothing to fear and you have not sinned but there is much to do. To begin, the strongbox and all it contains is yours, by right. It is your inheritance from your uncle. He may not have so intended but the laws support it. The strongbox and the shop and all its stores are yours - by right. But you cannot, nor do you wish to be a merchant as your uncle. You must take all that is yours and leave; to find a different life and a better one."

Edwige sniffled, "But I know not what to do. I am puzzled to find my way and the means to go."

Fouinon knelt before her.

"Edwige, I shall join you and see you safely to another place. I shall not leave you until you so say I should."

Edwige laughed and reaching down, she hugged Fouinon.

"I shall do as you tell me always."

Fouinon thought. *I hope I have not committed an error, but it is done. Now to arrange to leave this foul city. Once past its air I must arrange for Edwige to swim in some clean water. She will be a rank perfume after Avignon is not so near to disguise it.*

Chapter 35: The Potion

"Seamus!" Maeve was standing at the bottom of the stairs with the phone in her hand.

"I'm here Maeve" Seamus was outside the kitchen behind her.

"It's Meg - again." Seamus walked up and took the phone. "Thank you Maeve."

"Hi Meg, is there anything new?"

"No, I just wanted to call. So, what have you been doing lately?"

"Well, I'm still taking Latin lessons from Father Schmidt. He's quite a good teacher but I suppose he should be after all."

Meg chuckled, I would think so, it's his occupation. You are a bit older than his regular students though. Anything new on the book?"

"No, the status is quo."

Has the old man contacted you?"

Not since he confirmed the plan was accepted and he was going to proceed. He said he'd let me know as events unfolded."

"Well, then when are we going to Rome."

Seamus laughed. "Ah, you haven't forgotten."

"How could I do that. Oh drat, I have a patient. Sorry Seamus, I have to go."

"Sigh, I'll let you know when I'm ready to book plane tickets Meg."

"And hotel room. You'd better. Bye Seamus. I love you."

"That sounds soooo good. I love you, too Meg. Goodbye."

Seamus pushed 'off' on the phone and walked to Maeve's office.

"Here you are Maeve, thanks very much. I'm going back to the kitchen and do my homework."

Maeve smiled up at him as she took the phone. "Good, that will be very useful when you join the clergy."

Seamus shrugged his shoulders and just nodded.

An hour or so later Maeve came into the kitchen. Seamus was bent over his book and papers.

"Seamus you have a message from Nigel." Seamus head snapped up.

"What does he say?"

"You had better come read it for yourself."

They both went into Maeve's office and Maeve sat and pushed some buttons then she stood up and motioned Seamus to the chair.

"Here - it's on the screen."

Seamus sat and read -

"Seamus,

Well I have bad news - or rather non-news.

I mixed up a batch of each formula and when it was ready we introduced plague bacillus and watched it carefully.

There was no effect on the plague whatsoever.

This is not totally conclusive, however. You see the formula may generate a reaction within the body that does harm to the plague. Unfortunately, we don't feel inclined to catch plague to find out.

If we learn anything more, I'll let you know. Sorry it isn't promising at the moment.

All the best,

Nigel

Seamus leaned back and sighed. "Oh well, I suppose I should have expected this. I wish I'd seen this before Meg called. She will be interested."

Seamus was in the kitchen studying when Maeve walked in. She watched for a minute or so, then.

"So, how is the Latin scholar doing?"

"amo, amas, amat, amamus, amatis, amant."

"I love you too Seamus."

"Well, I hate declensions and you'll be sorry to hear I don't think I can say mass."

"Nevermind, you have another message from Nigel and I think it'll cheer you up."

"Oh my what does he say?"

"Come on, you should read it for yourself."
Seamus got up and followed Maeve to her office. She waved at the chair.

"There it is, go ahead."

Seamus sat and read.

Seamus,

This is amazing but I don't know yet what is going on.

By some strange fluke we had an opportunity to test your Greek's formula.

A dog was brought in, in desperation I think. The dog had bubonic plague. We think he caught it from a stoat he was chasing.

We gave him the potion - and IT WORKED.

The dog recovered in a couple of days. Obviously, the potion did something. I just don't know what.

We have blood samples taken before and during the dog's recovery.

We will be studying those intensely.

As remarkable as this is, it is useless unless we can uncover how the potion worked. Otherwise no pharmaceutical firm would take it up. I know - I worked for one. The idea of mixing up this revolting sauce would turn them right off.

I will write whenever I have anything more definite.

All the best,

Nigel

Seamus leaned back with his mouth open and looked up at Maeve.

"You read this?"

"Yes, I did. Amazing."

"Indeed it is, but as Nigel said, the bit that begs for an answer is - how?"

"Well, You'll have to leave that to Nigel. How did you come to know him?"

"It was long ago, Before I married Lena. I was working a job in England in concert with the Thames police. They found a murder. Two bodies in a small flat. There were many odd pieces of equipment. The police knew about Nigel and brought him in to identify what the gear was. I met him over that and we liked each other. Later on, I called him for other similar advice. He kept in touch - the little taps over time, you know, Christmas cards and such. He remembered my birthday and never failed to send me a card."

"So, what happened?"

"We just lost touch. He went over to the research labs. He was a natural scientist, I think and that was where he wanted to be. I kept working and didn't find any more need for him in the jobs I was doing. Sooo..." Seamus shrugged and stood up.

"Nevermind, I think it's time for a beer. Do you want one?"

Maeve shook her head. "No thank you, not just yet."

Seamus went downstairs to get a beer, well, two beers.

Maeve walked into the kitchen with the phone and handed it to Seamus.

"Its the old man's butler, Seamus."

Seamus took it from her.

"Hello Robert, what can I do for you?"

"Seamus, the master asked me to call. He is wondering if you would mind taking the book back to the Vatican library...in Rome. He told me to say he would pay all your expenses."

"Well, yes, of course I will. He is very generous."

Robert chuckled.

"The cost of anything doesn't come into his purview Seamus."

"I suppose not. Well thank him for me, all the same."

"I shall. You should call with an estimate and I will send you a check."

"That won't be necessary Robert. I'll just keep track of my expenses and he can cover my charges, whenever he likes."

"Thank you Seamus. He would appreciate a call on your return or, better yet, a visit to discuss the events."

"Of course, I would enjoy that myself."

"Well, enjoy the trip and we'll talk when you get back."

"I promise, Robert, goodbye."

Maeve had been standing next to the table all through the conversation. Seamus pushed the 'off' button on the phone and handed it back to her.

"Well, I'm to go to Rome at the old man's expense. I'd better call Meg."

Maeve raised an eyebrow.

"Indeed, you've the luck but it's a little early to call her now. She's not out of bed yet."

Seamus waited to call Meg until after his nap. He was trying to time it for Meg's lunch time.

"Meg?"

"Hullo Seamus what news?"

"We're going to Rome. I just need you to tell me when you can get away."

"I will be just about free and clear by the end of next week. How's that?"

"Wonderful, I'll tidy up the loose ends here and make the travel arrangements. Then I'll have Maeve e-mail you all the particulars."

"That will work. Don't arrange me from here. When I get the details I'll fly out to you and we can both leave from Cincinnati."

"As you wish; I can't wait."

"I can't either but we'll both have to. Sorry sweetheart, I have to go, I have a patient in five minutes. Bye"

"Bye love."

Maeve walked in and took the phone.

"I overheard some of that. What are the loose ends?"

"Ah well, I need to talk to Father Schmidt about his friend at the Vatican library. It would be well if he knew I was coming and how to reach him after I'm there. As I understand it, you can't just go strolling into the library without prior arrangement."

Maeve thought for a few seconds.

"I'm sure you're right. You need to bring it up at your next lesson."

"Oh lord, my next lesson; I need to crack the books."

"So, when do I arrange your flights to Rome?"

"No rush Maeve. Meg can't go until the week after next."

"Good, I'm behind again. I'll look into it tomorrow. Coach or first class?"

"Oh my, first class, I think, I want Meg to be comfortable."

Maeve smiled.

"Of course you do. So be it. For how long?"

"Oh, a week I think. Then we can see the sights; besides the Vatican."

"Alright, I'll set it up. But wait, are you coming back here?"

"Yes, of course. I still have to report to the old man and Meg hasn't actually said she wants to follow me to Ireland."

"Ah, there's the rub. All the best."

She turned and went back to her office.

—####—

"Seamus."

"Yes, Maeve I'm still in the kitchen."

Maeve walked in and sat down.

"Alright, here's the deal. You can't get first class; there's no such thing. I got you and Meg Business Class. Its still pretty good; not like economy. You're leaving a week from Friday at about quarter to two and coming back a week from the following Sunday. You get into Rome about ten thirty the next day. That's why I extended you till the Sunday. I actually had a call from Robert and he was very helpful. He wanted to be sure you had a pleasant trip and he told me he would make all the arrangements in Rome. I told him about Meg and he said he would include her. You will be a VIP when you arrive. I have it all here. Read it over and put it in your luggage. When you come back you get in during the day so I'll meet you at the airport and Meg can stay with us until she's ready to go back to San Francisco."

"Will you send all this to Meg?"

"I already have. You should expect a phone call any minute."

Seamus grinned.

Chapter 36: Rome

Seamus and Meg were on the plane.

"How can you sleep? It's so exciting. Seamus we're going to Rome."

"I know Meg. I've been there before. It was a long time ago, though, I expect it's changed a bit. I just can't help myself. I always fall asleep on airplanes."

"Well, you have *me* this time. Can't you stay awake and keep me company?"

"You're the reason I've stayed awake this long."

"Oh. I suppose I'll have to sleep too, then."

"That's a good idea. You get there more quickly you know."

"Right! Where are we staying?"

"The Marriott on the via Veneto. I think it's a good choice. The old man's butler set it all up. We're better off with a chain so there'll be a better chance they speak English."

"I imagine they all do. Americans are the only ones who don't speak English."

Seamus laughed.

"Sad but true, Meg."

"OK, how do we get to the hotel?"

"Taxi, of course. It'll cost a lot and scare the pants off us, but it's the simplest and easiest."

"I promise not to scream. You can go to sleep now."

Seamus closed his eyes.

"Oh, Seamus, wait, I forgot to tell you. Tony's going to meet us in Rome."

Seamus opened his eyes and sat up.

"What? When?"

"A couple of days after we get there. I told him to get details from Maeve."

Seamus thought for a minute.

"Well enough. We'll have plenty of privacy and it'll be good to see him."

Meg exhaled.

"Thank God you're not upset."

Seamus patted her shoulder.

"I couldn't be upset with you, Meg. Everything will be fine."

He slid down and closed his eyes…again.

It took an hour to get through customs and pickup their bags. As they came out of customs onto the concourse Meg nudged Seamus and pointed. There was a man holding a sign that said "Seamus & Meg." Seamus chuckled.

"I guess that must be for us. I can't believe there are two Seamuses and Megs."

They walked over to the sign and the man dropped the sign. He had a New York accent.

"Mr. Cash?"

"Yes, and this is Meg Farrell," he said, pointing at Meg.

"Robert thought I would be some help. He warned me you wouldn't be expecting me."

The ride in the car was about another hour. As they pulled up in front of the hotel, the driver turned and handed Seamus a business card.

"Turn my card in at the desk. If you need the car any time while you're here, just have them call me. I don't have a lot on this week so I'll be available."

Seamus thanked him and as they got out he unloaded the bags and put them on a luggage cart. A hotel bellman wheeled the cart into the lobby. When they checked-in, the man at the desk was expecting them.

"Ah, Signore Cash, your secretary has arranged your reception. He told us you would be arriving before normal check-in. Your room is ready."

"My secretary?"

"Si, Signore Robert."

"Ah, of course, thank you."

Seamus turned to Meg.

"Robert is smoothing our way, apparently. He prepared everything."

Meg smiled and they went up to the room; as soon as they walked in, Meg gasped.

"Oh, Seamus, it's beautiful. Good lord, it's a suite. Look it even has a fireplace. What must this be costing?"

"I shudder to think, Meg but Robert arranged this so he must know. I suppose, as he said, the financial affairs don't even come up on the old man's radar."

She was looking out the window.

"Seamus there's an antique ruin right outside. It looks like an aqueduct. What do you think it is?"

Seamus looked.

"I have no idea. So what's the attraction with an antique ruin outside when you've got one right here next to you?"

Meg laughed.

"You are not an antique and I intend to prove it before we leave Rome."

They unpacked a little, freshened up and then went down to the Cabiria bar. They had a quick lunch, a couple of drinks and went back to their room. Seamus missed his nap even after sleeping on the plane. Seamus got undressed and got into bed. Meg picked up one of her bags and went into the bathroom. After a few minutes she came out wearing a satin top that reached just below her waist and thigh-top stockings. Seamus looked, his mouth slightly open in wonder. Then,

"Meg you're breathtaking."

She giggled.

"I thought I should decorate myself and my shape isn't what it used to be."

"It's everything I ever dreamed of."

"You're sweet and you shall be rewarded."

She got into bed and reached over to him.

When they woke up they finished unpacking and chatted about what to do. Then they went down to the Cabiria bar followed by the restaurant for dinner. Meg was staring at the menu for a long time.

"Seamus, they have everything on this menu. All the gourmet dishes I expected but they even have a whole section of hamburgers and pizza."

Seamus raised his eyes over the menu.

"Well Meg, they did invent pizza after all." They laughed a bit. After dinner they went to the bar for a nightcap.

Seamus looked serious for a second.

"Right now, we are on a clock that feels like noon. So we have plenty of energy. Tomorrow morning we will be getting up at, say, eight in the morning here but it will feel like two in the morning. If we're going to get off the jet lag, we should go to bed early."

Meg saw the look.

"Good, you will have more energy." She smiled demurely.

Seamus smiled.

"Yes, I think I will."

After a few drinks, they went up to bed. The next morning they were woken with a call from the front desk at eight o'clock. Although they were groggy, as Seamus had predicted, they got up and showered.

Seamus was dressed, waiting for Meg to put on her face.

"I want to have breakfast on the roof at the Ailanto restaurant. It's a buffet but they say you can see all of Rome from up there."

Meg was excited.

"Ooo, that sounds wonderful, let's do that."

Sitting at the restaurant, they looked out over the city.

"Seamus, what's the dome over there?" She pointed.

"I think that's St. Peter's basilica."

"It's not very far away."

"No, it's not. Why don't we walk through the city after breakfast."

"All the way to the Vatican?"
"No, just down to the Spanish Steps, I think. It will take about a half hour, because we'll walk 'a la Sant Terre'."

"A la Sant Terre?"

"Yes, we'll saunter, slowly."

Meg giggled.

"Of course, 'to the holy land', now I get it. Is that where the word came from?"

"I think so; it's too much of a coincidence otherwise."

They stopped at their room, so Meg could change her shoes and then set off.

It was a beautiful morning, cool and sunny with a slight breeze.

Seamus knew where to go and in about fifteen minutes they were standing at the top of the Spanish steps. The steps had stone vases filled with flowers on every step. They covered both edges and the center. It was beautiful. Meg gasped and Seamus stopped and stared.

"Meg, this is very, very different than I remember. I don't think they had any flowers; the steps were just bare stone."

"Well, I like this better; it's breathtaking."

Meg was looking around brightly like a schoolgirl. Then she grabbed Seamus arm.

"So, onward, now what?"

"Well, how about a coffee to follow up on breakfast?"

"OK, where?"

Seamus pointed.

Just down there, the Cafe Greco. I read it's the oldest cafe in Rome. Keats and Shelley used to have lunch there. Oh, and write little stanzas of Poetry. I think that's how they paid their bills."

He started down the steps. At the bottom, Seamus fell back behind Meg and pinched her bottom.

"Ouch, what was that about?"

Seamus looked down.

"Well, when I was here last that was quite common. The Italian men were notorious for pinching pretty women. It was considered flattery. I don't know if they still do it though."

Meg gave him a crooked smile.

"Alright, but you walk behind me from now on. If I'm going to be pinched, I want to know who's doing it."

Sitting in the cafe, Meg leaned over to whisper.

"It's very nice and the coffee is great but it's not cheap. Lord, eight euros for a coffee."

Seamus nodded.

"Fortunately, we don't care. I'm sure the old man doesn't either."

They strolled back, well, sauntered back. At the hotel they realized they had only been gone a little more than two hours. Meg looked at Seamus.

"Well, now what?"

"Let's go up and relax."

"Ok"

They were in the room for only a few minutes and the phone rang. Meg looked at Seamus quizzically.

"Who could that be?"

"Any number of people. Maeve, Robert, perhaps even Tony."

He picked it up. "Hello?"

"Mr. Cash?"

"Yes?"

"This is Monsignor Ahern from the Vatican library."

"Ah, Monsignor, pleased to meet you, so to speak."

"Pleased to meet you too Mr. Cash."

"Please, Monsignor, call me Seamus."

"As you wish Seamus and, please, call me Mark. Honorifics are tiresome after a while. I'm so excited, I can hardly wait to see the book."

"As soon as you wish Mark. How did you know where I was staying?"

"Oh, I had a call from Father Schmidt. He had all the details from your sister."

"Of course, so what would you like to do?"

"I have a friend near you I promised to visit today. Could I stop in and see you after?"

"Of course, about what time?"

"Well, I'll be free by noon. Perhaps we could meet for lunch?"

"Good, we'll be at one of the tables outside. Myself and a very attractive lady. You should have no trouble spotting us."

"Well, Seamus there are a lot of couples in Rome where one is an attractive lady. I'm sure you've noticed."

Seamus chuckled. "Yes, I have Mark and, of course, there are as many clergy as well. Look for the table with a very old book on it."

"Excellent, that should be unique. I'll see you between noon and twelve thirty."

"Til then Mark, bye."

He turned to Meg as he hung up the phone.

"All right then, things are moving quickly."

Just before eleven thirty Meg and Seamus went down to the lobby restaurant and found a table outside. Sitting with a glass of wine, Meg leaned back and sighed.

"This feels almost morally wrong."

Seamus smiled and spoke from the side of his mouth as his head swiveled to watch a nun ride by on a Vespa.

"Why?"

"Oh, having a glass of wine in the middle of the day. I'm breaking all the health rules I give my patients."

"This is a very special occasion Meg. You're allowed to indulge."

"I'll take your guidance because I want to." She giggled.

Seamus thought, *She has been giggling a lot since we arrived here, I like it.*

After a half hour, Seamus noticed a clergyman walking towards them. He picked up the book and held it up. The clergyman smiled and waved.

Seamus shook Monsignor Ahern's hand and introduced Meg. The Monsignor sat down and Seamus gave him the book. He looked at the book with fascination, then set the book on the table and gingerly lifted the cover. Then he let it drop.

"I should have brought some gloves. Oh, Seamus it's beautiful."

"I thought you would like it."

"How could I not. The wonderful work those tireless monks produced. Do we know if the same monk did the binding?"

"Yes, we think he did. Of course, we can't prove it."

They ordered lunch and Monsignor Ahern talked about Rome and the Vatican library. With an insider's view, it was fascinating. Seamus and Meg were entranced, interrupting with only a few interjections and questions. Finally, lunch being over, the Monsignor stood up and left the book on the table. Seamus held his arm.

"Mark, don't forget the book."

"Oh, well, I was going to leave it with you and arrange an appointment to bring it to the library."

Seamus shook his head.

"I don't think that's necessary. Why don't you just take it back with you. Then all possible complications are avoided."

"As you wish. I must admit, my brownie points will be increased; walking in with this. I don't even have to prove ownership since it's identified as belonging to Pope Clement the sixth. How long do you plan to stay in Rome?"

"We are scheduled to leave a week from today."

"Good, I have time to see you both again."

"We'd like that, Mark. Whenever you like. Just call us."

Seamus shook hands. The Monsignor bent over and kissed Meg's hand.

"Until then, this has been my pleasure. Thank you."

"Our pleasure, uh, Mark and thank you. I may have been tangled up the whole week without your help."

Monsignor Ahern held up his hand and turned saying "Arrivederci," as he walked away.

Seamus sat down. "Ah Rome, there's magic in this city."

"So, now what do we do?"

"I'm going to have my nap. The sooner I get back on schedule, the sooner my clock will adjust."

"It's a good idea, you'll live longer."

"All the more important, since I now have so much to live for."

They went back to the room and both napped until about three o'clock.

When they got up. Meg dressed and went to the bathroom to touch up her makeup. She shouted out of the bathroom.

"OK, we still have some day left. What can we do?"

"How about we walk down to the Fontana di Trevi and throw some coins in?"

"Sounds great, but I will have difficulty coming up with a wish. I can't think of anything I have left to wish for. How far is it?"

Not much more than we walked this morning. We won't be stopping at Cafe Greco so it won't take longer."

They went out and started the walk.

Meg's head was swiveling around, trying to see everything.

"So Seamus, tell me what's different from when you were here before."

"The first thing I noticed was the light."

"The Light?"

"Yes, it may be my bad memory but I remember the light being very clear, almost blue, and, of course, very bright. Mind you, I was much younger then and my eyes were better. I suppose there are more people and cars and they may have some pollution now. There do seem to be more cars."

He turned to watch a very expensive car, a convertible, going by with a church prelate in the back. The chauffeur appeared to be a priest. *Is that a cardinal?* he wondered. He nodded toward the car.

"That looks familiar. I remember seeing that sort of thing when I was here last. But then, there was a whole motorcade with Alfa Romeos and a group of nuns on Vespa's."

Meg nodded.

"OK, but I was looking for, you know, insider information. Something from an expert. You're a detective, don't you know things the usual tourist doesn't know about?"

Seamus, with a bemused look, stopped and thought.

"No, sorry, wait a minute. There is the Pont Milvio bridge but that happened after I was here last."

"What's that?"

"It seems lovers would bring a padlock, presumably new, to this bridge, the Pont Milvio bridge, and lock it to, well, wherever they could. Then they would throw the key into the river. It was a sign that their love was locked inside them forever. The trouble was it grew so out of control, the bridge was being damaged. Some likened it to vandalism. So they banned it. Before they banned it entirely, the mayor imposed a fifty dollar fine on anyone caught. Rather sad really but it was all started by some book and, I suppose, characters in the book did it."

Meg smirked.

"Oh well, I don't want to be arrested and I don't think we need anything like that to reassure us, do you?"

Seamus pulled her over and kissed her.

"No, I don't think we do - or ever will."

Later, after they got back, they had dinner at the restaurant off the lobby, stopped at the Cabiria bar for a nightcap and called it a day.

Getting up the next morning was easier; their clocks were starting to adjust. Again they went up to the Ailanto breakfast buffet on the roof.

Meg held her coffee up between her hands and gave Seamus a smile and 'a look'.

"So, what do we do today? How about the Villa Borghese? all day?"

Seamus shook his head.

"Sorry love, it's closed on Mondays. We could do that tomorrow but we can't spend the whole day. They only allow you two hours. Beside that, we have to have tickets and they're for a specific time."

"Can we see everything in two hours?"

"Oh yes, it's not that large. I only want to see the first floor. That's where the sculpture is."

"Oh, I want to see it all."

Seamus reached over and patted here hand.

"Don't worry, you can see it all. But now what do we do today?"

"Something big - and not too far away."

"Alright, how about the Castle St. Angelo?"

"What's that?"

"It's the old fortress where the pope runs to whenever he's attacked. There's an enclosed walkway from the Vatican to the castle. I doubt it's been used much of late."

Meg grinned.

"I certainly hope not. Is it far?"

"Not really, I think we can do our usual sauntering."

"Done."

It was another beautiful day. They strolled around the city and visited the Castle St. Angelo. Everywhere they walked was something interesting. After a few hours, Meg stopped.

"I think we should go back now. I'm really tired. I had no idea my legs were so out of shape."

"Well, they may be tired but they're definitely not out of shape."

She grabbed his arm and kissed him.

"I'm so glad I found you."

He blushed.

"No no, I found you, remember?"

"Whichever way I'm very happy."

They walked back, holding hands. The Italians looked at them as they walked by (*ah, amore*).

Back at the hotel, Seamus went to the front desk and arranged tickets to the Villa Borghese. Then they had a nap. When they woke up, they decided to call room service for dinner. The suite was so elegant and the view so romantic, it seemed like a waste not to spend more time there. After a leisurely meal, Meg went to the bathroom and, once again, came out wearing the satin top and stockings. Once again, Seamus stared in wonder finally saying.

"Meg you're going to wear me out."

"Oh, I don't think you can be worn out. But if you can, I want to be the one to do it."

She got into bed and turned to him.

The next morning they had been sitting, with their coffee for a few minutes when a voice said, "Good morning."

They looked up and Tony was standing, looking at them with a very large grin.

Seamus stood up and leaned over to shake his hand and said, "Tony, sit down, join us."

"Thank you, I'd like that." He remained standing and looked around at the view.

"Wow, this is even better than I expected. I thought I'd find you two up here; it's l ."

He sat down; he already had a coffee. He looked back and forth between them.

"So, tell me everything that you've done that I missed. Then tell me everything you're going to do, that, I hope, I won't miss."

Seamus, nodded and told Tony everything they'd done. Finishing with,

"We plan on visiting the Villa Borghese today. You have to have tickets but you can get them through the front desk. The trouble is, they only allow you two hours and the ticket tells you what time you are supposed to show up."

Tony pursed his lips.

"All right, what time are your tickets for?"
"Three o'clock this afternoon."

"Then I will try for that time. If I can get it, all well and good. If not, I'll let you go on without me and I'll walk down to the Fontana di Trevi. That may be better, anyway, it will help me adjust my bioclock and I have some wishes that need help."

Seamus sipped his coffee and then told him about Monsignor Ahern and the book.

Tony took it all in and asked.

"Does this mean you don't have to go get access to the library?"

"Yes, it's all over, as easy as could be."

"Well then, you can spend the rest of the time enjoying Rome."

Seamus nodded, "um hum. Just so."

Tony looked a little disappointed.

"Well sometime during a break I want the story on the book and what's new about the Greek's potion."

"Good enough Tony. How about tomorrow morning?"

"Promise?"

"I swear by St. Peter."

After breakfast they went down to a table on the sidewalk. Tony stopped at the front desk to see about a ticket at three o'clock. A few minutes later he came out to the table and sat down. He had a long face.

"Well, I can't get a ticket for three o'clock so I'll just wait for another day. I'll walk around the town and meet you for dinner?" "Of course, Tony. We'll see you tonight. We put in reservations so ask for us if you don't see us."

Tony looked a little sheepish.

"I don't want to be in the way."

Meg touched Tony's arm.

"Don't be silly, we want you there. The conversation will be much more interesting."

Tony raised his eyes to heaven.

"I don't believe that for a minute. Well, I need to get on my walking shoes. I'll see you tonight."

He got up and started for the lobby.

"Six thirty, Tony," Seamus called after him.

Tony nodded and kept walking.

Seamus and Meg sat for a few more minutes and finished their coffee. Up in the room they were talking about what to do with the day before going to the Villa Borghese. The phone rang.

Seamus picked up the phone mumbling "Who could this be?"

"Seamus?"

"Mark! To what do I owe the honor?"

He put his hand over the mouthpiece and whispered to Meg.

"It's Monsignor Ahern."

"I thought you would be interested. After we started to look at your book, I noticed something odd.

"Oh, what was that?"

"Your book was written on vellum but the unbound manuscript was written on parchment."

"Good Lord, how can you tell?"

Mark chuckled, to the trained eye, you can tell. The vellum tends to be thinner and smoother on both sides. Parchment will be a little rougher on one side. That's the side where the wool was."

"Ugh, alright. I bow to superior knowledge. But what does that mean?"

"It may mean nothing but I thought the monk may have run out of vellum and had to find something else. Seamus, I think it's a palimpsest."

"A palimpsest, is that important?"

"Perhaps, it depends on what is underneath. Fortunately, the monk erased the original with Limewater. That means we can uncover the original chemically. If he had actually scraped it clean, it would be much more difficult, if not impossible but why don't you come to the library and let me show you the difference. I should have invited you when we met."

Seamus cupped the phone and turned to Meg - "Want to go to the Vatican Library?" She nodded eagerly. "Mark, we'd love to - are you free this morning?"

"I was hoping you'd say that - I don't have any appointments until two this afternoon so any time this morning is good."

"Well then, why don't we take a cab and be there around 11."

"Better yet Seamus, why don't I send a car and bring you here - it's the least we can do after giving us this treasure."

"A Vatican limo to the Vatican Library…how can we refuse?"

Monsignor Ahern was waiting for them at what seemed to be a private entrance. Quickly, he guided them through a maze of stairs and corridors until they emerged into a room furnished with long tables but empty of people.

"Welcome, to the Manuscript Reading Room."

Did he imagine it? Seamus swore he could sense an aroma of incense combined with must - with perhaps a hint of that distinctive Ronuk polish scent forever implanted in his memory from boarding school days. Meg just stood still, looking around - awe struck seemingly by the simplicity of the room and perhaps entertaining the thought of what the scholars might have looked at within these walls.

"Come, sit down," said Mark, guiding them to a table near the front of the room. They spotted the book immediately - and three pairs of white gloves.

The Monsignor pointed out the differences between the vellum and the parchment - so subtle, they would be easily overlooked. Seamus was bursting with curiosity.

"So when will you know what you have?"

"Oh, it'll be a couple of months at least. I expect it will be a few weeks before we can actually start on it."

"Hum, that's a shame. I don't know where I'll be in a couple of months. Can I contact you, around November? I'm really curious."

"Of course, I hope you will. You can get all my contact information from Father Schmidt. I won't be going anywhere, that's for sure."

Excellent, thanks for letting me know Mark. We'll talk in November."

Mark, gave them a tour of the rest of the Library. It was beautiful. Finally, they all shook hands and Mark walked them out to the car, waiting outside where they left it.

In the car, on the way back to the hotel Meg tapped Seamus' arm. She was obviously surprised.

"I didn't know about the unbound manuscript. When did that turn up?"

Seamus explained the whole story of the multiple books and the unbound portion found in the Vatican Library. Meg thought furiously and then,

"So, we still don't know what happened to the books that are supposed to be there. Your book is, now, the only one."

"That's right but, at least, there is one. Mark can uncover the palimpsest without worrying about losing the contents of the book."

Meg nodded then shook it off.

"When we get back, let's just relax until we have to leave. That will make us well rested for the villa Borghese."

Seamus agreed. I'm happy with that; we'll be on our feet all afternoon."

That evening in the restaurant, Seamus, Meg and Tony talked about Rome. Meg was full of what she had seen at the Villa Borghese. Tony told anecdotes about his walk around the city. Seamus just listened, for the most part. Finally it was time to go. As they all stood up Seamus pointed at Tony.

"Tomorrow morning at eight o'clock we'll meet at an outdoor table and I'll bring you up to date on the book."

"Goodness Seamus, it's about time. I'm bursting with curiosity."

"Never mind, all your questions will be answered. All the questions I have answers to , anyway."

They all said 'goodnight'.

The next morning Tony and Seamus were sipping their coffee. Tony looked around.

"Where's Meg?"

"She's getting ready. It takes her a while to put her face on."

Tony chuckled.

"So, how's it all going?"

"She's wearing me out Tony and she's rather proud of it."

"Oh, I doubt you're too upset. This is what I hoped for and, as I recall, so did you."

Seamus nodded and looked up. Meg was walking over. Seamus poured Meg some coffee as she sat down.

Tony looked hard at Seamus and stuck out his jaw.

"OK, come on and tell me the story. I've waited long enough."

Seamus took his coffee in both hands.

"Well, let's see, you left it with the book and potion puzzle. You knew that there were two other books. I'll pickup from there and fill in the gaps before going forward."

Seamus told them about the old man, the three drug dealers and the portion in the Vatican Library.

Tony interrupted.

"Wait a minute, there were, uh are, no other copies of the book in the Vatican Library?"

"That's right and we don't know why not. Of course, there's one there now - mine."

Tony went on.

"Let me make sure I have this right. The original book and the copy for the pope have just vanished. There were additional copies, two of them, one of which was yours. That one is now safely in the library. That still leaves one unaccounted for. Do I have that right?"

Seamus nodded and started to continue but Meg touched him on the arm.

"Tell him about Nigel."

Seamus told the story of Nigel and the e-mails. Then he nodded at Meg.

"Now Meg, there's more. I received an e-mail from Nigel, just before you came in from San Francisco. He thinks he knows how the potion works but it's so amazing he's not quite ready to believe it. It turns out the potion, somehow, creates a benign virus."

Meg blurted, "A virus!?"

"Yes, and this virus has only one purpose: to add a gene to the DNA of every cell it finds. Of course, that is most likely blood cells to start - red and white. That extra gene, sometimes two copies, makes the cell immune to plague."

Tony and Meg sat with their mouths open.

Seamus looked at them.

"Yes, amazing is too weak a word. There's even more. That genetic modification could, I stress could, also protect the cell from another, even worse, disease of modern times.

Tony interrupted.

"HIV?"

"Full marks Tony, yes, HIV."

"Omigod."

Seamus glanced from one to the other of them.

"You should see your faces."

Meg spoke first.

"Good Lord Seamus, this all sounds impossible. Of course I'm stunned."

Tony laughed.

"All the same, what a wonderful discovery. If only it's true."

Seamus lowered his eyes and almost mumbled.

"Yes, if only..."

Then Tony shook his head.

"Hang on, what about the last book, the copy like yours?"

Seamus smiled.

"Well, there is a search going on right now, as we sit here."

"What? By who? Where?"

"In Ireland, of course. By those three young, worthless drug dealers."

Tony leaned back liking the sound of it.

"That's perfect. If they don't get pneumonia and they can stick it out, they will actually do something useful. I like it."

—####—

Ireland

"God, I'm freezing. Let's go to a warm pub and have a cold beer."

Jock looked at him.

"You're freezing and you want a cold beer. Steve, you're weird."

—####—

Jimmy and Jock were sitting in a 'snug'. Jock slid around closer to Jimmy and said, "Where's Steve?" looking around,

"He's out having a smoke."

"Gawd, in this rain. It's coming down in buckets."

"Yeah, he'll smell bad when he comes in."

Jock's face became serious. "Jimmy, remember I told you that Irish detective at the old man's looked familiar."

"Yeah."

"Well, I finally ken'd why."

"How's that?"
Before I went to America , I was a runner for a group, you know, in the business - in England."

"OK, so."

"Well the boss was a real brain. He worked for a big drug company and could lift whatever he wanted. He gathered a few of us he could trust and told us that Interpol was getting too close. Then he said he'd heard they'd hired an Irish detective who was very good. That detective was coming closer and closer but he didn't know who he was."

"So what did he want to do?"
"Well, that's it. He wanted us to find out who he was and get rid of him."

"And did you?"

"We turned him out through a friend I had in the Dublin Gardai. A coupla mates and I watched for him and held a spot we knew he'd walked through."

"And"

"It didna go well. The paddy killed two of my mates and I ran for it. But we did get the skirt he was with."

"So what then?"

We all went back to England and told Nigel."

"The boss?"

"Ya, that's when he said he was shutting everything down - and then he scarpered."

"Scarpered?"

"Aye, he broke up the network; destroyed any evidence; he even quit his job and went to work for some government research lab. He went honest. The rest of us were out of a job. That's when I went to America and ran into you."

"It sounds like he overreacted to me."

"I couldna blame him much. The police were almost at his doorstep. He had plenty of brass. Why should he take the chance?"

"So now what?"

"Nothing, I'm all right and I don't really like guns much. Not like Steve. Watching my mates killed was it for me."

Jimmy put his hand on Jock's shoulder.

"Good for you, Jock. You might make a businessman yet."

Cincinnati

Back in Cincinnati, Seamus and Meg picked up their luggage and were finally through the customs line.

The customs official asked, with a bored look.

"Anything to declare?"

Seamus did all the talking.

"No."

The official was surprised.

"You went to Rome and didn't bring anything back?"

"That's right, we actually went to deliver a book to the Vatican Library."

"You flew all the way to Rome to give the Vatican a book? That must be some book."

Seamus looked at Meg. The last few months flashed through his mind. He turned back to the customs man.

"Yes sir, it was - some book and quite a good story too."

The End

Epilogue

The palimpsest

Made in the USA
Charleston, SC
16 April 2013